THE LAST THEOREM

∞

BALLANTINE BOOKS ▪ DEL REY ▪ NEW YORK

THE
LAST
THΣORΣM

∞

Arthur C. Clarke and
Frederik Pohl

Published in the United States by Del Rey Books, an imprint of The Random House Publishing Group, a division of Random House, Inc., New York.

DEL REY is a registered trademark and the Del Rey colophon is a trademark of Random House, Inc.

LIBRARY OF CONGRESS CATALOGING-IN-PUBLICATION DATA

Clarke, Arthur C. (Arthur Charles), 1917–2008.
The last theorem / Arthur C. Clarke and Frederik Pohl—1st ed.
p. cm.
ISBN 978-0-345-47021-8
1. Mathematicians—Fiction. 2. Physicists—Fiction. 3. Fermat's last theorem—Fiction. 4. Space vehicles—Propulsion systems—Fiction. 5. Sri Lanka—Fiction. I. Pohl, Frederik. II. Title.
PR6005.L36L37 2008   823'.914—dc22   2008021262

Printed in the United States of America on acid-free paper

www.delreybooks.com

2 4 6 8 9 7 5 3 1

First Edition

Book design by Liz Cosgrove

∞

THE FIRST PREAMBLE

Arthur C. Clarke says:

The incidents at Pearl Harbor lay in the future and the United States was still at peace when a British warship steamed into Nantucket with what was later called "the most valuable cargo ever to reach American shores." It was not very impressive, a metal cylinder about an inch high, fitted with connections and cooling fins. It could easily be carried in one hand. Yet this small object had a strong claim to being responsible for winning the war in Europe and Asia—though it did take the atom bomb to finish the last of the Axis powers off.

That just-invented object was the cavity magnetron.

The magnetron was not in principle a new idea. For some time it had been known that a powerful magnetic field could keep electrons racing in tight circles, thus generating radio waves. However, this fact remained little more than a laboratory curiosity until it was realized that those radio waves could be used for a military purpose.

When it had such a military use, it was called radar.

When the American scientists working at the Massachusetts Institute of Technology received that first device, they subjected it to many tests. They were surprised to find that the magnetron's power output was so great that none of their laboratory instruments could measure it. A little later, powering the giant antennae that had quickly been erected along the Channel coast, that British radar did a fine job of spotting the Luftwaffe's myriad warplanes as they formed up to attack England. Indeed, radar was responsible, more than any other one thing, for allowing the Royal Air Force to win the Battle of Britain.

It was soon realized that radar could be used not only to detect enemy aircraft in the sky, but to make electronic maps of the ground over which a plane was flying. That meant that, even in total darkness or complete overcast, the land below could be imaged in recognizable shape on a cathode-ray tube, thus helping navigation—and bombing missions. And as soon as the magnetron was available at MIT, a team headed by future Nobel Laureate Luis Alvarez asked the next question: "Can't we use radar to land aircraft safely, as well as to shoot them down?"

So began GCA, or ground-controlled approach, the landing of aircraft in bad weather using precision approach radar.

The experimental Mark 1 GCA used two separate radars, one working at ten centimeters to locate the plane's direction in azimuth, and the other—the world's first three-centimeter radar—to measure height above ground. An operator seated before the two screens could then talk the aircraft down, telling the pilot when to fly right or left—or sometimes, more urgently, when to increase altitude—fast.

GCA was welcomed enthusiastically by the RAF Bomber Command, which every day was losing more aircraft over Europe through bad weather than through enemy action. In 1943 the Mark 1 and its crew were stationed at an airfield in St. Eval, Cornwall. An RAF crew headed by Flight Lieutenant Lavington was dispatched to join them. Lavington was assisted by the newly commissioned Pilot Officer Arthur C. Clarke.

Actually, Clarke should not have been in the Royal Air Force at all. As a civilian he had been a civil servant in H.M. Exchequer and Audit Department and hence had been in a reserved occupation. However, he had rightly suspected that he would soon be unreserved, so one day he sneaked away from the office and volunteered at the nearest RAF recruiting station. He was just in time. A few weeks later the army started looking for him— as an army deserter who was wanted by the medical corps! As he was unable to bear the sight of blood, particularly his own, he obviously had a very narrow escape.

By that time Arthur Clarke was already a keen space-cadet, having joined the British Interplanetary Society soon after it was formed in 1933. Now, realizing that he had at his command the world's most powerful radar, producing beams only a fraction of a degree wide, one night he aimed it at the rising moon and counted for three seconds to see if there would be a returning echo.

Sadly, there wasn't. It was years later before anyone did actually receive radar echoes from the moon.

However, although no one could have known it at the time, something else may have happened.

∞

THE SECOND PREAMBLE

Frederik Pohl says:

There are two things in my life that I think have a bearing on the subject matter of this book, so perhaps this would be a good time to set them down.

The first: By the time I was in my early thirties, I had been exposed to a fair amount of mathematics—algebra, geometry, trigonometry, a little elementary calculus—either at Brooklyn Tech, where for a brief period in my youth I had the mistaken notion that I might become a chemical engineer, or, during World War IJ, in the U.S. Air Force Weather School at Chanute Field in Illinois, where the instructors tried to teach me something about the mathematical bases of meteorology.

None of those kinds of math made a great impression on me. What changed that, radically and permanently, was an article in *Scientific American* in the early 1950s that spoke of a sort of mathematics I had never before heard of. It was called "number theory." It had to do with describing and cataloging the properties of that basic unit of all mathematics, the number, and it tickled my imagination.

I sent my secretary out to the nearest bookstore to buy me copies of all the books cited in the article, and I read them, and I was addicted. Over the next year and more I spent all the time I could squeeze out of a busy life in scribbling interminable calculations on ream upon ream of paper. (We're talking about the 1950s, remember. No computers. Not even a pocket calculator. If I wanted to try factoring a number that I thought might be prime, I did it the way Fermat or Kepler or, for that matter, probably old Aristarchus himself had done it, which is to say, by means of interminably repetitious and laborious handwritten arithmetic.)

I never did find Fermat's lost proof, or solve any other of the great mathematical puzzles. I didn't even get very far with the one endeavor that, I thought for a time, I might actually make some headway with, namely, finding a formula for generating prime numbers. What I did accomplish—and little enough it is, for all that work—was to invent a couple of what you might call mathematical parlor tricks. One was a technique for counting on your fingers. (Hey, anybody can count on his fingers, you say. Well, sure, but up to 1,023?) The other was accomplishing an apparently impossible task.

I'll give you the patter that goes with that trick:

If you draw a row of coins, it doesn't matter how long a row, I will in ten seconds or less write down the exact number of permutations (heads-tails-heads, heads-tails-tails, etc.) that number of coins produces when flipped. And just to make it a little tougher on me, I will do it even if you cover up as many coins in the row as you like, from either end, so that I won't be able to tell how many there are in the row.

Impossible, right? Care to try to figure it out? I'll come back to you on this, but not right away.

The second thing that I think might be relevant happened some twenty years later, when I found myself for the first time in my life spending a few weeks in the island empire of Japan. I was there as a guest of Japanese science-fiction fandom, and so was Brian Aldiss, representing Britain, Yuli Kagarlitski, representing what then was still the Union of Soviet Socialist Republics, Judith Merril, representing Canada, and Arthur C. Clarke, representing Sri Lanka and most of the rest of the inhabited parts of the earth. Along with a contingent of Japanese writers and editors, the bunch of us had been touring Japanese cities, lecturing, being interviewed, and, on request, showing our silly sides. (Arthur did a sort of Sri Lankan version of a Hawaiian hula. Brian got involved in trying to pronounce a long list of Japanese words, most of which—for our hosts loved a good prank—turned out to be violently obscene. I won't tell you what I did.) For a reward we were all treated to a decompressing weekend on Lake Biwa, where we lounged about in our kimonos and depleted the hotel's bar.

We spent most of the time catching one another up on what we'd been doing since the last time we had been together. I thought Judy Merril had the most interesting story to tell. She had come early to Japan, and had sneaked a couple of days in Hiroshima before the rest of us had arrived. She was good at describing things, too, and she kept us interested while she told us what she had seen. Well, everyone knows about the twisted ironwork the Japanese preserved as a memorial when every other part of that building had been blown away by that first-ever-deployed-in-anger nuclear bomb, and about the melted-down face on the stone Buddha. And everyone knows about—the one that nobody can forget once that picture enters their minds—

the shadow of a man that had been permanently etched, onto the stone stairs where he had been sitting, by the intolerably brilliant nuclear blast from the overhead sky.

"That must have been bright," someone said—I think Brian.

Arthur said, "Bright enough that it could have been seen by a dozen nearby stars by now."

"If anyone lives there to be looking," someone else said—I think it was me.

And, we agreed, maybe someone might indeed be looking . . . or at least it was pretty to think so.

As to those mathematical parlor tricks:

I don't think I should explain them to you just yet, but I promise that before this book is ended, someone will.

That someone will probably be a bright young man named Ranjit Subramanian, whom you are bound to meet in just a few pages.

After all, this book is basically Ranjit's story.

∞

THE THIRD PREAMBLE

Atmospheric Testing

In the spring of the year 1946, in a (previously) unspoiled South Pacific atoll named Bikini, the American navy put together a fleet of ninety-odd vessels. They were battleships, cruisers, destroyers, submarines, and assorted support craft, and they came from many sources. Some were captured German or Japanese ships, the spoils of battle from the recently ended World War II; most were war-weary or technologically outmoded American vessels.

This fleet was not meant to sail off into a giant naval battle against any-one, or indeed to go anywhere at all. Bikini Atoll was the vessels' last stop. The reason the fleet had been assembled was simply so that a couple of atomic bombs could be inflicted on it. One would come from the air, the other from under the sea. The hope was that this travail could give the admirals some idea of what their navy might suffer in some future nuclear war.

Bikini Atoll, of course, wasn't the end of nuclear weapons testing. It was just the beginning. Over the next dozen years and more the Americans exploded bomb after bomb in the atmosphere, diligently noting yield and damage done and every other number that could be extracted from a test. So did the Soviets and the Brits a little later, the French and the Chinese later still. Altogether the first five nuclear powers (who also happened, not by chance, to be the five permanent members of the United Nations Security Council) set off a total of more than fifteen hundred nuclear weapons in the atmosphere. They did this in places such as the Marshall Islands in the Pacific, in Algeria and French Polynesia, in desert areas of Australia, in Semipalatinsk in Soviet Kazakhstan and Novaya Zemlya in the Arctic Ocean, in the marshy waste of Lop Nor in China, and in many other places all around the world.

It did not greatly matter where the blasts originated. Each one of them produced an inconceivably brilliant flash—"brighter than a thousand suns," was how the physicist Hans Thirring described it—a flash that swelled out into space in a hemispheric shell of photons, expanding at the rate of three hundred thousand kilometers in each second.

By then the photons of that first puny radar flash that young Arthur Clarke had aimed at the moon had traveled a long way from the place in the galaxy where Earth had been when the photons were launched.

How far had they gone? Well, by then it had been some thirty years since that radar flash of his had returned no data. Light—or radio waves, or electronic radiation of any kind—travels at, well, at that velocity of 186,000 miles (or some 300,000 kilometers) per second that is the speed of light. So each year those photons had traveled one light-year farther away, and in their passage they had already swept through the systems of several hundred stars. Many of those stars had planets. A few had planets capable of supporting life. A small fraction of that life was intelligent.

Human beings never did know which star's beings first detected what was happening on Earth. Was it Groombridge 1618? Alpha Centauri B? (Or, for that matter, A?) Or Lalande 21185, Epsilon Eridani, perhaps even Tau Ceti?

The humans never knew, and perhaps that was just as well. It would only have worried them.

Whichever star's system they had inhabited, the astronomers among those creatures (they didn't call themselves astronomers; their term for what they did was something like "inventoriers of externalities") paid close attention to that first weak pulse. It troubled them.

These people did not look in the least like humans, but they had certain nearly human "emotions," and among them was something quite like fear. The microwave emanations from Earth were the first things to worry them. Then came those far brighter fire bursts that arrived a little later—the ones from the first nuclear test from White Sands Proving Ground, and then from Hiroshima and Nagasaki, and then from everywhere. Those flashes set those alien skywatchers to clattering and squealing at one another. Such flashes represented trouble, and potentially very big trouble.

It wasn't that those first observers felt fear at what humanity was doing on its remote little planet. They didn't care in the least what happened to planet Earth. What worried them was that that same expanding hemisphere of radiation would not die out once it passed their star. It would keep going on, farther and deeper into the galaxy. And sooner or later it would reach certain other individuals who were likely to take it very seriously indeed.

THE LAST THΣORΣM

∞

ster's developing muscles were used to, not to mention the splinters and the scrapes and the endless cuts from the broken glass that was everywhere.

Those were the bad parts, and there were plenty of them. But there were good parts, too. Like the time when Ranjit and some other boy around his own age finally got down to the source of some plaintive sounds that were coming from a debris pile, and released the headmaster's terrified, but intact, elderly Siamese cat.

When a teacher had carried the cat off to its owner, the two boys had stood grinning at each other. Ranjit had stuck his hand out, English fashion. "I'm Ranjit Subramanian," he'd said.

"And I'm Gamini Bandara," the other boy had said, pumping his hand gleefully, "and, hey, we did a pretty good job here, didn't we?"

They agreed that they had. When at last they had been allowed to quit work for the day, they had lined up together for the sort of porridge that was their evening meal, and plopped their sleeping bags next to each other that night, and they had been best friends ever since. Helped out, to be sure, by the fact that Gamini's school had been made uninhabitable by the fire and so its students had to double up at Ranjit's. Gamini turned out to be pretty much everything a best friend could be, including the fact that the one great obsession in Ranjit's life, the one for which there was no room for another person to share, didn't interest Gamini at all.

And, of course, there was one other thing that Gamini was. That was the part of Ranjit's impending talk with his father that Ranjit least wanted to have.

Ranjit grimaced to himself. As instructed, Ranjit went straight to one of the temple's side doors, but it wasn't his father who met him there. It was an elderly monk named Surash who told Ranjit—rather officiously, Ranjit thought—only that he would have to wait a bit. So Ranjit waited, for what he considered quite a long time, with nothing to do but listen to the bustle that came from within his father's temple, about which Ranjit had mixed emotions.

The temple had given his father purpose, position, and a rewarding career, all of which was good. However, it had also encouraged the old man in the vain hope that his son would follow in his footsteps. That was not going to happen. Even as a boy, Ranjit had not been able to believe in the complex Hindu pantheon of gods and goddesses, some with their various animal heads and unusual number of arms, whose sculptured figures encrusted the temple walls. Ranjit had been able to name every one of them, and to list its special powers and principal fast days as well, by the time he

1

ON SWAMI ROCK

And so now, at last, we meet this Ranjit Subramanian, the one whose long
and remarkable life this book is all about.

At this time Ranjit was sixteen years old, a freshman at Sri Lanka's
principal university, in the city of Colombo, and more full of himself than
even your average sixteen-year-old. He wasn't at the university now,
though. At his father's bidding he had made the long trip from Colombo
slantwise across the island of Sri Lanka to the district of Trincomalee,
where his father had the distinction of being chief priest at the Hindu temple called Tiru Koneswaram. Ranjit actually loved his father very much.
He was almost always glad to see him. This time, however, he was a bit less
so, because this time Ranjit had a pretty good idea of what the revered
Ganesh Subramanian wanted to talk to him about.

Ranjit was an intelligent boy, in fact one who was quite close to being
as smart as he thought he was. He was a good-looking one, too. He wasn't
terribly tall, but most Sri Lankans aren't. Ethnically he was a Tamil, and
his skin color was the rich dark brown of a spoonful of cocoa powder, just
before it went into the hot milk. The skin color wasn't because he was a
Tamil, though. Sri Lankans have a rich palette of complexions from near-
Scandinavian white to a black so dark it seems almost purple. Ranjit's bes'
friend, Gamini Bandara, was pure Sinhalese for as many generations bac'
as anyone had bothered to count, but the boys were the same in skin hue

The boys had been friends for a long time—since that scary nig
when Gamini's school had burned to the ground, probably put to the to'
by a couple of upperclassmen smoking forbidden cigarettes in a stor
room.

Like every other nearby human being capable of picking up a sp
tered piece of plywood and throwing it on the back of a truck, Ranji'
been drafted for emergency relief work. So had all the rest of the st'
body of his own school. It had been a dirty job, a lot harder than a y

was six. It hadn't been out of religious fervor. It had been simply because he had wanted to please the father he loved.

Ranjit remembered waking early in the morning when he was a small child, still living at home, and his father getting up at sunrise to bathe in the temple pool. He would see his father, naked to the waist as he faced the rising sun, and hear his long, reverberating Om. When he was a little older, Ranjit himself learned to say the mantra, and the location of the six parts of the body that he touched, and to offer water to the statues in the puja room. But then he went away to school. His religious observances were not required, and therefore ended. By the time he was ten, he knew he would never follow in his father's faith.

Not that his father's was not a fine profession. True, Ganesh Subramanian's temple was neither as ancient nor as vast as the one it had attempted to replace. Although it had been bravely given the same name as the original—Tiru Koneswaram—even its chief priest rarely called it anything but "the new temple." It hadn't been completed until 1983, and in size it was not a patch on the original Tiru Koneswaram, the famous "temple with a thousand columns," whose beginnings had been shrouded by two thousand years of history.

And then, when at last Ranjit was met, it was not by his father but by old Surash. He was apologetic. "It is these pilgrims," he said. "So many of them! More than one hundred, and your father, the chief priest, is determined to greet each one. Go, Ranjit. Sit on Swami Rock and watch the sea. In an hour, perhaps, your father will join you there, but just now—" He sighed, and shook his head, and turned away to the task of helping his boss cope with the flood of pilgrims. Leaving Ranjit to his own resources.

Which, as a matter of fact, was just fine, because for Ranjit an hour or so to himself on Swami Rock was a welcome gift.

An hour or so earlier Swami Rock would have been crowded with couples and whole families picnicking, sightseeing, or simply enjoying the cooling breeze that came off the Bay of Bengal. Now, with the sun lowering behind the hills to the west, it was almost deserted.

That was the way Ranjit preferred it. He loved Swami Rock. Had loved it all his life, in fact—or no, he amended the thought, at six or seven he hadn't actually loved the rock itself nearly as much as he had the surrounding lagoons and beaches, where you could catch little star tortoises and make them race against one another.

But that was then. Now, at sixteen, he considered himself a fully adult man, and he had more important things to think about.

Ranjit found an unoccupied stone bench and leaned back, enjoying both the warmth of the setting sun at his back and the sea breeze on his face, as he prepared to think about the two subjects that were on his mind.

The first, actually, took little thinking. Ranjit wasn't really disappointed at his father's absence. Ganesh had not told his sixteen-year-old son just what it was that he wanted to discuss. Ranjit, however, was depressingly confident that he knew what it was.

What it was was an embarrassment, and the worst part of it was that it was a wholly unnecessary one. It could have been avoided entirely if he had only remembered to lock his bedroom door so that the porter at his university lodgings would not have been able to blunder in on the two of them that afternoon. But Ranjit hadn't locked his door. The porter had indeed walked in on them, and Ranjit knew that Ganesh Subramanian had long since interviewed the man. He had talked to the porter only for the purpose, Ganesh would have said, of making sure that Ranjit lacked nothing he needed. But it did carry the collateral benefit of ensuring that Ganesh was kept well informed of what was going on in his son's life.

Ranjit sighed. He would have wished to avoid the coming discussion. But he couldn't, and so he turned his attention to the second subject on his mind—the important one—the one that was nearly always at the top of his thoughts.

From his perch atop Swami Rock, a hundred meters above the restless waters of the Bay of Bengal, he looked eastward. On the surface, at twilight, there was nothing to see but water—in fact nothing at all for more than a thousand kilometers, apart from a few scattered islands, until you reached the coast of Thailand. Tonight there had been a lull in the northeast monsoon, and the sky was perfectly clear. A brilliant star, its light slightly tinged with orangey-red, lay low in the east, the brightest star in the sky. Idly, Ranjit wondered what it was named. His father would know, of course. Ganesh Subramanian was a devout and sincere believer in astrology, as a temple priest should be. But he had also had a lifelong interest in secular science of all kinds. He knew the planets of the solar system, and the names of many of the elements, and how it was that a few rods of metallic uranium could be made to manufacture the electrical power that could light a city, and he had passed some of that love on to his son. What remained with Ranjit, though, was not so much about the astronomy and physics and biology of the world, but most of all that one subject that bound everything else together, mathematics.

That, Ranjit knew, he owed to his father because of the book his father had given him on his thirteenth birthday. The book was G. H. Hardy's *A Mathematician's Apology*. It was in that book that Ranjit first encountered the name of Srinivasa Ramanujan, the impoverished Indian clerk, with no formal training in mathematics, who had been the wonder of the mathematical world in the dark years of World War I. It was Hardy who received a letter from Ramanujan with some hundred of the theorems he had discovered, and Hardy who brought him to England and to world fame.

Ramanujan was an inspiration to Ranjit—clearly mathematical genius could come from anyone—and the book had left him with a specific, dominating interest in number theory. Not just number theory: in particular the wonderful insights that were the work of the centuries-old genius Pierre de Fermat, and even more in particular that towering question Fermat had left for his successors, the proof—or the proof that there was no proof—of Fermat's celebrated Last Theorem.

That was Ranjit's obsession, and it was the subject he proposed to devote the next hour to thinking about. It was too bad that he didn't have his calculator in his pocket, but his best friend had talked him out of that. "You remember my cousin Charitha?" Gamini had said. "The one who is a captain in the army? He says that some of the guards in the trains are confiscating calculators. They sell them for what they can get. Your two-hundred-dollar Texas Instruments calculator they would sell for perhaps ten dollars to somebody who only wants to keep track of his cash outlays, so leave it at home." Which Ranjit sensibly had done.

The calculator's absence was an annoyance, but not a particularly important one, for the wonderful thing about Fermat's Last Theorem was its simplicity. After all, what could be simpler than $a^2 + b^2 = c^2$? That is, the length of one arm of a right triangle, squared, added to the squared length of the other arm equals the square of the hypotenuse. (The simplest case is when the arms are three units and four units in length and the hypotenuse is then five units, but there are many other cases with unitary answers.)

This simple equation anyone could prove for himself with a ruler and a little arithmetic. What Fermat had done to obsess generations of mathematicians was to claim that such a relationship worked only for squares, not for cubes or for any higher power. He could prove it, he said.

But he didn't publish his proof.

(If you would like a fuller discussion of the "last" theorem, one is included at the end of this book, under the title "The Third Postamble.")

．　．　．

Ranjit stretched, yawned, and shook himself out of his reverie. He picked up a pebble and threw it as hard as he could, losing sight of it in the dusk long before it struck the water below. He smiled. All right, he confessed to himself, some part of what he knew other people said about him wasn't totally untrue. For instance, it wasn't entirely wrong to say that he was obsessed. He had chosen his loyalties early, and he stayed with them, and now he was what one might call a Fermatian. If Fermat claimed he had a proof, then Ranjit Subramanian, like many a mathematician before him, took it as an article of faith that that proof did exist.

By that, however, Ranjit certainly did not mean an aberration like the so-called Wiles proof that he had tried to get his math professor to discuss at the university. If that cumbersome old turkey (it dated from the closing years of the twentieth century) could be called a proof at all—and Ranjit hesitated to use "proof" for something no biological human could read—Ranjit didn't deny its technical validity. He simply thought it was trash. In fact, as he had told Gamini Bandara just before that confounded porter had opened the door on the two of them, it certainly was not the proof that Pierre de Fermat had boasted of when he'd scribbled in the margin of his volume of Diophantus's *Arithmetica*.

Ranjit grinned again, wryly, because the next thing he had said to Gamini was that he was going to find Fermat's proof for himself. And that was what had started the laughing put-downs and the friendly horseplay that had led directly to what the porter had walked in on. And Ranjit's mind was so filled with the memories of that time that he never heard his father's footsteps, and didn't know his father was there until the old man put a hand on his shoulder and said, "Lost in thought, is that what you are?"

The pressure of Ganesh's hand kept his son from rising. Ganesh seated himself beside him, methodically studying Ranjit's face, dress, and body. "You are thin," he complained.

"So are you," Ranjit told him, smiling, but a little worried, too, because on his father's face was a look he had never seen before, a worry and a sorrow that did not befit the usually upbeat old man. He added, "Don't worry. They feed me well enough at the university."

His father nodded. "Yes," he said, acknowledging the accuracy of the statement as well as the fact that he knew quite well just how adequately his son was fed. "Tell me what else they do for you there."

That might have been taken to be an invitation to say something about a boy's right to a personal life and some freedom from being spied upon by servants. Ranjit elected to postpone that subject as long as he could. "Mainly," he said, improvising hastily, "it's been math that has kept me busy. You know about Fermat's Last Theorem—" And then, when the look on Ganesh's face showed real amusement for the first time, Ranjit said, "Well, of course you do. You're the one who gave me the Hardy book in the first place, aren't you? Anyway, there's this so-called proof of Wiles. It's an abomination. How does Wiles construct his proof? He goes back to Ken Ribet's announcement that he had proved a link between Fermat and Taniyama-Shimura. That's a conjecture that says—"

Ganesh patted his shoulder. "Yes, Ranjit," he said gently. "You needn't bother to try to explain this Taniyama-Shimura thing to me."

"All right." Ranjit thought for a moment. "Well, I'll make it simple. The crux of Wiles's argument lies in two theorems. The first is that a particular elliptical curve is semi-stable but it isn't modular. The second says that all semi-stable elliptical curves that possess rational coefficients really are modular. That means there is a flat contradiction, and—"

Ganesh sighed fondly. "You are really deeply involved in this, aren't you?" he observed. "But you know your mathematics is far beyond me, so let's talk about something else. What about the rest of your studies?"

"Ah," Ranjit said, faintly puzzled; it was not to talk about his classes, he was quite sure, that his father had brought him to Trincomalee. "Yes. My other classes." As conversational subjects went, that one was not nearly as bad as the one about what the porter would have passed along. It wasn't really wonderful, though. Ranjit sighed and bit the bullet. "Really," he said, "why must I learn French? So I can go to the airport and sell souvenirs to tourists from Madagascar or Quebec?"

His father smiled. "French is a language of culture," he pointed out. "And also of your hero, Monsieur Fermat."

"Huh," Ranjit said, recognizing the debating point but still unconvinced. "All right, but what about history? Who cares? Why do I need to know what the king of Kandy said to the Portuguese? Or whether the Dutch threw the English out of Trinco, or the other way around?"

His father patted him again. "There is an easy answer to your question. The reason is because the university requires those credits of you before they will grant you your degree. After that, in graduate school, you can specialize as much as you like. Isn't the university teaching you anything you enjoy other than math?"

Ranjit brightened slightly. "Not now, no, but by next year I'll be through with this really boring biology. Then I can take a different science course, and I'm going to do astronomy." Reminded, he glanced up at the bright red star, now dominating the eastern horizon.

His father did not disappoint him. "Yes, that's Mars," he said, following Ranjit's line of sight. "It's unusually bright; there's good seeing tonight." He turned his gaze back to his son. "Speaking of the planet Mars, do you remember who Percy Molesworth was? The one whose grave we used to visit?"

Ranjit reached back into his recollections of childhood and was pleased to find a clue. "Oh, right. The astronomer." They were speaking of Percy Molesworth, the British army captain who had been stationed at Trincomalee around the end of the nineteenth century. "Mars was his specialty, right?" he went on, happy to be talking about something that would please his father. "He was the one who proved that, uh . . ."

"The canals," his father assisted.

"Right, the canals! He proved that they weren't actual canals built by an advanced Martian civilization but just an example of the kind of tricks our eyes can play on us."

Ganesh gave him an encouraging nod. "He was the astronomer—the very great astronomer—who did most of his work right here in Trinco, and he—"

Then Ganesh stopped midsentence. He turned to peer into Ranjit's face. Then he sighed. "Do you see what I am doing, Ranjit? I am delaying the inevitable. It was not to talk about astronomers that I asked you to come here tonight. What we must discuss is something a great deal more serious. That is your relationship with Gamini Bandara."

It had come.

Ranjit took a deep breath before bursting out: "Father, believe me! It is not what you think! We just play at that sort of thing, Gamini and I. It means nothing."

Unexpectedly, his father looked surprised. "Means nothing? Of course what you were doing means nothing. Did you think I did not know all the ways in which young boys like to experiment with kinds of behavior?" He shook his head reproachfully, and then said in a burst, "You must believe me in this, Ranjit. It isn't the experimenting with sexual behavior that matters. It is the person you were sharing it with." His voice was stressed again, as though it were hard for these words to come out. "Remember, my son, you are a Tamil. Bandara is Sinhalese."

Ranjit's first reaction was that he could not believe what he was hearing from his father's lips. How could his father, who had always taught him that all men were brothers, say such things now? Ganesh Subramanian had been faithful to his beliefs in spite of the fact that the ethnic riots that began in the 1980s had left scars that would take generations to heal. Ganesh had lost close relatives to rampaging mobs. He himself had narrowly escaped death more than once.

But that was ancient history. Ranjit hadn't been born yet in those days—even his deceased mother had hardly been born yet—and for years now there had been a well-kept truce. Ranjit raised a hand. "Father," he begged, "please! This is not like you. Gamini hasn't murdered anyone."

Inexorably Ganesh Subramanian repeated the terrible words. "Gamini is Sinhalese."

"But Father! What about all the things you taught me? About that poem you made me learn by heart, the one from the Purananuru. 'To us all towns are one, all men our kin, thus we have seen in the visions of the wise.'"

He was clutching at straws. His father was not to be moved by two-thousand-year-old Tamil verses. He didn't answer, just shook his head, though Ranjit could see from the expression on his face that he was suffering, too.

"All right," Ranjit said miserably. "What do you want me to do?"

His father's voice was heavy. "What you must, Ranjit. You cannot remain so close to a Sinhalese."

"But why? Why now?"

"I have no choice in this," his father said. "I must put my duties as high priest of the temple first, and this matter is causing dissension." He sighed and then said, "You were raised to be loyal, Ranjit. I am not surprised that you want to stand with your friend. I only hoped that you could find a way to be loyal to your father as well, but perhaps that is impossible." He shook his head and then stood up, looking down at his son. "Ranjit," he said, "I must tell you that you are not now welcome in my house. One of the monks will find you a place to sleep tonight. If you finally choose to sever your relationship with Bandara, phone or write me to tell me so. Until you do, there is no reason for you to contact me again."

As his father turned and walked away, Ranjit dropped quite suddenly into a state of misery. . . .

Perhaps that state needs to be examined more closely. Ranjit was certainly miserable with the sudden distance that had opened between himself and his beloved father. Nothing in that fact, however, led him to think that he himself was in any way in the wrong. He was, after all, just sixteen years old.

. . .

And some twenty light-years away, on a planet so corrupted and befouled that it was very difficult to believe any organic creature could survive there, an odd-looking race known as the One Point Fives was nevertheless surviving.

The question now on the collective minds of the One Point Fives, as they prepared themselves to meet the inevitable orders from the Grand Galactics who were their masters, was how much longer that survival would go on.

True, the One Point Fives hadn't received their marching orders yet. But they knew what was coming. They themselves had detected the troublesome emissions from Earth as the successive waves of photons had swept by. They knew as well just when those photons would reach the Grand Galactics.

Most of all, they knew just how the Grand Galactics were likely to respond. The thought of what that response might mean for them made them shudder within their body armor.

The One Point Fives had only one real hope. That was that they would be able to accomplish everything the Grand Galactics would demand of them and, when that task was completed, that they would have enough survivors among their own people to keep the race alive.

2

UNIVERSITY

That year's first few months of university classes had been the best kind of holiday for Ranjit Subramanian. Not because of the classes themselves, of course. They were totally boring. But they took up only a few hours a day, and then he and Gamini Bandara had all the time that the university hadn't already claimed, with a whole exciting city to explore and each other to explore it with. They did it all, from the Pinnewala Elephant Orphanage and the Dehiwala Zoo to the cricket club and a dozen less reputable places. Gamini, of course, had lived in Colombo much of his life. He had long since explored all of those places and many more, but introducing Ranjit to them made them all fresh. The boys even managed to take in a few museums and one or two theaters—cheaply done, because Gamini's parents had memberships or season tickets to everything in Colombo. Or at least to everything respectable; and the attractions that weren't respectable the boys found for themselves. There were of course plenty of the bars, toddy joints, and casinos that gave Colombo its nickname as "the Las Vegas of the Indian Ocean." The boys naturally sampled them, but didn't care much for gambling and certainly didn't need a whole lot of alcohol to feel good. Feeling good was their natural state.

They usually met for lunch in the students' dining hall as soon as their morning classes were over. Unfortunately none of their classes were shared. Given Gamini's father-inspired emphasis on government and law, that had been pretty much inevitable.

When they didn't have time to go into the city proper, there was nearly as much fun to be had exploring the campus of the university itself. Early on they found a penetrable service entrance to the school of medicine's faculty lounge. That was a promising target, with platters of goodies always laid out, along with endless supplies of (nonalcoholic) drinks. Unfortunately, it was—permanently, it seemed—out of the boys' reach; the faculty lounge was almost always full of faculty. It was Gamini who found the ventilation louvers for the girls' changing room in the school of education's gym—and Gamini who made the most use of them, leaving Ranjit somewhat puzzled. And at a not quite finished, apparently abandoned structure attached to the Queens Road building they found a treasure. According to the decaying signage it had been intended to be the school of indigenous law, set up during one of the periods when the government had been extending olive branches not only to Tamils but to Muslims, Christians, and Jews as well.

The structure itself had been nearly completed, with a row of unfurnished faculty offices and classrooms that had barely been begun. The library was much further along. It even had books. According to Gamini, whose father had insisted on his learning simple Arabic at an early age, the authors were such as Hanafi, Maliki, and Hanbali on the side of the room meant for Sunnis, and mostly devoted to Jaafari on the side for the Shia. And in a little alcove between the two sides sat a pair of silent but fully operational computer terminals.

This whole unoccupied structure called out for the boys to take advantage of it. They did. In short time they had discovered a reception room, furnished but not lavishly; the receptionist's desk was plywood and the chairs ranked against the wall were the foldaway kind usually found in funeral parlors. That wasn't their most interesting discovery, though. On top of that plywood desk was an American picture magazine, one of the kind devoted to the lives of Hollywood stars, next to an electric kettle bubbling away and a foil-wrapped container of somebody's lunch.

The boys' private little den had not been as private as they had thought. But they hadn't been caught, and they had chuckled to themselves as they hastened to leave.

Exploring this new territory was a delight for Ranjit. Studying at the university, however, wasn't. By the time he neared the end of his first year, he had learned a good many things, few of which he considered worth the trouble of knowing. Not in the worth-knowing category, in his opinion, was his newfound ability to conjugate most regular French verbs and even to do the same for a few of the most important irregular ones, such as *être*. On the positive side, though, was the fact that he had somehow eked out a passing grade in his French class anyway, thus helping to preserve his status as a student for another year.

Even the much-disliked biology course became almost interesting when the (equally disliked) instructor ran out of frogs to dissect and then turned from the theoretical discussion of disease vectors to some actual news stories from the Colombo media. The stories were about a fast-spreading new pestilence called chikungunya. The name was a Swahili word meaning "what bends up," thus describing the stooped-over posture of patients suffering from its ruinous joint pain. The chikungunya virus, it seemed, had been around for some time, but in relatively trivial amounts. Now it was suddenly reemerging, and infecting the region's always available swarms of *Aedes aegypti* mosquitoes. Thousands of people in the Seychelles and other Indian Ocean islands were coming down with rash, fever, and incapacitating joint pain . . . and, the instructor reminded them, Sri Lanka still possessed countless swamps and stagnant ponds that were ideal breeding spots for *A. aegypti*. He did not endorse, but did not deny, either, the rumor that the chikungunya organism might have been "weaponized"— that is, tailor-made to be used in biological warfare (by what country, and intended to be used against what other country, no one would say)—and had somehow escaped to the lands of the Indian Ocean.

It was the most interesting thing Ranjit had found in the wasteland of Biology 101. Rogue nations? Weaponized disease? Those were things he wanted to talk about with Gamini, but that wasn't possible. Gamini had one of those poli-sci classes just before lunch and thus would not be available for sharing for at least another hour.

Bored, Ranjit did what he had avoided doing for most of the term. There was an open-attendance seminar for do-gooders, something about the world's water problems. All students were encouraged to attend, and, of course, most students resolutely stayed away. That made it a place where he could maybe drowse with nobody talking to him.

But the lecturer began talking about the Dead Sea.

Ranjit had given very little thought to the Dead Sea, but to the lecturer it was a hidden treasure. What you could do, he said, was dig aqueducts from the Mediterranean to the Dead Sea, four hundred meters below sea level, and use the height difference to generate electricity.

Ranjit found his mind racing at the idea. It was problem solving on a huge scale, and it was something worth doing! Ranjit couldn't wait to tell Gamini about it.

But when Gamini finally showed up for lunch, he wasn't impressed. "Old stuff," Gamini informed him. "My father's friend Dr. Al-Zasr—he's an Egyptian; they went to school together in England—told us about it once at dinner. Only it's never going to happen. It was an Israeli idea, and the other nations around there don't like Israeli ideas."

"Huh," Ranjit said. The lecturer hadn't mentioned that it was an Israeli idea. Or that it was twenty years old, and that if it hadn't been built in twenty years, it wasn't likely to be built now.

Gamini wasn't all that interested in chikungunya, either, and then it was his turn to educate Ranjit. "Your problem," he informed his friend, "is what they call the GSSM syndrome. Know what that is? No, you don't, but it's what you're doing. It's your multitasking, Ranj. You're cutting yourself into too many pieces. My psych teacher says there's a good chance it makes you stupid, because, you know, every time you switch from one thing to another, you're interrupting yourself, and you can do that just so much before there's a permanent effect on your prefrontal cortex and you've got ADD."

Ranjit frowned. He was fiddling around on Gamini's laptop. Recently, Ranjit had begun learning everything he could about computers. "What's ADD? And while we're at it, what's the GSSM syndrome?"

Gamini gave him a reproving look. "You really should try to keep up, Ranj. ADD is attention deficit disorder, and GSSM is the initials of the four people who led the research into the multitasking syndrome. There was somebody named Grafman, plus people named Stone, Schwartz, and Meyer. There was a woman named Yuhong Jiang, too, but I guess they didn't have room for any more initials. Anyway, it sounds to me like you're too concerned with events beyond your control."

It was a fair cop. Nevertheless, that night, before turning in, Ranjit made a point of watching the news, just to show that he wasn't ruled by his friend's notions. Not much of it was good. At least a score of countries were still truculently declaring that they had every right to whatever nuclear programs they chose to implement, and most of them were in fact implementing them. North Korea was, as usual, displaying itself as the very model of a rogue state. In endlessly troubled Iraq a Shiite incursion into oil-rich Kurdish territory threatened to set off another round of the turmoil that characterized that troubled country.

And so it went.

There was a personal item about to come up on the bad-news list at the next day's lunch, too.

Ranjit was not immediately aware of that. When he caught his first sight of Gamini, there ahead of him and skeptically investigating what the cafeteria rather charitably called their special of the day, all he felt was the pleasure of seeing his friend again. But as he was seating himself, he became aware of the expression on Gamini's face. "Is something wrong?" Ranjit demanded.

"Wrong? No, of course not," Gamini said at once, and then sighed. "Oh, hell," he said. "As a matter of fact, Ranjit, there is something I need to tell you about. It's a promise I made my father years ago."

Ranjit was instantly suspicious. Nothing good could be coming of that sort of promise, told in that tone of voice. "What promise?"

"I promised the old man that I would apply to transfer to the London School of Economics after my first year here. He visited there years ago and he thought it was the best school in the world to learn about government."

Indignation fought with surprise in Ranjit's voice. "About government? In a school of economics?"

"That's not its whole name, Ranjit. It's really called the London School of Economics and Political Science."

To that Ranjit could only respond with his all-purpose "Huh." But then he added morosely, "So you're going to apply to this foreign school, just so you can keep some promise you made to your father?"

Gamini coughed. "Not exactly. I mean, it's not what I'm going to do. It's what I already did. I actually applied years ago. It was my father's idea. He said that the earlier I put my name in, the better my chances would be, and it looks like he was right. The thing is, Ranjit, they accepted me. We got the letter last week. I start at London as soon as the school year is finished here."

And that was the second of the bad things that happened to the friendship of Ranjit Subramanian and Gamini Bandara, and by a long way the worse of the two.

Things did not get better for Ranjit. The biology teacher's shipment of embalmed white mice finally arrived, and so the grisly business of dissection started again, and interesting subjects like chikungunya didn't come up again. Even his math course, the one he had counted on to make the others worth enduring, was letting him down.

By the end of his first week at university, Ranjit had been pretty sure he already knew all the algebra he would ever require. Solving Fermat's great puzzle would not depend on conic sections or summation notation. Still, he had breezed through the first few months; such things as finding the factoring of polynomials and the use of logarithmic functions were at least moderately entertaining. But by the third month it became clear that

Dr. Christopher Dabare, the mathematics instructor, not only was not planning to teach anything relating to number theory, but didn't really know a lot about it himself. And, worse, didn't want either to learn or to help Ranjit to learn.

For a time Ranjit made do with the resources of the university library, but the books in the stacks were finite in number. When they ran out, Ranjit's last recourse would have been some or all of the number theory journals, such as the *Journal of Number Theory* itself, from Ohio State University in the United States, or the *Journal de Théorie des Nombres de Bordeaux,* for which that hard-won sketchy knowledge of French might have been useful after all. But the university library did not subscribe to any of those journals, and Ranjit could not access them himself. Oh, Dr. Dabare could, just by permitting the use of his private faculty member password. But he wouldn't do that.

As the end of the year approached, Ranjit needed a friend to unload his disappointments on. But he didn't have that, either.

It was bad enough that Gamini was going nine thousand kilometers away. But to make it worse for Ranjit even those last few weeks were not going to be reserved for the two boys to share. Gamini's family obligations, as it turned out, had to come first. First there was a weekend in Kandy, the "great city" that had once been the island's capital. One branch of Gamini's family had doggedly stayed on in what had been the family home before the mighty "Great Attractor" that was the bustling city of Colombo had drawn the intellectual, the powerful, and even the merely ambitious to where power now resided. Then another weekend to Ratnapura, where a cousin supervised the family's interests in the precious stone mines; still another to where Gamini's ancient grandmother ruled their cinnamon plantations. And even when he was still in the city, Gamini had duty calls to make, and no realistic chance of bringing Ranjit along with him when he made them.

While Ranjit himself had nothing at all to do . . . except to attend his boring classes in the uninteresting subjects that he didn't care about in the first place. And then nearer worries appeared.

It happened at the end of the sociology class Ranjit had never liked. The teacher, whom Ranjit had liked even less, was a Dr. Mendis, and as Ranjit was about to leave, Mendis was standing in the doorway, holding the black-covered notebook he entered grades into. "I've just been going over the grades from last week's exam," he told Ranjit. "Yours was unsatisfactory."

That wasn't surprising to Ranjit. "Sorry, sir," he said absently, peering after his rapidly disappearing classmates. "I'll try to do better," he added, poised to follow them.

But Dr. Mendis wasn't through with him. "If you remember," he said, "at the beginning of term I explained to the class how your final grade would be calculated. It is made up of the midterm examination, the spot quizzes given out from time to time, your classroom attendance and participation, and the final exam, in the proportion of 25 percent, 20 percent, 25 percent, and 30 percent. I must now inform you that, although you did do reasonably well on the midterm, your performance in the classroom and the spot quizzes is so far below an acceptable standard that you would have to get at least 80 percent on the final examination to get a low C for the course. I truthfully don't think you are capable of that." He studied the entries in his book for a moment, and then nodded and snapped it shut. "So what I suggest is that you consider taking an Incomplete for the course." He raised a hand as though to ward off objections from Ranjit, although Ranjit had not been planning any. "I am aware, of course, that that will naturally cause a problem with your hopes for a continuing scholarship. But it would be better than an outright failure, would it not?"

It would, Ranjit was forced to agree—but not out loud, because he didn't want to give Dr. Mendis the satisfaction. By the time he got out of the classroom, the one fellow student left in the hall was a Burgher girl, nice enough looking, some years older than himself. Ranjit was aware that she had been in the sociology class with him, but to him she had been simply another item in the lecture hall's furnishings. He hadn't had much to do in his life with Burghers, the name given to that small fraction of the Sri Lankan population who traced a significant part of their ancestry to one or another of the old European colonizers. Particularly with the female ones.

This particular female Burgher was talking on a cell phone, but closed it up as he approached. "Mr. Subramanian?" she said.

Ranjit stopped, in no mood for casual conversation. "Yes?" he barked.

She did not seem to take offense at his tone. "My name is Myra de Soyza. I heard what Dr. Mendis was saying to you. Are you going to do what he said and take an Incomplete?"

She was really annoying him. He said, "I hope not. Why should I?"

"Oh, you shouldn't. All you need is a little study help. I don't know if you've been noticing, but I've been getting straight A's. I could tutor you, if you liked."

That wasn't anything Ranjit had expected to hear, and it immediately triggered his most suspicious reactions. He demanded, "Why do you want to do that?"

Whatever answer might have been true—perhaps simply that he was a good-looking young man—the one she gave was, "Because I don't think Dr. Mendis is fair to you." But she looked disappointed at his response, perhaps even offended. As she went on, her tone grew sharp. "If you don't want help, just say it. But, you know, what Dr. Mendis calls sociology is just memorizing what it says in the books, and almost always only the parts that are about Sri Lanka. I could walk you through it in plenty of time for the final."

For a moment Ranjit actually considered her offer. Habit won; she was still irrevocably female. "Thanks," he said, "but I'll be all right." He gave her a nod to express enough gratitude to be polite, then turned and walked away.

But, although he left the woman behind him, he carried away with him what she had said.

There was wisdom in it—from a woman, yes, but still wisdom. Who was this professor to tell him that he could not do well on the final exam? There were others besides a Sinhalese schoolteacher and a Burgher woman who knew Sri Lankan history. And there was one particular place, Ranjit was quite sure, where such knowledge was stored, and those in charge would be glad to share it with him.

Pass he did. Not with the "impossible" 80 percent on the final that Dr. Mendis had found so amusing, but with a 91 percent—one of the five highest marks for those taking the test that year. And what would Dr. Mendis say now?

Ranjit had been confident that the fact that his father wasn't speaking to him did not mean he would refuse his son help. He'd been right. When he'd explained his need to Surash, the old monk who had taken his call, he'd got the response he had expected. "I must consult with the high priest about this," Surash had said cautiously. "Please call me back in one hour." But Ranjit had had no doubt of the answer, and had already filled his backpack with toothbrush, clean underwear, and everything else he would need for a stay in Trincomalee before he'd called back. "Yes, Ranjit," the old monk had said. "Come as soon as you can. We will give you what you need."

The only way for Ranjit to get to Trincomalee had been to hitchhike in a truck that smelled of the driver's curry and its cargo of fragrant cinnamon bark. That had meant arriving at the temple well after midnight. His father had of course been long asleep, and the assistant priest on duty did not offer to disturb him. What the assistant priest was willing to do, however, was everything Ranjit asked for: give him a cell and a bed and three plain (but adequate) meals a day—and access to the temple's archives.

The archives weren't written on ancient parchment or animal skins, as Ranjit had feared; this was his father's temple, right up to speed with all the modern necessities. When Ranjit woke that morning, there was a laptop on the table by his cot, and through it he had access to all the history of Sri Lanka, from the days of the tribal Veddas who were the island's first inhabitants, to the present. There was much that his teacher had not touched on, but Ranjit had brought his textbook along—not to study, but to give him a guide to the parts of the nation's past he could safely ignore. He had only five days before he had to go back to the university. But five days of total dedication to one subject was quite enough for a young man as bright and motivated as Ranjit Subramanian. (Nor was he interrupting himself by multitasking. Score one for the theory of the GSSM syndrome.) And he had learned a number of things that would not appear on the final exam, too. He had learned about the vast treasure of pearls and gold and ivory that the Portuguese had looted from his father's temple, just before they tore it down. He learned that once, for fifty years, the Tamils had ruled all of the island—and that the general who had finally defeated the Tamil forces and "freed" his own people evidently was still held in respect by the modern Sinhalese—even by Gamini's own family, because his own father, Dhatusena Bandara, was named after him.

Ranjit headed straight for Gamini's room when the temple van dropped him at the university. He was grinning to himself as he knocked on Gamini's door, thinking of how amusing it would be to tell him that.

That didn't happen. Gamini wasn't there.

When Ranjit roused the night porter, the man said sleepily that Mr. Bandara had left two days earlier. For his family's house in Fort? No, not at all. For London, England, where Mr. Bandara was going to complete his studies.

When at last Ranjit got back to his own room, there was a waiting letter that Gamini had left for him, but all it said was what Ranjit already knew. Gamini's flight to England had been moved up a few days. He would be on it. And he would miss Ranjit.

That was not Ranjit's only disappointment. It was natural enough that the temple staff hadn't disturbed his father when Ranjit had arrived so late. It was not quite as natural, perhaps, that his father had not chosen to disturb himself even enough to look in on his son once in any other of the five days he was living in the temple.

It was almost funny, Ranjit told himself as he turned out the light by his bed. His father had not forgiven him for his closeness to Gamini Bandara. But now Gamini was not close to him at all, not by nine thousand kilometers.

So he had lost the two dearest people in his life, and what was he to do with that life now?

There was one other significant event at that time. Neither Ranjit nor any other human being alive knew of it, however. It took place many light-years away, in the vicinity of a star that human astronomers knew only by its right ascension and declination numbers. One of those great expanding hemispheres of photons, perhaps the one from Eniwetok, perhaps from one of the Soviet monster bombs, finally reached the place where the photon pulses caused a major decision that meant bad news for the people of Earth. The pulses had alerted certain high-performance sapients (or one such sapient, their nature making it difficult to say which it should properly be called) who (or at least some fraction of whom) inhabited a vortex of dark-matter rivulets in that part of the galaxy.

These sentients were known as the Grand Galactics. Once alerted they constructed a fan of probability projections. The display that resulted matched some of their worst speculations.

These Grand Galactics had many plans and objectives, few of which would then have been comprehensible to an Earth human. One of their principal concerns was observing the working out of the galaxy's natural physical laws. Humans did that, too, but humans' reason for doing so was an effort to understand them. The Grand Galactics' primary concern was to make sure those laws did not require changing. Other interests were more arcane still.

However, at least one of their concerns would have been quite clear. It could have been translated somewhat like, "Protect the harmless. Quarantine the dangerous. Destroy the malevolent—after storing a backup in a secure location."

That was what troubled the Grand Galactics here. Species that developed weaponry were all too likely to try it out on some other species, and that could not be tolerated.

Accordingly the Grand Galactics by unanimous agreement (that being the only kind of agreement they ever had) sent a directive to one of their newest, but also most useful, client races, the Nine-Limbeds. The directive came in two parts. The first was to prepare a radio message for Earth, in as many of Earth's several thousand dialects and languages as were broadcast in electronic form so that Nine-Limbed experts could pick them up and learn to communicate in them. The message was to say, basically, "Cease and desist." (Languages were what the Nine-Limbeds were especially good at. This was quite unusual among the client races of the Grand Galactics. They did not encourage their clients to speak to one another.)

The second part required the Nine-Limbeds to continue, and indeed to increase, their intensive close-range surveillance of Earth.

It was a curious thing (an outside observer might have thought) for the Grand Galactics to give so much responsibility to a species that was, after all, relatively new to their employ. However, the Grand Galactics had employed them on other matters in the handful of millennia since they had been added to the roster of client races, and the Grand Galactics had observed that the Nine-Limbeds displayed persistence, curiosity, and thoroughness in carrying out their assignments. These were qualities the Grand Galactics prized. It did not occur to them that the Nine-Limbeds might also have other qualities, such as a sense of humor.

3

AN ADVENTURE IN
CODE-CRACKING

There were nearly two months of summer vacation between the end of Ranjit's first school year and the beginning of his second. This tinkering with the calendar was still regarded as a rather radical new experiment by much of the university's faculty. Until recently they had never allowed a summer vacation on the grounds that, Sri Lanka being as close to the equator as it was, it never had seasons. But a few years of student unrest, followed by the realization that college-age young men and women need a break from discipline now and then, led to the experiment of following Western university practices.

For Ranjit, the experiment was not so successful. Gamini was away, so he had no one to enjoy it with, and world news remained bad.

What made it worse was that for a time things had looked good. There had been a promise of a superpower meeting to stamp out some of the world's deadly little wars. That had sounded like a promising development, but the selection of a site for the meeting went badly. Russia proposed Kiev, in Ukraine, but when it came to a vote, Kiev lost by two votes to one. China offered Ho Chi Minh City, in Vietnam, but it, too, was defeated, by the same margin. As was the American proposal, Vancouver, in Canada. After which the Chinese representatives stormed out of the UN building, declaring that the Western powers had no real interest in world peace after all.

But the American and Russian delegates had expected that, and had made a plan in readiness. In joint statements they deplored the Chinese failure to subordinate national vanity to the needs of peace and announced their intention to set aside their often-expressed and irreconcilable differences to go ahead with the meeting without China's presence.

For a locale they chose that beautiful Venice of the north, the city of Stockholm, Sweden. Their effort almost succeeded. They agreed on the urgent need to put an immediate stop to the ongoing fighting between Israel and the Palestinians, between the Muslim and the Christian fragments of what had once been Yugoslavia, between Ecuador and Colombia—well, between every pair of nations that was making war, declared or otherwise, on each other all around the globe. There were plenty of candidates, and there was no doubt that a few rockets in the right place could have made any of them stop fighting. The Americans and the Russians agreed that it was their simple duty, as the biggest bullies on the block, to do the job.

But there was one thing they couldn't agree on. That was, in each combative pair, which one to aim their rockets at.

Ranjit Subramanian decided to do his best to ignore all that sort of thing. It was spoiling his summer, which was cherished, unprogrammed time for Ranjit, meaning he could do pretty much whatever he wanted to do, and he knew exactly what that would be. But when he trapped Dr. Christopher Dabare in his office, the math teacher took offense. "If I would not allow you to use my password during the school year, what gives you the lunatic notion that I will let you have it while I'm in Kuwait?"

Ranjit blinked at him. "Kuwait?"

"Where I have a contract to teach summer sessions each year for the oil sheikhs' sons, at, I might mention, a rate of payment quite a bit more impressive than I receive trying to beat simple mathematical truths into the heads of you people."

To which Ranjit, thinking fast, responded only, "Oh, I'm sorry. I didn't know you'd be away. I wish you a pleasant trip," and headed out of the professor's office for the nearest computer. If bloody Dr. Dabare wouldn't give up his password voluntarily, there were other possibilities. Specifically there were the kind of possibilities that existed in the case of a teacher who would be making his fortune a couple of thousand kilometers away, and Ranjit had instantly conceived a plan for taking advantage of them.

Step one in the plan was easy. Every faculty member at the university kept a potted biography on file. It took only a moment for Ranjit to pull Dabare's up. Ten minutes later he was walking away, folding into his pocket the printout that held a healthy beginning for all the preliminary data he wanted—Dabare's birth date, his personal phone extension number, his e-mail address, his passport number, his wife's name—and the names of her parents, too—his own parents' names, and even the name of his paternal grandfather, included because he had once been mayor of a small town somewhere in the south. Plus the name of his Jack Russell terrier, Millie, and the address of his beach house down the shore in Uppuveli. It wasn't everything. It almost certainly would not even be enough. But it was certainly a good chunk of data to be starting with.

The question was, where could he find a place to run the necessary programs?

Certainly none of the terminals he was in the habit of using for his schoolwork would do. They were far too public. Ranjit had no doubt that when he finished programming the computer to do what he wanted, it would need to chug along for a significant period of time as it worked all the required combinations and permutations. He did not want some casual passerby wondering what that computer was up to.

But there was an ideal place! The one he and Gamini had discovered in the unfinished school of indigenous law!

When he got there, though, he got a shock. He came in the usual way for Gamini and himself—the back way—and was pleased to see the two computers still sitting there and lighting up at once when he hit the power key. But he could hear a distant sound of music, the kind of tuneless this-year's trash that he and Gamini had agreed they hated, and when he peered in at the reception room, the actual receptionist was there. An elderly woman, rather fat. Making herself a cup of tea to go with the supermarket special "newspaper" in her hand.

She seemed to have the ears of a bat. She looked up at once to where Ranjit lurked. "Hello?" she called. "Is someone there?"

For a time it seemed to Ranjit that he was going to have to find another perfect spot for his computing, but it turned out that the receptionist did not consider her duties to include security checks. Her name, she said, was Mrs. Wanniarachchi. (To which Ranjit inventively responded that his was Sumil Bandaranaga.) She was glad to have company in the stacks, because sometimes it got lonesome. Mr. Bandaranaga did of course have at least a minor in comparative religions? Ranjit assured her that he did, and that was all it took. Mrs. Wanniarachchi gave him a friendly wave and went back to her scandal sheet, and Ranjit had the freedom of the library.

Nothing had changed. The pair of computer terminals still sat ready, and it didn't take Ranjit long to set up his program and feed in the bits and pieces he had collected. As he left, the woman at the desk, already standing up and putting on her raincoat, said idly, "You've turned everything off, haven't you?"

"Oh, of course," Ranjit reassured her. Actually, he hadn't; but the computer would turn itself off when it had found the password Ranjit was looking for, or when it concluded that the password could not be generated from any of the data he had supplied. And in the morning he could get the results.

Which were, as he had more or less expected, nonexistent.

There had not been enough data for the program to do its job. By then he already had more data to feed it, though, having spent one hour of the night wearing the rough clothes of a garbageman and collecting all the refuse Dr. Dabare's household had set out for the real collectors of everything unwanted. Most of what Ranjit acquired was not only worthless but offensive to the nose, but there had been several dozen sheets of paper— statements of account from various shops and service providers; offers for tours, car rentals, and e-bank lending facilities; and, best of all, a dozen or so personal letters. Tragically most of them were in German, the language of the country where the professor had taken some graduate courses, a language as opaque to Ranjit as Inuit or Choctaw, but from the letters in English or Sinhalese he extracted Dabare's driver's license number, his exact height in centimeters, and the PIN for his cash machine card. (And wouldn't it be only fair if Ranjit took a thousand rupees or so for the trouble the math professor was causing him? No, he concluded, it wouldn't. Such a thing was feloniously illegal. But it was amusing to think about.)

The computer of course had long since run out of permutations to try and so had stopped. Ranjit typed in all the new candidates, hit the go button, and left once more. Yes, he might be divorcing himself from the real world. But the real world seemed to have very little to offer a friendless and—at least temporarily—fatherless Tamil boy.

But then, when he got to his room to get a long-delayed sleep, there waiting for him was something that brightened the whole day. It was a letter with a London postmark, and it was from Gamini.

Dear Old Ranjit:
Got here safe and sound, also totally exhausted. It was a nine-hour flight, counting changing planes twice, but when I got to London, it was only four and a half hours later, which meant it was nearly another eight hours before I could get to bed, and I was a physical wreck. Oh, and missed you like hell.

It had taken long enough for Gamini to get around to saying the good part, but there it was. Ranjit took the time to read that sentence over three or four times before going on with the rest of the letter. Which was newsy but not very personal. Gamini's classes were interesting but maybe more demanding than he would have liked. The food at the London School was, naturally, horrible, but there were plenty of Indian take-out places everywhere, and some of them knew what to do with a curry. The school's housing wasn't much better than the food, but Gamini wasn't going to have to stay in it forever. As soon as he got the go-ahead from his father's London lawyers, he was going to sign a lease on what the landlord called "a superb maisonette" just a five-minute walk from most of his classrooms. Such things you could do, Ranjit thought as he looked without enjoyment around his own bleak room, when you were lucky enough to possess a rich father. And, oh, yes, Ranjit, the letter went on, you'd be thrilled to be here because the school is no more than ten minutes away from the cluster of theaters and restaurants around Leicester Square. Gamini had already found time to see a revival of *She Stoops to Conquer* and a couple of musicals.

So Gamini Bandara, though nine thousand kilometers away, was having fun.

Ranjit sighed, spared a moment to be glad that his absent friend was doing so well—or, at least, spared a moment to tell himself that he was glad—crawled into his lonesome bed, and went to sleep.

It took Ranjit long enough to get the code-cracking job done—eleven days, actually, with much of each day devoted to dredging up additional possible entries or inventing new ways for the computer to mix and match them. But then there was the morning when he came in, expecting little, and got the supreme delight of seeing his computer screen announcing "Dr. Dabare password identified." What it turned out to be was the motto of the University of Colombo, *Buddhih Sarvatra Bhrajate*—"wisdom shines forth everywhere"—with his wife's birthday cut in half and interpolated between the words:

Buddhih.4-14.Sarvatra.1984.Bhrajate

And the world of mathematical documents was open to him!

4

FORTY DAYS OF
DATA DOWNPOUR

So in the remaining six weeks before the new school year began, Ranjit for the first time in his life found himself very nearly drowning in the cascades of the precise sort of information he most desired.

To begin with there were the journals of number theory. There were two major ones in the English language and one or two apiece in French, German, and even Chinese (but he decided early on not to bother with anything he would need to get translated). And the books—so many books! And all now available to him through the interlibrary loan! Ones that looked interesting, though perhaps not directly relevant to his quest, were those such as Scharlau and Opolka's *From Fermat to Minkowski* and Weil's *Basic Number Theory,* which according to the reviews was not all that basic, indeed quite advanced even for Ranjit. Less promising, because apparently written for an audience not as informed as Ranjit himself, were Simon Singh's *Fermat's Enigma* and Yves Hellegouarch's *Invitation to the Mathematics of Fermat-Wiles* and the book by Cornell, Silverman, and Stevens called *Modular Forms and Fermat's Last Theorem.* Well, the list was long, and that was only the books! What about the papers, the hundreds, maybe even the thousands, of papers that had been written on this most famous of mathematical conundrums and published—well, everywhere: in England's *Nature* and the American *Science,* in mathematical journals refereed and respected and circulated around the world, and in mathematical journals issued in obscure universities in places such as Nepal and Chile and the Duchy of Luxembourg, and perhaps hardly respected at all.

Somewhat saddeningly he kept finding little curiosities that he would have liked to share with his father. There was, it seemed, a strong tradition of elements of number theory in Hindu literature as far back as the seventh century A.D. and even earlier—Brahmagupta, Varahamihira, Pingala, and, in the Lilavati of all places, Bhaskara. As well as that seminal Arab figure abu-i-Fath Omar bin Ibrahim Khayyám, best known to those who had ever heard of him at all, a number which had not previously included Ranjit Subramanian, as Omar Khayyám, the author of the long collection of poetic quatrains called *The Rubaiyat*.

None of this was particularly helpful in Ranjit's dogged pursuit of Fermat. Even Brahmagupta's famous theorem meant nothing to him since he did not particularly care that in a certain kind of quadrilateral a certain kind of perpendicular would always bisect its opposite side. However, when Ranjit came across the fourth or fifth mention of Pascal's triangle and the taking of roots in connection with Khayyám, he sat down and composed an e-mail to his father telling of his discoveries. And then he sat for some time with his finger poised over the send button before he sighed and pushed cancel instead. If Ganesh Subramanian wanted to have a social relation with his son, it was his duty, not his son's, to make the first move.

Four weeks later Ranjit had read, or read part of, every one of the seventeen books and nearly one hundred and eighty papers in his bibliography. It hadn't been rewarding. He had hoped for some stray insight that would clarify everything else. That didn't come. He found himself led up a dozen different blind alleys—over and over, because many of the mathematician authors were following the same paper trails as himself. Five or six times each he was reexamining Wieferich's relatively prime exponents and Sophie Germain's work on certain odd primes and Kummer's theory of ideals and, of course, Euler, and, of course, every other mathematician who had innocently ambled into Fermat's lethally inviting tar pit and, bellowing in fear and pain like any other trapped dire wolf, mastodon, or saber-toothed cat, had never escaped.

The plan was not working. With less than a week before the new school year began, Ranjit faced the fact that he was trying to work too many angles at once. It was something like the very GSSM syndrome Gamini had warned him against.

So he determined to simplify his attack. Being Ranjit Subramanian, his idea of simplifying was to make a head-on attack on that hated and endlessly long Wiles proof, the one that only a handful of the world's leading mathematicians dared claim they understood.

He gritted his teeth and began.

The first steps were easy. But then he worked further into Wiles's ugly chain of reasoning and it began to get—well, not hard, exactly, not for the likes of Ranjit Subramanian, but at least it began to require concentrated attention for every line. Because that was when Wiles began considering the equations for curves in the x-y plane, and for elliptical curves, and for the many solutions to the equation for modularity. Which was when Wiles, for the first time ever, was able to demonstrate that what was called the Taniyama-Shimura-Weil conjecture—namely, that any infinite class of elliptical curves was modular—was valid. And then, while Gerhard Frey and Kenneth Ribet had demonstrated that a certain elliptical curve could not be modular, Wiles himself was able to demonstrate that that same curve necessarily had to be modular. . . .

And, aha! There it was! A veritable contradiction!

A contradiction was the mathematical pot of gold that—sometimes!—lay at the end of some interminable mathematical trail. A contradiction was the thing that mathematicians gladly devoted their lives to finding, because if logical deductions from your starting equation wind up with two conclusions that contradict each other, then your starting equation itself must be wrong!

And so it was proved—sort of proved—that Fermat had spoken truth. The square was the limit. The sum of no two cubes would ever be another cube, and so on for every other exponent this side of infinity. But Ranjit was no nearer to finding his own less daunting proof of what Fermat had so casually mentioned so long ago.

And—oh, yes—he was not aware that his picture was being taken.

The beings that were doing the picture taking were another of those client races of the Grand Galactics. These were called the Machine-Stored, and of course Ranjit never saw them. They didn't intend to be seen. They generally weren't ever seen, either, although under certain rare combinations of starlight, moonlight, and gegenschein, a few of them had occasionally been detected by an occasional human being. When reported, these sightings were generally referred to as sightings of flying saucers, thus adding to the vast catalog of fakes, mistakes, and downright lies that made it nearly certain no respectable scientist would ever pay any attention to them.

What the Machine-Stored were doing on Earth at that time was anticipating a need of the Grand Galactics, whose needs and wishes the Machine-Stored always catered to. The Grand Galactics hadn't ordered this activity, but the Machine-Stored were permitted to use their own discretion in certain limited circumstances. The special quality of the Machine-Stored lay in the fact that they had trashed their planet even more diligently than the One Point Fives, to the point where organic life on its surface was now completely impossible. The One Point Fives had dealt with the problem by adding infinite prostheses to their vulnerable organic bodies. The Machine-Stored took a different tack. They abandoned their physical planet, and indeed abandoned everything physical at all. They reconstituted themselves as something like computer programs and allowed their now quite frail and sickly bodies the privilege of death, while the individuals lived on in cyberspace. (Since which their despoiled planet had begun to show the beginning signs of regeneration. Not all of its liquid water was now toxic, for instance—though it still would have been pretty much a hellhole for anything organic.)

And the Machine-Stored themselves?

Why, they made themselves useful. Sometimes, when the Grand Galactics chose to move a certain quantity of objects or beings from one star system to another, the Machine-Stored were instructed to do the moving. And when they had detected those first microwave and then nuclear pulses from Earth, they'd known the Grand Galactics would take an interest. They didn't wait for orders. They at once began to survey the planet and everything on it, and to pass those findings at once to the corner of the galaxy where the Grand Galactics swam in their dark energy streams.

Of course, the Machine-Stored had no good idea of just what the human race was up to in its various activities. For that, they would have needed to understand human languages. That didn't happen. The Grand Galactics preferred that their client races be ignorant of any languages but their own, because if the races could freely talk to one another, who knew what they might be saying?

Ranjit would have been astonished to know that his own picture had been flashed across interstellar space in that manner. It had, though. So had the pictures of everyone, and almost everything, on Earth, because the Machine-Stored—if not omnipotent—were diligent.

And hoped that the Grand Galactics would appreciate, or at least tolerate, that diligence.

When Ranjit's bedside radio woke him for the first day of his new term, he leaped out of bed in order to turn it off. His first class, Astronomy 101: The Geography of the Solar System, was also pretty close to his last hope that the university would provide him with anything interesting over the next three years. That was mildly cheering in itself. And then, as he was leaving the building, the porter handed him a letter—from London, and therefore from Gamini—and Ranjit actually did feel a little bit cheerful.

Hunched over his breakfast, he read the letter. It didn't take very much time. The letter was even shorter than its predecessor and almost entirely devoted to describing Gamini's "superb maisonette":

You enter from the street and go up a flight of stairs. Then you're in the living room (the Brits call it the "reception"). Next to that room is a doll-size kitchen, and that's all there is on that floor. There's a separate flight of stairs going down from the reception to the back, where there's a spare room that looks out on a few square meters of mud that might be supposed to be a garden. I guess I'll call that the guest room, but I don't plan to be putting up any overnight guests in it. (Unless, my man, you want to drop by for a weekend sometime!) Going back to the reception floor, there's another flight of stairs that takes you up to the bedroom and bath. Not very convenient for anybody sleeping in the guest room if he needs to have a pee in the middle of the night. And let's go back to the kitchen. It's got everything you'd want in a modern kitchen, but in dollhouse sizes: tiny fridge, tiny stove, tiny sink, and the tiniest washer-dryer you've ever seen. I said it was about big enough to handle a pair of socks, but Madge said it could only if you did just one sock at a time.

Anyway, such as it is, it's mine! Even if all the furnishing is Early Cheap. Only now I've got to run, because a bunch of us are going to see the new Stoppard revival and we want to have dinner first.

Ranjit managed a smile at the thought of Gamini doing laundry—the Gamini for whom laundry had always been what you took home and gave to the servants, who the next morning would return it to you, cleaned, ironed, and folded.

That did not keep him from wondering just who this Madge was.

So he showed up for his first class prepared for disappointment. . . .

But then, wonderfully, miraculously, that was not at all what happened!

5

FROM MERCURY
TO THE OORT

The place where Astronomy 101 was given wasn't a regular classroom. It was one of the rooms that were designed like miniature theaters, with curved rows of seats enough for a hundred students. Almost every seat was occupied, too, right down to the level that held a desk, a chair, and a lecturer who didn't look to be much older than Ranjit himself. His name was Joris Vorhulst. He was obviously a Burgher, and it was almost as obvious that he had chosen to leave the island for his graduate schooling.

The schools he had gone to impressed Ranjit, too. They were hallowed names for astronomers. Dr. Vorhulst had got his master's at the University of Hawaii at Hilo, where he had interned on the vast old Keck telescopes, and he'd gone on to his doctorate at Caltech, with a side order of working at the Jet Propulsion Laboratory in Pasadena. At JPL he had been part of the team that ran *Faraway,* the spacecraft that had flown by Pluto into the Kuiper Belt—or into the rest of the Kuiper Belt, as Vorhulst would say, because he was loyal to the old profession-wide decision that had stripped Pluto of its claim to true planethood, so that now it was just one more of the countless millions of Kuiper snowballs. (Actually, Vorhulst told the class, *Faraway* had gone pretty much all the way through the Kuiper Belt by now and was already taking aim at the nearer fringes of the Oort cloud.)

Vorhulst went on to explain what all those unfamiliar (at least to Ranjit) things were, and the boy was fascinated.

And then, when the class was nearly over, Vorhulst gave them some good news. Everyone in the class, he announced, would have the privilege of looking through Sri Lanka's best telescope at the observatory on the slopes of Piduruthalagala. "A really neat two-meter reflector," he said. And then he added, "It was a present from the government of Japan, replacing a smaller one they'd given us earlier." That got a smattering of applause from the students, but that was nothing compared to what they did when he said, "Oh, and by the way, my computer password is 'Faraway.' You're all welcome to use it to access any astronomical material on the Web." Then

there were actual cheers, among the loudest the ones that came from the Sinhalese boy in the seat next to Ranjit. And when the professor looked at the timer on the wall and said the remaining ten minutes could be used for questions, Ranjit was one of the first to have a hand up. "Yes," Vorhulst said, looking at the identifying board on his desk, "Ranjit?"

Ranjit stood up. "I'm just wondering if you've ever heard of Percy Molesworth."

"Molesworth, eh?" Vorhulst shaded his eyes to get a better look at Ranjit. "Are you from Trincomalee?" Ranjit nodded. "Yes, he's buried there, isn't he? And yes, I have heard of him. Did you ever look up his crater on the moon? Go ahead. 'Faraway' will give you access to the JPL page."

That was precisely what Ranjit did, the minute the class was over. He quickly located Jet Propulsion Laboratory on the World Wide Web on the rank of computers in the hall and downloaded a splendid image of the lunar crater named Molesworth.

It was indeed impressive, nearly two hundred kilometers across. Though an almost flat plain, its interior was dotted with a dozen genuine meteor-made craters, including one with a magnificent central peak. Ranjit thought of his visits to Molesworth's grave in Trincomalee with his father. How nice it would have been to let his father know that he had seen the lunar crater for himself. But to do that seemed impossible.

The rest of Ranjit's courses, naturally, were nowhere near as interesting as Astronomy 101. He'd signed up for anthropology because he'd expected it would be easy for him to get through without actually thinking much about it. As it developed, it was easy, although the other salient fact about it, as Ranjit learned, was that it was very nearly terminally tedious. And he'd signed up for psychology because he'd wanted to hear more about this GSSM syndrome. But in the first session the teacher informed him that he didn't believe in GSSM, no matter what some other professor in some other class might say. ("Because if multitasking made you stupid, how would any of you ever manage to graduate?") Finally, he was taking philosophy because it looked like the kind of thing you could bluff your way through without the necessity of a lot of studying.

There he had been wrong. Professor de Silva was a devotee of the practice of giving spot quizzes almost every week. That would have been tolerable enough, perhaps, but Ranjit quickly also learned that the professor was the kind who required his classes to memorize dates.

For a while Ranjit tried to take an interest in the subject. Plato was not a total waste of time, he thought, nor Aristotle. But when Professor de Silva began getting up to the Middle Ages, with Peter Abelard and Thomas Aquinas and all those people, things got worse. Ranjit did not really care about the difference between epistemology and metaphysics, or whether God existed, or what "reality" really was, exactly. So his flicker of interest flickered a bit more and then went out.

But, wonderfully, the joy of exploring Sol's other worlds kept getting better and better. Especially when, in the second session, Dr. Vorhulst got into the possibilities of actually visiting some of the planets, at least perhaps one or two of the least forbidding ones.

Vorhulst ran through the list for them. Mercury, no; you would hardly want to go there because it was far too hot and dry, even though there did appear to be some water—actually, ice—at one pole. Venus looked to be even worse, wrapped in that carbon dioxide blanket that trapped heat. "The same kind of blanket," Vorhulst told the class, "that is causing the global warming right here on Earth that I hope we may actually, one day, escape. Or at least the worst parts of it." On Venus, he added, those "worst parts" had added up to a surface temperature that would melt lead.

Next out was the Earth, "which we don't actually need to colonize anymore," Vorhulst joked, "because apparently someone, or something, did already, a good long time ago." He didn't give them a chance to react to that but went right on: "So let's look at Mars. Do we want to visit Mars? More interesting, is there life there? That argument went back and forth for years." The American astronomer Percival Lowell, he said, had thought not only that there was life on Mars but that it was a highly civilized, massively technological kind of life, capable of building the enormous network of canals Giovanni Schiaparelli had observed on its surface. Better telescopes—with the help of the late Captain Percy Molesworth of Trincomalee—ruined that idea when it was established that Schiaparelli's "canali" were only random markings that his eye had tricked him into linking into straight lines. Then the first three Mariner missions ended that debate by sending back pictures of a surface that was arid, cratered, and cold. "But," Dr. Vorhulst finished, "better photographs of the surface of Mars since then have shown indications of actual flowing water. Not flowing anymore now, of course, but pretty definitely real water that did flow sometime in the past. So the life-on-Mars people were riding high again. But," he added, "then the pendulum swung back. So which way is right?" Dr. Vorhulst swept the audience with his glance, then grinned. "I think the only way

we'll know is to send some people there, preferably with a lot of digging equipment."

He paused. Then he said, "I guess your next question is, 'What would they be digging for?' But before I answer that, do any of you know of a place in the solar system that we have left out so far?"

Silence for a moment while a hundred students counted on their fingers—Mercury, Venus, Earth, Mars—until a young woman in the front row called, "Are you talking about the moon, Dr. Vorhulst?"

He glanced at his finder plate for her name, then tipped her a salute. "Right on, Roshini. But before we get to the moon let me show you some pictures of a place I've actually been to, namely, Hawaii."

He turned to the wall screen behind him, which had begun to display a nighttime shot of a dark hillside running down to the sea. The slope was dotted with splotches of red fires, like the campsite of an army, and where the splotches reached the shoreline there were violent pyrotechnics with fiery meteors flying above the surface.

"That's Hawaii," Vorhulst said. "The big island. The volcano Kilauea is erupting, and what you see is its lava flowing into the sea. As it flows along, each little stream begins to cool on the outside, and so it forms a sort of a pipe of hardened stone that the liquid lava flows on through. Only, sometimes the lava breaks through the pipe. Then you see these isolated patches of red-hot lava shining out." He gave the class time to wonder why they were looking at Hawaii when the subject had ostensibly been the moon. Then he touched his controller again. Now the screen displayed Dr. Vorhulst himself along with a rather good-looking young woman in a skimpy sunsuit. They were standing at the entrance to what looked like an overgrown cave in the middle of a tropical rain forest.

"That's Annie Shkoda there with me," Vorhulst told the class. "She was my thesis adviser in Hilo—and don't get any ideas, because about a month after that picture was taken she married somebody else. What we're just about to go into there is what Americans call the Thurston Lava Tube. I prefer the Hawaiian name, which is Nahuku, because actually the man named Thurston that the other name comes from had nothing to do with the tube. He was just a newspaper publisher who campaigned for creating the Volcanoes National Park. Anyway, what happened was that maybe four or five hundred years ago Kilauea—or possibly the earlier volcano, Mauna Loa—was in eruption. It poured out lava; the lava formed tubes. When the lava stopped flowing, the liquid stuff ran out of the tubes. But the tubes remained as great big pipes of rock. Over time they got covered up with mud and dirt and God knows what, but they were still there." He paused, look-ing up at the rows of students. "Anyone care to guess what this has to do with the moon?" Twenty hands went up at once. Vorhulst picked the boy next to Ranjit. "Yes, Jude?"

The boy stood up eagerly. "There were volcanoes on the moon, too."

The professor nodded. "You bet there were. Not very recently, because the moon is so small it cooled off long ago. But we can still see where there were humongous ones, where the basaltic lava flows still cover hundreds of square kilometers, and there are plenty of domes on the moon—on the plains or actually inside a crater—that are probably volcanic in origin. And if there are flows and domes, there was lava, and if there was lava, there was what?"

"Lava tubes!" a dozen students said at once—Ranjit being one of them.

"Lava tubes, exactly," Vorhulst agreed. "On Earth, tubes like Nahuku rarely grow to more than a couple of meters in diameter, but the moon is a different matter. In the moon's trivial gravity they could grow ten times as big—could grow to the size of the Chunnel between England and France. And they're sitting there, waiting for some human being to come along and dig down to one of them and caulk it—very thoroughly caulk it—and fill it with air . . . and then rent out bedroom space in it to immigrants from Earth." He looked up at the timing light over the screen, which had gone from green to amber and was now flashing red. "And that's the end of today's session," he said.

But, as a matter of fact, it really wasn't because at least a dozen hands were still up. Dr. Vorhulst cast a rueful glance at the implacably red timing light, but surrendered. "All right," he said. "One more question. What is it?"

Several of the hand raisers dropped their own hands to turn eagerly toward a boy Ranjit had seen in the company of the boy who was his seat-mate, Jude. He spoke right up, as though he had been waiting for his chance. "Dr. Vorhulst," he said, "a few of us would like to know your opin-ion on something. What you say often sounds as though you think intelli-gent life might be quite common in the galaxy. Do you think that is true?"

Vorhulst gave him a quizzical look. "Come on, guys! How do I know some of you don't have brothers-in-law who work as newspaper reporters? And if I say what you want me to say, what's the story going to be, 'Uni-versity Stargazer Claims Countless Alien Races Will Compete with Hu-manity'?"

The boy stood his ground. "Do you?" he asked.

Vorhulst sighed. "All right," he said. "It's a fair question and I'll give you a fair answer. I know of no scientific reason why there could not be a number, perhaps a quite large number, of life-bearing planets in our galaxy, nor of any scientific reason why some number of them have not developed scientifically advanced civilizations. That's the truth. I have never denied it. Of course," he added, "I'm not talking about your crazy superbeings out of the comics who want to make us humans their slaves, or maybe exterminate us entirely. Like—what were their names? Superman's enemies that his father had captured before their planet blew up and put into a floating space prison that looked sort of like a cubical paperweight, only something happened and they all got loose?"

A voice from the back row was already shouting, "You mean General Zod?" And another voice came up with, "And the girl, Urna." And then half a dozen others put in, "And Non!"

The professor gave them all a grin. "I'm happy to see that so many of you are so well versed in the classics. Anyway, trust me on this. They don't exist. No hideous space aliens are going to decide to exterminate us, and now let's get out of here before they call the campus police."

Although Dr. Joris Vorhulst had never heard of the Grand Galactics or any of their client species—and would have been likely to give a very different answer if he had—he, technically, was still quite right in what he said. No space aliens were going to decide to exterminate the human race. The only space aliens interested in the subject had already made the decision to do so and had then gone on to more entertaining matters.

The Grand Galactics were not motivated to keep their turf clear of inimical species out of any notion of living in peace and amity. What they desired, and attained, was an existence with the least possible distraction from their main interests. Some of these interests had to do with their plans for an ideal galactic environment, which they had some hope of attaining in another ten or twenty billion years. Other interests were more like what humans might call the appreciation of beauty.

The Grand Galactics found many things "beautiful," including what humans would describe as numbering, nucleonics, cosmology, string (and non-string) theory, causality, and many other areas. In their enjoyment of the fundamental aspects of nature, they might spend centuries—millennia, if they chose—contemplating the rich spectral changes as, one by one, some single atom lost its orbital electrons. Or they might study the distribution of prime numbers greater than 10^{50}, or the slow maturation of a star from wispy gas and thin-scattered particles through the initiation of nuclear burning to its terminal state as a cooling white dwarf or, again, as a cloud of wisps and particles.

Oh, they did have other concerns. One, for example, was their project of increasing the proportion of heavy elements relative to primordial hydrogen in the galaxy's chemical makeup. (They had a valid reason for this program, but not one that contemporary human beings would have understood.) Their other concerns were even less comprehensible to the likes of humanity. But, yes, they did consider the suppression of potentially dangerous civilizations worth doing.

Therefore the data concerning planet Earth required action. Their cease and desist order radioed to the human planet at light's lazy stroll was still years from reaching its target. It would not be enough. Would not matter at all, in fact, because more urgent action was required. These upstart bipedal vertebrates not only possessed the technology of nuclear fission and fusion to an extent capable of creating inconveniencing weaponry, they already possessed a vast planetwide weapons industry to build on. The situation was even more annoying than the Grand Galactics had supposed, and they did not tolerate annoyance well.

They elected to terminate this particular annoyance.

When the Grand Galactics wished to convey an instruction to one of their client races, they had several delivery systems available. There was, for example, simple radio, efficient but ponderously slow. No electromagnetic signal—light, radar, that kind of thing—could go any faster than Dr. Einstein's beloved c, which is to say an absolute maximum speed of some three hundred thousand kilometers a second. The Grand Galactics had devised some faster machines, sneaking through loopholes in relativity, but those were at most four or five times more speedy.

The Grand Galactics themselves, however—or any detachable fragment of them—being what ineffably nonbaryonic beings they were, suffered no such limitations. For reasons connected with the geometry of ten-dimensional space-time, their travel was composed of a number of laps, a to b, then b to c, then from c perhaps a straight shot to their destination. For each lap, however, transit time was always zero, whether across the diameter of a proton or from the galaxy's core to its farthest-flung spiral arm.

So they took the inconvenient step of detaching a fragment of themselves to carry the instruction to the One Point Fives, and so the One Point Fives had their marching orders almost as soon as the Grand Galactics had decided to give them. And because the One Point Fives had anticipated what the decision would be, they were already in full marching order by the time the orders came.

The One Point Fives saw no reason to delay. Their invasion armada was quite ready to launch. They launched it.

To be sure, the One Point Fives were wholly material and thus not exempted from the speed-of-light rule. Roughly a human generation would pass before the armada could reach its destination and exterminate the undesirable species. But it was on its way.

6

MEANWHILE, BACK ON EARTH

Things were looking up for Ranjit Subramanian—well, they were, that is, if you didn't count the fact that Gamini was still nine thousand kilometers away and Ranjit's own father might almost as well have been. And things were hotting up again in Iraq, where muscular Christian thugs with assault rifles were guarding one end of a bridge that they didn't want crossed by Islamists; the bridge was guarded at the other side by equally husky and well-armed Islamists who didn't want Christians polluting their side of the river.

There were many more such things going on, but those certainly weren't the things that were giving some provisional happiness to Ranjit.

Such things did exist, though. He was not only enjoying Astronomy 101, he was doing very well in it. The worst of his quizzes received scores in the upper eighties, the goodwill of his teacher (as measured in the compliments he gave Ranjit's questions and discussion) scoring perhaps even higher. Of course, Dr. Vorhulst found some way to compliment nearly everyone else in the class, too. It wasn't just that he was an indulgent or lazy teacher, Ranjit decided. More likely it was that no one would sign up for his class who wasn't fascinated by the idea of sometime, somehow seeing human beings going off to visit some of those bizarre other worlds. When Ranjit got his third straight hundred on a quiz, it occurred to him for the first time that perhaps he might actually have the makings of the kind of student who would make his father proud.

So as an experiment he tried taking his other classes a bit more seriously. He checked his philosophy teacher's list of extra-credit reading and picked a book that had at least an interesting title. But when he took Thomas Hobbes's great work *Leviathan* home, it quickly stopped being interesting. Was Hobbes saying that the human mind was like a machine? Ranjit wasn't sure. Nor could he make sense of, say, the distinction between *meritum congrui* and *meritum condigni*. And while he was quite confident he knew what Hobbes was saying when he praised a "Christian state" as the highest form of government, that was not a notion that appealed to the doggedly agnostic son of the head priest of a Hindu temple. Nothing in Hobbes, for that matter, seemed very relevant to the life of anybody Ranjit knew. Glumly he took the book back to the library and headed to his room, hoping for nothing but a peaceful hour's nap.

He found two letters waiting for him. One was in a creamy-textured envelope embossed with the university's golden seal. Most likely, Ranjit thought, a notice from the student banking people to inform him that his father had sent along another quarter's dorm rent. But the other was from London and thus from Gamini. Ranjit ripped it open at once.

If he had hoped that hearing from Gamini would brighten this unsatisfactory day, he was disappointed once more. It didn't. The letter was short and it did not at any point say that Gamini was missing him. What it principally talked about was attending a performance of one of Shakespeare's less amusing comedies at something called the Barbican. For some reason, Gamini said, the director had dressed the entire cast in featureless white, so that half the time neither he nor Madge had been able to tell who was speaking.

It was, Ranjit realized as he reached for the letter on university stationery, the third, maybe the fourth, time Gamini had mentioned this Madge person. He was contemplating the possible implications of this fact while extracting a letter on the same creamy paper as the envelope, and then Gamini's possible failing went right out of his mind. The stationery was engraved with the name of the dean of students, and the letter said:

> Please present yourself at the office of the Dean at 2:00 P.M. on Tuesday next. It is alleged that during the school year just past you made unlawful use of the computer password of a faculty member. You are urged to bring with you any documents or other material that you consider relevant to this charge.

And it was signed by the dean of students.

According to her nameplate the woman at the dean's reception desk was a Tamil, which was encouraging, but she was also as old as Ranjit's father. Her look was cold. "You are expected," she informed him. "You may go right into the dean's private office."

Never before had Ranjit had occasion to visit the dean of students. He knew what the man looked like, though—the faculty file on the university's home page supplied photos—and the elderly man reading a newspaper at the huge mahogany desk definitely was not him. But he put down his paper and rose, not exactly with a smile but certainly without the hanging-judge look Ranjit had expected. "Come in, Mr. Subramanian," he called. "Sit down. I'm Dr. Denzel Davoodbhoy, chairman of the mathematics department, and as mathematical matters seem to play a significant role here, the dean asked me to conduct this interview for him."

That hadn't been a question, and Ranjit had no idea what response would have been appropriate. He simply went on gazing at the mathematician with an expression that, he hoped, conveyed attentive concern but no admission of guilt.

Dr. Davoodbhoy didn't seem to mind. "First," he said, "there are a couple of formal questions I must put to you. Did you use Dr. Dabare's password to earn money you were not otherwise entitled to?"

"Certainly not, sir!"

"Or to alter your math grades?"

This time Ranjit was offended. "No! I mean, no, sir, I wouldn't have done that!"

Dr. Davoodbhoy nodded as though he had expected both answers. "I think I can tell you that no evidence has been presented to suggest either charge. Finally, how, exactly, did you obtain his password?"

As far as Ranjit could see, there did not appear to be any reason to try to conceal anything. Hoping that this was so, he began with his discovery that the teacher would be out of the country for a prolonged visit and ended with that return to the library computer when he found the solution waiting on the screen.

When he finished, Davoodbhoy gazed at him in silence for a moment. Then he said, "You know, Subramanian, you might have a future in cryptography. It would be a better chance than continuing to spend your life trying to prove Fermat's Last Theorem."

He looked at Ranjit as though expecting a response. Ranjit didn't choose to give him one, so Davoodbhoy added, "You're not alone, you know. When I was your age, like every other math major in the world, I got interested in the final theorem myself. It is compelling, isn't it? But then, when I was a little older, I gave up on it because—you know this, don't you? Because the odds are pretty great that Fermat never did have the proof he was claiming."

Unwilling to be baited, Ranjit kept his attention set at politely attentive and his mouth closed. "I mean," Davoodbhoy added, "look at it this way. You do know, I suppose, that Fermat spent a lot of his time, right up to the day he died, trying to prove that his theorem held true for third-, fourth-, and fifth-power exponents. Well, think about it. Does doing that make any sense at all? I mean, if the man already did possess a general proof that the rule was true for all exponents greater than two, why would he bother trying to prove a few isolated examples?"

Ranjit gritted his teeth. It was a question that, on dark nights and disappointing days, he had asked himself often enough. Without ever finding a good answer, either. He gave Davoodbhoy the not wholly good answer he had usually tried to content himself with: "Who knows? How can someone like you or me try to guess why a mind like Fermat's went in any direction it liked?"

The mathematician looked at him with an expression that somewhat resembled tolerance but also resembled, to some degree, respect. He sighed and spread his hands. "Let me offer you a different theory of what happened, Subramanian. Let's suppose that in—what was it, 1637?—in 1637 Monsieur Fermat had just completed what he thought was a proof. Then later that night, while he was reading himself to sleep in his library, let's suppose he just couldn't help himself, and in a fit of exuberance he scribbled that note in his book." He paused there for a moment, giving Ranjit what could only be described as a quizzical look. When he went on, however, his tone would have been appropriate for a respected colleague as much as for an undergraduate expecting to be disciplined. "Then let's suppose that sometime later he went over his proof to double-check it, and found it possessed a fatal error. It wouldn't have been the first time, would it? Because that had already happened with other 'proofs' of his that he later admitted were wrong, hadn't it?" Mercifully he didn't require an answer from Ranjit but kept right on going. "So he tried to repair his proof every way he could. Unfortunately, he failed. So, trying to salvage something from his mistake, he then tried the more limited task of proving the argument for an easier case like p equals three, and there he succeeded; and for p equals four, and succeeded again. He never did get a proof of the p equals five case, but he was still pretty sure that one existed. He was right, too, because somebody else proved it after Fermat died. And all that time his scribble in Diophantus was sitting on a shelf in his library. If he ever remembered he'd written it, he thought, well, he probably ought to go back and erase that bad guess. But, after all, what's the chance that anyone would ever see it? And then he died, and somebody was riffling through his books and did see it . . . and didn't know that the great man had changed his mind."

Ranjit didn't change expression. "That," he said, "is a perfectly sensible theory. I just don't happen to believe that it's what happened."

Davoodbhoy laughed. "All right, Subramanian. Let's leave it at that. Just don't do it again." He thumbed through the papers before him, then nodded and closed the file. "Now you can go back to your classes."

"All right, sir." He tarried for a moment after picking up his backpack, then asked the question: "But am I going to be expelled?"

The mathematician looked surprised. "Expelled? Oh, no, nothing like that. It was only a first offense, you know. We don't expel for that unless it's something a lot worse than stealing a password, and anyway the dean received some extremely glowing letters of support for you." He opened Ranjit's folder again and thumbed through the papers. "Yes. Here we are. One is from your father. He is quite positive you are basically of good character. In itself, to be sure, a father's opinion of his only son might not carry great weight, but then there is this other one. It is very nearly as commending as your father's, but it comes from someone who is, I think, not very close to you but who is a person of considerable importance in the university. In fact, he's the university's attorney, Dhatusena Bandara."

And now Ranjit had a new puzzle to mull over. Who would have suspected that Gamini's father would have exerted himself to save his son's friend?

7

GETTING THERE

The school year limped toward its end. It picked up speed remarkably in the all too brief periods when Ranjit was in his astronomy class, but the remainder of each week's hours were in no hurry to move on at all.

For a little while Ranjit thought he had hopes of one bright—fairly bright—spot. Remembering the lecture on what they'd called the hydrosolar plan for Israel's Dead Sea, he went back to the lecture series. But then what the lecturer was talking about was the increasing salinity of a lot of oceanfront wells, all over the world, and then about how some of the world's great rivers no longer ran to the sea, any sea, because they were drained for farming and flushing city toilets and watering city folks' front lawns first. Ranjit didn't need more discouragement. After that he stayed away.

He even briefly considered trying to take, or at least pretend to take, his schooling seriously. Studying, for example, could be considered a game, and a fairly easy one to win. It did not at all resemble that insatiable thirst for learning that had marked his early consecration to the Fermat theorem. Now all he had to do was guess what questions each of his instructors would ask on each test and look up the answers. He didn't always get it right, but then to attain a merely passing grade he didn't have to.

None of this, of course, applied to Astronomy 101.

There Dr. Vorhulst managed to make every session a pleasure. Like what happened when they were talking about terraforming—that is, reworking planetary surfaces so that human beings could live on them. And, if you were going to do that, how did you get there to do the terraforming?

Ranjit's answer would have been "rocket ships." His hand was already halfway toward the raised position so that he could offer that answer when the teacher froze it mid-motion. "You're going to say 'rocket ships,' aren't you?" Dr. Vorhulst asked, addressing the whole class and particularly the dozen or so who, like Ranjit, had been putting their hands up. "All right. Let's think about that for a bit. Let's suppose that we want to start terraforming Mars, but all we have to work with is an absolute minimum of heavy-duty earthmoving machinery. One very big backhoe, for instance. One bulldozer. A couple of medium-size dump trucks. Fuel enough to run them all for, let's say, six months or so. Long enough to get the job started, anyway." He paused, eyes on a hand from the second row that had just sprouted. "Yes, Janaka?"

The boy named Janaka eagerly shot to his feet. "But, Dr. Vorhulst, there's a whole plan to make fuel from Martian resources that are already there!"

The professor beamed at him. "You're absolutely right, Janaka. For instance, if there really is a large amount of methane under Mars's permafrost, as many people think there is, then we could burn that for fuel, assuming we could find some oxygen to burn it with. Of course, to do that we'd really have to have a bunch more heavy machinery, which would need a bunch more fuel to run it until the extraction plants were working." Vorhulst gave the boy a friendly smile. "So, Janaka," he said, "I think that if you wanted to start any terraforming in the near future, probably you'd want to fly your fuel in after all. So let's see."

He turned to the whiteboard and began writing. "Say six or eight tons of fuel to start. The earthmoving machines themselves—what would you say, at least another twenty or thirty tons? Now to get those at least twenty-eight tons of cargo from low earth orbit, known as LEO, to Mars, we need to put them into some kind of spaceship. I don't know what that would mass, but let's say the ship itself would run fifty or sixty tons, plus the fuel to get it from LEO to Mars." He stepped back to look at his figures on the board and frowned. "I'm afraid we have a problem," he said to the class, addressing it over his shoulder. "All that stuff won't start out in low earth orbit, will it? Before the ship can start heading for Mars, we have to get it into LEO. And I'm afraid that's going to be expensive."

He paused, looking with a sorrowful expression at his class. He was waiting for some student to rise to the occasion, and after a bit, one of the girls did. "That's because it has to get out of the Earth's gravity well, isn't it, Dr. Vorhulst?"

He gave her a big smile. "Exactly right, Roshini," he said, looking up at the class timer that had just turned amber. "So you see, it's that first step that's a killer. Is there anything we can do to make it easier? We'll try to find out next time. But if any of you guys just can't wait for the answer, hey, that's what search engines are for."

And then, as everybody began to rise, he said, "Oh, one more thing. You're all invited to the end-of-term party at my house. Don't dress any

differently than you do for class, and don't bring any house gifts but your-
selves. But do come. You'll hurt my mother's feelings if you don't."

One of the things that Ranjit liked best about his astronomy teacher—apart
from such unexpected surprising joys as end-of-term parties—was that Dr.
Vorhulst didn't actually spend a lot of time in the normal practice of teaching. When, at the end of each session, Dr. Vorhulst told the class what the
next session was going to be about, Vorhulst knew perfectly well that his
hundred eagerly motivated space-cadets would look all that material up
long before the next session started. (The few who hadn't started out all
that motivated—the ones who had entertained the false hope of a snap
course and an easy A—either soon dropped or were reformed by the en-
thusiasm of their fellows.) Thus, each time, Dr. Vorhulst had that next session to play.

This time, however, Ranjit couldn't hit the search engines right away.
He had other obligations. First there was the terminally tedious hour and
fifty minutes of philosophy to get through. Then came the quick gulping of
a detestable sandwich and a lukewarm bag of some anonymous variety of
juice, which was lunch, all swallowed in a hurry so he could get to the two
o'clock bus that would take him to the library.

But just outside the lunchroom his seatmate in Astronomy 101 was
standing with a few of his fellows, and he had news for Ranjit. "You didn't
hear what Dr. Vorhulst had promised for our next session? I was just telling
my friends the news about it. The Artsutanov project, you know. Vorhulst
says we might get the project built right here! In Sri Lanka! Because the
World Bank's just announced that it has received a request for financing a
study of a Sri Lankan terminal!"

Ranjit was just opening his mouth to ask what all that meant when one
of the others said, "But you said it might not pass, Jude."

Jude looked suddenly brought down. "Well, yes," he admitted. "It's the
damn Americans and the damn Russians and the damn Chinese that have
all the power—and all the money, too. They're just as likely as not to hold
it up, because once you've got an Artsutanov lifter going, any damn little
pipsqueak country in the world can have a space program of its own. Even
us! And there goes their monopoly! Don't you think?"

Ranjit was saved the embarrassment of not having an answer for
that—indeed, of not having any really good idea of what Jude was talking
about in the first place—by the Sinhalese group's growing hunger. And
then in the library—search engines working—Ranjit was soaking up in-

formation at a high rate of knots. The more he learned, the more he shared Jude's excitement. That tough first step of getting from Earth's surface to LEO? With an Artsutanov skyhook it was no problem at all!

True, feasibility studies were a long way from an actual car that you could hop into and have drawn at high speed up to low earth orbit, no million-liter oceans of explosive liquid propellant required. But it might happen. Probably would happen, sooner or later, and then even Ranjit Subramanian might be one of those lucky ones who would circle the moon and cruise among Jupiter's satellites and perhaps even walk across the hopelessly dry deserts of Mars.

According to what the search engines turned up for Ranjit, as far back as 1895 Russia's first thinker on space travel, Konstantin Tsiolkovsky, got a look at Paris's Eiffel Tower and then came up with his idea. A good way to get a spacecraft into orbit, he said, was to build a really tall tower with a built-in elevator and hike your ship up to the top before turning it loose to roam.

However, in 1960 a Leningrad engineer named Yuri Artsutanov read Tsiolkovsky's book and quickly saw that the plan wouldn't work. It was a lesson the ancient Egyptians had learned long ago—as had the Maya, a few thousand years later and on the other side of the world. The lesson was that there is a limit to how tall you can build a tower or a pyramid, and that limit is set by compression.

In a compression structure—which is to say, any structure that is built from the ground up—each level must support the weight of all the levels above it. That would be hundreds of kilometers of levels, to reach low earth orbit, and no imaginable structural material could support that weight without crumbling.

Artsutanov's inspiration was to realize that compression was only one possible way to build a structure. Another equally viable way was tension.

A structure based on tension—one made up of cables attached to some orbiting body, for example—was a theoretically elegant but practically un-attainable notion when considered from the point of view of an engineer who had only mid-twentieth-century materials to make the cables out of. But, Artsutanov contended, who was to say that the advanced cable materials that might be developed a few decades on wouldn't be up to that challenge?

When at last Ranjit got himself to go to bed that night, he was smiling—and kept on smiling even in his sleep, because for the first time in quite a while he had found something that was really worth smiling about.

. . .

He was still smiling the next morning at breakfast, and was counting the hours (there would be almost a hundred and forty of them) until the next session of Astronomy 101. There was no doubt in Ranjit's mind that his astronomy sessions were the brightest spots in his academic year. . . .

That being so, why not change his major from math to astronomy?

He stopped chewing long enough to think that over, but not to any successful conclusion. There was something in his head that wouldn't let him take the official step of giving up on math. Rightly or wrongly that felt too much like giving up on Fermat's theorem.

On the other hand, it was pretty strange—as his guidance counselor had pointed out in the one session he had been willing to allow her—to be a math major who wasn't taking any mathematics courses.

Ranjit knew what to do about that, and he had a whole free morning to do it in. As soon as the counselor was in her office, Ranjit was there to clear up his status with her, and by noon he was officially registered as a late entry into the course in basic statistics. Why statistics? Well, it was, after all, a kind of mathematics. But entering the class so late, how would that work? No problem, Ranjit assured the counselor; there was no undergraduate math course that he couldn't pick up in no time at all. And so by lunchtime Ranjit had solved at least one of his problems, even though it was a problem he hadn't really thought important enough to be worth solving. All in all, Ranjit attacked his boring lunch quite cheerfully.

Then things went bad.

Some fool had left the radio news on at high volume instead of the murmur of music the college students were willing to put up with at their meals. Nobody seemed to know how to turn it off, either.

Of course, it was inevitable that the principal news stories that day were exactly the sort of stories Ranjit didn't want to hear, because that was pretty much all the world news there was.

Now that the news was on, however, Ranjit dutifully listened to it. Predictably the news was bad—all the little wars were still thriving, and new ones were being promised, just like always. And then the news turned to local Colombo stories. These were not of much interest to Ranjit, until one word caught his attention. The word was "Trincomalee."

Then he gave the news his full attention. It seemed that a man from Trincomalee had been stopped because he had failed to give way in his old van to a police car with its siren going. (Actually the police in the car had

been heading toward a place to eat lunch.) When they pulled him over, the police naturally looked around the van. That was when they caught him with a load of toasters, blenders, and other small domestic appliances, and no good explanation for how they came to be in his possession.

Ranjit had stopped with his spoonful of rice halfway to his mouth, just as the news reader mentioned the suspect's name. Kirthis Kanakaratnam.

That left Ranjit worse off than before. He couldn't place the name. It did sound vaguely familiar, but from where? School? His father's temple? It could have been from almost anywhere, and try as he might, Ranjit could not fit a face to the name. A later news story, long after lunch, after Ranjit had nearly given up, said the suspect had left a wife and four small children behind him.

It really was not his business, Ranjit told himself. He wasn't successful in convincing himself, though, because if he didn't know for sure just who this Kirthis Kanakaratnam was, how could he know it wasn't someone who had in some context been a friend?

That was why Ranjit called the police. He called their central headquarters number, and he did it from a phone in a part of the campus he rarely visited. The voice was a woman, not young, and not in the habit of giving information away. A prisoner named Kirthis Kanakaratnam? Yes, perhaps so. They had a good many persons held in one Colombo jail or another, and they didn't always give their right names. Could the caller give more information about this person? The names of some of his associates, for example? And was the caller himself related to him? Or perhaps associated with him in some enterprise? Or—

Ranjit quietly hung the phone up and departed that area. He didn't really think that a squad of Colombo police was likely to come racing down the hallway any minute. But he was also far from positive that they weren't, and saw no reason to wait around to find out.

When Ranjit got back to his rooms that night, there was the next best thing to Gamini's actual presence waiting for him, namely, an e-letter from London. (There was also a message that Ranjit's father had called and wished to be called back—very good news, Ranjit thought, because at least the old man seemed willing to speak to him again . . . but, all the same, it was the e-letter from Gamini that he looked at first.)

Gamini was showing every sign of having a wonderful time in London. Just yesterday (he wrote) he had walked over to the campus of University College London because Madge had told him that there was

something she wanted him to see. Well, it was interesting, all right, assuming you liked looking at dead—even long-dead—bodies, because what was there to see was the waxed and mummified corpse of the two-hundred-years-ago English utilitarian philosopher, Jeremy Bentham. He was always there, Gamini said, but usually locked away in the wooden cabinet he called his "Auto-Icon." As a special favor to Madge it had been unlocked for her by a smitten junior faculty member. This Bentham, Gamini went on to explain, had been a really ahead-of-his-time early-nineteenth-century thinker, had even once written a carefully thought out argument for extending tolerance—well, some tolerance, anyway—to homosexuals. Bentham was revolutionary, Gamini added, but he was also somewhat cautious. He didn't publish the argument. He locked it away, and so it stayed for a century and a half, until someone finally put it into print in 1978.

By then Ranjit was getting tired of Jeremy Bentham, and a little curious about why Gamini was telling him so much. Could it be because Bentham had been one of the first significant figures to write with some sympathy about homosexuals? And if so, what was it that Gamini wanted Ranjit to understand about that subject? It certainly wasn't that either of the young men considered himself homosexual, because they certainly did not.

He found that subject uneasy to think about and went on. There wasn't much more of the letter anyway. A bunch of Gamini's fellow students—Gamini didn't mention this Madge there, but Ranjit would have bet a large sum that she had been in the group—had gone up to Stratford-upon-Avon for a day. And then at the very end, in a brief afterthought, the big news: "Oh, listen, I've got some summer courses I need to take, but Dad wants me home for a few days this summer so I can see Gram one more time before she goes. He says she's doing poorly. So I'll be back in Lanka for a bit. Where will you be? I don't know if I'll have time to get to Trinco—but somewhere?"

Well, wasn't that grand news? It was. And the only thing that slowed Ranjit's quiet exultation was the fact that his father's call needed to be returned.

The old man picked the phone up on its first ring. His voice was cheerful, too, as he said, "Ah, Ranjit"—affectionate, pleased—"why do you keep secrets from your father? You didn't tell me that Gamini Bandara had gone to England!"

Though no one was there to see, Ranjit rolled his eyes. If he had failed to tell his father the news, it was almost entirely because he had been confident his father's watchers would make sure it got to him. The only surprising thing was that it had taken so long. Ranjit considered for a moment whether or not to mention that Gamini would at least briefly be coming home, and decided not to do the dormitory staff's work for them. He said guardedly, "Yes, he's going to school there. London School of Economics. His father thinks it's the best school in the world, I think."

"And I'm sure it is," his father agreed, "at least for certain kinds of studies. And I know you must miss him, Ranjit, but I have to say that it goes a long way toward solving a major problem for me. No one is going to be worrying about your closeness with a Sinhalese boy when there's an ocean or two between you."

Ranjit didn't know what to say to that and sensibly said nothing. His father went on. "The thing is, I've missed you very much, Ranjit. Can you forgive me, Ranjit?"

Ranjit had no need to think over his answer to that. "I love you, Father," he said at once, "and there is nothing to forgive. I understand why you had to do what you did."

"Then," his father said, "will you come and spend your summer holidays here in Trinco?"

Ranjit assured him he would like nothing better, but he was beginning to feel uneasy. The conversation was getting sticky. He was glad when he remembered the question his father might be able to answer. "Dad? There's a man from Trinco who's been arrested in Colombo, Kirthis Kanakaratnam, and I have a feeling I might have known him at some time. Do you know who he is?"

Ganesh Subramanian sighed deeply—whether because the question was troubling to him or because he, too, was grateful for the change of subject, Ranjit could not tell. "Yes, of course. Kirthis. Don't you remember him, Ranjit? My tenant? The one with all those little children, and a wife in somewhat poor health? He usually worked as a coach driver for one of the hotels along the beach. His father used to do odd jobs around the temple until he died—"

"I remember now," said Ranjit, and he did. The man they were talking about was short and as black as Ranjit himself. He had lived, family and all, in the tiny house at the edge of Ganesh Subramanian's property: by the most optimistic count, three rooms all told, for two adults and four tiny kids, and no interior plumbing. Ranjit's clearest memory was of the mother despondently washing children's clothes in a huge tin tub . . . and the children whining around her feet as they assiduously dirtied more clothes, and themselves.

When Ranjit got off the phone, he readied himself for bed, feeling pretty good about the world. Things were going well. He had made up with his father. He was going to see Gamini, at least briefly. And that mystery concerning the identity of this Kirthis Kanakaratnam was solved, and he would never have to think of the man again, he thought.

Statistics wasn't quite as boring as Ranjit had feared it might be. It wasn't much fun, either. Long before Ranjit entered the class, he had a pretty good understanding of the differences between mean, median, and mode and knew what a standard deviation was, and it didn't take him long to learn how to draw any kind of histogram the teacher wanted. But the teacher surprisingly turned out to have a sense of humor, and when she wasn't teaching the class what stem-and-leaf and other statistical plots were, she was almost—well, sometimes she was almost—as entertaining to listen to as Joris Vorhulst himself.

But on second thought, Ranjit told himself, no. That was going too far. She was a nice enough person, but she just didn't have the material of Astronomy 101 to work with. Such as the space elevator and its wondrous ways.

Even Artsutanov's lift wasn't the only game in town. What (asked one of the students one day in astronomy class) about something like the Lofstrom loop? For that you didn't have to start by putting some humongous satellite into orbit because the thing just sat on Earth's surface, from which it flung your space capsules into orbit.

But there Dr. Vorhulst began to rein in the class's speculation. "Friction," he said succinctly. "Don't forget friction. Remember what reentry did to a lot of the early spacecraft. If you used a Lofstrom loop, you'd need to accelerate your capsule to that seven miles a second of escape velocity that I was talking about the other day before you let go of it, and then the air friction would burn it right up."

He paused, eyes roving over his class, expression as good-natured as always but with a faint twinkle that made Ranjit expect some sort of surprise was coming. "So," the teacher said sociably, "have any of you junior-grade astronauts figured out what kind of rocket drive your ship is going to have yet?"

Ranjit hadn't thought of anything beyond the usual fuel-plus-oxidizer. He kept his mouth shut, though, because he knew, from the fact that the professor had raised the question in the first place, that Dr. Vorhulst had something else in mind.

So did his seatmate, but he responded in a different way. His hand went right up. "You're not talking about a chemical rocket, are you, Dr. Vorhulst? So, then, what do you think? Maybe a nuclear-powered one?"

"Good guess," the teacher said, "but, no, I don't think a nuclear-powered rocket would be your best bet, at least not the kind of nuclear power you mean. Oh, there are designs around for rockets that were driven by exploding atom bombs, one after another. We can talk about them if you like, but for getting from LEO to Mars I think there are two much better possibilities. Both of them are tailor-made to be used with some kind of space elevator to boost them into low earth orbit because they're both way too feeble to lift anything off Earth's surface and into space. One is the solar sail. The other is the electric rocket."

Ten minutes later Dr. Vorhulst had given short and convincing reasons for avoiding nuclear explosions as rocket propellants—the need for heavy shielding to protect astronauts from the deadly radiation, and anyway who wants to shoot a few hundred atomic bombs off into space? Solar sails had a lot to recommend them, he conceded, but they were dreadfully slow and not very maneuverable. However, the electric rocket, while also pretty slow to accelerate, required no fuel storage and produced no undesired by-products. Where did the electricity come from? Perhaps from an onboard nuclear power plant, Vorhulst conceded, but just as easily from solar power—that is, from solar power in space, where there were no nights or cloudy weather, so that the sun always shone. "And what do you do with that electricity? You use it to ionize some working fluid—a gas like xenon, for instance—and the gas fires itself out of your rocket nozzles at very high velocity, and off you go."

He paused for a breath. "All right," he admitted, "an electric rocket would not accelerate very fast." But it would keep right on accelerating as long as you liked, and the longer the acceleration, the greater its velocity would be. You could accelerate until you were halfway there. Then you could turn around and decelerate until you arrived. Did anyone see what that implied?

Vorhulst gave them a few moments to figure it out, but no one did. "It means," he told them, "that the farther your trip, the faster the speed that you'll attain. You wouldn't want to use an electric rocket to go to the moon. Short trip; you don't really have time to get going very fast. For Mars, though, it's optimal. And for the outer planets, say Uranus or Neptune, why, that trip doesn't take much longer than to Mars! And if you're really going to go a far piece, say to the Oort cloud, you build up so much velocity with all that acceleration that that enormous journey in fact becomes feasible!"

Then he stopped and grinned. "Well," he said, "I don't want to oversell you on the electric rocket, because it has one serious fault. That is, we don't have any." He overrode the faint groans of disappointment. "Oh, it's legitimate in principle, all right. But nobody has ever built one because if you have to start your flight from Earth's surface, they won't work. They need something to lift them into low earth orbit first, and then they can strut their stuff. Something like an Artsutanov space elevator, and, as you know, we just don't have one of those around anywhere."

He gave them a rueful smile. "Oh, one day we will," he promised. "Then we'll have electric rockets by the zillion, and I'd be willing to bet that more than one of you will be riding to all sorts of weird and wonderful places. But not yet, because at the present time they don't exist."

Which, when you stopped to think about it, was true enough, at least for the little volume of space near Earth, though it wouldn't be for long.

Actually, somewhat farther away, there were 154 of those electric rockets that were already taking direct aim for Earth, and the individuals aboard them didn't think they were unusual at all.

These individuals were the One Point Fives, and they (or their ancestors) had been traveling from star to star in spacecraft just like these for many, many generations. Always on much the same errand, too. The fact of the matter was that the One Point Fives had a unique place among the subordinate sapient species of the galaxy.

Basically they were the Grand Galactics' hit men.

To a casual observer the One Point Fives might not have seemed to be good candidates for that sort of employment. Stripped of their shields and prostheses the average One Point Five wasn't much bigger than a terrestrial cat. That casual observer would not be likely, however, to see a One Point Five in that stripped-down condition. A One Point Five's indispensable protective devices massed just about half as much as his body itself (hence the name One Point Five), and every last bit of these devices was vitally necessary. Some of the devices guarded the fragile organic being inside against radiation—from the ionizing spillover from their nuclear power plants or from the residues of their many long-ago nuclear wars. Or even against the lethally high ultraviolet rays that came from their star and were no longer warded off by their planet's ozone layer because their earlier activities had resulted in their planet's no longer having one. Some of their chemical processors removed poisons from the air they breathed or the food and water they ingested. Some merely kept them from going insane from the unbearable din that suffused every part of their world (that took blanketing sound absorbers backed up with frequency nullifiers). Other processors toned down the maddening flashes and flares that accompanied their industry.

There were a few isolated spots on their planet where a One Point Five could strip naked and survive. Those places were the breeding rooms and the birthing rooms, as well as a scattering of spots where medical and surgical procedures were performed. There weren't many of those. Because there was so much to guard against, neutralize, or prevent on that ravaged world, such places were not only scarce but expensive.

That being so, one might wonder why a species as technologically savvy as the One Point Fives didn't just go ahead and build themselves a fleet of spaceships and proceed to start a new life on some unspoiled planet somewhere else in space.

Actually, the One Point Fives had done that . . . once.

The project had not been a success, however. Oh, the ships had got invented and built, all right, and a benign enough planet had been located. But the Grand Galactics had stepped in. After that happened, it had been so little of a success that, though many thousands of years had passed, the One Point Fives had never considered trying it again.

8

SUMMER

By and large the school year had been a disappointment, but the summer began well for Ranjit Subramanian. Take his grades, for instance. When they were posted, he was not surprised at the gentleman's C he got in philosophy (his grade in psychology didn't matter, because he'd dropped it out of boredom) and not particularly surprised, either, though pleased, by his A in astronomy. But the A in statistics had been a total mystery. Ranjit could only conjecture that it was the result of the advanced reading he had picked up for himself when he couldn't stand to see one more box plot or density histogram. The library had saved him, with advanced texts on such matters as stochastic methods and Bayesian analysis.

The bad part about the term's end, of course, was that the astronomy course was over as well. But there was at least a postscript in the form of the party at Professor Vorhulst's home.

Still, as he walked from the bus to the address that had been on his invitation, Ranjit was beginning to have second thoughts. In the first place, the neighborhood was refined and therefore unfamiliar to him because he and Gamini had avoided it in their browsings in the city. (Gamini's family lived in this neighborhood, too.) Then, the Vorhulst home was not only bigger than any single-family home needed to be, it was surrounded by totally unnecessary columned verandas and set in an exquisitely maintained garden.

Ranjit took a deep breath before he pushed the gate open and climbed the couple of steps to the veranda. The first thing he noticed once inside the door was the cooling breeze from overhead fans. That was welcome in Colombo's heat. More welcome still was catching sight of Joris Vorhulst himself, standing next to a woman almost as ostentatiously oversize as the house they lived in. The professor greeted Ranjit with a wink and a nod. "Ranjit," he said, steering him down to where the woman stood, "we're so glad you could come. I'd like you to meet Mevrouw Beatrix Vorhulst, my mother."

Unsure of what action to take in greeting a woman—and an exceedingly fair-skinned one—who towered over him by at least three or four centimeters and outmassed him by more kilos than that, Ranjit experimentally offered a small bow. Mevrouw Vorhulst was having none of that. She took his hand and held it. "My dear Ranjit, I am delighted to meet you. My son doesn't have favorites in his classes, but if he did—please don't let him know I said this—I'm sure you would be one of them. And I've had the pleasure of meeting your father. A wonderful man. We worked together on one of the truce commissions, back when we needed truce commissions."

Ranjit sent a quick glance to Dr. Vorhulst in the hope of getting some clue as to what he should be saying to this good-looking perfumed force of nature. He got no help there. The professor was already bantering with three or four new arrivals, but Mevrouw Vorhulst, well aware of Ranjit's difficulty, helped him out. "Don't waste your time with an old widow lady," she advised. "There are quite a few nice-looking girls inside, not to mention things to eat and drink. There are even some of those horrid American sports drinks that Joris came back from California addicted to, but I would not myself recommend them." She relinquished his hand with a final pat. "But you must join us for dinner one of these days, after Joris gets back from New York. He'll be depressed. He always is after he's tried one more time to get the UN to act on the Artsutanov lift. But of course," she added, already turning toward the next guests, "you can't entirely blame them, can you? People just haven't learned how to play nicely together."

Entering the house's wide salon, Ranjit observed that there were indeed some nice-looking girls present, though most of them seemed to be already taken by one or more young men. He exchanged nods with three or four classmates, but what most interested him at that moment was the house itself. It was very little like his father's modest home in Trincomalee. The floor was made of polished white cement, and the walls were punctuated with open doors leading out to the vast garden with its palms and frangipani and an inviting pool. As a precaution Ranjit had already eaten lunch, so the great spread of food the Vorhulsts had set out was superfluous. The American sports drink Mevrouw Vorhulst had spoken of he passed with a shudder, but was glad to find a supply of good old-fashioned Cokes. When he looked for an opener, a servant appeared from nowhere, whisked the bottle out of his hand, snapped the cap off, and emptied the soda into a tall glass, already iced, that also came from nowhere.

The servant left Ranjit blinking after him until, from another direction, a female voice said, "You were breaking his rice bowl, you know. If the guests opened their own Coke bottles, the beverage wallah would be out of a job. So, Ranjit, how are you?"

When he turned, he recognized the young Burgher woman from his unhappy first year's sociology class, Mary—Martha—no, "Myra de Soyza," she supplied. "We met in sociology last year, and it's nice to see you again. I heard you were working with Fermat's theorem. How is it going?"

It was not a question Ranjit had expected to be asked, especially by a young woman as good-looking as this one was. He gave her a noncommittal answer. "Pretty slowly, I'm afraid. I didn't know you were interested in Fermat."

She looked faintly embarrassed. "Well, I suppose I'd have to say that you were the one who got me interested. After we heard that you'd stolen the math professor's password—oh, are you surprised? But of course all of his classes heard about it. I think if the semester hadn't been over, there would have been a movement to elect you class president." She gave him a friendly smile. "At any rate, I couldn't help wondering what would so obsess a person like you—is 'obsession' too strong a word?" Ranjit, who had long since come to terms with the technical description of his so-far-failed quest, shrugged. "Well," she went on, "let's just say I couldn't help wondering what would account for your strong interest in trying to find a proof for Fermat's claim. Wiles's work was certainly not what Fermat had had in mind, was it? If only because nearly every step in Wiles comes from work somebody else did long after Fermat was dead and gone, and there was no way Fermat could have known— Oh, Ranjit, please be careful of your drink!"

Ranjit blinked and saw what she was talking about. He had been so taken aback by the turn the conversation had taken that he had allowed his Coke glass a dangerous tilt. He straightened it and took a quick swallow to clear his head. "What do you know about the Wiles proof?" he demanded, past the point of caring if he was being polite.

Myra de Soyza didn't seem to mind. "Not a great deal, really. Just enough to get an idea of what it was all about. Certainly not as much as a real mathematician might. Do you know who Dr. Wilkinson is? From the Drexel Math Forum? I think his was the best and simplest explanation of what Wiles really accomplished."

The thing that was now paralyzing Ranjit's vocal cords was that he himself, in the days when he had just begun to try to comprehend the Wiles proof, had been really grateful for that same Dr. Wilkinson's analysis.

He realized that he must have made some sort of vocal sound, because the de Soyza woman was looking at him inquiringly. "I mean," he clarified, "are you telling me that you can follow Wilkinson's gloss?"

"Of course I can follow it," she told him sweetly. "He was very clear. I just had to read his explanation—well," she admitted, "five times, actually. And had to look up quite a lot in the reference books. And I don't doubt that I missed a lot, but I do think I got a sort of approximate understanding." She looked at him silently for a moment before she asked, "Do you know what I might do if I were you?"

With total truth Ranjit said, "I have no idea."

"Well, I wouldn't bother with any part of Wiles. I'd take a look at what other mathematicians had done in, say, the first thirty or forty years after Fermat died. You know. I'm talking about work that Fermat might have heard some anticipations of, or perhaps even worked on himself. And— Ah," she said, with an abrupt change of subject, looking past Ranjit's right shoulder, "and here is my long-lost Brian Harrigan, with my long delayed champagne."

The long-lost Brian Harrigan was another of those outsize Americans, and he came trailing a pretty girl of about twenty. He gave Ranjit a one-microsecond glance. Then, "Sorry, hon," he said to Myra de Soyza, talking through the space occupied by Ranjit Subramanian as though it were empty, "but I got to talking to, uh, Devika? She more or less grew up in this house and she promised to show me around. It's got some great design features—have you noticed the cement floors? So if you don't mind . . ."

"Go," Myra said. "Just give me the champagne if it isn't warm by now, and then go." And he went, arm in arm with the girl, who hadn't said a word to either Ranjit or Myra de Soyza.

The best part of Brian Harrigan's departure was that it left Ranjit in exclusive possession of the company of this surprising, perplexing, altogether quite unusual young woman. (Although Ranjit was pretty sure she wasn't all that young. At least two or three years older than himself, he conjectured. Maybe even more than that.) He did not regard their tête-à-tête as a romantic event. He was too ill-informed on boy-girl dating to take that leap, and anyway there was the matter of this Brian Harrigan, who routinely addressed her as "hon." Given a hint or two, de Soyza filled in part of the Brian Harrigan portrait for him. Turned out he wasn't American after all. He was Canadian. Worked for one of those world-girdling hotel chains, currently doing some sort of planning for another luxury hotel on one of Trincomalee's beaches. She did not, however, supply the one datum about which Ranjit was most curious. Still, he told himself, it really was none of his business whether they were sleeping together.

When Ranjit picked up on the name Trincomalee, de Soyza looked embarrassed. "Oh, of course. I didn't think. That's your home. Do you know the hotel Brian was talking about?"

Ranjit admitted that about all he knew about Trinco's tourist hotels was that they were really expensive. But then she asked him about his father's temple, about which she, again astonishingly, seemed to know a great deal. She knew that it was built on what was called Shiva's holy hill, knew that it had—or at least the big temple that the Portuguese had sacked in 1624 had—been one of the richest houses of worship in all of Southeast Asia, with the vast stores of gold, silk, jewels, and every other sort of thing that the monks had amassed over its thousand-year history. Knew even about that terrible 1624 day when the Portuguese commander, Constantine de Sa de Menzes, ordered the temple's head priest to strip the temple of everything of value and deliver the treasures to the Portuguese ships in the harbor, because if he didn't, de Sa would turn his ship's cannon on the temple. The head priest had had no choice. He did as ordered . . . and then de Sa cannonaded the temple into rubble anyway.

"Huh," Ranjit said when she had stopped. "You really know a lot about that time, don't you?"

She looked embarrassed. "I suppose, but I imagine what I know isn't quite the same as you do. Actually, my ancestors were generally some of the looters."

For that Ranjit had no better response than another "Huh." They had strolled out into the garden with its frangipani and flowering ginger, and were sitting companionably side by side in a cluster of palms. They were within sight of the Vorhulsts' vast swimming pool, where a few of Ranjit's classmates, somehow having obtained the right swimsuits, were playing aquatic volleyball. One of the Vorhulst servants had brought refills of Myra's champagne and Ranjit's Coke. Other guests had greeted Myra as they'd strolled past, and one or two had said hello to Ranjit as well. Still, de Soyza showed no interest in ending their tête-à-tête. Ranjit had no interest, either. Which was, he reflected, a bit curious, since he had seldom been willing to protract any other chat with a young woman.

De Soyza, Ranjit discovered, had traveled all over the island of Sri Lanka with her parents, and loved every centimeter of it. And was astonished to hear that Ranjit had seldom been away from Trincomalee, apart from his present time in Colombo and a few school trips. "But you've never been to Kandy? Or seen the way the tappers climb the trees to get the palm wine they make toddy from?" And no, in each case the answer was the same. He hadn't.

At about that time Mevrouw Vorhulst passed by, making the rounds to ensure her guests were well cared for. "You two seem to be doing all right," she offered, peering in at them. "Is there anything I can get you?"

"Not a thing, Aunt Bea," de Soyza said. "It's a fine party." And then when Mevrouw Vorhulst had moved on, she responded to the question in Ranjit's look. "Well, all we Burghers know one another, of course, and Aunt Bea really is some kind of a relative. When I was little, I spent about as much time here as I did in my own house, and Joris was the big brother I never had. Made sure I didn't drown when he took me to the beach, and got me back home in time for my nap." Then she noticed the signs of puzzlement on Ranjit's face. "Is something wrong?"

Apologetically he said, "I'm just a little confused. You called her Bea. I thought her name was—what is it?—Mevrouw."

Myra was polite enough not to smile very much. "Mevrouw just means Mrs. in Dutch. Her name is Beatrix, all right." Then she glanced at her watch and looked concerned. "But I don't mean to keep you from your friends. Are you sure you wouldn't rather take a dip in the pool? The Vorhulsts keep a selection of bathing suits in the changing rooms. . . ."

He was sure, no doubt of that. How long they would have gone on talking, Ranjit could not have said. Myra de Soyza didn't seem in any hurry to terminate it, but that was taken care of, sometime later, by the nearly forgotten Brian Harrigan. He reminded them of his existence by peering into, then entering, their little palm garden. He looked annoyed. "I've been all over this place trying to find you," he told Myra.

She stood up and gave him a smile. "It looked to me as though you had plenty of company," she said.

"You mean the girl who was showing me around? She was very helpful. It's a grand old house. Walls three feet thick, all sand and coral and plaster, and what would they need air-conditioning for? But did you forget we had a dinner reservation?"

Myra had forgotten, and apologized for it, and told Ranjit how much she had enjoyed their talk, and was gone.

Ranjit didn't leave the party. He stayed on, but it didn't seem to be as much fun as it had been. He considered, and rejected, the idea of a dip in the pool; spent a little time in the cluster of students that had formed around

Joris Vorhulst, which was discussing pretty much the whole range of things they had already discussed in class; sat in for a bit with a handful of guests who were watching, and talking about, the news program on the TV in the little tent by the garden wall. The news, of course, wasn't amusing. In Korea some of those troublesome North Koreans had, apparently deliberately, released a pack of vicious and perhaps rabid dogs near the boundary between north and south. Nobody had been bitten. Three of the dogs died when one stepped on a land mine, and the rest were quickly machine-gunned by a Republic of South Korea guard detachment, and everybody agreed that something needed to be done about North Korea.

Actually, Ranjit found it surprisingly easy to have conversations with these strangers—on the parlous state of the world, on the need for Artsutanov skyhooks to be deployed so ordinary people could have some hope of traveling in space, on what nice people the Vorhulsts were, on a dozen other topics. What finally put an end to it was when the guests began to thin out. Ranjit took that to mean that it was time for him to go as well.

He had enjoyed the party, especially the first part of it, and he had no doubt that what had made it so good was the meeting with Myra de Soyza.

On the way back to the campus Ranjit found himself thinking—not in any boy-girl way, of course—about what an interesting person Myra de Soyza was. And wondering what the best way would be to go about murdering Brian Harrigan.

All the same, Ranjit was glad when he got back to Trincomalee for the summer. Ganesh Subramanian had assumed his son would want to spend the time on fresh attacks on that bafflingly elusive Fermat conundrum. He was only partly right. Ranjit hadn't forgotten Fermat's theorem. It kept popping up in his mind at inopportune moments, more often than ever since Myra de Soyza had reawakened the memories. But each time it did, Ranjit did his best to dismiss it. Ranjit Subramanian knew when he was licked.

In any case he had other things to occupy his mind. One of the monks had told him that, down on the beach, where they were refurbishing one of Trincomalee's older tourist hotels, vacationing college students could get easy jobs that paid good money. Ranjit checked. There were such jobs. He got one, and for the first time in his eighteen-year-old life, Ranjit Subramanian was able to pay his own way in the world.

The job was, as promised, not at all difficult. Its technical title was "supply expediter." Its duties were, one, to make a note of the contents every time a truckload of material arrived; two, to run and tell the foreman at once if any one of those trucks attempted to leave the premises with part of the goods still on board; and, three, each morning upon arriving at the workplace to quickly scan all the stacks of building material that had arrived the day before to make sure that no large fraction of them had disappeared during the night. The private security guards hired by the hotel corporation had orders to assist him whenever necessary. They were well motivated to do a good job, too, because they had been informed that any losses due to pilfering would come out of their pay.

And Ranjit also had four small but very active assistants of his own.

They weren't on the hotel company's payroll, and neither they nor their mother had figured in Ranjit's plans for the summer. In fact, Ranjit had acquired them one day when old Ganesh Subramanian had given his son a couple of sacks of food that his cook had said would spoil if not eaten soon. "Take them to Mrs. Kanakaratnam," he said. "You know, Kirthis Kanakaratnam's wife. You remember Kirthis? He was arrested in Colombo for possession of what they called stolen goods?" Memory refreshed, Ranjit nodded. "I'm afraid the family is having a rather hard time," his father went on. "I'm letting them use my old guest house. You remember where it is, I'm sure? Well, just drop these off for me, please."

Ranjit had no objection. Had no trouble finding the place, either. One of his earliest playmates, the son of a railroad engineer who had done odd jobs for the temple, had lived there when Ranjit was small, and Ranjit remembered the house well.

It had not changed much. The little garden the railway man's wife had kept up in the front yard was now partly used for growing vegetables and partly reverted to weeds. The building itself, Ranjit thought, could use a fresh paint job. It was smaller than Ranjit had remembered, though, three little rooms with a privy out back and a pumped well at the farthest edge of the property.

The house, however, was empty. Ranjit debated the propriety of going inside when no one was at home, but he couldn't just drop the food on the ground. He knocked on the unlocked door, called a greeting, and then entered.

The first room he came to was the kitchen—propane stove; sink with no faucets but a drain and a large plastic water jug, nearly empty; table and chairs; not much else. Just off it was a smaller room, evidently a bedroom for someone because of the couch with the pillows and the pile of folded sheets at one end of it. And the third room was the largest yet, but also the most crowded: two cribs, two cots, three or four chests of drawers, a couple of chairs . . .

And something else.

Something was different from the way it had been when Ranjit had been there as a boy. Then he saw that in the corner of the children's room there was a trace of something on the wall, and when he looked more carefully, he saw that it was a nearly obliterated religious poster, written in Sanskrit.

Well, of course! This was the house's northeast corner, and this had once been the home's puja corner, the sacrosanct space for devotion and prayer that every gods-fearing Hindu household possessed. But what had become of it now? Where was the idol of Shiva—of any one of the gods, anyway—on its little stand? Where was the incense container or the plate to hold flowers for the offering or any other of the ritual necessities for worship? There was nothing! It had been a good many years since Ranjit had thought of himself as in any sense religious, but when he looked on the heap of washed but unfolded children's clothing in what had once been the home's immaculate and holy puja space, he did feel a sense of, well, almost revulsion. It just wasn't the way a proper Hindu family, atheist or not, should conduct itself.

When he heard voices approaching from outside and went out to introduce himself, he became less sure that this was a proper Hindu family. Its head, the wife of Kirthis Kanakaratnam, did not dress like a proper Hindu woman. She was wearing men's overalls and a pair of men's boots, and she was pulling a child's coaster wagon that held, along with some smaller items, two of those big plastic jugs of water and one small female child. There were three more children, a ten- or twelve-year-old girl bearing another girl, the tiniest one yet, on her back and a boy, gamely shouldering a canvas sack of something. "Hello," Ranjit said in general to them all. "I'm Ranjit Subramanian, Ganesh Subramanian's son, and he sent me down with some stuff for you. It's inside on the table. You must be Mrs. Kanakaratnam."

The woman didn't deny the charge. She dropped the handle of the cart and cast a glance at the sleeping passenger to make sure she was still sleeping. Then she held out her hand to be shaken. "I am Kanakaratnam's wife," she agreed. "Thanks. Your father has been very good to us. Can I offer you a drink of water? We don't have any ice, but you must be thirsty after carrying that stuff all the way down here."

He was, and gratefully drank the tumblerful she poured him out of one of the jugs. (All of their drinking water, she explained, had to be portaged in. The long-ago Boxing Day tsunami had flooded their well water with salt from the bay, and it had never recovered. It was all right for washing and for some kinds of cooking, but not to quench thirst.)

Mrs. Kanakaratnam, he observed, was a woman in her thirties, apparently healthy, not unattractive, not particularly stupid, either, but seriously at odds with a world that had turned against her. Another thing about Mrs. Kanakaratnam was that she didn't especially like to be called Mrs. Kanakaratnam. She explained that both she and her husband really had not liked being stuck in this tropical nowhere that was called Sri Lanka. They wanted to be where things were happening—which was to say, probably America. But they had had to settle for another country because the American embassy had turned down their request for visas. They had immigrated to a different place entirely—it was Poland—and then that hadn't worked out, either. "So," she said, her tone something close to defiant, "we did the best we could. We took American names. He wouldn't let me call him Kirthis anymore. He took the name George, and I was Dorothy. Dot for short."

"It's a nice name," Ranjit volunteered. He didn't actually have an opinion about the name. He simply wanted to cool down the hostility in her voice.

Apparently he was successful, because she became chatty, explaining that they had given the same sorts of names to the children when they came along. It seemed that for a time Dot Kanakaratnam had popped one out in every even-numbered year. First Tiffany, the oldest at eleven, then the only boy, Harold, now nine, and Rosie and Betsy, seven and five. In a very off-hand way, she mentioned that her husband was now in jail; she announced the news in such a manner that Ranjit thought it best to reserve judgment.

When he did have a chance to make a judgment, Ranjit thought they were reasonably nice kids, sometimes sweet and sometimes entertainingly impudent, and always working hard at the tricky and difficult, but amusing, business of growing up. Ranjit found himself liking them. So much so that before he left the Kanakaratnam house he volunteered to take the children to the beach on his next day off.

That was forty-eight hours in the future. Ranjit spent a fair share of that time wondering whether he could handle the responsibilities that went with it. For instance, what if one of them had to, you know, go?

In the event, Tiffany took over without being asked. When Rosie had to pee, Tiffany directed her into the gentle surf, where the massive dilution afforded by the Bay of Bengal took care of the sanitary requirements. And when Harold had to do the other thing, Tiffany led him by the hand to one of the construction workers' portable toilets without bothering Ranjit about it at all. Between times they marched splashingly around the shallows together, Ranjit leading the procession as gander of the group, the kids his gosling train. They lunched on sandwiches swiped from the workers' buffet. (The workers didn't seem to mind. They liked the kids, too.) In the hottest hours of the day the children napped in the palms above the high tide mark, and when Tiffany ordered a taking-it-easy time, they sat and listened while Ranjit told them wonderful stories about Mars and the moon and the great brood of Jovian satellites.

Of course, in other parts of the world things were less amiable.

In Israeli school yards ten-year-old Palestinian girls were blowing up themselves and everybody around them. In Paris four husky North Africans demonstrated their feelings about French politics by killing two Eiffel Tower guards and hurling eleven tourists off the top platform. Things just as bad were going on in Venice, Italy, and Belgrade, Serbia, and even worse ones in Reykjavik, Iceland . . . and those few of the world leaders whose own countries didn't happen to be in flames—yet—were at their wits' ends trying to find some way of dealing with it.

Ranjit, however, didn't really care. . . .

Well, no. He cared quite a lot about such things when he thought about them, but he did his best not to think about them very much.

In this he somewhat resembled the giddy revelers in Edgar Allan Poe's story "The Masque of the Red Death." His world, like theirs, was terminally unwell. But meanwhile the sun was warm and the children were thrilled when he showed them how to capture star turtles and try to get them to race, and told them stories. The kids enjoyed hearing Ranjit's stories very nearly as much as he enjoyed telling them.

Funnily enough, at that same time some, or all (it was rarely possible to say which), of the Grand Galactics were trying to teach a wholly other phylum of living things a somewhat similar lesson.

These other creatures of course were not turtles, though they did have turtlish hard shells and turtlishly low IQs. What the Grand Galactics were trying to teach them was the use of tools.

This was one of the many, many matters that were the self-imposed concerns of the Grand Galactics. A human might think of it as an attempt to raise the standards of the galaxy's living things.

Their idea was that if the hard shells learned to use a lever, a hook, and a striking stone, they might be taking the first steps toward dawning intelligence. And if that happened, then under the micromanaging tutelage of the Grand Galactics they might go further. Indeed, they might go all the way to primo technology, without ever having discovered such unwanted distractions as subjugation, exploitation, or war.

Well, this program would take a long, long time. But the Grand Galactics had plenty of time to spend, and they thought it was worth a try. They considered that it would be worth their while if, in the long future history of the universe, just one species could manage to evolve all the way to matter transmission and space colonies without having learned the art of murder along the way. The Grand Galactics were assuredly intelligent and powerful. But sometimes they were also naïve.

9

LAZY DAYS

Everything considered, Ranjit was reasonably pleased with his summer. The job was easy, and no one seemed to mind if he brought his four goslings along to work. He was only to bother with babysitting them, Dot insisted, on the days when she absolutely had to be away from the house. There were a fair number of those days, though. Sometimes that was because she needed to look for work, although there she didn't have much luck. More often she had to sell off a few more of their possessions to keep the children fed and clothed.

Ranjit noted that the absences did get more frequent. He thought that perhaps Dot was gaining confidence in him. He didn't mind. Whether it was interest or mere politeness, the kids seemed enthralled by both his stories and his mathematical tricks. Ranjit's years of puzzling over number theory had not been entirely for nothing. With his fellow students he had learned ways of playing with numbers that the average layman had never heard of.

There was, for instance, the one called Russian peasant multiplication. To begin with Ranjit determined that only Tiffany had got far enough in school to learn to multiply. To the others he said, "Don't feel bad if you don't know how to multiply numbers. In the old days there were plenty of grown-ups, particularly in places like Russia, who didn't know how to do it, either. So they invented a trick. They called it 'Russian multiplication,' and it goes like this. First write down the two numbers side by side, like this. Say you want to multiply twenty-one by thirty-seven."

He pulled from his pocket the little notebook he had had the forethought to take with him, wrote quickly, and displayed the page:

21   37

"Then—do you know how to double a number? Fine. Then double the number on the left, that's the twenty-one, and halve the number on the right, and write them under the first numbers. So then you get . . ."

$$
\begin{array}{cc}
21 & 37 \\
42 & 18
\end{array}
$$

"There's a one left after you halve that number on the right, but don't worry about it. Just throw that leftover one away. Then you do the same halving and doubling thing with the next numbers, and the ones after that, until the number on the right side gets down to a one."

$$
\begin{array}{cc}
21 & 37 \\
42 & 18 \\
84 & 9 \\
168 & 4 \\
336 & 2 \\
672 & 1
\end{array}
$$

"And whenever the number in the right-hand column is even, you just strike out that whole line."

$$
\begin{array}{cc}
21 & 37 \\
84 & 9 \\
672 & 1
\end{array}
$$

"And you add up the numbers in the left-hand column."

$$
\begin{array}{cc}
21 & 37 \\
84 & 9 \\
\underline{672} & \underline{1} \\
777 &
\end{array}
$$

Under it Ranjit wrote triumphantly "21 × 37 = 777" and said, "And that's the answer!"

Ranjit waited for a response. Actually, he got four different ones. Little Betsy took her cue to clap her hands, applauding Ranjit's success. Rosie looked pleased but puzzled, Harold was frowning, and Tiffany politely asked if she could borrow Ranjit's pen and paper. He peered over her shoulder as she wrote:

$$
\begin{array}{r}
37 \\
\times 21 \\
\hline
37 \\
74 \\
\hline
777
\end{array}
$$

"Yes," she announced, "that's right. Give me two other numbers, please, Ranjit."

He gave her an easy one, eight times nine, and then another even easier one when Harold demanded a chance. He got it, and seemed as though he would gladly have gone on doing elementary Russian multiplication for some time longer, but the youngest girls were beginning to look rebellious. Ranjit deferred the thought of showing them why Russian multiplication was an example of binary arithmetic for another time. Well pleased at the success of his first infliction of number theory on the kids, he said, "That was fun. Now let's catch some more turtles."

Gamini Bandara got to Sri Lanka right on schedule, but when he called Ranjit, he was apologetic. His time was even more overprogrammed than he had realized. He wouldn't be able to visit Tricomalee at this particular time, so would Ranjit very much mind coming up to Colombo for their visit instead?

Actually, Ranjit was a little put out, and didn't very well conceal it. "Well," he said, "I don't know if I can get away from my job." But Gamini was persuasive and, in the event, the foreman at the construction job was glad enough to let Ranjit take as many days as he liked (having a brother-in-law who would gladly take Ranjit's place, and paycheck, while he was away). And Ganesh Subramanian positively went all out to help him. Ranjit had been afraid his father would be upset at the prospect of Gamini coming back into the picture. He wasn't. Apparently a short visit, especially one that took place a considerable distance away, was not a problem. Ganesh made it as easy as possible for his son. "Bus?" he said with a dismissive gesture. "Certainly you won't take the bus. I've got a van that's assigned to me and I don't use it. Take it, Ranjit. Keep it as long as you like. Who knows, the temple insignia on its doors may discourage some ill-intentioned people from letting the air out of your tires."

So Ranjit arrived in Colombo with a bag in the back of the van packed with several days' worth of clothes. Puzzlingly, Gamini had let him know that he would be staying at a hotel instead of his father's house. Ranjit understood the choice of that particular hotel—it had a bar the two boys had visited frequently enough in their explorations of the city—but it surprised him that Gamini's father had let him get away for even one night.

When Ranjit asked to be announced, the desk clerk shook his head, pointing to the bar. And indeed there in the bar was Gamini, and not alone. He had a girl on either side of him, and a nearly empty wine bottle on his table.

All three got up to greet Ranjit. The blond girl was named Pru; the other, whose name was Maggie, had hair of a lipstick color that had never been produced by human genes. "Met them on the plane," Gamini said when he had finished the introductions. "They're Americans. They're students in London, they say, but the school they go to is the University of the Arts—that's the one where the only thing you learn is how to look good. Ouch!"

That last part was because Maggie, the improbably redheaded one, had pinched his ear. "Pay no attention to this slanderer," she instructed Ranjit. "Pru and I are at Camberwell. That's the college at Arts where the instructors make you work. Gamini wouldn't last a week there."

Making an assumption, Ranjit stuck out his hand. The two girls pumped it earnestly, one after the other. "I'm Ranjit Subramanian," he said.

The one named Maggie spoke up. "Oh, we know who you are," she informed him. "Gamini told us everything there is to know about you. You're a short person with a long name, and you spend all your time solving one single math problem. Gamini says if anybody ever does, you'll be the one who does it."

Ranjit, who still suffered occasional attacks of guilt for having neglected the Fermat problem, wasn't sure how to respond to that. He looked to Gamini for help, but actually the expression on Gamini's face was itself a little like guilt. "Listen, Ranj," he began, his tone even more remorseful than his face, "I'd better tell you the bad news right away. When I wrote you, I was hoping you and I would have at least a couple of days together." He shook his head. "Won't happen. My dad's got both of us booked up solid for every day, starting tomorrow. Family, you know."

Ranjit did know, remembering those days before Gamini left for London. He let his disappointment show on his face. "I've got a week, car and all."

Gamini gave him a rebellious shrug. "Can't be helped. He even wanted me for dinner tonight, but I told him positively no." He studied Ranjit for a moment, then grinned. "But, damn, I'm happy to see you! Give us a hug!"

That Ranjit was willing to do, first so as not to embarrass Gamini in front of the girls, then, as Gamini's lean, hot body pressed against his own, with a return of real affection. "Anyway," Gamini said, "you haven't even had a drink yet. Pru, take care of that for me, will you?"

Aware that both girls had been studying something or other artistic, Ranjit tried conversation. "So you want to be an artist?" he asked Maggie.

She gave him an incredulous look. "What, and starve to death? No way! I'm pretty sure that what I'll be doing is teaching art in some community college near Trenton, New Jersey, where my folks live. Or wherever my husband's job is, when I have a husband."

The blonde, Pru, spoke up. "Oh, I'd love to be an artist, Ranjit. I won't make it, though. I have no artistic talent at all, and I don't want to go back to the family in Shaker Heights. What I'm hoping for is a job as auctioneer at someplace like Sotheby's. Good money, interesting people to work with, and I'd be around art even if I wasn't creating any."

Maggie handed Ranjit his arrack and Coke, laughing. "Fat chance," she said.

Pru reached around Gamini's legs with one of her own and kicked her. "Pig," she said. "I don't mean right away. You start out as an intern, and maybe the first thing they give you to do is get the numbers from the bid paddles that people at the back of the room are holding up—you know, where the actual auctioneer won't be looking. Ranjit? Don't you like arrack and Coke?"

Ranjit didn't have a good answer to that. Actually, he had liked it pretty well when he and Gamini had been exploring Colombo but hadn't had any of that particular drink since Gamini had left. But when he tasted it, it went down pretty agreeably. So did the next one.

Although the evening wasn't what Ranjit had expected, it wasn't turning out badly at all. At some point the girl named Pru had detached herself from Gamini and settled in next to Ranjit himself. He immediately noticed three things about her. She was warm, she was soft, and she smelled quite nice. Oh, not as nice as Myra de Soyza, or perhaps even as nice—in a quite different way, of course—as Mevrouw Beatrix Vorhulst, but still quite pleasing.

Ranjit not being a fool, he was quite aware that the way women smelled was primarily an artifact purchasable at any pharmacy. No matter. It was still quite pleasing, and Pru had other virtues as well, which included feeling good against his arm and, quite often, saying amusing things. Taken all in all, Ranjit decided that he was having quite a good time.

But as the evening wore on, he was aware that he had some unanswered questions in his mind. When the two girls went off to the powder room, he had a chance to approach some of the questions. As a beginning he asked Gamini if he had seen much of them in London. Gamini looked surprised. "Never set eyes on either one of them until they turned up on the plane from Dubai and we got to talking."

"Oh, I see," Ranjit said, although he wasn't sure he did. For clarification he asked, "What about your friend Madge?"

Gamini gave him a long and amused look. "You know what your problem is, Ranjit? You worry too much. Madge is in Barcelona, I guess with whoever it is that sends her texts every other hour. Have another drink."

Ranjit did. In fact they both did, and so did the two girls when they returned. It wasn't quite the same as before, however. Ranjit's drink sat unfinished before him, and so did most of the others. And then Maggie whispered something in Gamini's ear. "Oh, all right," Gamini said to her; and then to Ranjit he said, "I'm afraid it's about that time. It's been good seeing you again, but my father and I have to take off for Grandma's first thing in the morning. So we're going to pack it in." He stood up, smiling. "Give us a hug, will you?"

Ranjit obliged, and got one from Maggie as well. "By the way," Gamini added as they turned to go, "don't worry about the check. It all goes on my father's tab. Come on, sweets." And as he and Maggie threaded their way between tables to the door, Ranjit understood what the plural pronoun had implied.

And there Ranjit was, just him and the girl named Pru.

He lacked experience to tell him what was expected of him under these circumstances. He had, however, seen enough American films to get a clue. "Would you like another drink?" he said politely.

She shook her head, grinning. She nodded at the nearly full glass in front of her. "I've barely wounded the last one. Anyway, I think another drink would be pretty superfluous, don't you?"

He did, but he was running out of ideas for the next step. In the films, at this point the man might ask the woman if she would care to dance. That wasn't an option here; no dancing was going on in this hotel bar, and anyway Ranjit didn't know how.

Pru saved him. "It's been a very nice evening, Ranjit Subramanian," she told him, "but I want to get up and do some sightseeing tomorrow. Do you think the waiter can get me a taxi?"

Ranjit was surprised. "You aren't in this hotel?"

"Booked the accommodation before we left London, and we took what they gave us. It's only about a five-minute ride away."

At that point Ranjit knew what to do, and did. Pru was glad to be given a ride in the temple's van—even if Ranjit was a little drunk behind the wheel—and she was interested to hear about Ranjit's father's position in the temple, along with a sketchy outline of the long and colorful history of Tiru Koneswaram. Enough so that she invited him in to sober up with a cup of coffee when they got to her hotel.

The travel agency in London had given the girls a young people's hotel, with a lot of young people making the lobby a bit too noisy for a conversation, so Pru invited Ranjit up to her room. They talked, sitting companionably close, and propinquity worked its magic. Within an hour Ranjit had lost his virginity, or at least his cross-gender virginity. He enjoyed it very much. So did Pru, enough so that they did it twice more before they finally got to sleep.

The sun was high and hot when the sound of a key in the lock woke them. It was Maggie, and she did not seem surprised to find both Ranjit and Pru in one of the room's twin beds. Gamini? Oh, he was long gone, had jumped out of the bed and into his clothes when reception called to say that his father was waiting for him in the lobby. "And anyway," Maggie said, giving Pru an inquiring look, "we're supposed to be taken to lunch by your life-drawing instructor's cousin at the embassy, and it's a quarter after ten."

Ranjit, who was getting into his clothes as fast as he could, took that for an exit cue. What he wasn't sure of was how to take leave of Pru, and this time she was not helpful. She did give him a hearty good-bye kiss. But when he tentatively suggested that if they wanted sightseeing he was available, she couldn't see a way of fitting him into their other obligations that day, or any other day, for that matter.

Ranjit got the message. He kissed her again, with the intensity dimmed down much lower this time, waved a farewell to Maggie, and left.

Back in the van, he considered. He had the van and his own freedom for at least a week. But there was nothing to keep him in Colombo, and nothing to attract him to any other part of Sri Lanka. So he shrugged and started the engine and began the long drive back to Trinco.

An hour later he was outside of the Colombo city limits, and wondering what his father would say when he returned the van so early. Most of his wondering, though, was devoted to the subject of Ms. Pru Never-Did-

Know-Her-Last-Name. Why had she behaved in the way—no, in the several contradictorily different ways—that she had in their short but, at least for Ranjit, highly significant relationship? He was nearly thirty kilometers down the road before he came to a satisfactory answer.

Well, "satisfactory" wasn't the best word to use. He was fairly sure he had the explanation, but he didn't like it at all. His conclusion was that Pru's actions were a function of his skin color. Having sex with a short and dark-skinned Asian man—what was the name people in Pru's social class used for that sort of person? Oh, yes. "Wog." For wily Oriental gentleman. Having sex with such a man might be an enjoyable experiment when no one knew about it except another young woman engaged in doing the same thing. But it was not acceptable where one might be seen by people who might speak of it to people in London, or to people in Shaker Heights, whatever Shaker Heights might happen to be.

So for the next hour or so Ranjit's thoughts were glum. They didn't stay that way, though. Whatever thoughts might have been in Pru's mind, the things her body had been doing while she was thinking them were quite pleasing for him to remember. It had been, Ranjit admitted to himself, one of the most intensely pleasurable experiences of his life. All right, it appeared that it was to be a one-time-only event with that particular partner, but there were other women in the world, were there not? Including some who were not concerned about the color of his skin?

Including, for instance, Myra de Soyza?

That was an interesting new thought for Ranjit. Experimentally he set his imagination a new task, which was to replay his memories of the night in bed with Pru Something, but replace Pru in the role of Female Partner with Myra herself.

Ranjit had not previously been thinking of Myra in that way, exactly, but he discovered that it wasn't hard to do. It was pretty enjoyable, too, until, unfortunately, the thought of the Canadian hotel man, Brian Harrigan, began to come up in his mind. That part wasn't pleasant at all.

Reluctantly Ranjit gave up that experiment and, doing his best not to think of anything at all, simply drove on.

The sun was nearly setting by the time he at last got to Trincomalee. Ranjit thought about going back to his lonely room, but what he wanted was someone to talk to about—well, not about Pru Last-Nameless, of course, but anyway just to talk. He took a chance on driving to the Kanakaratnam house, and won.

They were all inside. Though the door was closed, he could hear Dot Kanakaratnam's voice, but no one else's. When Tiffany answered his knock and let him in, he saw that her mother was sitting at the table and talking into a cell phone. (Ranjit hadn't known she owned one.) When she saw him in the doorway, she said a few quick words into the phone and folded it shut. There was something in the look on her face that troubled Ranjit—anger? Sadness? He couldn't tell. What she said was "You're early, Ranjit. We thought you'd be spending more time with your friend."

"So did I," he said, a tad ruefully, "but it didn't work out. I had a good time, though." He had not been intending to tell them exactly how good, more about what an interesting place Colombo was, but the expressions on the faces of the children stopped him. "Is something wrong?" he asked.

Dot answered for the whole family. "It's George. My husband. He's escaped."

That was news that trumped anything Ranjit might have said. He pressed for details. George Kanakaratnam, for some inscrutable police reason, had been in the process of being transferred from one prison to another. There had been a car crash. The guard and the driver had been killed. Kanakaratnam had not, and he had simply walked away.

"The Trinco police were here all day," Harold volunteered when his mother paused to breathe. "They said Da might have got away on a boat. There was a bridge that went over a pretty big river right down the road."

"But there wasn't any blood there," Rosie said triumphantly, puzzling Ranjit. It seemed to him that with two dead, there had to be some spilled blood somewhere around the scene.

Tiffany clarified the matter. "She means there wasn't any blood inside the bus, except for right around the front seats. So our father probably didn't get hurt."

Dot met Ranjit's look with a hostile look of her own. "You're thinking of George as a jailbird, but to them he's their father. Naturally they love him," she informed Ranjit. Then, in a friendly tone, "Can I give you a cup of tea? And we'd like to hear all about your trip."

Obeying her gesture, Ranjit sat at the table. He didn't get a chance to tell them his story, though, because Tiffany was waving her hand. When the girl spoke, it wasn't to Ranjit but to her mother. "Is this when we should tell him about the letter?" she asked.

Dot gave Ranjit a stricken look. "Oh, I'm sorry. There was so much going on here that I just forgot." She scrabbled in the litter of papers on the table for a moment, then pulled out an envelope and handed it to Ranjit.

"One of the monks brought it. It's been sitting in the temple mail room for a week because nobody told them where you were staying."

"And then this morning, when they figured it out, they tried to deliver it to your room, but you weren't there," Tiffany put in. "And our mother told them they could leave it here and we'd see that you got it."

Dot looked embarrassed. "I did, yes. The police were here, and I just wanted everybody to go away. . . ."

She stopped when she realized Ranjit was no longer listening to her. The envelope had the return address of the beach hotel nearest the construction site. So did the sheet of notepaper inside, and what it said was:

Dear Ranjit,
I'll be here for a few days. Is there any chance we could get together for a cup of tea or something of the sort?

It was signed Myra de Soyza.

Ranjit didn't wait for the tea with the Kanakaratnams. "I'll see you later," he said, already on his way out the door.

Driving to the hotel didn't take longer than twenty minutes. The young woman at the desk was as helpful as she could be, but when it came down to it, all she could tell him was, "Oh, but they checked out yesterday, Ms. de Soyza and Mr. Harrigan. I think they may have gone back to Colombo."

Back in the van Ranjit allowed himself to admit how much he regretted having missed her—and how much he disliked the fact that she and the Canadian were traveling together. His mood depressed, he drove slowly back. At the turn that would have taken him to the Kanakaratnam house he paused, then turned the other way. It was interesting, in a way, that Dot's husband had managed to escape from a federal prison. Ranjit had looked forward to telling the children about his trip, too. Well, about parts of it.

But not right now. Right now he didn't want to talk to anybody about anything.

The next day he went back to his job. The foreman's brother-in-law was not at all happy to see him, but when Ranjit picked up the Kanakaratnam children, they were happy enough that it made up for it. When it became story time, they loved hearing about how the kings of Kandy had fought off the European invaders for so many years (as Ranjit had read off his computer first thing that morning) and did not seem to want to talk about their escapee father.

Neither did their mother, not for several days, at least, and then when he stopped off for the kids one morning, he didn't get them.

Dot Kanakaratnam was seated at the table, putting clothes and household goods into sacks, and all four of the children were packing little bundles of their own. When she saw the question in Ranjit's eyes, she gave him a great smile. "I have wonderful news, Ranjit! Some old friends have found me a job! It's right here in Trinco, too, although down by the port. I'm not sure what the work is, exactly, but they say it will pay well and an apartment of our own comes with it!"

She gave Ranjit an expectant look. "That's—wonderful," he said, doing his best to supply what she wanted. He found himself wondering how she couldn't know what job she was taking, but he realized she was desperate, so he didn't pursue it. "When would you start?"

"Almost immediately. There is one thing, though, Ranjit. You still have your father's van, don't you? And taxis are so expensive. Could you give us a lift to the port?"

10

A NEW LIFE FOR
THE KANAKARATNAMS

He did have the van, because his father had told him to keep it for commuting to work, so he could drive them. At least he could as soon as he had notified the foreman that his brother-in-law could have his payday a little longer. By the time he got back to Dot's house, everything was ready. Twenty minutes later he had the children, squealing with excitement in the back of the van, while Dot sat beside him, studying the harbor as they approached.

The port was not a sight Ranjit had seen much of since Sri Lanka had attained peace. True, there were reminders of the unruly outside world. On the far side of the harbor he could make out the shark shapes of a couple of nuclear submarines, probably Indian, and so much else! There were fishing vessels, of course, and not of the four- or five-man kind that were pulled up on every beach around the island. These were the deepwater craft that would sail a hundred kilometers or more from land for the commercially valuable schools. There were freighters of all kinds and sizes, being relieved of their containers or bulk cargoes or having new ones loaded. And Ranjit saw with astonishment that there were several ships of a different kind entirely—painted brilliant white, festooned with lifeboats hanging in their davits, lined with rows of portholes. Why, the cruise ships were back! Ranjit couldn't help pulling over to let the children get a look. He expected childish whoops of excitement and was puzzled when what he got instead was the children's endless whispering in each other's ears.

Dot, however, was having no delays. "Settle down," she ordered the children. Then to Ranjit, "I'd like to get there as soon as I can. Do you see the souvenir shop next to where those white ships are docked? I think that's the place."

It was a fairly shabby little kiosk, not particularly busy, either. A few elderly tourists in bright-colored shorts and imitation Hawaiian shirts were desultorily studying its picture postcards and plastic elephant figurines.

But it was where Dot Kanakaratnam insisted on going, children and all. She reassured him. "Yes, this is the place. Our friends will come for us, and now, Ranjit, you must go. And," she added, suddenly flinging her arms around him, "the children will miss you, and so will I!" One after another the children gave him their own hugs. And, as Ranjit drove away, he could see that they were all crying.

Of course Ranjit didn't cry. He was a grown man. Anyway, people were looking at him.

Ranjit was in no hurry to get back to his job on the beach, no longer with any small children there to amuse him. Four or five little restaurants and snack shops were nearby, ready for the custom of the cruise ship passengers. He parked near the least unattractive of them for a cup of tea and sat for a time musing over how rapidly little children could win over a heart.

It was odd, he thought, that Dot should know details such as, for instance, that she was going to get an apartment with the job but not seem to know what the job itself was going to be. It almost made Ranjit wonder if Dot was being less than truthful with him.

But that was a thought easy to dismiss. What reason could the woman have to keep secrets from him? When he left the shop he cast a quick glance at where he had left them.

They were gone.

Ranjit wished them a silent good-bye and good luck, and drove unhurriedly along the bay front. He passed a sweet-smelling little freighter being loaded with cinnamon for export, next to a container ship from Singapore now unloading (it was safe to assume) cars, computers, and domestic appliances from the factories of China. Next was the cluster of cruise ships, a good deal more bedraggled at close range than they had at first seemed. A few passengers who apparently had had no interest in the ground tours to Swami Rock or his father's temple lounged around the railings of the upper decks. One was a little girl who was waving joyously in his direction. . . .

No! It wasn't just any little girl. It was tiny Betsy Kanakaratnam! And running rapidly toward her, apparently with the intention to scold her, was her big sister, Tiffany, and a few meters away was the one boy in the family, holding the hand of a squat, dark man.

Could that be Kirthis Kanakaratnam? It could hardly be anyone else. Tiffany was already calling to the man, dragging her baby sister toward him.

The man nodded consideringly. Then he turned toward Ranjit, who was leaning out of the van window below. Grinning broadly, the man gestured to him.

What he was trying to say was not hard to understand: He was waving Ranjit to come aboard the ship, pointing to a parking space not far away, pointing to himself and then to the gangway that linked the ship to the dock. Ranjit didn't hesitate. He turned toward the indicated parking space, shut off the engine, slammed the van door, and trotted up the gangway.

As he climbed, he saw that this ship was clearly not one of the fifty-thousand-ton behemoths that cruised the Caribbean and the Greek islands. It was a lot smaller, a lot dirtier, and had a lot more places in its paint job where chipping indicated the need for a new coat. At the head of the gangway a large black-bearded man in a white ship's uniform stood before a badge reader and a little gate. Next to him, however, stood the presumed George Kanakaratnam, who said something in the man's ear and then spoke welcomingly to Ranjit. "Come aboard, come aboard! It's grand to meet you, Mr. Subramanian. The kids have had so much to say about you! Now—this way, please—we'll go down and have a word with Dot, and you can see what a nice stateroom the children have, all their own! And I'm getting good pay, and it looks like they'll find a job for Dot, too. It's just the luckiest break we ever had!"

"Well," Ranjit said, "I guess you were pretty lucky—"

Kanakaratnam wasn't slowing down for interruptions, especially ambiguous ones that could refer to a jailbreak. "You bet," he said. "Good pay, too! Now we just go down these steps—"

They did, and walked through another passage, and down more steps, with Kirthis (or George) Kanakaratnam never stopping his recital of how lucky his family was and how fond his children were of Ranjit Subramanian. They passed through seven or eight doors, all of the kind that would spring irrevocably closed in an emergency, and most marked NO ADMITTANCE. Until at last they came to a door of a quite different kind, a kind that Kanakaratnam stopped before and knocked on. It was opened by a large bearded man. "He's Somalian," Kanakaratnam told Ranjit. "They all look like that, pretty much."

And he gave the bearded man a nod, and the man nodded back. Then, in a quite different tone, Kanakaratnam said, "Now sit down. You're going to have to stay here for a day or two. You don't want to make any loud noises or try to leave, because if you do, he'll kill you."

He gestured at the Somalian. Evidently the man understood enough of what was going on, because he patted a wide-bladed kind of knife that he carried thrust into his belt.

"Have you got all that?" Kanakaratnam asked. "No noise, don't try to leave, you stay here until somebody tells you it's all right to leave. So don't make trouble and you'll turn out to have an interesting trip—after we take over the ship."

11

PIRATE LIFE

It was a little longer than Kanakaratnam had suggested before Ranjit was freed. It took long enough, anyway, for him to be fed several times—quite well, actually, because the kitchen was after all on a cruise ship. At least twice Ranjit fell restlessly asleep on the hard cot that stood against the wall. The Somalian left him alone several times, but not without locking the door behind him. Ranjit thought it over carefully before taking the risk of trying it; it was thoroughly locked. Kanakaratnam looked in a couple of times, apparently just to be sociable. He was quite willing to explain to Ranjit what was going on. On the second day the pirates—that was the word Kanakaratnam himself used, "pirates"—stormed the bridge, disarmed those of the crew who were not actually already colleagues, and announced that the ship was changing course for the port of Bosaso in, yes, Somalia. Before Ranjit was released, the pirates looted everything of value from the ship's strong room and everything easily portable from the staterooms of the passengers—who, they were informed, would fairly soon be on their way home, unharmed, provided only that their families or friends came up with the appropriate ransom money. ("You would be surprised," Kanakaratnam told Ranjit, "what some people will pay to get Grandma back.") And then there was the ship itself. If they got it safely to the right port in Somalia, a paint job and some decent false papers could make it the most saleable item of all.

It was all very businesslike. It was, in fact, Kanakaratnam explained, pretty much like any other commercial enterprise. Since the beginnings of the twenty-first century, piracy had become a fairly big business on its own, with established brokerage houses prepared to collect a ransom and pass it on to those demanding it, in return for which they guaranteed the safe return of captives. "In fact," Kanakaratnam told Ranjit with satisfaction, "getting caught with that stolen junk was the luckiest thing that ever happened to me. My cell mate at Batticaloa was supposed to be in on this, but he got picked up for something else. But he told me all about it, and when I got a chance to get away, I knew just where to go."

Even businesslike piracy did, of course, sometimes have its unpleasant side. One bad side, Ranjit was pretty sure, was what the pirates did with any crew members who resisted them too vigorously. (Ranjit asked Kanakaratnam, but he simply didn't answer. Which was answer enough for Ranjit.)

When Kanakaratnam told Ranjit that the takeover was complete and he could come out of his cell, Ranjit found out there had been at least one unsavory occurrence. It was because of the ship's captain, who had possessed an excessive sense of duty. He hadn't wanted to turn over the keys to the strong room. Of course, that problem had been readily solved. The pirates had shot the captain on the shuffleboard court and promoted the much more cooperative first officer, who himself had pulled the keys out of the deceased man's pocket and handed them over.

Ranjit had never been on a cruise ship before. Despite the grim circumstances, this one still offered all sorts of absurd amenities. There was a swimming pool on the top deck (though not conveniently usable when there was any significant wave action, which was almost always). The kitchen produced quite good meals, even if the actual passengers were clumped despondently together on one side of the dining room, watched over by pirates with assault rifles. The casino was closed, but that made little difference since all the passengers had already been relieved of the cash and credit cards they might have gambled with. The bars were closed, too, and there was no nightly show in the barroom theater. But there were canned movies on the TV screens in every stateroom, and the weather was balmy.

Too balmy, according to Kanakaratnam. "I'd rather have more clouds," he said. "You don't know how many eyes are up there, watching us. Satellites," he clarified, when Ranjit looked puzzled. "Of course, they don't pay much attention to an old rust bucket like this, but you never know. Oh," he added, reminding himself of an obligation, "and Tiffany's looking for you. Wants to know if you'll help her with the kids up on the sundeck."

"Why not?" Ranjit said agreeably, in fact rather looking forward to seeing his four playmates again. He was miserable, yes, but doing everything he could to hide it. When he came out of the stairwell into the bright tropical daylight of the sundeck, he couldn't help casting a quick look at the sky.

Of course he couldn't see any of those eyes in the sky. He hadn't expected to but could not help wondering just who it might be whose eyes were staring down at them at that moment. . . .

And, of course, he had no idea of what totally nonhuman eyes some of them were.

There turned out to be about twenty children among the ship's passengers, ranging from six or seven up to about fourteen. Most of them spoke reasonable approximations of English, and what Tiffany wanted Ranjit to do—of course—was tell them stories so that they would forget having seen the murdered captain's body exposed all day near the shuffleboard courts.

That turned out to be a tall order. Two of the ten-year-olds never stopped crying, and several of the others could not seem to take their eyes off the rifle-carrying pirate who patrolled the deck. It may have been that Ranjit made it even harder on himself, because rather than doing the simple and never-failing Russian multiplication thing again, he decided to show the children how to count on their fingers, binary style.

It was not a success. Clearly none of the passenger children had ever heard of binary numbers before. When Ranjit informed them that if you wanted to say you had one of something in binary, you could just write the old familiar one, but if you had two, you had to write it as one-zero, and three as one-one, the incomprehension was palpable.

He pressed on gamely. "Now we come to the counting-on-your-fingers part," he told them, holding up his two hands. "What you have to do now is assume that every one of your fingers represents a numeral—and, yes, Tiffany, I know what you're going to ask. Yes, we do count the thumb as a finger." (Tiffany hadn't said anything, but cheerfully nodded.) "Each numeral has to be a one or a zero because that's all you have to work with in binary arithmetic. When the fingers are retracted"—he made two fists— "each finger is a zero. So now look here." He laid his two fists on the tabletop before him. "In binary these ten retracted fingers represent the number zero zero zero zero zero zero zero zero zero zero. Which is just another way of saying that zero is the number all ten of the zeros represent, because no matter how many zeros you write down, it's still just zero. But now look at this."

He stuck out all the fingers on both hands. "Now they're all ones, and the binary number I'm displaying is one one one one one one one one one one. And that means, if you want to express it in the decimal equivalent, that you're writing a one for the last numeral one in the line, plus a two for the numeral one next to it. Plus a four for the one next to that—doubling each time, you see, all the way up to five hundred and twelve for the last numeral one at the end of the left hand. And so you have written—"

He did the arithmetic with a crayon on a scrap of paper:

1
2
4
8
16
32
64
128
256
+512

"And if you add them all up together you get—"

———
1,023

"And so you've counted on your fingers all the way up to one thousand and twenty-three!"

Ranjit paused to look around at his audience. What he got back was not what he had hoped for. The number of weepers had risen to four or five, and the expressions on the other faces ranged from simple confusion to resentful bafflement.

Then, tardily, questions did begin.

"Do you mean—"

"Wait a minute, Ranjit, are you trying to say—"

And finally, rewardingly, "Oh, let's see if I got it right. Let's say we're counting fish. So what that numeral one at the right-hand edge means is that there's one pile of fish that has only one fish in it, and the numeral one next to it means there's another pile that has two fish, and piles with four fish and eight fish, all the way up to the pile—that's the numeral one at the other end—that has five hundred and twelve fish in it. And you add all the piles together, and altogether you've got one thousand and twenty-three fish. Is that it?"

"It is," Ranjit said, gratified in spite of himself. Gratified despite the fact that the only children who had responded at all were Dot and Kirthis Kanakaratnam's kids, and the one who had really understood was, of course, Tiffany.

Kanakaratnam himself didn't seem to worry about Ranjit's poor reception. When he joined Ranjit for lunch—two kinds of soup, three different salads, and at least half a dozen entrées on the menu—he said approvingly, "You did yourself some good today." He did not say in what way, though Ranjit—who had also caught a glimpse of the late captain's splayed and riddled corpse—had a pretty good idea of what it was.

When Kanakaratnam returned, an hour later, he made it explicit. "You need to keep on showing my friends that you're cooperating with us," he told Ranjit. "There's been questions. So look, here's the thing. We need to get biographical information about every passenger—to know how high to set the ransom—and most of our guys don't speak any language the passengers can understand. So you can help us out that way, right?"

There was a question in the tone of Kanakaratnam's voice, but in the realities of the situation Ranjit faced, there was none. It was clear to him that his best hope of survival was to be useful to the pirates, so he spent a few hours of each of the next two days questioning elderly couples— sometimes terrified, more often belligerent—about their bank accounts, pensions, real-estate holdings, and possibly wealthy relatives.

That only lasted for a couple of days, though, just until the trouble struck.

It was still dark when a change in the ship's noise level woke Ranjit. The comforting sound of the ship's engines was no longer the languid *kerplum, kerplum* but had become a fast and frantic *beggabegga! beggabegga!* Even louder was the yelling back and forth that came from the passage outside his room. When he peered out, he saw members of the original crew trotting as fast as they could toward the exits. Each of the men was carrying two or three suitcases, obviously purloined from the passengers' staterooms—and, Ranjit was quite sure, stuffed full of passengers' stolen valuables. Most of the yelling came from one of the pirates, urging the crew members along with a rope's end. The pirates looked angry and worried. The captive crew members looked scared to death.

Once again it seemed to Ranjit that it would be a good idea to make himself useful. He backtracked the bag carriers to one of the ship's stairwells, where other crewmen were throwing stolen bags down to his level. As Ranjit was about to pick up a couple of the bags to carry, he heard a childish voice calling his name, and when he looked up, Dot Kanakaratnam and her brood were coming down the steps toward him. All of them, even the tiny Betsy, were carrying a share of the loot, and Tiffany was full of information. An hour or two earlier, one of the pirates had spotted what looked like ship's lights far astern. "But nothing showed on the radar," Tiffany informed him excitedly, "so you know what that means?"

Ranjit didn't, but he was capable of a decent guess. "A naval vessel with stealth antiradar?"

"Exactly! We're being followed by some destroyer or something! That means we can't make it to Somalia anymore, so we're going to have to beach this ship somewhere—I guess it'll be India or Pakistan, probably—and then just disappear into the woods. Up on the bridge they're working the radio now, trying to arrange for one of the local gangs to help us."

"And why would a local gang of crooks want to do that, when they can just take the loot away from us?" Ranjit asked.

But the children didn't even try to answer that, and Dot said only, "Come on. Let's get some of this stuff down to the departure place."

Once everything worth stealing had been lugged to the B deck exit, there was nothing useful for any of the pirates to do. They mostly wound up on one of the outside decks, worriedly scanning the horizon for some trace of their radar-blind pursuer, or even more worriedly studying the horizon ahead for a glimpse of where the ship would be run aground.

There wasn't actually much to see but water. If there was another craft or point of land anywhere near them, it did not reveal itself to Ranjit. Around noon he tired of the sport, went down to find something for lunch, and then returned to throw himself onto his bed. He was asleep in minutes. . . .

And then awakened again when a violent metallic screeching and a rocking and bouncing motion that almost threw him to the floor told Ranjit they had arrived.

Then the ship was at rest, though tilted a half dozen degrees from the vertical. Ranjit looked around to make sure there was nothing for him to take—there wasn't—and then, clutching the safety rails, made his way to the exit port. Nearly all of the spoils were already off the ship and being licked by wavelets from the sea behind them. So were most of the people—pirates, passengers, and captive crew alike. Some of the pirates were, quite ungently, ordering the crew and the passengers to carry the wet suitcases above the high-water mark.

Ranjit cast one look around, found no human beings on the shore, and let himself down into the warm calf-deep water.

Humans had been on that shore at one time. They had left unmistakable signs of their presence. This was one of those deserted Indian Ocean beaches that once had been used for low-cost (and low-safety) ship breaking. The whole place stank of oil and rust. All up and down the edge of the water were fragments of old hulls, or of discarded bits of ship's furnishings—chairs, beds, tables—too old and damaged to be worth removing. What was nowhere in sight, though Ranjit knew they had once been there, was any trace of the desperately poor men who had taken the jobs of cutting up the hulls and separating out the commercially profitable sections of engines and drive shafts . . . the men who had died on that beach, as often as not, from the toxic substances that would have made the job too expensive on any better-policed stretch of coast. How much of those trapped poisons and carcinogens might remain in the sands and waters around him, Ranjit could not guess.

The best way to deal with that problem, Ranjit knew, was to get off that beach as quickly as possible.

There didn't seem to be any good way of doing that. If there was to be help from local gangs, Ranjit could see no signs of it. Well, there might have been something—a quick glimpse of some shadowy something half-concealed by the brush, but when he looked again, nothing was there.

Wading just behind Ranjit, Dot Kanakaratnam was doing her best to keep hold of four little hands at once without letting go of her loot bags. Finally she gave up and shoved one of the bags at Ranjit. "Here," she said. "It's George's spare clothes. You hang on to them until he shows up; I want to get these kids out of the water."

She didn't wait for his consent. Kids attached, she shuffled through the hot sands to the high-water mark, where she stood and looked all around for her husband. Ranjit himself was suddenly the target of one of the pirates, waving his gun approximately at a cluster of the captive crew but clearly shouting at Ranjit. Who wasn't sure what the man was ordering but thought it was not likely to be anything he wanted to do. So he bobbed his head as though in agreement, while turning and running, as fast as he could, around the stern of the beached ship. He didn't stop until he was out of sight of the pirate. . . .

That was when he heard the first distant, mournful hooting.

It was a scary sound, not musical exactly but reminiscent of the background to a horror film, as the undead begin to clamber out of their coffins. Nor was he the only one who heard it. Up on the beach a pirate who had flung himself to the sand, panting with the exertion of getting there, sat up and looked wonderingly around. So did another pirate, and a couple of the crew, all sitting or standing and trying to see where the sound had come from.

Then Ranjit saw them, a string of distant aircraft coming toward them from the sea. Helicopters. At least a dozen of them, and every one fitted with curious soup plate–like disks, all rotating with every shift in the choppers' course to remain pointed at the people on the beach . . . and the sound grew louder. . . .

And kept on growing louder and louder.

For all the rest of his very long life Ranjit Subramanian never managed to forget that day on the beach. True, there were even worse days that followed it, but those terrifying and degrading moments under the acoustic barrage from the helicopters were bad enough for anyone. Ranjit had never before been exposed to the sublethal armorarium of a modern assault force. He had not known what it would mean for the sound to bypass the brain. It was the belly that caught the worst of its effects, the bowels loosened, the vomiting profuse, the sick pain remorseless.

Nor was the attack entirely sublethal. At least two of the pirates managed to fight back the miseries of their bodies long enough to fire a few rounds at the helicopters from their assault rifles. (Unfortunately for Ranjit, this included Kirthis Kanakaratnam.) That was a mistake. Each of the choppers contained two open doorways, one occupied by a machine gunner, the other by an equally death-dealing man with a grenade launcher, and neither pirate survived firing his weapon by more than a minute.

And as to those other watchers from the skies . . .

They found this incident puzzling, even the ones called the Nine-Limbeds.

Oh, the Nine-Limbeds had seen human firefights before. The Nine-Limbeds were the only client race the Grand Galactics encouraged to be linguists, and their main mission was to tell their masters what these humans said to one another—but you couldn't spy on humans for very long without encountering violence. The Nine-Limbeds had thought they knew what was coming this time. When they had identified a surface craft abristle with chemical explosive weapons lurking in slow-motion pursuit of another that was apparently unarmed, they had supposed the outcome would be another human bloodbath. They had even wondered if it was worth their while to stick around to observe just one more example of human mass murder.

It was a surprise to them that so few of the humans on the beach were put to death as a result of having their integuments penetrated by the projectile weapons from the aircraft.

They recognized the nature of the choppers' primary weapons—the compression air device, the ring vortex cannon, and all the others—because they had seen their like before. After all, there were few weapons employed by the human race that had not been employed, over and over, by other races at other places and times in the galaxy. And the Nine-Limbeds well understood, from the histories of other species who had employed similar weapons in the long galactic past, what unpleasant and debilitating effects such weaponry might have on an undefendable animal body.

The puzzle for the Nine-Limbeds was this: Why would these primitives employ such weapons in preference to their usual armorarium of explosively propelled penetrants, which produced even more destructive effects on organic bodies?

When the encounter on the surface was over, the decision makers among the Nine-Limbed crew debated for many minutes before deciding whether to report what they had seen.

In the long run they did. They reported it exactly and in detail, letting the Grand Galactics make of it what they would, although the Nine-Limbeds did attempt to give themselves a little wiggle room by the title they gave the report: "An Example of an Anomalous Encounter."

12

JUDGMENT

Ranjit didn't see much of the actual bloodshed, being totally absorbed by his own humiliatingly nasty problems. Apart from the fact that he felt as though a herd of mad swine had been stampeding through his digestive system, the subsonics had, as they were programmed to do, caused him voluminously to foul himself. He had not done anything like that since early childhood, and he had forgotten how repulsive a process it was.

He managed to strip off the soiled garments and stagger back into the warm wavelets, using the least filthy of his own clothing to scrub himself nearly clean. After that he had a plan. He looted the bag of George Kanakaratnam's clothing that Dot had given him. There were no shoes in the bag, and Ranjit chose not to put on another man's underwear, but all the rest was there: slacks, and pullover shirts, and thick woolly socks that Ranjit hoped might protect his feet from the sharp-edged pebbles of the beach. Then he stepped out of concealment to take stock of the situation.

It looked bad and smelled worse. The choppers had landed and positioned themselves in orderly ranks, and now they disgorged at least a hundred armed troops—probably either Indian or Pakistani, Ranjit guessed, though he was not familiar enough with either to guess which. Whoever they were, they had efficiently separated the former cruise ship population into four clusters. Two were made up of the former passengers, one group for men, one for women, and what the clusters amounted to were enclosures made up of hastily strung-up sheets along the water's edge. Half a dozen soldiers were handing out towels and blankets to the passengers who had cleaned themselves as much as they intended to. Ranjit noted that the soldiers helping the female passengers were female themselves; in the uniforms, wielding their weapons, they had all looked interchangeably sexless.

A couple of dozen meters down the shore twenty or thirty men and women, unguarded, were doing their best to clean themselves as well.

They didn't have anyone to hand them towels, but a stack of the things was available for the taking on the beach. Ranjit could identify them as rescued crew by the few he recognized . . . but he actually would have known who they were anyway, by the rapturous looks of relief these saved-at-the-last-minute souls wore on their faces.

There was one other cluster. These had not been allowed to clean themselves or change their clothes. They lay flat on their faces, fingers locked atop their heads, and they were guarded by three or four of the soldiers, weapons at the ready.

There was no doubt which group they represented. Ranjit scanned the prostrate forms, but if any of the Kanakaratnams were there, he could not recognize them from their backs. None looked small enough to be any of the younger children, either.

One of the soldiers guarding them was taking an interest in Ranjit, shouting something Ranjit could not make out and waving his rifle meaningfully.

It seemed to Ranjit that walking around on his own made the soldiers suspicious. "Right," he called to the soldier, hoping he knew what he was agreeing to, and looked around at his options.

Which group Ranjit actually belonged to was hard to say. Still, there was no doubt that the former passengers were getting the best treatment, so he flipped a soft salute to the soldier and then strolled over to those waiting for fresh clothing at the men's side and attached himself to the line, nodding pleasantly to the oldster just ahead of him.

Who didn't nod back. Instead he scowled at Ranjit for a moment and then opened his mouth and let out a yell for the soldiers. When a couple of them came running, the man was shouting, "This one's no passenger! He's one of them! He's the one who was trying to get me to tell how much my kids would pay to ransom me!"

Which is why, a moment later, Ranjit wound up lying facedown, his hands on his head, between a pair of the largest and—because they had been given no chance to clean themselves up—smelliest of the pirates.

He kept on lying there, for hours.

Those hours were not totally without anything happening, because in the first of them Ranjit learned two important lessons. The first was that he shouldn't try to lift his head enough to try to look for the Kanakaratnams, because when he did, he was hit with a stick just above his left ear, while whoever was wielding the stick yelled, "Lie still!" The pain of the strike was like a lightning bolt. The second was that he shouldn't try whispering to his neighbors for information. That got him a serious kick right about where his lowest right-hand rib was. The pain from the kick was indescribable. And the kicker was a soldier, all right, because he was definitely wearing steel-braced army shoes.

After about two hours—when the tropical sun had mounted high in the sky and Ranjit was beginning to feel as though he were being baked alive—something did happen. A new fleet of helicopters arrived, bigger and a good deal more comfortable-looking than the first, and immediately boarded all the passengers—and all those passengers' reclaimed possessions—to take them to what no doubt would be a nicer place than this. An hour or so more and there was a sound of heavy-duty engines from the brush, and a couple of flatbed trucks pushed their way onto the sand to take the rescued crew away. And later still—much later, when the sun had done its best to parboil the helpless pirates, Ranjit included—it was their turn. It was helicopters again this time, big ones that didn't look comfortable at all. The man in charge was identifiable by the amount of metallic embroidery on his uniform and cap and by the facts that he arrived in his own helicopter and that before he got out of it, other soldiers had immediately prepared a chair and a table—well, an upended box, to be more accurate—for him to sit at as he dispensed judgment.

Each of the pirates, one by one, was commanded to stand up and answer the officer's questions. Ranjit couldn't hear the questions or answers, but the verdicts were delivered clearly enough to be heard by all. "Rawalpindi, central jail," the officer said to the first prisoner, and again, "Rawalpindi, central jail," to the second and the third.

Ranjit was next to be summoned before the dispenser of justice. He took advantage of the few moments he had between getting to his feet and facing the officer to hastily look over the remaining pirates for a sign of the children, but if they were there, Ranjit could not identify them.

Then he was standing before the officer and did not dare look farther. His questioning was brief. The officer listened while another soldier spoke in his ear, then addressed Ranjit. "What is your name?" he asked—gratefully, in English.

"I am Ranjit Subramanian, son of Ganesh Subramanian, who is the high priest of the Tiru temple in Trincomalee in Sri Lanka. I was not one of the pirates—"

The officer stopped him. "Wait," he said, and said something inaudible to his aide, who equally inaudibly replied. The officer mulled over that information in silence for a moment. Then he leaned forward, his head close to Ranjit, and inhaled deeply.

Then he nodded; Ranjit had passed the smell test and could therefore be tolerated as a traveling companion. "Interrogation," he said. "Put him in my aircraft. Next!"

13

A CONVENIENT PLACE
FOR QUESTIONING

Beginning to end, Ranjit was in the hands of the interrogators for just over two years, but it was only in the first six months that much actual interrogation went on. His stay, however, was not at any point comfortable.

Ranjit's first inkling that this would be the case was when he was blindfolded, gagged, and handcuffed to a seat in the judging officer's helo before it took off. Where he was then flown to he could not say, although it took less than an hour to get there. Then, still blindfolded, he was helped down the steps to some sort of paved surface and then was walked twenty or thirty meters to some other steps, these going up into some other aircraft. There he was cuffed once more to his seat, and then the new plane took off.

This one wasn't a helicopter. Ranjit could feel the bumps in the runway as the aircraft gained speed, and then the sudden transition to bumpless free flight. It wasn't a short flight, either, and it certainly wasn't a sociable one. Ranjit could hear the aircrew talking to one another, though in what language he could not say, but when he tried calling out to let them know he needed to go to the bathroom, the answer he got was not in words. It was a sudden, hard blow to the side of his face, unexpected and unbraced-for.

Nevertheless they did, ultimately, let him use the plane's little toilet, though still blindfolded and with the door kept open. They fed him, too—that is, they opened his seat's tray and put something on it and ordered, "Eat!" By feel he determined that it was some kind of sandwich, possibly cheese of an unfamiliar variety, but by then it had been nearly twenty hours since Ranjit had had anything to eat and he devoured it, dry. He did take a chance to ask for water, and got a repeat of the blow to the side of the head.

How long they flew, Ranjit could not say because he drifted off to an uneasy sleep, waking only when the jittery bouncing of the aircraft told him they were landing, and on a much worse runway than before. He didn't get the blindfold removed. He did get helped out of the plane and into some kind of vehicle, in which he was driven for more than an hour.

He wound up being led, still blindfolded, into some sort of building, down a hall, and into a room where his captors sat him down. Then one of them spoke to him in a gruff, accented English: "Hold out hands in front of you. No, with palms up!" And when he did, he was struck on the palms with something brutally heavy.

The pain was sharp. Ranjit couldn't help crying out. Then the voice again: "Now you tell truth. What is name?"

That was the first question Ranjit was asked under duress, and the one asked most often of all. His questioners did not choose to believe the simple fact that he was Ranjit Subramanian, who chanced to be wearing some garments belonging to somebody else, whose name, as shown by the labels stitched to the garments, was Kirthis Kanakaratnam. Each time he gave the truthful answer, they exacted the penalty for lying.

This was different for each of the questioners. When it was the stubby, sweaty man named Bruno asking the questions, his favorite weapon for gaining truth was a length of electrical cable, four or five centimeters thick and capable of inflicting extreme pain wherever it was employed. Alternatively Bruno would give Ranjit a violent open-handed slap on his bare belly; this was not only painful, it made Ranjit wonder every time it was applied if it might not be rupturing his appendix or spleen. But there was something comforting about Bruno's technique. No fingernails were extracted, no bones broken, no eyes gouged out; it seemed, hopefully, to Ranjit that they were not doing anything that would leave a permanent mark, and what that suggested to Ranjit was that they might ultimately be planning to let him go.

That hope, however, didn't last. It vanished when, one day, Bruno exasperatedly threw his electrical cable across the room, grabbed up a short wooden club from the table of useful implements, and repeatedly smashed Ranjit across the face with it. That cost Ranjit a black eye and a knocked-out front tooth, as well as most of his tenuously held hope for ultimate release.

The other main torturer was an elderly man who never gave a name but had one eye always half-closed. (Ranjit thought of him as "Squinty.") He seldom left a mark on Ranjit, and he was curiously reassuring in his conversation. On the very first day Ranjit met him, Ranjit held by two powerful assistants flat on his back, Squinty held up a square of cloth. "What we will do to you now," he warned politely, "will make you think you are going to die. You won't. I won't let that happen. Only you must answer my questions truthfully." And then he spread the cloth over Ranjit's face and poured cold water over it from a metal pitcher.

Ranjit had never experienced anything quite like it. The effect wasn't so much pain as brutalizing, incapacitating terror. Ranjit had not failed to hear and understand that Squinty had promised he wouldn't die of this experience, but his body had understandings of its own. It knew that it was being terminally, lethally drowned, and it wanted the process stopped at once. "Help!" Ranjit cried, or tried to cry. "Stop! Let me up!" And all that came out was a bubbly, choky splatter of watery parts of sound, none of them like any English words—

The trickle of poured water stopped, the cloth was pulled off his face, and Ranjit was lifted to sitting position. "Now, what is your name?" Squinty asked politely.

Ranjit tried to stop coughing long enough to get the words out. "I'm Ranjit Sub—" he began, but he didn't even finish saying his name before his shoulders were slammed back onto the floor, the cloth was over his face again, and the terrible pouring of water began once more.

Ranjit managed to hold out four times more before the heart was gone out of him, further resistance was impossible, and he gasped and managed to say, "I'm whoever you want me to be. Just stop!"

"Good," said Squinty encouragingly. "We are making progress, Kirthis Kanakaratnam. So now tell me, what country were you working for?"

There were, of course, many other ways of making a subject become cooperative, but, of course, none of them produced any truthful confessions from Ranjit since he had no crimes to confess.

This exasperated his interrogators. The one he called Squinty complained. "You are making us look bad, Ranjit, or Kirthis, or whoever you are. Listen to me. It will go easier for you if you just stop denying you are Kirthis Kanakaratnam."

Ranjit tried taking the advice. Then it did go easier, a little.

14

RENDITION TO THE
HIGHEST BIDDER

Although Ranjit hadn't known any part of it, quite a few things had been going on outside the walls of his place of detention. Cathedrals had been blown up, railroad trains derailed, office buildings poisoned with radioactive dust in their ventilation systems. And assassinations? Oh, yes, there had been plenty of assassinations, by throat-cutting or defenestration from an upper floor; by handgun, shotgun, and assault rifle; quite often by poisoning, administered in sometimes quite ingenious ways. Not to mention, in one case, assassination by dropping a piano on the victim's head, and in another, by standing on the victim's chest to hold him to the bottom of his bathtub as its taps filled it with lukewarm water. And, of course, there were the wars. Perhaps the most violent of the new ones revived an old plague spot as a Sunni incursion into Kurdish territory threatened to set off another round of the turmoil that characterized post-occupation Iraq.

However, not everything that had transpired had been bad. Under the close supervision of four of the five Scandinavian nations—Iceland, with its own domestic unrest, stayed outside the group—several of the most bitterly fought wars were in, however brief, remission. Even Myanmar, the country that was more commonly called Burma (except by its own intransigent governing clique), had without warning released all of its political prisoners and invited foreign diplomats to monitor its next set of elections. Finally—a development that would have greatly pleased Ranjit, if he could have known of it—after endless stalling, the World Bank had come through with a decent billion-dollar start-up grant for an actual Artsutanov space elevator. True, a World Bank grant was a long way from the actual wheels turning, with the cars going up and down the cables, the hardware that you could hop onto and be drawn to low earth orbit at three hundred kilometers an hour. But it was a real first step.

Those, of course, were not the only data with a significant bearing on his own life that Ranjit did not know. For example, he didn't know why he had been taken to this place and why he had been tortured in it. And then, when the torturing had stopped, he didn't know why that had happened, either. Ranjit had never heard of extraordinary rendition or the momentous decision that had been handed down, decades earlier, by the British Law Lords.

Of course, Ranjit's torturers could have helped him out with some information if they had chosen to. They didn't choose to.

After the first day without inflicted pain, he didn't see Bruno, the belly-slap and electrical-cable guy, again at all. He did see Squinty quite often, but only after Squinty had extracted a promise from him that he would stop asking why he had been tortured and whether he would ever be released, and indeed pretty much any question that Ranjit really wanted answered. Squinty did supply a tiny bit of information. ("Bruno? Oh, he's been promoted upstairs. He just doesn't know what to do with a prisoner unless he's hurting him, and it doesn't look like we're going to be hurting you anymore.")

That was, Ranjit reminded himself, a fact of life not to be scorned. It was a big improvement over the previous diet of thrashings and waterboardings. But it was, especially after Squinty quit coming around because Ranjit couldn't keep his promise to stop asking forbidden questions, pretty damn boring. Ranjit wasn't left entirely without human company. There was a limping old man who brought him his food and carried away his slop buckets, but that one was no use for conversation. He no doubt spoke some language or other, but it didn't seem to be one that Ranjit possessed.

Ranjit didn't know when he first began to have long one-sided talks with his friends. With his absent friends, that is, since none of them was physically present in his cell.

Of course, none of them could hear what he said to them. It would have been interesting if, for example, Myra de Soyza could have, or Pru No-Name. Less interesting for Gamini Bandara because, after reporting on his own emptily monotonous existence, about all Ranjit had to say to his absent lifelong friend was that he really should have budgeted more time to be with Ranjit and less for the American woman, who, after all, would never see him again.

Some of Ranjit's best absent friends were people he had never known in the flesh. For instance, there was the no-longer-living Paul Wolfskehl. Wolfskehl had been a nineteenth-century German business tycoon whose best-beloved sweetheart had turned down his proposal of marriage. That meant that, in spite of all his wealth and power, life was no longer worth living for Wolfskehl, so he sensibly decided to commit suicide. That didn't work out, though. While Wolfskehl was waiting for the exact right moment to do himself in, he idly picked up a book to read.

The book chanced to concern Fermat's Last Theorem, written by a man named Ernst Kummer. As it happened, Wolfskehl had attended a couple of Kummer's lectures on number theory; curiosity made him read the new essay. . . .

And, like many other amateur mathematicians, before and after, Wolfskehl was immediately hooked. He forgot about killing himself, being too busy trying to plumb the mysteries of a-squared plus b-squared equals c-squared, and the paradox that if the quantities were cubed, they never did equal each other.

Then there was the also long deceased Sophie Germain, whose teenage years had been spent during the frightening time of the French Revolution. Why this should have persuaded young Sophie to resolve on a career in mathematics is not immediately obvious. But it did.

Of course, that was not an easy ambition for a female to accomplish. As Elizabeth I of England had once put it, Sophie was cursed by being split rather than fringed, and so everything she tried to do was vastly harder for her than for her fringed colleagues.

Then, when his imaginary conversation partners ran out of steam, something Myra de Soyza had said began to cudgel Ranjit's mind.

What had it been? Something about seeing what tools other mathematicians had possessed at the time Fermat had jotted his cursed boast in the margin of his book?

Well, what tools were they?

He remembered that Sophie Germain was said to have been the first mathematician of any gender to make any headway at all with the Fermat proof. So just what headway had she made?

Ranjit, of course, had no way of looking that up. Back at the university, equipped with a password, all he would have had to do was hit a few keys on the handiest computer and the damn woman's entire life production would have been laid out for him to study.

But he didn't have the computer. All he had was his memory, and he was not sure that it was adequate to the task at hand.

He did remember what a "Sophie Germain prime" was—that is, any prime, p, such that $2p + 1$ was also a prime. Three was the littlest Sophie Germain prime: $3 \times 2 + 1 = 7$, and seven was a prime, all right. (Most of the other Sophie Germain primes were much larger, and thus hardly any fun at all.) Ranjit was quite pleased with himself for remembering this, though no matter how much he thought about it, he could not see any way in which a Sophie Germain prime could lead him to a solution of the Fermat problem.

There was one other thing. After profound labor Germain had produced a theorem of her own:

If x, y, and z are integers, and if $x^5 + y^5 = z^5$, then x, y, or z must be divisible by five.

Like every other stepping-stone toward a proof that Ranjit had managed to quarry out of the refractory stone of his mind, this one was a disappointment. The equation made no sense. Fermat's whole theorem was supposed to prove that no such equality as $x^5 + y^5 = z^5$ could ever exist in the first place. So it wasn't of any use at all. . . .

Or was it? That is, forget Sophie Germain's useless theorem itself, but how did she get to it?

And wasn't that what Myra had suggested to him at Dr. Vorhulst's party, back in the days when Ranjit could sometimes go to a party?

There was one other person (well, sort of person) with whom Ranjit had never, or never yet, had any personal dealings, but who (or which) could have supplied him with very useful data. It is probably about time that we spent a little more time with him (or them, or it, or maybe even her).

15

INTRODUCTION TO ONE (OR MORE) GRAND GALACTICS

The first thing we need to straighten out about this Grand Galactic person is whether in fact he was a he, or indeed a person, or, ultimately, "a" (rather than some fraction of "a") Grand Galactic.

None of those questions has an easy answer. So what we're going to do here is, we're going to ignore the facts and settle for answers that are no problem for us to deal with, apart from their being just plain wrong. First, we will say that this person is really a person, in spite of also being a part of that larger "person" that was all the Grand Galactics combined.

There were Grand Galactics all over the place, from the galaxy's accelerating fringes to its relatively motionless core, and just about everywhere in between. How many Grand Galactics were there? That's also a meaningless question. There were many, many of them, but when you came right down to it, the many were also one, because whenever he chose, every Grand Galactic was instantly merged with any or every other.

As you have noticed, we just arbitrarily assigned gender to the Grand Galactics' pronoun. Don't assume from this that they practiced sexual intercourse in any sense understandable by a human being. They didn't. It is just that we can't go on with that "it" or "he" or "they" business forever, so we just cut the Gordian knot and made him a "he."

We have just taken one rather large liberty. Let's take another. Let's give "him" a name. We'll call him "Bill." (Not Bill. "Bill." It is a major liberty that we have taken, and we should acknowledge that we know it to be so by the use of the quotation marks.)

Now, what else would it be useful for us to know about the Grand Galactics at this time?

For example, would it be helpful to know how big they are? Or at least, since one node of Grand Galactics may be thousands, or billions, of light-years from some particular other node, how they measure distance?

Let's assume it would indeed be helpful, but we must also recognize that, as with all questions about the Grand Galactics, the answer is going to be complicated. Start with the fact that the Grand Galactics don't like the kind of arbitrary units of measurement human beings use. When you track those down, they are always based on some human value, such as the distance from a man's fingertip to his armpit, or some calculated fraction of the distance from a pole to the equator on the particular planet that humans chance to occupy. Grand Galactic measurements are always made on the Planck scale, which is actually quite tiny. The measure of a single Planck unit is 1.616×10^{-35} meters. The easiest way to understand how little that is is to remember that it's so small it is impossible to measure anything smaller.

(Why impossible? Because you can't measure anything you can't see, and nothing can be seen without employing those light-carrying particles called photons. And any photon that was powerful enough to illuminate a Planck-scale distance would be so extremely powerful—and thus so extremely massive—that it would immediately transform itself into a black hole. The word "impossible" is sometimes taken as a challenge. In this case, though, it's just a fact.)

So to measure anything in any of the three dimensions, whether it's the circumference of an electron or the diameter of the universe itself, Grand Galactics simply count the number of Planck distances along a line from point A to point B.

That is invariably a large number, but that's all right with the Grand Galactics. Looked at in one way, they are pretty large numbers themselves.

So, having found ways of at least identifying the un-understandable, let's get back to that much simpler being, Ranjit Subramanian.

When Ranjit was quite young, his highly ecumenical father encouraged him to read some rather strange books, one of which, by a writer named James Branch Cabell, was about the nature of writing and writers. (For a time Ganesh Subramanian thought that might be a career choice for his son.) What some would-be writers were trying to say to the world, Cabell wrote, was, "I am pregnant with words, and I must have lexicological parturition or I die."

And, curiously, that is almost exactly the condition Ranjit now felt himself to be in.

For days now Ranjit had been pleading for help, shouting into the empty hallways, explaining, though no one seemed to be listening, that he had something that absolutely had to be communicated to a journal at once. There were no answers. Even the limping old man was now just putting Ranjit's meals inside the door and limping away as fast as he could.

So when Ranjit heard the old man's step-slide coming along the empty corridors, he felt little interest, except that this time there was, along with it, the *rap-tap-tap* of the footsteps of someone who wasn't limping at all. A moment later Ranjit's cell door opened. The old man was there, but deferentially a step or two behind another man—a man who wore an expression of shock and dismay on a face whose lineaments Ranjit knew as well as he knew his own. "Sweet God Almighty, Ranj," Gamini Bandara said wonderingly, "is that really you?"

Of all the questions Ranjit might have asked this unexpected visitor from his past, he chose the simplest. "What are you doing here, Gamini?"

"What the hell do you think I'm doing? I'm going to get you out of here, and if you think that was easy, you're crazier than you look. Then we'll get you to a dentist—what happened to your front teeth? Or, no, I suppose first you need to see a doctor— What?"

Ranjit was standing now, almost quivering with excitement. "Not a doctor! If you can get me out of here, get me to a computer!"

Gamini looked puzzled. "A computer? Well, sure, that can be arranged, but first we need to make sure you're all right—"

"Damn it, Gamini!" Ranjit cried. "Can't you understand what I'm saying? I think I've got the proof! I need a computer, and I need it right now! Do you have any idea how terrified I am that I'll forget some part of the proof before I can get it refereed?"

Ranjit got the doctor. He got the computer, too—in fact got both of them at the same time, but not until Gamini had walked him out of his prison to where a helicopter waited, its vane turning over. As Ranjit climbed into the chopper, he saw a couple of men standing nearby. Squinty was one of them; Squinty looked astonished and worried but didn't even gesture a good-bye. Then a twenty-minute downhill flight, among great mountains that wore brilliant caps of ice. In the helicopter Ranjit could not help turning to Gamini with questions, but this time it was Gamini who didn't want to talk. "Later," he said, nodding at the chopper pilot, who wore a uniform Ranjit had never seen before.

They landed at a real airport, a scant dozen meters from a plane—and not just any plane, Ranjit saw, but a BAB-2200, the fastest and, in some configurations, the most luxurious aircraft Boeing-Airbus had ever built, and it wore the blue globe-and-wreath United Nations insignia. Inside, it was even more so. Its seating was in leather armchairs. And its crew consisted of a pilot (wearing the uniform of a colonel in the American air force) and two very pretty flight attendants (wearing the same uniforms but with captain's bars, and over the uniform fluffy white aprons). "Heading for home now, sir?" the pilot asked Gamini. He got a nod for an answer and immediately disappeared into the cockpit. One of the attendants led Ranjit to a chair (which, he discovered, swiveled) and belted him in. "That's Jeannie," Gamini informed him, while himself being belted into another chair. "She's a doctor, too, so you better let her check you out—"

"The computer—" Ranjit started to object.

"Oh, you'll get your damn computer, Ranj, but first we have to get airborne. It'll just be a minute."

By then the two women had already retreated to their fold-down seats against a bulkhead and, sure enough, the plane had begun to move. And as soon as the seat belt sign went off, the second of the attendants—"I'm Amy. Hi!"—was magicking a laptop out of the table next to Ranjit's chair, while the one named Jeannie was approaching with stethoscope, blood pressure machine, and several other instruments at the ready.

Ranjit didn't protest. He let the doctor poke and prod and listen as much as she liked while he himself slowly and clumsily typed out pages of a nearly six-page manuscript, pausing every couple of lines to ask Gamini if he could find the address of the magazine called *Nature* for him. "Their offices are in England somewhere." Or just to scowl at the keyboard until memory at last told him what the next line should be. It was a slow process, but when Gamini ventured to ask him if he wanted anything to eat, Ranjit ferociously and unarguably told him to shut up. "Just give me ten minutes," he demanded. "Oh, maybe half an hour at the most. I can't stop now."

It wasn't ten minutes, of course. Wasn't half an hour, either. It was well over an hour before Ranjit looked up, sighed, and said to Gamini, "I need to check everything, so I'd better send a copy to your house. Tell me your e-mail address."

And when he had typed that in, he at last pushed the icon marked send and then sat back.

"Thanks," he said. "I'm sorry to have been such a pest, but it was pretty important to me. Ever since I figured it out, five or six months ago, I've been terrified that I might forget some part of it before I could get it refereed." He paused, suddenly licking his lips. "And one other thing. For a long time I've been thinking about real food. Do you have, say, any fresh fruit juice on this plane, any kind? And maybe something like a ham sandwich, or maybe a couple of scrambled eggs?"

16

HOMEGOING

Gamini refused to listen to any talk of American breakfasts but simply signaled to the flight attendants. Who produced a fine Sri Lankan meal—string hoppers of woven rice, a rich curry of meat and potatoes, and a plate of poppadoms—causing Ranjit's eyes to bulge in wonder. "Tell me, Gamini," he ordered, already chewing, "when did you get to be God? Isn't this an American plane?"

Gamini, sipping a cup of tea that had come from the fields around Kandy, shook his head. "It's a United Nations plane," he said, "which happens to have an American crew, only it's not on either UN or U.S. business right now. We just borrowed it to go after you."

"And 'we' is—?"

Gamini shook his head again, grinning. "Can't tell you, or anyway not right now. Pity. I knew you'd be interested, and as a matter of fact, I was considering asking you if you wanted to join us, when you went off on your little cruise."

Ranjit didn't put his spoon down, but he held it motionless while he gave his friend a long and not entirely friendly look. "You're telling me that you're such an important person that you can just borrow a plane like this to run your errands for you?"

This time Gamini laughed out loud. "Me? No. They didn't do it for me. They did it because my dad requested it. He's got this high-up UN job, you see."

"And what job is that?"

"Can't tell you that, either, so don't ask. And don't ask what country you've just got out of, either. Finding where you were wasn't hard, after we got hold of Tiffany Kanakaratnam— Oh," he said, taking note of Ranjit's response to the child's name, "that's something I can tell you about, anyway, at least up to a point. I, uh, used my father's position to run my own computer search for you. Sort of the way you got your math teacher's password; I fed in every name I could think of that might possibly know anything about where you were—Myra de Soyza, and Maggie and Pru, and all your teachers, and all the monks that worked for your father, and the Kanakaratnams. No," he said, again answering the look that had appeared on Ranjit's face, "there wasn't anything to embarrass you. We were just looking for meetings or conversations you'd had, after the day you disappeared. We got nothing. Didn't get any data on the adult Kanakaratnams at all, which I think means they were shot out of hand along with the rest of the pirates by the first court that tried them. But I kept adding names as I thought of them, and when I put the names of the four children in, we found them. They'd been arrested, of course, but they were too young to be tried even on a piracy charge, so they were taken to some relatives near Killinochchi, and Tiffany gave us a description of the people who took you away. She described the helicopters and where you washed ashore; it took a lot of searching after that, to be sure, but at last I located you. You might have sat there for years more."

"And the people who took me were?"

"Oh, Ranj," Gamini said, "there you go again. I can't exactly tell you that, except, I guess, in sort of general terms, without mentioning any specifics. Have you ever heard of extraordinary rendition? Or the Law Lords' findings on torture?"

Ranjit hadn't, but Gamini filled him in after his friend had woken from a deep sleep that had lasted hours. Back in the bad old days some great powers, such as the United States, were on record as opposed to using torture to extract information. However, they kept finding themselves in possession of some captives who surely knew things that were important but that they would never voluntarily say. Torture was an unreliable way of making people give truthful answers—at a certain stage almost anyone would say whatever their interrogators wanted to hear, true or not, just to make it stop—but these great powers had no better way available. So they worked out a little plan. Captives of that sort were handed over to the intelligence services of some other country, one that had never promised to abjure the infliction of pain as a technique in questioning, and then the information would be passed back to the United States or whatever other great power had requested it. "And that," Gamini finished, "was extraordinary rendition. 'Extraordinary' because that's what it was. 'Rendition' in the sense of rendering—meaning, 'turning over'—like rendering unto Caesar the things that are Caesar's, as the Christians say."

"Huh," Ranjit said thoughtfully. "And that's still going on?"

"Well, sort of. The superpowers don't commission it anymore. There's been too much publicity. Anyway, they don't have to because there are plenty of uncommitted countries that automatically pick up and question people with inexplicable criminal records. Like pirates, who are beyond the pale for them anyway, and especially like pirates who seem to be hiding their identities. Like you, they thought, because of the name business. And then they trade off information to the sanctimonious countries, because that's where the Law Lords' decision comes in. The Lords did a commission on information derived from torture way back when, and concluded that, for moral reasons, such information could never be used in any legal proceedings. On the other hand, it would be perfectly proper, they said, to turn it over to, say, the police." He looked up as the two women were advancing on them. "And now we have to buckle up because I guess we're coming in to Bandaranaike. Only, listen. You wouldn't believe what deals we had to make and what promises we had to give to spring you loose from where you were. So help me keep those promises. No matter what, you don't ever tell anybody anything that can identify any of the people who held you. Or I'll be in deep trouble, and so will my dad."

"I promise," Ranjit said, meaning it. And then he added mischievously, "You said you checked on the girls. How's good old Maggie doing?"

Gamini gave him a pained look. "Oh, good old Maggie's fine," he said. "She married a U.S. senator a couple of months ago. Sent me an invitation to the reception, as a matter of fact. So I went to Harrods and picked out a nice fish slice to send her, but I didn't go myself."

17

HEAVEN

As the BAB-2200 rapidly taxied toward a gate, Captain-Doctor Jeannie delivered her verdict: What Ranjit really needed was rest, kindly care, and food, enough food to put back the eight or ten kilos of body mass that his extraordinary-rendition diet had taken from him, although (she added) it wouldn't hurt for him to spend the next couple days in a hospital, either. The party waiting to greet him at the gate, however, vetoed that. That party was only one person, but that person was Mevrouw Beatrix Vorhulst, and she was not in a mood to be contradicted. The place for Ranjit to recuperate, Mevrouw Vorhulst declared, was not some impersonal factory that generated quantities of medical care but very little love. No. The right place for Ranjit to regain his strength was a comfortable, caring home. Hers, for instance.

So it was. Beatrix Vorhulst was certainly right about her promise of great care, too, because at the moment Ranjit arrived, every resource of their quite resourceful household was devoted to 'him. He had a room as vast and cool as his hottest and sweatiest prison night could have imagined. He had three wonderful meals a day—no, more like a dozen of them, because every time he closed his eyes for a moment, he woke to find a perfect apple or banana or icy-cold pineapple spear waiting beside his bed. Better still, in the long run he won his argument with the doctors that Gamini had ordered to double-check him. True, he first had to convince them that for all the time of his captivity he had been up and about every day without harm, or at least every day when he wasn't so bruised and beat-up that walking hurt more than it was worth. But then he had the freedom of that grand house and its grander gardens. Including the swimming pool, and what a delight it was to backstroke dreamily across that gently cool water, with the hot sun blessing him from the sky and the palms swaying overhead. And he had access to the news.

That was not altogether a good thing. His time without access to print or television had not prepared him for the details of all the things that had been going on around the planet Earth—the murders, the riots, the car bombings, the wars.

None of those were the worst of the bad news, though. That came when Gamini looked in for a minute before leaving Sri Lanka for some more urgent (but, of course, unspecified) errand. As he was actually at the door to leave, he paused. "There's one thing I didn't tell you, Ranj. It's about your father."

"Oh, right," Ranjit said remorsefully. "I'd better call him right away."

But Gamini was shaking his head. "Wish you could," he said. "The thing is, he had a stroke. He's dead."

There was only one person in the world Ranjit wanted to speak to at that moment, and he had him on the phone before Gamini was out of the Vorhulst house. That was the old monk Surash, and he was overjoyed to hear Ranjit's voice. Less so, of course, to discuss the death of Ganesh Subramanian, but curiously not particularly sad about it, either. "Yes, Ranjit," he said, "your father was moving heaven and earth to find you, and I think he just wore out. Anyway, he came back from another visit to the police complaining he felt tired, and the next morning he was dead in his bed. He had not been in really good health for some time, you know."

"Actually, I didn't know," Ranjit said sorrowfully. "He never said."

"He did not wish to worry you—and, Ranjit, you must not be worried. His *jiva* will be greeted with honor, and his funeral was good. Since you had been taken from us, I was the one who said the prayers, and made sure there were flowers and rice balls in his coffin, and when he had been burned, I myself carried his ashes to the sea. Death is not the end, you know."

"I know," Ranjit said, more for the monk's sake than his own.

"He may never even need to be born again. And if he is, I am sure it will be as someone or some creature near you. And, oh, Ranjit, when you can travel, please come and see us. And do you have a lawyer? There is a little bit in your father's estate. Of course it all goes to you, but there are documents to file."

That troubled Ranjit. He had no lawyer. But when he mentioned it to Mevrouw Vorhulst, she said that wasn't a problem, and from then on he did have a lawyer. Not just any lawyer, either, but a partner in Gamini's father's firm, whose name was Nigel De Saram. What troubled Ranjit a good deal more was the stabbing guilt he felt. He hadn't known of his father's death, and the reason for that was that he had not bothered to ask.

Oh, sure, he told himself, he had been full of a thousand other ⟨
cerns.

But if it had been the other way around, would Ranjit have slipped
father's mind?

Not counting servants, Mevrouw Vorhulst was his only visitor for the ⟨
few days, but then he argued (and the doctors had to agree) that no sti
any visitor might cause him would come anywhere near the stress cau
by strong young jailers hitting him with clubs. The barriers were reduc
The next morning, while Ranjit was experimenting with some of
Vorhulsts' exercise machines, the Vorhulsts' butler came into the gɣ
cleared his throat, and said, "You have a visitor, sir."

Ranjit's mind had been far away. "Have there been any messages
me?" he asked.

The butler sighed. "No, sir. If any messages come, they will
brought to you at once, as you requested. Now Dr. De Saram would like
see you. Shall I show him in?"

Ranjit quickly put on one of the Vorhulsts' infinite supply of dressi
gowns. Lawyer De Saram quickly took charge. He didn't seem very jun
to Ranjit—he was maybe fifty or sixty, maybe more—and he was clea
good at what he did. He didn't have to be told about the bequest from Ra
jit's father. Although he had been asked to handle Ranjit's affairs bare
forty-eight hours before, he had already established Ranjit's existence wi
the appropriate Trincomalee court and had a pretty good idea of the valɩ
of the bequest. "Not quite twenty million rupees, Mr. Subramanian," ⟨
said, "but not far under it, either—or, at the current rate of exchange, abo
ten thousand U.S. dollars. The bulk of it is two pieces of property, your fɑ
ther's home and a smaller house that is currently unoccupied."

"I know the house," Ranjit told him. "Is there anything I have to do?

"Not just now," De Saram told him, "although there is one possibilit
that you may wish to give some thought to. Dr. Bandara himself woul
have wished to do this for you, but, as you know, he is involved in som
highly classified matters with the United Nations."

"I do know, but I don't know much," Ranjit said.

"Of course. The thing is that you might normally have a claim fo
damages against the people who, ah, prevented you from coming home foɩ
so long, but—"

Ranjit said, "I know. We aren't to talk about those people."

"Exactly so," De Saram declared, sounding relieved. "However, there

is another avenue you may wish to take. It would be possible for you to bring an action against the cruise line company on the grounds that they should not have allowed their ship to be taken over by pirates. That would not be for as large a sum as the other, of course, both because their responsibility is a little harder to establish and also because their solvency is not very strong—"

"No, wait a minute," Ranjit said. "They had their ship stolen, which I was on because of my own stupidity, and now I should sue them for letting it happen? That doesn't sound fair."

For the first time De Saram gave him a friendly grin. "Dr. Bandara said you would say that," he announced. "Now I think my car should be about ready. . . ."

And indeed just then there was a knock on the door. It was Vass, the butler, to announce that that was the case. And then, before Ranjit could say anything, the butler addressed him directly: "There are no messages for you, sir," he added. "And, if I may—I didn't want to trouble you before—we were all deeply saddened to learn of the loss of your father."

It wasn't that what the butler said reminded Ranjit of his father's death. He didn't need reminding. The loss was part of him, day and night, a wound that did not heal.

The worst thing about death was that it irrevocably ended communication. Ranjit was left with a long list of things he should have said to his father and never had. Now that the opportunity was lost, all those unsaid expressions of love and respect were silting up inside Ranjit's heart.

And, of course, there was no more cheer to be found in the news. Fighting had flared up between Ecuador and Colombia, new squabbles were arising over the division of Nile water, and North Korea had filed a complaint before the Security Council accusing China of diverting rain clouds from Korean rice paddies to their own.

Nothing had changed. It was just that the world population was now irretrievably one person short.

But there was one thing he could do—should have done long since—and by his sixth day as a guest in the Vorhulst home, Ranjit finally demanded, and got, a copy of that frantic communication he had rushed off from the plane. He studied it as critically, as demandingly and as judgingly, as any freshman composition teacher had ever looked over a student's final term

paper. If the kind of mistakes that might disqualify him were there, he was going to find them. He was crushed to discover that there indeed were some—two of them on his first look, then four, then one or two additional passages that weren't entirely wrong but did seem to be not entirely clear, either.

Ranjit had excuses. It was all due to that last stretch of seven or eight weeks, when he had at last completed the proof in his mind—all that he could manage to complete, since he was lacking paper, ink, or computer—and only kept rehearsing it, step by step, terrified that he might forget some crucial step.

The question was, what to do about those mistaken bits?

Ranjit worried over that question for all of one day and much of that night. Should he send the magazine a list of corrections? That would seem the sensible thing to do . . . but then Ranjit's pride got in the way, because the "mistakes" were really rather trivial, things that any decent mathematician would spot at once and almost as quickly see how to repair. And he had a horror of seeming to beg.

He did not send another communication to *Nature,* though most nights after that, while trying to go to sleep, he all over again worried the question of whether he should have.

Ranjit wished he had a better idea of what a publication such as *Nature* did with submissions like the one he had sent them. He was pretty sure that if they had any idea of publishing it, their first step would be to send copies of it to three or four—or more—experts in that particular area to see that there weren't any glaring mistakes in it.

How long could that take?

Ranjit didn't know. What he did know was that it had already taken a lot longer than he would have liked.

So every time the butler knocked on the door to announce a visitor, Ranjit's hopes soared, and every time the butler announced that visitor's trivial errand, his hopes crashed again.

18

COMPANY

On the seventh day of Ranjit's stay with the Vorhulsts the butler announced another visitor, and it was Myra de Soyza. "Am I intruding, Ranjit?" she asked at once. "Aunt Bea said I could look in on you as long as I didn't keep you from resting."

Actually he had in fact been resting, and Myra de Soyza was certainly keeping him from it. He didn't want to say that and did his best to manufacture conversation. "What are you doing now?" he asked. "I mean, are you still at the university?"

She wasn't. Hadn't been since that sociology class they had shared; had in fact just come back from a postdoc session (postdoc! He had had no idea how far up the academic ladder she had climbed) at MIT in America, and naturally he asked, "Studying what?"

"Well . . . artificial intelligence, more or less."

He decided to ignore the cryptic "more or less." "So how's artificial intelligence doing?"

She grinned at last. "If you mean how close are we to getting a computer to have a reasonable chat with us, terrible. If you go back to the kinds of artificial intelligence projects that the people who started the field were trying to solve, not bad at all. Did you ever hear of a man named Marvin Minsky?"

Ranjit consulted his memory and came up empty. "I don't think so."

"Pity. He was one of the best minds ever to try to define what thought was, and to find ways of getting a computer to actually do something you could call thinking. He used to tell a story that cheers me up sometimes." She paused there, as though unsure of her audience's interest. Ranjit, who would have taken pleasure in hearing her announce train delays or closing stock prices, made the right sounds, and she went on. "Well, the thing is that in the beginning of AI studies, he, and all the other pioneers, too, considered pattern recognition as one of the hallmarks of AI. Then pattern recognition got solved in a rather everyday way. Checkout counters in every supermarket in the world began reading the prices of every item from bar codes. So what happened? AI simply got redefined. Pattern recognition got left out of the recipe because they'd solved that one, even if the computers still couldn't make up a joke or figure out from the way you looked that you had a hangover."

Ranjit said, "So can you get a computer to make up a joke now?"

She sat up. "I *wish*," she said moodily. And then she sighed. "Actually, my main interest isn't in that kind of thing anymore. It's more in applications. Autonomous prostheses, mostly." Then she changed expression, and the subject. Without warning she asked, "Ranjit, why do you keep covering your mouth like that?"

It was a more personal question than he had expected from her. He was, however, quite aware of the way his hand kept covering his face. She persisted. "Is it your teeth that bother you?"

He conceded, "I know what I look like."

"Well, so do I, Ranjit. You look like an honest, decent, and extremely intelligent man who hasn't gotten around to letting a dentist repair his bite." She shook her head at him. "It's the easiest thing in the world, Ranjit, and you will not only look better, you'll chew better." She stood up. "I promised Aunt Bea that I wouldn't stay longer than ten minutes, and she promised me that I could ask you if you wanted to swim in the ocean for a change. On Nilaweli beach. Do you know where that is? We've got a little beach house there, so if you'd care to . . ."

Oh, yes, Ranjit would care to. "We'll work it out," she said, and surprised him by giving him a hug. "We missed you," she said, and then drew back to look at him. "Gamini said you asked him about his old girlfriend. Do you have any of that kind of question for me?"

"Uh," he said. And then, "Well, yes, I suppose you mean about that Canadian."

She grinned. "Yes, I suppose I do. Well, the Canadian was in Bora-Bora, last I heard, where they were building an even bigger hotel. But that was long ago. We don't keep in touch."

Ranjit hadn't even known that Gamini and Myra were aware of each other's existence, much less that they were apparently on easy chatting terms. That wasn't all he hadn't known. His density of visitors was getting more so, with the lawyer from Dr. Bandara's office coming in with more documents to sign—"It's not that your father's estate is at all complicated," he told Ranjit apologetically. "It's just that you were reported missing and somebody in the bureaucracy interpreted that to mean presumed dead. So we have to clear that up."

And then there were the police. Not that anybody was filing any charges against Ranjit himself. De Saram made sure of that, before he would allow any questioning at all. But they had loose ends to tie up about the piracy, and Ranjit was the only one who could help tie them.

Then there was the question of Myra de Soyza's "autonomous prostheses," whatever they were. His data searches were of limited help. True, they coached him to the right spelling, but what had AI to do with artificial limbs or hearing aids?

Beatrix Vorhulst helped him out there. "Oh, they're not talking about smart wooden legs, Ranjit," she told him. "It's more subtle than that. The idea is to manufacture a lot of really tiny robots that they inject into your bloodstream, and they're programmed to recognize and destroy, say, cancer cells."

"Huh," he said, considering the idea and liking it. It was, of course, the exact right kind of project to interest Myra de Soyza. "And these little robots, are they working out?"

Mevrouw Vorhulst gave him a sad little smile. "If they'd had them a few years ago, I might not be a widow today. No, they're still just hopes. There just isn't the funding for the research—even Myra has been waiting and waiting for her own project to be funded, and it just doesn't happen. Oh, there's plenty of money for research—as long as what is being researched is some kind of a weapon."

When at last Ranjit was able to take Myra de Soyza up on her invitation, Beatrix Vorhulst was happy to provide him with a car and driver. When they were well along the road to the beach, he began to recognize landmarks. He and Gamini had of course checked this beach out in their exploration of everything the area had to offer. Not much had changed. The beaches still had their quota of good-looking young women in trivial bathing costumes, of which there were quite a few.

Ranjit had no idea what the de Soyza beach house would look like, until the driver pointed it out: tile roof, screened lanai around the door, nicely planted with bright flowers. It was only when the door opened and Myra de Soyza came out, wearing a light robe over a bikini that was fully as fashionable, and trivial, as any other along the beach, that he was sure he was in the right place.

Then not quite so sure, because right behind her was a five- or six-year-old girl. Ranjit experienced a quick, dismaying reality shift.

Six-year-old girl?

Myra's?

Had he been gone quite that long?

He hadn't. Ada Labrooy was the child of Myra's sister, now seriously pregnant with another and for that reason quite happy to grant her daughter's wish to spend as much time as possible with her favorite aunt. Myra herself was happy to have Ada there, not least because Ada's mother had sent along Ada's nanny to make sure the child was no inconvenience. When Ranjit had changed and been anointed with UV-repellent cream by Myra, which in itself was one of his nicer recent experiences, the two of them minced across the hot sands to the pleasingly cool waters of the gulf.

What was most wonderful about a Sri Lankan beach, apart from the company, was that the water deepened so gradually. Many dozens of meters from the shoreline he could still stand up straight.

He and Myra didn't go much farther than waist-deep, and they didn't swim as much as they happily threw themselves about in the water. Ranjit didn't resist the temptation to show how far he could swim underwater—nearly a hundred meters; a lot less than he had done as a teenager near Swami Rock, but still enough to get compliments from Myra, which was what the purpose had basically been.

The shrewdness of Myra's deal with the nanny then became evident. By the time they were showered and changed, a pleasant luncheon had been laid out for them. When they finished with that, the nanny took Ada away for a nap, and herself away to wherever it was she went when not visibly on duty.

By and large, that was one of the pleasantest parts of the day for Ranjit. However, when Myra announced that she really needed to put in the exercise of at least a couple hundred yards of actual swimming—and, no, Ranjit shouldn't come with her, because he needed to keep his time in bright sunlight down to a safe minimum until his skin got used to the stuff again—he was comfortably aware that she would be back. And for the last twenty minutes or so he had been beginning to wonder if he had properly expanded one of Sophie Germain's terms.

He had just about convinced himself there had been no mistake when little Ada came back from her nap. She looked around for her aunt, but was sufficiently reassured when Ranjit waved an arm in the direction of where Myra's arms and kicks were propelling her along.

Then Ada got herself a fruit juice and sat down to oversee whatever it was that Ranjit was doing.

By and large Ranjit preferred to be unwatched during his tussles with mathematics. Ada, however, seemed to have her own rules of audienceship. She didn't wail about being kept on the beach, wasn't even morose about it. When Ranjit bought her an ice from one of the beach's wandering vendors, she ate it slowly, her eyes fixed on the things he was writing in his notebook. When she finished, she ran down to the water's edge to wash the stickiness off her fingers before she asked politely, "Can I see what you're doing?"

By then Ranjit was quite reassured about his use of the Germain formulation. He opened the notebook on the table before him, interested to see what she would make of the Germain Identity.

She studied the line of symbols for a moment, then announced, "I don't think I understand that."

"It's difficult," Ranjit agreed. "I don't think I can explain it to you just now, either. However—"

He paused, examining her. She was a lot younger than Tiffany Kanakaratnam, of course, but then she had the advantage of a better educated and more sophisticated family. "Maybe I can show you something," he said. "Can you count on your fingers?"

"Of course I can," she said, just one moiety of courtesy short of indignation. "Look," she said, raising one finger at a time. "One, two, three, four, five, six, seven, eight, nine, ten."

"Yes, that's very good," Ranjit said, "but you're only counting up to ten. Would you like to know how to count to one thousand and twenty-three?"

By the time he finished showing the child the all-fingers-extended binary representation of 1,023, Myra was back from her swim and listening as intently as Ada.

When he was done, the child looked at her aunt, now toweling her hair dry. "That's quite good, don't you think, Aunt Myra?" And to Ranjit, "Do you know any other tricks?"

Ranjit hesitated. His one other trick he had never even shown to Tiffany Kanakaratnam, but Myra was in this audience.

"Actually," he said, "I do," and moved off the boarded part of the bungalow's lanai so he could scratch a circle in the sand:

O

"That's a rupee," he said. "Well, of course it's really just a picture of a rupee, but let's say it's a real coin. If you flip it, there are two possible ways it can come down, either as heads or as tails."

"Or, if it fell in the sand, it could land on edge," Ada said.

He looked at her, but the child Ada's expression was innocent. "So we don't flip on the beach. We flip on a craps table in the casino. Now, if you flip two coins—"

$$\bigcirc \quad \bigcirc$$

"—each of the coins can come down either heads or tails. That means there are four possible outcomes. They can be heads-heads, heads-tails, tails-heads, or tails-tails. While if there are three coins—"

$$\bigcirc \quad \bigcirc \quad \bigcirc$$

"—there are eight possibilities: heads-heads-heads, heads-heads-tails, heads—"

"Ranjit," Myra interrupted him, smiling but with the faintest hint of annoyance in her voice, "Ada does know what two to the third power is."

"Well, of course she does," he said meekly. "Now, here's the thing. You take this stick and draw in as many more coins to the line as you want to. I won't look. Then when you're done, within ten seconds or less, I will undertake to write down the exact number of possible outcomes if that number of coins are flipped. And," he added, holding up one finger, "just to make it more interesting, what I'm going to do is let you cover up as many of the coins as you like, from either end of the line, so I won't be able to tell how many coins are there."

Ada, who had been listening carefully, said, "Wow. Can he do that, Aunt Myra?"

Myra said firmly, "No. Not if he doesn't peek or cheat in some other way." Then, to Ranjit, "You aren't going to peek?"

"No."

"And you won't know how many coins are actually in the row?"

He pursed his lips. "I didn't say anything about what I would *know* . . . but, no, I won't."

"Then it's impossible," she declared. But when Ranjit invited her to put him to the test, she made him turn around and set Ada to watch his eyes to see that he wasn't making use of some accidental window that could serve as a mirror. Then she swiftly smoothed most of the coins out of existence, leaving just three. She winked at Ada, and then draped her beach towel so that it covered two of the remaining three, and also covered a full meter of no coins at all—

○

—and said, "You're on."

Ranjit turned slowly, as though he had all the time in the world, while Ada squealed, "Hurry, Ranjit! You only have ten seconds! Or five, now. Or maybe only two—"

He gave the child a smile. "Don't worry," he admonished. He leaned forward and for the first time glanced at where the row of circles had been, took the stick, and at one end of the row scratched a straight line. Then, as he was removing Myra's towel, he said, "There's your answer," and grinned. "Huh," he said, admiring the result. "Very clever." He waited for a reaction from Myra to the drawing in the sand—

1000

Myra stared in puzzlement for a moment, and then her expression cleared. "Oh my God! Yes! It's the binary number for—wait a minute—for the decimal number eight! And that's the right answer, too!"

Ranjit, still grinning, nodded and turned to Ada, now a little apprehensive. Should he explain again how binary notation worked—1, 10, 11, 100 for one, two, three, four? He hesitated.

But the child's lips had broken into a smile. "You didn't say you were going to go binary, Ranjit, but then you didn't say you weren't, either, so I guess that's all right. It's a good trick."

She delivered her verdict with enough adult gravity to sustain Ranjit's smile. His curiosity was piqued, though. "Tell me something, Ada. Do you really know what binary numbers are?"

She became mock-indignant. "But of course I do, Ranjit! Don't you know who Aunt Myra made my parents name me after?"

Myra was the one who responded to Ranjit's puzzled look. "I'm guilty," she admitted. "When my sister and her husband couldn't agree on a name for the baby, I suggested Ada. Ada Lovelace was my heroine and role model, you know. All of my friends fixated on women like Shiva or Wonder Woman or Joan of Arc, but the only woman I wanted to be just like when I grew up was Countess Ada Lovelace."

"Countess—" Ranjit began, and then snapped his fingers. "Of course!

The computer woman in, when was it, the 1800s? Lord Byron's daughter, who wrote the first computer program ever for Charles Babbage's calculating machine!"

"That one, yes," Myra agreed. "Of course, that machine never got built—they didn't have the technology—but the program was good. She's why they named the software language Ada."

The daily beach drive had become a fixed date, and then Ranjit thought of a way to make it even better. De Saram had opened a line of bank credit for him, based on the anticipation of his father's estate, which meant not only that he then had an actual bank account with actual rupees in it that he could spend, but meant he had a credit card as well. Ranjit had noticed the beachside restaurants up above the tree line, and decided to take Myra to dinner.

His driver stopped at one of the restaurants along the road, but when Ranjit opened the door to investigate, the smells were not encouraging. The second he tried was better. He actually went inside, got a menu, sniffed thoughtfully, and told the person who gave him the menu that he'd probably be back, but he made no promises about when. But in the third, Ranjit got a menu but hardly looked at it. The aroma from the kitchen, the way the few diners were lingering over their tea and sweets . . . Ranjit inhaled deeply and made a reservation. And when he issued the actual invitation to Myra, she looked uncertain for only a moment, and then said, "Of course. It would be lovely."

Which meant Ranjit had only the day to get through before he could have the pleasure of being the one who provided something for her.

Ada wasn't there, so they actually swam together, farther out than usual, and when they came back, they dressed and sat with drinks on the lanai, idly talking. Well, Myra was doing most of the talking. "It used to be a lot livelier here," she said, gazing out over the nearly empty sand. "When I was tiny, there were two deluxe hotels right down the beach, and a lot more restaurants."

Ranjit looked at her curiously. "You miss the lively times?"

"Oh, not really. I like it peaceful, the way it is. But my parents used to go dancing there, and now there's nothing."

Ranjit nodded. "The Boxing Day tsunami," he said wisely.

But she was shaking her head. "Long before that," she said. "It was 1984. The beginning of the civil war. Some of the first battles were fought right here, Sea Tigers making a landing so they could launch an attack on the airport. The army took the hotels over as firing positions, so the Tigers took care of the hotels. My parents were right here, couldn't get away until things calmed down a little and the roads reopened. My mom said the tracers were like a fireworks display, screaming in from the assault boats and back out from the hotels. They called it 'the entertainment.' "

Ranjit wanted to make a response but didn't know how to do it. Not in words, maybe. What he really wanted to do was put an arm around her. He settled for a sort of first step, putting his hand over hers as it rested on the arm of her chair.

She didn't seem to mind. "The ruined old buildings were still there while I was growing up," she said. "You know what finally took care of them? That was the tsunami. Otherwise I think they'd still be right there."

She turned toward him, smiling . . . and looking quite a lot as though she wanted to be kissed.

He put it to the test.

It turned out that his estimate had been correct. She had. And she was the one who took his hand and led him back into the beach house, with that welcoming couch, just right for two, and Ranjit discovered that sexual intercourse with a woman was not only a good thing in itself, but was several times better when the woman was someone you liked, and respected, and really wanted to spend a lot of time in the company of.

And then there was the dinner that he hosted, and that was great, too. So all in all that day on the beach was a great success, and Myra and Ranjit at once made plans to do it again. Often.

It didn't quite work out that way, though, because the very next day something happened to change their plans.

Ada Labrooy was with them that day, and so was her nanny, who kept giving sidelong glances at Myra and Ranjit, convincing Ranjit that what the two of them had done was written all over their faces. It was a perfectly normal day, though—if you didn't count that when he arrived, Myra kissed him on the lips instead of the usual cheek—until they were back from their outing in the water, and wearing their robes and helping themselves to their drinks.

And then Ada saw something. Hand shading her eyes from the sun, she asked, "Is that that man who works for the Vorhulsts again?"

And when Ranjit stood up to get a better look, yes, it was the Vorhulst butler, moving a great deal faster than Ranjit had ever seen him move before, and holding a sheaf of papers clenched tightly in one hand. He seemed excited. Not just excited, impatient to get the pages to Ranjit, so that he was still five or six meters away when he called, "Sir! I think this may be what you've been waiting for!"

And it was.

Well, it sort of was. Well, what it was was a lengthy analysis of Ranjit's paper, or actually five different analyses of the paper, each apparently written by a different (but unnamed) person, and what they'd done—in exacting and almost unreadable detail—was go over every last passage that Ranjit himself had already found to contain a mistake or an unclarity. Plus, they'd found no fewer than eleven other passages that needed cleaning up just as much but that Ranjit hadn't caught in his own reading. There were forty-two sheets of paper in all, each densely written over with words and equations. As Ranjit quickly scanned each one and hurried to the next, he passed the sheets to Myra, his frown getting deeper with every page. "Holy gods," he said at last, "what are they saying? Are they just telling me all the reasons they have for rejecting the bloody thing?"

Myra was biting her lip as she reread the final page for the fourth or fifth time. Then a smile broke through. She handed the page back to Ranjit. "Dear," she said—in the excitement of the moment neither of them noticed that she had never used that word to him before—"what's the very last word at the end of the message?"

Ranjit snatched the page from her. "What word?" he demanded. "You mean at the very bottom here? Where it says 'Congratulations'?"

"That is exactly what I mean," she informed him, the smile now broad and tender and in every way exactly the best kind of smile he could ever have wished for from Myra de Soyza. "Have you ever heard of anyone being congratulated for a failure? They're publishing your paper, Ranjit! They think you've finally done it!"

19

FAME

"As soon as that magazine prints your article, you're going to be famous. Really famous!" Beatrix Vorhulst declared as soon as Ranjit was back in her house that night.

She was wrong, though. It didn't take that long. Days before the magazine's printing presses began to turn out the hundreds of thousands of copies that would bring Ranjit's fame to the world, the fame had already arrived. Someone—perhaps someone on *Nature*'s staff, or among their referees—had leaked the story and so reporters began to call. First it was the BBC, then someone from *The New York Times,* and then it was everybody, all of them wanting Ranjit to explain just what it was that Monsieur Fermat had been playing at, and why it had taken all this time to prove he'd been right.

All that was easy enough for Ranjit to answer. What was harder was what to say when the callers asked about the rumor that he'd been jailed for something or other, too, but there De Saram was a help. "Simply tell them that your attorney has instructed you not to discuss any of that because there is a suit pending. I'll make that true by bringing an action on your behalf against the cruise line."

"But I don't want to take their money," Ranjit objected.

"Don't worry. You won't get any. I'll make sure of that, but that's a sufficient reason for anybody to refuse to answer any question . . . since Dr. Bandara has impressed on me that that whole matter is not to be discussed."

That stratagem worked fine, but did nothing to decrease the number of people who wanted him to sit down in a quiet one-on-one with them—that is, with them and their team of anything up to a dozen recording technicians—and tell them all about this Fermat person and why he had behaved so peculiarly. For that, explained De Saram when Ranjit again turned to him for help, the only way to temper their curiosity about him was to go public. That is, to have a press conference and tell the whole story at once to everyone who wanted to hear.

They were sitting by the Vorhulsts' pool, De Saram and Ranjit and Myra de Soyza and Beatrix Vorhulst herself; trips to the de Soyza beach house were no longer much fun for Ranjit and Myra, because the press pests had found them there, so Myra now came to swim with Ranjit in the pool. "I've spoken to Dr. Bandara about it," De Saram said, inching his chair closer to the shade of the great pool umbrella. "He is confident the university will make a space available for you to hold your press conference. Indeed, he says it would be an honor for the school."

Ranjit said uncomfortably, "What would I say?"

"You'll tell them what you did," De Saram answered. "Leaving out, of course, all the specifics that Dr. Bandara feels must be kept secure." He set his cup down and smiled at Mevrouw Vorhulst. "No, no more tea, thank you. I need to get back to the office. And I'll find my way out."

Mevrouw Vorhulst let him shake her hand, but didn't protest as he left. "Actually," she observed to Ranjit and Myra, "that sounds like an excellent idea. I'd love to hear that talk." Then, turning to Myra, she said, "Dear, do you remember the room we used to put you to sleep in when your parents were going to be really late? It's still there, right next to Ranjit's. If you'd like to use it from time to time—or as often as you like—it's yours."

So when he went to sleep that night, Ranjit had to count that a good day. He had very little experience in public speaking, and that worried him a bit. But right there was Myra's head on the pillow next to his own, and, all in all, things seemed to be going very well for him at last.

The auditorium that the university donated for Ranjit's press conference was quite big, and needed to be. Every one of its 4,350 seats was filled, and not just with newspeople. There were several hundred of those, but it seemed half of Sri Lanka had decided it wanted to be there as well. Besides the lucky 4,350, an additional 1,000, nearly, watched on closed-circuit television in another campus hall, leaving quite a few extremely important (or so self-described) other people consumed with indignation over having to watch the event on (ugh!) broadcast television.

To Ranjit Subramanian, peering out at them through a peephole in the curtain, they looked like a great many people. It wasn't just the number of the human beings in the room, either. It was the particular human beings they were! The president of Sri Lanka was seated in the front row. Two or three possible candidates for the next election were there, and so was the Vorhulst family, and—believe it or not!—so was Ranjit's old math professor, not having the grace even to look as embarrassed as he should have felt but instead smiling and nodding to everyone in a less favored seat than his.

As the curtain began to rise, the man sitting in the armchair next to Ranjit's gave him a reassuring look. "You'll be fine," said the august Dr. Dhatusena Bandara, unexpectedly having flown in from his hush-hush UN job just to introduce Ranjit. "I wish Gamini could have been here, and so does he, but he's busy recruiting in Nepal," he added, and then the curtain was up and the lights were on him, and—without explaining just what it was that Gamini had to go to Nepal to recruit—Dr. Bandara moved to the lectern.

And then, sooner thereafter than Ranjit would have imagined possible, it was he who was at the lectern, and every pair of hands in that hall began to clap.

Ranjit waited patiently for the sound to stop. When it didn't seem to be stopping, he cleared his throat. "Thank you," he said. "Thank you all." And then, as it abated only slightly, he began:

"The man who presented this problem to me—well, to the world—was named Fermat, an advocate, or lawyer, in France a few centuries ago—"

By the time he got to the famous jotting in the margin of a page of Diophantus the applause had subsided, and the audience was intent. They weren't quiet throughout the talk. They laughed when he commented that a lot of trouble could have been saved if the book Fermat had been reading had had larger margins. And they applauded again, though not in quite as unruly a fashion, as he described each step in his growing comprehension of what Fermat had been talking about. Then, when he described Sophie Germain's work and how that turned out to be the key at last, they applauded a lot. And kept on doing so at every opportunity until Ranjit reached the moment when he had become pretty sure, or at least pretty nearly sure, that he had by-God actually completed a defensible proof of Fermat's Last Theorem.

He stopped, smiled, and shook his head at them. "Do you have any idea how hard it is to memorize a five-page mathematical proof?" he asked. "I didn't have anything to write with, you see. I couldn't write it out. All I could do was go over it, over and over again, repeating each little step, I don't know, hundreds of times, or thousands. . . . And then when I was rescued, all I could think of was getting to a computer and getting it all down at once. . . .

"And I did," Ranjit finished, and let them clap the skin off their silly hands at that until they got tired of it. Which took a long time, until he managed to cut in again to say, "And so Gamini Bandara, my oldest and dearest friend, is one of the people I have to thank, and so is his father, Dr. Dhatusena Bandara." He gestured toward the older man, who politely accepted his share of applause. "And there are two other persons I owe. One is my late father, Ganesh Subramanian of the Tiru Koneswaram temple in Trincomalee. The other person is hiding backstage here, but she is the one who first suggested to me that the clue to finding out what Fermat had discovered lay in looking at the mathematical procedures known to have been in use at around that time, and trying to figure out what other procedures Fermat might have deduced from them. I don't know what I might have done without her, and I don't intend to take that chance again. So come out here, Dr. Myra de Soyza, and take my hand—"

Which she did, and though Ranjit was still speaking when she appeared, it was hard to make out just what he was saying. Myra got easily the biggest hand of anyone other than Ranjit himself, perhaps because the audience could read what was written all over his face when he spoke of her, perhaps only because she was definitely the best-looking.

Ranjit might have let her applause go on forever, but Myra was shaking her head. "Thank you," she called, "but let's hear the rest of what Ranjit has to say." She stepped back, and sat down in Ranjit's own chair to listen.

He turned back to the crowd. "That's the end of what I wanted to say," he informed them, "but I promised I would take a few questions. . . ."

And then it was over, and he had successfully ducked all the questions about where he had been jailed and why. They were back in the Vorhulst residence, along with a pared-to-the-bone residue of guests from the university hall. That included nearly all of the first two rows of the auditorium and a scattering of others, as well as a hired-for-the-occasion staff of servants to pass around the drinks and snacks. (That was so the actual Vorhulst household staff, each one of whom felt personally responsible for some part of the event, could attend as guests.) Ranjit and Myra sat side by side, holding hands, and quite remarkably happy to be there. All of the guests were just as happy, so that the champagne the hired staff was passing out was very nearly superfluous.

Dr. Bandara, of course, was already on his way back to New York in his own BAB-2200, but before he'd left, he had taken Ranjit aside for a few words. "You'll be wanting a job, of course," he began, and Ranjit nodded.

"Gamini said something about going to work with him," Ranjit said.

Dhatusena Bandara said, "And I hope that will happen, but I'm afraid not right away. Meanwhile, I understand the university is prepared to offer you a faculty position, teaching a few advanced classes and doing your own research, if you wish."

"But I'm not a professor! I haven't even graduated!"

Dr. Bandara said patiently, "A professor is just a person the university has hired in that grade. And don't worry about degrees you may lack. I expect people will be offering you all the degrees you could wish for."

All of this, naturally, Ranjit passed on to Myra. But Beatrix Vorhulst, sitting on the other side of her, was looking dubious. "You know," she said, "I'm not sure you even need a job. Look at these." She held up a sheaf of printouts, vetted by her personal secretary, who was now supplemented by an assistant just to handle the traffic Ranjit was generating. "People want you to come and speak to them, or to be interviewed, or just to say that you drink their beer or wear their shirts. And they're willing to pay for it! If you'll wear their track shoes, these people will give you a good many American dollars. And if you'll let them interview you, *60 Minutes* will pay, too. Harvard University will pay you to come and talk to them—they don't say how much, but I understand they're rich."

"Whoa," said Myra, laughing. "Let the poor man catch his breath."

But the secretary-screener was waving another piece of paper just off the printer at Mevrouw, who glanced at it, bit her lip, and said, "Well, this one isn't about money, but I think you'll want to see it, Ranjit. And you, too, Myra."

"Me?" asked Myra. "Why me?"

But when it had been passed to Ranjit, who looked thunderstruck but handed it over to her, Myra quickly understood why. The note was from the old monk at his father's former temple, and what it said was:

Your father would be even more proud of you, and as delighted as we all are, that you are going to marry. Please don't delay too long! You don't want to wait until the unlucky months of Aashad, Bhadrapad, or Shunya. And of course, please, not on a Tuesday or a Saturday.

Myra looked up at Ranjit, who was staring in confusion at her. "Did I say anything about getting married?" he asked.

This brought about a faint blush. "Well, you did say some nice things about me," she admitted.

"I have no recollection of saying anything like that," he said. "Must have been my subconscious." And, taking a deep breath, he said, "Which proves that my subconscious is smarter than I am. So what about it, Myra? Will you?"

"Of course I will," she said, as though that had been the dumbest question she had ever heard. And that was that.

Later, when the two of them played news clips of the speech out of curiosity, they found that what he had said was simply the obvious truism that he could not imagine spending the rest of his life without her . . . but that was enough, and anyway, by then they were already thoroughly married.

Was everything perfect for the loving pair?

Well, pretty close. The one big question that had to be settled was not about whether they should get married, because there wasn't the slightest doubt about that, or even when, because the answer to that was as soon as could be. The real questions were where, and by whom. For a time it looked like that was easily answered, too, because the Vorhulsts and the Bandaras and the de Soyzas among them had access to every church in the city of Colombo, not to mention every registrar's office, and were well along the process of eliminating the less attractive of them when Myra noticed the faraway look in Ranjit's eyes.

When she asked, he shrugged it off. "Nothing, really," he said. "No. Nothing at all."

But, since Myra did not give up easily, at last he relented and showed her yet another text from the old monk: "Your father would have been so happy to see you marry in his temple."

Myra read it twice and then smiled. "What the hell," she said. "I don't think the presbytery of Ceylon is going to care. I'll tell everybody."

And, of course, "everybody" understood at once that what Ranjit wanted was what Myra would enforce, and so it was. If there was a little disappointment in some circles in Colombo, there was wild delight among others in Trincomalee. The old monk quickly understood that it would have to be a stripped-down ceremony. He wistfully considered what a wonderful Paalikali Thalippu they could have had for the bride—if they could have had them at all—and how the groom's Janavasanam arrival at the temple would have been decorated with the finest fruits and flowers. Well, that would have pretty nearly amounted to a full-scale parade, wouldn't it? And anything like that would have attracted vast attention just when the couple wanted to be ignored. So no Paalikali Thalippu and no Janavasanam, though the monk did make sure that the bride's party carried the requisite supply of *parupputenga* and other sweetmeats to give to the groom.

The good part of the stripped-downness of the wedding was that it could all be done quite quickly, for which reason it was less than a week before the bride and the groom were in Trincomalee—well, in hiding in Trincomalee, to be exact, because they tried to avoid showing their instantly recognizable faces in public.

For that reason there were few people at the ceremony, as Ranjit spoke the words the old monk had written out for him and Myra allowed the monk to tie around her wrist the holy thread that would ward off evil, with the endless flowers all over the room and the unending blare of the Naathaswaram horns and the *melam* drums. Then it was all over and the two of them, now indissolubly wed, got back into their police car for the long ride back to the Vorhulst estate. "Long life!" called the monks as they left, and indeed Ranjit and Myra felt confident that that was what lay ahead of them.

However, other persons, farther away, had quite different expectations.

Those persons included the One Point Fives, the designated assassins for the Grand Galactics. They were executing their order to clean up the mess on Planet 3 of that trivial yellow star, and their armada was progressing on its flight. Since their vessels were material, they could not go faster than light speed. There would be many years of transit time, followed by a few days of actual extermination, after which the newlyweds, and every other human being anywhere, would be dead.

It might not be a very long life after all.

20

MARRIAGE

Now that he was everything that he had dared to dream of being, namely, free, famous, and married to Myra de Soyza, it seemed to Ranjit that his personal world just kept getting better and better. There was, however, a larger perspective that kept intruding itself on his private musings, and in many ways that wasn't good at all.

Take the situation in North Korea, for instance. First off, there seemed to have been a regime change. Blustery luxury-loving Kim Jong Il was gone.

In some ways that was almost a pity. Kim might have been a nut, but he had been the kind of nut that had always stopped just short of an actual large-scale attack on his neighbors. Now there was this new guy. He was always referred to as "the Adorable Leader." If he had a proper name, it seemed to be too precious to share with the decadent West.

But if the Adorable Leader's identity was secret, what he did was all too public. Their latest generation of nuclear rockets, the Adorable Leader's generals claimed, could easily cross the northern stretches of the Pacific Ocean. This meant that they could strike actual United States of America soil—at least Alaska, perhaps even the northern corner of Washington State. What's more, the generals boasted, the new rockets were definitely reliable. This talk made all of their neighbors increasingly nervous. Those that didn't already have their own nuclear stocks were under increasing pressure to acquire them.

Nor was the rest of the world much better off. In Africa the continent had backslid to some of the worst days of the twentieth century. Once again they were seeing the armies of boy soldiers, some of them barely into their teens, drafted when their families were murdered, and fighting for stocks of illicit diamonds and even less licit ivory. . . .

It was discouraging.

.   .   .

There was, though, one thing that did trouble Ranjit when he let himself think of it, and it came up when Mevrouw Beatrix Vorhulst looked in on a conversation with lawyer De Saram to ask, "What would anyone like for dinner?"

It was the same question that someone had to ask every morning, but this time it got a different reception. Myra turned to look inquiringly at Ranjit, who cocked an eyebrow at her, sighed, and spoke to their hostess. "That's something we've been talking about, Aunt Bea. We think you'd probably like to have your house back."

It was the first time Ranjit had ever seen Beatrix Vorhulst look indignant. "Dear boy, not at all! We're glad to have you stay here as long as you like. You're family, you know. We like having you here, and we're honored, besides, and—"

But De Saram, having studied Myra's face, was shaking his head. "Perhaps we've missed the point, Mevrouw," he said. "They're married. They want their own home, not a piece of yours, and they're absolutely right about it. Let's all have another cup of tea and consider the options. And as to a place for the two of you to live, you already have one, Ranjit. What used to be your father's home in Trincomalee is now yours, you know."

Ranjit turned to examine Myra's face. The expression on it was very much what he had been expecting. "I don't think Myra wants to live in Trinco," he reported sorrowfully to the group, but she was already shaking her head.

"Trinco's beautiful," she said. "I'd love to have a place there, but—"

She didn't finish. "What then?" De Saram asked, puzzled.

Ranjit answered for her. "It was a very nice house for one elderly man," he said. "But for us—that is, for a couple who are probably going to want washing machines, dishwashers, all sorts of appliances that my father had no reason to bother with—well, what do you say, Myra? Do you want to start making changes in my father's house?"

She took a deep breath, but managed to compress her reply to one word: "Yes."

"Of course you do," he said. "You wouldn't rather tear it down and start over from scratch? No? All right. Then the first thing we do is get Surash to find us an architect who can make floor plans of what we've got to work with—he knows every Tamil in Trinco—and we invite him here with the plans and you and he start creating. With," he added, "me available for creative inputs any time I'm asked. Meanwhile, Myra, you and I move our bodies into a hotel. How does that sound?"

Mevrouw was frowning more deeply than Ranjit had ever seen her. "There's no reason for that," she declared. "We're perfectly comfortable with you here until the place in Trincomalee is ready for you."

Ranjit looked at his wife, then spread his hands. "All right, but I do have another suggestion. Myra, love? Didn't I once hear you say something about a honeymoon?"

Myra looked surprised. "No. You haven't. I admit I think a honeymoon would be grand, but I haven't said a single word about it—"

"Not since we were married," Ranjit agreed, "but I remember exactly what you said to me, right in this room, a few years ago. You told me about all the wonderful parts of Lanka that I'd never visited. So let's go visit them, Myra. While everybody's getting the rest of our lives ready for us."

The best place to start was the easiest, Myra declared, so the first place they tried was the turtle hatchery in Kosgoda, because Myra had loved it as a child and, mostly, because it was close enough for practice, then Kandy, the island's grand old city. But a week later, when they had done them both and were back in the Vorhulst house and the staff wanted to know how they'd liked it, their responses were tepid. They had been recognized in Kosgoda, and small crowds had followed them about all day. Kandy had been worse. The local police had taken them around the town in a police car. They had seen everything, but hadn't once been allowed to wander at will.

Over the dinner table Beatrix Vorhulst listened sympathetically as Ranjit explained that it was nice to be driven around, but they really would have liked to mingle with the crowds. She sighed. "I don't know if that can happen," she said. "You're the best sight the people have for sightseeing purposes. You see, the trouble is that we're a bit short on world-famous celebrities here in Lanka. You're about all we've got."

Myra disagreed. "Not really. There's the writer—"

"Well, yes, but he hardly ever comes out of his house. Anyway, it's not the same. If we were somewhere thick with movie stars and all kinds of famous people—Los Angeles, for instance, or London—you two could just put on some dark glasses and you'd hardly be noticed." And then her expression changed. She said, "Well, come to think of it, why not?"

And when everyone was looking at her, she explained: "You've got all these invitations from all over the world, Ranjit. Why not accept a few?"

Ranjit blinked at her, then turned to Myra. "What do you think? Should we try to have a real honeymoon—Europe, America, whatever you like?"

She glanced at him, then around the table thoughtfully. She finally said, "I think that would be wonderful, Ranjit. If we're going to do it, let's do it soon."

He gave her a curious look, but turned at once to questioning about what specific invitations were available. It wasn't until they were heading to bed that he thought to ask her, "You do want to do this, don't you? Because if you don't want to—"

She laid a finger across his lips and then, unexpectedly, followed with a kiss. "It's just that I think if we're going to do long-distance traveling, it might be better to do it soon. Might be a little more difficult later on. I wasn't going to tell you until the doctor confirmed it, but I won't see her until Friday. The thing is, I'm pretty sure I'm pregnant."

21

HONEYMOON, PART TWO

While Myra and Ranjit were making their way to London, a trip as long and wearing as Gamini had described it years before, the world was going on its own way. Which was, of course, the way of death and destruction. They had booked their flight the long way around, by way of Mumbai, so Ranjit could get a quick look at the city. But their plane was forty minutes late because of circling before being allowed to land. Artillery fighting had broken out again in the Vale of Kashmir. No one knew what underground Pakistani agents might be planning to do to targets in India's heartland, so the couple spent their whole time in the old city in their hotel room, watching television. That didn't have much good news, either. Units of the Adorable Leader's North Korean army, no longer limiting themselves to creating incidents along the border with South Korea, had plucked up the courage to have a few incidents with the country that fed it, the one that was pretty nearly its only real friend in the world, the People's Republic of China. What they were up to no one seemed able to guess, but four separate incursions, no more than a dozen or so troops each, crossed into PRC territory, where there was nothing but hills and rocks, and set up camp.

Myra and Ranjit were three hours later boarding their London plane, too, but by the time they were airborne, skirting Pakistan's shoreline en route to Heathrow in England, the Kashmir fighting had died down and the North Korean army had turned around and gone back to its barracks, and no one could figure out what they had been up to in the first place.

And then there they were, in London.

It did not disappoint, exactly. The great sights of the city were as fascinating to Ranjit as they had been to millions of visitors for hundreds of years. All of them—huge old St. Paul's, the Tower of London, the Houses of Parliament, Westminster Abbey—all the famous ones that every tourist had to see and a fair number of sights that were not really famous at all but were of particular interest to Ranjit—like the London School of Economics and a certain superb maisonette a few squares away on Arundel Street, because both had once been inhabited by Gamini Bandara at a time when Ranjit himself had had no hope of ever visiting them. When Myra persuaded him to take an excursion to Kew Gardens, he really loved the vast greenhouses. He loved all the great and famous structures of the city, almost without exception. What he did not love in the least, however, was all the open and unroofed spaces that lay between them, the spaces that he had to traverse in order to get from one to another.

And which were, without exception in this month of November, terribly, unbearably *cold*.

This soul-searing experience was one that Ranjit had never before encountered in all of his life. Oh, perhaps sometimes he had suffered a brief chill, maybe at the tip of Swami Rock when the winds were strong, or when he was just coming out of a plunge in the surf in the early, early morning. Not like this! Not when it was so cold that the sparse snows of the week before, and even the ones of the week before that, still left their blackened remains on the margins of parking lots and the edges of lawns because it had never warmed up enough since to finish melting them away.

Still, London's shops were full of garments designed to keep the coldest visitor toasty, or anyway somewhat warm. Thermal underwear, gloves, and a fur-collared topcoat made the London streets bearable to Ranjit, while the first mink coat of her life improved things for Myra.

Then they met Sir Tariq. It was he, on behalf of the Royal Mathematical Society, who had invited Ranjit to become a member, and to come to London to tell them about his feat. (And had produced a foundation that paid their expenses.) Sir Tariq al Diwani turned out to be a plump elderly man with unruly Albert Einstein hair, a kindly heart, and no trace of any accent but the purest OxCam. ("Well," he explained when pressed, "I'm fourth generation London, after all.") And when he found that Ranjit was freezing most of the time, he struck his forehead. "Oh, blast," he said. "I let them give you posh instead of comfort. I'll have you moved."

What they were moved to was a brand-shiny-new but not particularly fashionable hotel in South Kensington. Which puzzled Myra a bit until she had a talk with the concierge and, grinning, reported to Ranjit that Sir Tariq had chosen this particular hotel because, a, it was convenient to some of the city's best museums, if that should interest them while they were there, and, b, it was frequently occupied by Arab oil sheikhs and their large retinues, an entire floor or two at a time. The importance of that was that what the oil sheikhs hated most, even more than Ranjit did, was being cold, not just in their private rooms but in a hotel's lobbies, fire stairs, and even elevators as well. And what the owners of the hotel hated even more than that was to fail to give those free-spending Arabs every last thing they might desire.

Though not himself a free-spending oil sheikh, Ranjit was happy to receive the fallout from their spending. Over the next couple of months, his mood improved visibly—improved enough, indeed, for him to take a shot at that other reason for the particular hotel they were in, its proximity to Museum Row. The Natural History Museum (though drafty) was a delight, inspiring Ranjit to agree to the crosstown odyssey to the great British Museum itself, back in Gamini's part of town—even grander (if even draftier) and making him agree that yes, cold countries might after all have some advantages over the hot ones.

It wasn't all tourism. The lecture for the Royal Mathematical Society took some thought, though actually what Ranjit said in London was pretty much what he had said at the press conference in Colombo. Two magazines had urgently requested a visit, *Nature* because they were the ones who had published his paper and *New Scientist* because (they promised) they would take him to the best pub on their side of the Thames. And there were a couple of press conferences, too, set up at long range by De Saram in Colombo. And even so, with their pictures in print on every newsstand and occasionally on the telly as well, Myra persuaded Ranjit to put his thermal underwear to the test by standing outside Buckingham Palace one evening to observe the changing of the guard. When they were back in their hotel, and Ranjit had to admit none of his parts seemed to be at all frostbitten from the ordeal, he also pointed out that, of all the cameras held by their fellow tourists, every last one had been pointed at the guards, and not one at them. "So it's true," he said. "We can move around London all we like, and no one pays any attention to us at all. I'd really like this place if they'd just move it a thousand kilometers or so south."

Well, they wouldn't do that, so after a few hours of bundling up to get from the hotel lobby to a taxi, and from the taxi to some other lobby somewhere else, Ranjit gave up. He took Sir Tariq aside. Then he got on the phone with De Saram in Colombo, and then, grinning, reported to Myra, "We're going to America. It's what they call the Triple-A-S—the American Association for the Advancement of Science?—and next month they're having their annual convention and De Saram has it all worked out. Oh, we're not through here, Myra. Not permanently. We'll do everything there is to do here, but not until the weather's a little warmer." So they were booked first class—another of those generous foundations—to leave on the American-Delta flight to New York City (Kennedy) at two P.M. that afternoon.

Which they did, though with many sincere protestations of thanks to Sir Tariq, and by two-twenty they were leaving England behind and approaching the eastern coast of Ireland.

Ranjit was all solicitude. "I haven't rushed you too much, have I? You're not—?" The whoopsing gesture he made at his mouth elucidated the question for Myra, who laughed. She held up her glass for an orange juice refill from the attendant, who was quick to oblige.

"I'm fine," she said. "And yes, you and I can come back to England when it's nice and warm—say June. But are you sure you're doing the right thing now, going to America?"

Ranjit finished spreading the clotted cream and strawberry preserves on his scone and popped the product into his mouth. "Of course I am," he told her, chewing. "I checked the New York weather reports for myself. Right now they've got a low of nine, looking to a high for the day of eighteen. I've been colder than that in Trinco."

Uncertain whether to laugh or cry, Myra set down her glass. "Oh, my darling," she said. "You've never been in America, have you?"

Suddenly worried, Ranjit turned to face her. "What do you mean?"

She reached out to stroke his hand. "Just that you haven't noticed that they're pretty old-fashioned there in some ways. The way they still use miles instead of kilometers, for instance. And—I hope this won't upset you—the way they cling to the Fahrenheit thermometer scale instead of going to Celsius along with the rest of the world?"

22

THE NEW WORLD

Apart from the great thermal disappointment that the climate of New York represented for Ranjit, the news that kept coming over their hotel suite's large supply of TV sets was even more disheartening than usual. For example, South America had been relatively quiet, war-wise, for some time. No longer. Now (as one of their American hosts explained it to Myra and Ranjit) what had changed was the fact that the United States had revised most drug crimes down from felonies to, at most, misdemeanors. That had decriminalized nearly all the stock in trade of the Colombian drug merchants. That change in the laws made it possible for any American addict to get what he needed for his habit, cheap and without gangster intervention, at any local pharmacy, thus effectively putting the gangsters out of business. (It also made it pointless for any neighborhood pusher to hand out free samples to twelve-year-olds. That would no longer ensure him a supply of addicted customers for the future, since none of those future customers, if there were any, would be buying from him anyway. And so each year the census of American addicts slowly dwindled as the oldest ones died or went dry, and few new ones came along as replacements.)

But that was only the good part of drug decriminalization. There was a bad part as well.

The bad part, or the worst of the bad parts, was that the drug cartels, deprived of the profits from their coca plantations, began to look longingly at the equally addictive stuff that was being exported by their neighbors in Venezuela. Why, there was even more money in oil than there ever had been in drugs! And so armed parties from the Colombian drug citadels were infiltrating the oil fields of their neighbor. The relatively small (and often quite purchasable) Venezuelan army was putting up a show of resistance, sometimes, but the powerful motivation was all on the Colombian side, and so were almost all the victories.

All this, of course, in addition to the latest list of vicious little escapades from the Adorable Leader's North Korea, and in addition to the renewal of violence in the irreconcilable fragments of what had once been Yugoslavia, and more and more heavy fighting in parts of what had once been the Soviet Union, and the Middle East. . . .

It was all bad. What made up for it, a little, was the city of New York itself, not in the least like Trincomalee, or even Colombo, and in fact not all that much like London. "It's so vertical," Ranjit told his wife, as they stood at the sixty-sixth-floor picture window of their hotel suite. "Whoever heard of sleeping this high up?" And yet in the panorama of the city that lay before them there were a dozen or more buildings much taller, and when they walked in the city streets, there were times when the sun seldom appeared because steep concrete walls shut it out except when it was directly overhead.

"But it does have that beautiful park," Myra pointed out, gazing at the lake, the giant apartments that lined the far side of the park, and the distant roofs of the Central Park Zoo.

"Oh, I'm not complaining," Ranjit told her, and indeed he had little to complain about. Though Dr. Dhatusena Bandara's office in the UN building was just across town, the doctor himself was somewhere else, on some errand that no one chose to discuss. His office had, though, provided them with a young lady who had taken them to the top of the Empire State Building and introduced them to the Lucullan joys of oyster stew in the old Grand Central railroad station, and who stood ready to get tickets for them for any show on Broadway. Which wasn't a great thrill to Ranjit, whose entire lifetime experience of performances had been on a flat screen, but greatly pleased Myra. Which itself much pleased Ranjit, not to mention that he had discovered the American Museum of Natural History, only a few blocks away—wonderful in its own right as an exemplar of that new delight in Ranjit's life, its museumness, but thrilling in the great planetarium that filled its northern space. "Planetarium" was hardly the right word, in fact; the structure on Central Park West was so much more than that. "I wish Joris could be with us!" Ranjit said, more than once, as he strolled its thrilling exhibits.

And then, following a long enough interval that Ranjit had stopped thinking he might actually show up, appeared the one person, totally unexpected, who could make a pleasant visit unforgettable. When Ranjit opened the door of their suite to a knock, supposing there would be no more than a chambermaid with an armload of fresh towels on the other side of it, there in fact, grinning, stood Gamini Bandara, with a spray of fresh roses in one hand for Myra and in the other a bottle of good old Sri Lanka arrack for the two of them. It was the first time they had been together since the wedding, and the questions came thick and fast. How had they liked England? What did they think of America? What was it like back in Lanka these days? It wasn't until the men had poured their third round of arrack that Myra noticed that all the conversation went in the same direction, questions coming from Gamini, answers from her husband and herself. "So," she said at last, "tell us, then, Gamini, what are you doing in New York?"

He grinned and spread his hands. "One damn meeting after another. It's what I do."

"But I thought you were based in California," Ranjit put in.

"I am, right. But there's all sorts of international stuff going on, and this is where the UN is, isn't it?" Then he swallowed his third shot and looked serious. "Actually, the reason I'm here, Ranjit, is that I want to ask you to do me a favor."

Ranjit said promptly, "Name it."

"Don't say yes so fast," Gamini chided. "It means making a commitment for some time. But it's not a bad commitment, either. So let me get right down to it. When you're in Washington, you will be contacted by a man named Orion Bledsoe. He's a cloak-and-dagger guy, and he's high up in the part of the government most people never hear about. For that matter, he has quite a record of his own. He's a veteran of the first Gulf War, and of the troubles in what used to be Yugoslavia, and then of the second, and much worse, war in the Gulf, the one in Iraq. That's where he got, in that order, the wound that cost him his right arm, the Purple Heart, the Navy Cross, and, finally, the job he's got now."

"Which is what?" Ranjit asked, as Gamini seemed to pause for a moment.

Gamini shook his head. "Come on, Ranj. I'll have to let Bledsoe tell you that—there are rules I have to follow, you know."

Ranjit tried again. "Is it going to be about a real job?"

That made Gamini pause for thought again. "Well, yes, but I can't tell you what that is right now, either," he said at last. "The important thing about that job is that you'll be doing something useful for the world. All we need Bledsoe for is to see that you get the security clearance you need."

"Need for what?" Ranjit asked.

Gamini, smiling, shook his head. Then, looking faintly embarrassed, he said, "I have to warn you that Bledsoe is a kind of old-fashioned Cold Warrior and a bit of a silly ass, too. But once you're in the job, you won't have to see much of him. And," he added, "since when I'm in America I'm usually based less than half an hour's drive from his part of the world, you probably will be seeing a lot more of me, if you can stand that." He winked at Myra. And then reported that he was late for another of those damn meetings way on the other side of town, and he hoped they'd all see one another one day soon in Pasadena, and was gone.

Ranjit and Myra looked at each other. "Where's Pasadena?" he asked.

"In California, I'm pretty sure," she said. "Do you suppose that's where you'd be based? If you took this job, I mean."

He gave her an exasperated grin. "You know what? Maybe we should ask Gamini's father about all this."

Which they did, or at least left a query at his office. They didn't get an answer right away, though. They didn't get an answer at all until they had made the short hop from New York (LaGuardia) to Washington National (Reagan) and were already welcomed by the people from the Triple-A-S and booked into their new hotel, in sight of the Capitol and walking distance from the Mall. And all Dr. Bandara's communication said was "Gamini assures me this person he wants you to see can be of great help to you." But it didn't say great help in doing what, or why Gamini cared in the first place, and so Ranjit sighed and gave up. Which actually was not a great disappointment, because Washington turned out to be full of things that interested him more than some unspecified job to be offered by some still unmet person named Orion Bledsoe.

The first thing—with Ranjit and Myra escorted there by enthusiastic volunteers from the AAAS—was the famous (which, actually, Ranjit had never heard of before coming to Washington) cluster of museums collectively known as the Smithsonian Institution. London's British Museum and New York's American Museum of Natural History had delighted him; this Smithsonian, not just one fabulous structure but a whole row of the things, staggered his imagination. All he could make time for was the Air and Space Museum and a quick peek into one or two of the others, but the space collection had, among countless other things, an actual working model (though not to scale) of the Artsutanov space elevator, which was even now beginning to be spun out in the skies above Sri Lanka. And then he had his own keynote speech to give the Triple-A-S convention, and (that having been done, and once again declared a triumph) he had their whole damn convention to pick and choose among. Bear in mind that this celebrated genius among Earth's most honored scientific minds, world famous and already possessed of three actual doctoral degrees given by three of the world's most prestigious schools (although in fact he had never quite achieved even a bachelor's degree for himself)—this modern Fermat or even Newton had never in his not very long life been lucky enough to sit in on a single scientific convention of any kind, except ones for which he was the principal speaker. He had no idea so much could be learned on so many subjects. His own chores attended to, he had the freedom of the convention, and he used it, attending sessions on cosmology and Martian (and Venusian and Europan) tectonics and something called "Machine Intelligence: Awareness of Self" (that primarily for Myra, but it fascinated Ranjit almost as much when he listened), and heaven only knew what arcane aspects of what previously unexplored (by Ranjit) other areas of human investigation turned up somewhere on the vast and challenging menu of events.

Myra kept right up with him, too, as fascinated by the panoply of human learning as he, with a few exceptions. The principal exception was the daily nap after lunch that he insisted on, because one of their doctors had insisted. "You are getting ready to have a baby, you know!" he informed her every day, although in fact she was never in any doubt of it. And then, on almost the last day of the convention, when Ranjit was tucking her in, they heard a gentle *beep-beep* from their telephone. It was a fresh text message, and what it said was:

I would be grateful if you could join me in my suite sometime today to discuss a proposal that I think will interest you.
                    T. O. Bledsoe, Lt. Col. USMC (ret.)

Ranjit and Myra looked at each other. "It's the man Gamini was talking about in New York," Ranjit said, and Myra nodded briskly.

"Of course it is. Go ahead, call him, see what he wants. And then come back here and tell me all about it."

The suite belonging to Lt. Col. (ret.) T. Orion Bledsoe was noticeably bigger than the one the AAAS convention had provided for Ranjit and Myra. Even the bowl of fruit on the conference table in the drawing room was larger, and it wasn't alone on the table, either. Next to it was an unopened bottle of Jack Daniel's whiskey, with the ice, glasses, and mixers to go with it.

T. Orion Bledsoe himself was not much taller than Ranjit, which for an American was hardly tall at all, and at least a couple of decades older. But he still had all his hair, and a pretty muscular handshake, though it was the left hand he offered and used to pull Ranjit in. "Come in, come in, Mr. uh—have a seat. Are you enjoying our District of Confusion?"

He didn't wait for an answer, either, but led the way to the conference table. "Care for a drink, Mr. Subra—uh—? I mean, if Jack isn't going to be too strong for you?"

Ranjit repressed a smile. Anyone who had spent his wild sixteenth year ingesting arrack was not likely to find some American tipple too strong. "That would be fine," he said. "Your message said something about a proposal."

Bledsoe gave him a reproachful look. "They say we Americans are always in a hurry, but in my experience it's you foreigners that are always jumping the gun. Sure, I want to talk about something with you, but I like to get to know a man a little bit before we do business." And all the time his previously neglected right hand was gripping the whiskey bottle while the other was opening the seal. Bledsoe noticed where Ranjit's eyes were focused and gave a little chuckle. "Prosthetic," he admitted—or boasted. "Pretty good design, too. I could even shake hands with it if I wanted to, but I don't. I can't feel your hand if I do, so what's the point? And if I got absentminded and squeezed a little too hard, you could suddenly be in the market for one of your own."

The artificial arm was actually quite efficient, Ranjit observed, reminding himself to tell Myra about it. The bottle open, the hand was pouring an even two centimeters of whiskey into each glass, and then passing Ranjit's over to him. Bledsoe watched attentively to see if Ranjit was going to use any of the mixers. When he didn't, Bledsoe gave a little nod of approval and took a taste from his own glass. "This is what we call sippin' whiskey," he said. "You can chug it down if you want to—hey, it's a free country—but you ought to give it a chance. Ever been in Iraq?"

Ranjit, sipping a little of the sippin' whiskey out of politeness to his host, shook his head.

"It's where I got this." He tapped the imitation arm with his good one. "With all the Shiites and the Sunnis doing their best to kill each other, but taking time out to kill as many of us as they could along the way. It was the wrong war, in the wrong place, for the wrong reasons."

Ranjit tried his best to sound interested enough to be polite, wondering whether Bledsoe was going to say the right war would have been Afghanistan, or maybe Iran. It wasn't, though. "North Korea," Bledsoe proclaimed. "They're the ones we should've pulverized. Ten missiles in the ten right places and they'd have been right out of the game."

Ranjit coughed. "As I understand it," he said, swallowing a little more of his Jack Daniel's, "the trouble with fighting North Korea is that they have a very large and very modern army and they've got it sitting right on the border, less than fifty kilometers from Seoul."

Bledsoe waved a dismissive hand. "Hell, sure there'd be losses. A lot of them, no doubt. So what? They'd be South Korean losses, not Americans. Well," he corrected himself, grimacing at the annoyance, "all right, there are quite a few American troops right up there, sure. But you can't make an omelette without breaking eggs, can you?"

It seemed to Ranjit that the party was getting unpleasant, and then as Bledsoe tossed a crumpled napkin into a wastebasket, he thought he saw a reason. The napkin bounced off an empty whiskey bottle. Apparently his was not the first conference Bledsoe had convened that day.

Ranjit cleared his throat. "Well, Mr. Bledsoe, I come from a small country with problems of its own. I don't want to criticize American policy."

Bledsoe bobbed his head in agreement. "And that's another thing," he said, and interrupted himself to offer a refill with the bottle. Ranjit shook his head. Bledsoe shrugged and recharged his own glass. "Your little island," he said. "Shree— Shree—"

"Sri Lanka," Ranjit politely corrected.

"That's the one. D'you know what you've got there?"

Ranjit considered. "Well, I think it's probably the most beautiful island in the—"

"I'm not talking about the whole damn island, for Christ's sake! My God, there's a million beautiful islands around all over the world and I wouldn't give you a nickel for any of them. I'm just talking about one little harbor you've got there, Trinkum— Trinco—"

Ranjit took pity. "I think you mean Trincomalee. I was born there."

"Really?" Bledsoe considered that datum, found no use for it, and continued. "Anyway, I don't give a damn about the town. It's the harbor that's a world-beater! Do you know what that could be? It could be the world's best base for a nuclear submarine navy, Mr. Sub— Subra—"

He had refilled his glass once again, and the sippin' whiskey was beginning to show its effects. Ranjit sighed and rescued him again. "It's Subramanian, Mr. Bledsoe, and, yes, we know what a base it could be. In World War II it was headquarters for the Allied fleet, and before that Lord Nelson himself said it was one of the world's greatest harbors."

"Oh, crap, what does Lord Nelson have to do with it? He was talking about a place for sailing ships, for God's sake. I'm talking nukes! That harbor's deep enough that submarines can dive well below what any enemy could find, much less attack! Dozens of them! Maybe hundreds. And what did we do about it? We let goddamn India snap up treaty rights for the whole damn port. India, for God's sake! And what the hell India needs a navy for in the first place, I can't—"

Ranjit was getting tired of this opinionated drunk. Gamini was Gamini, but Ranjit couldn't be expected to put up with much more of this. He stood up. "Thanks for the drink, Mr. Bledsoe, but I'm afraid I have to be getting along."

He held out a hand to be shaken in farewell, but Bledsoe didn't reciprocate. He glared up at Ranjit, then deliberately put the top back on the whiskey bottle. "Excuse me one second," he said. "We have some unfinished business."

He disappeared into one of the suite's bathrooms. Ranjit heard running water, thought it over, shrugged, and sat down. It was more than one second, though. It was close to five minutes before T. Orion Bledsoe appeared again, and he hardly seemed the same man. His face was scrubbed, his hair was brushed, and he was carrying a partial cup of steaming black coffee— no doubt from the coffee machine that seemed to be standard equipment in any American hotel bathroom.

He didn't offer Ranjit any of the coffee. He didn't offer any explanations, either, just sat down, glanced at the whiskey bottle as though astonished to find it there, and said briskly, "Mr. Subramanian, if I should mention the names Whitfield Diffic and Martin Hellman, what would they mean to you?"

Slightly confused by the abrupt change in both subject and demeanor—but a little encouraged by the fact that the conversation had suddenly entered into an area he knew something about—Ranjit said, "Public-key cryptography, of course. The Diffie-Hellman-Merkle procedures."

"Exactly," Bledsoe said. "I don't think I need tell you that Diffie-Hellman is in serious trouble, because of the quantum computers."

He didn't. Although Ranjit had never taken any particular interest in codes or code-cracking himself—not counting his exploits in learning one professor's computer password—every mathematician in the world had a pretty good idea of what had gone on.

Diffie-Hellman was based on a very simple idea, but one that had been so difficult to execute that the idea had been useless until the age of really powerful computers. The first step in encoding any message that one wished to keep private was to represent it as a series of numbers. The simplest way to do that, of course, would be to replace the letter *A* with a one, the *B* with a two, and so on through *Z* equals twenty-six. (Naturally, no cryptographer in the world, or at least none over the age of ten, would take seriously such a trivial system of substitutions.) Then these numbers could be combined with an enormous number—call it "N"—in such a way that the original simple substitution was concealed. Simply adding the substituted numbers to giant N might do the trick by itself.

But N had a secret of its own. The way it was generated by cryptographers was by multiplying two large prime numbers together. Any decent computer could do that kind of multiplication in a fraction of a second, but once the two large primes were multiplied together, trying to discover what the primes themselves had been was a brutal job that, even with the best computers, could take many years. Hence the description "trapdoor cipher"—easy to get into, virtually impossible to get out of again. Still, public-key cryptography, as it was called, possessed one great virtue. Anybody could encrypt any message from the product of the primes—even, say, some harried member of the French Resistance in World War II, one step ahead of the Gestapo, with some crucial knowledge of where a bunch of panzer divisions were moving to. But only the people who knew what both those primes were could read the message.

Bledsoe took a sip of his rapidly cooling coffee. "The thing is, Subramanian," he said, "we have some pretty important traffic going around the world right now—don't ask me what it is. I have only a bare glimmering of a notion, and I can't tell you even that much. But at this moment it is more important than ever that our code be unbreakable. Maybe there's some way of decrypting that doesn't involve all this factoring of prime numbers hocus-pocus. And if there is, we would like you to help us figure out what it is."

Ranjit tried his best not to laugh. What he was being asked to do was what every code agency in the world had been working on ever since Diffie-Hellman had published their paper way back in 1975. "Why me?" he asked.

Bledsoe looked pleased with himself. "When I saw the news stories about your proof of Fermat's Last Theorem, it rang a bell. All those mathematicians that work on this public-key stuff use what they call the Fermat test, right? So who would know more about that than the man who just proved his theorem? And there were others around who liked you, so we started the machinery going to recruit you for our team."

When Ranjit considered all the ways in which Bledsoe's notion was ridiculous, he was tempted to get up and walk away. Fermat's test was certainly the basis for many more recent ways of identifying prime numbers. But to leap from that to the notion that the man who proved Fermat's theorem would be any good at public-key code-cracking was, well, simply preposterous.

All the same, this was exactly the offer that Gamini had asked him to accept. Ranjit controlled the impulse to laugh in Bledsoe's face and said only, " 'Recruit' me. Does that mean you're offering me a job?"

"Damn straight it does, Subramanian. You'll be provided with all the resources you need—and the U.S. government has plenty of resources—and a generous salary. How about—?"

Ranjit could not help blinking at the figure mentioned. It would have supported several generations of Subramanians. "That seems adequate," he commented drily. "When should I start?"

"Ah, well," Bledsoe said moodily, "not right away, I'm afraid. It's a matter of your security clearance. You did, after all, spend a couple of months in the slammer back home, under suspicion of being associated in terrorist activities."

Then Ranjit did come close to blowing his top. "That's ridiculous! I wasn't involved in any—"

Bledsoe raised his hand. "I know. Do you think I'd be offering you this kind of a job if I didn't know that? But the security clearance people get real antsy when there's a connection with a certified terrorist bunch like your pirates. Don't worry. It's all just about straightened out. We had to go right to the top. It took actual White House intervention, but you'll get your clearance. Only it will take a bit more time."

Ranjit sighed and bit the bullet. "How long?"

"Three weeks, maybe. At most a month. So what I suggest is you go ahead and do all those speaking dates you've accepted, and when the word comes through, I'll get in touch with you and arrange for your coming to California."

There didn't seem to be much help for it. "All right," Ranjit said. "I'll need an address for you so I can keep you posted on where to reach me."

Bledsoe grinned. He showed a lot of teeth, a lot of sharklike teeth, when he smiled, Ranjit observed. "Don't worry," he said. "I'll know where you are."

Three weeks turned into six, and then into two months. Ranjit was beginning to wonder how long the generosity of the foundation that paid their hotel bills would last, and he still had not heard from Bledsoe again. "It's just typical government red tape," Myra said, consoling. "Gamini said to take the job. You took it. Now we just have to live by their timetable."

"But where the hell is Gamini?" Ranjit said sulkily. He hadn't appeared again, and when Ranjit e-mailed his father's office to see if they could supply an address, they had simply replied, "He is in the field and can't be reached."

At least Myra had the visits to her old friends at MIT to amuse her. Ranjit didn't have that much. When she came back to the hotel, puffing and—yes, you'd have to say it—waddling but full of news about the great new accomplishments of some of her old buddies, he greeted her with an unexpected question: "What would you think about catching the next plane back to Lanka?"

She eased herself and her great belly into a chair. "What's the matter, dear?"

"This is going nowhere," he announced, not adding that it was also very cold outside. "I've been thinking about what Dr. Bandara said. Being a full professor at the university wouldn't be a bad life. I'd have a chance to do research, too, and you know there are plenty of other big problems that nobody has solved. If you wanted to be rich, I could see if I could work the bugs out of the Black-Scholes equation. Or, if I wanted a real challenge, there's always P equals NP. If anybody could solve that, it would revolutionize mathematics."

Myra shifted her weight around in the chair, trying to find a comfortable position. She decided there wasn't one and leaned over to press her husband's hand. "What's P equals NP?" she asked. "Or that other equation?"

It was worse than she'd thought; Ranjit didn't take the bait. "The thing is," he said, "we're just wasting our time here. We might as well give it up and go home."

"You promised Gamini," she reminded him. "Just give it a few more days."

"A very few," he said stubbornly. "A week at the most, and then we're out of here."

It didn't come to that. It was the very next day that the teletext message came from ex–Lt. Col. T. Orion Bledsoe. "Clearance granted. Report to Pasadena ASAP."

And they were certainly about ready to get out of Boston's worst-yet climate. But when they were all packed up, and just waiting for the limo that was to take them to Logan Airport for the flight to LAX, Myra suddenly put her hand to her belly. "Oh, my," she said. "I think that was a contraction."

It was.

Once she made Ranjit understand what was happening, it was no problem to divert their limousine from the airport to Massachusetts General Hospital. Where, six hours later, little Natasha de Soyza Subramanian made her first appearance in the world.

23

FARMER "BILL"

And in another part of the galaxy, far, far away . . .

You couldn't say that the Grand Galactics had forgotten about unruly Earth. That never happened. They were constitutionally incapable of forgetting anything. All the same, Earth had certainly slipped into the farther recesses of their collective mind, and their attention was concentrated on more important, or anyway more interesting, issues.

In the case of "Bill" himself, for example, there was the task of tending to their farm—or, perhaps it should be "farm" in quotation marks, since nothing organic grew there.

We wouldn't usually think of the Grand Galactics as farmers of any kind. Nevertheless there were certain kinds of crops that they encouraged, and it is a curious fact that medieval human peasants had done something very similar with their own tiny plots.

The plot that interested Bill enough to cause him to visit it was a volume of space several light-years on a side.

At first look, any astronomer might have thought it was nothing but empty space. As a matter of fact, that is exactly what human astronomers had thought when they'd first observed it. It wasn't entirely empty, though. Better observations, achieved when humans had managed to acquire better telescopes, showed that there was something in that patch of space that bent light, refracting blue in one direction, red in the other.

That something, as the Grand Galactics had always known, was interstellar dust.

This trip was not, of course, Bill's first visit to his farm. Not long before—oh, a matter of a few million years or so before—he had explored it in detail, making a careful census of the dust. What percentage of the dust particles (as humans might measure them) were less than a hundredth of a micron in size? What percentage, indeed, were in all the size ranges all the way up to the giants, which were as much as ten microns across, or even larger? He took note as well of the chemical composition of the dust particles, and of their neutron counts and ionization status.

All this was a simple and quite easy part of the self-imposed duties of a Grand Galactic. Bill however had always found it among what one could call the most enjoyable duties. After all, his census would ultimately contribute to one of the great goals the Grand Galactics possessed.

So, like some eleventh-century Norman baron, what Bill was doing was riding his fields. The dust patch was what the baron's Saxon serfs would have called a fallow field, allowed to remain unplanted so that the soil could rest and regain its fertility.

Bill's patch didn't raise corn or oats. It raised only stars—big ones, little ones, all kinds; but the Grand Galactics preferred the big ones. Those giants—what humans would call the A's and B's and O's—could be counted on to rapidly burn up their initial stocks of hydrogen in the nuclear furnaces at their cores. Then, when that was gone, they would do the same with their helium, carbon, neon, magnesium—each element heavier than the one that came before, until they came to iron, which was the end of the line.

When a star's core has turned to iron, the nuclear furnace at its core weakens, until it can no longer fight off the terrible gravitational squeeze of the dead weight of its outer layers. The star collapses on itself. . . .

And then it rebounds in a titanic explosion, pouring out new treasuries of heavier elements still, manufactured in the condign heat of that explosion, to turn into tiny particles that will enrich the next patch of interstellar gas.

That was what would inevitably happen, sooner or later, in the normal course of events, and it didn't require any action on the part of Bill. It would be taken care of by those simple Newtonian-Einsteinian laws of gravitation that the Grand Galactics had never seen any reason to change.

As we say, "sooner or later," but the Grand Galactics preferred sooner. Bill chose to speed things up. He scanned a considerable volume of adjacent space and was lucky enough to find a trickle of nearby dark matter . . . coaxed it to flow into his patch . . . and was pleased. One of the Grand Galactics' main objectives was being helped along.

And what was that objective?

There is no way of expressing it in terms a human being could understand, but one step in its achievement was known to be an increase in the proportion of heavy elements to light—in this case "heavy" meaning those elements with at least twenty or so protons in their nuclei, along with crowds of neutrons. The kind of elements, that is, that the original creation of the universe had omitted entirely.

Changing all those light elements to heavy would take much work, and vast amounts of time . . . but time, after all, belonged to the Grand Galactics.

24

CALIFORNIA

The American East Coast might consider itself the center of power, of government, or of culture. (Of course, that would depend on which East Coast city you were talking about, New York, Washington, or Boston.) But in one very important way it was definitely inferior to the other edge of the North American continent. Oh, it wasn't the palm trees and the flowers blooming everywhere that thrilled the Subramanians. After all, Myra and Ranjit were Lankans, and a riot of exotic vegetation was their natural ambience. No, the best thing about California was that it was warm! It never got painfully cold, especially around the Los Angeles area, where it wasn't ever really cold at all.

So Pasadena, where Ranjit discovered he was based, was a great place to live. Well, it was if you didn't count the possibility of earthquakes. Or wildfires that could flatten a whole subdivision of homes in a dry year. Or floods that could pull down some other subdivision, one that had been built on precipitous lots because all the flat lots had been built on already, floods that were always ready to do this in a year when some relatively minor fire had killed off enough of the brush to weaken the ground's hold on the substrate.

Never mind. Those things might not happen. At least they might not before the Subramanian family had packed up and gone somewhere else. Meanwhile it was a splendid place to raise a child. Myra happily pushed Natasha's carriage through the local supermarket, along with all the other mothers doing the same, and thought she had never been so lucky in her life.

Ranjit, on the other hand, had some doubts.

Oh, he loved the good parts of their life in Southern California as much as Myra did. Took pleasure in their excursions to the points of interest that were so unlike anything in Sri Lanka, the La Brea tar pits in the heart of the city, where millennia of ancient beasts had been trapped and preserved for humans to wonder over well into this twenty-first century. The movie studios, with their brilliantly engineered rides and exhibits. (Myra had been a little doubtful about taking Tashy to such a chancy place, but in the event, Natasha chortled and loved it.) Griffith Observatory with its seismographs and telescopes and its grand picnic area overlooking the city.

What he didn't like was his job.

It gave him everything T. Orion Bledsoe had promised, that was true, and even a fair number of things Ranjit hadn't expected at all. He had his own private office, which was spacious (three meters by more than five) if windowless (because, like all the rest of this installation, it was nearly twenty meters underground) and furnished with a large desk and a large leather armchair for his own use and several less pricey other chairs, at a clear oak table, for guests and meetings. And no fewer than three separate computer terminals, with unlimited access to almost everything. Now all it took was pushing a few keys for Ranjit to get his personal copies of just about every mathematical journal there was in the world. Not only did he get the journals themselves—hard copies when there were hard copies to begin with, electronic copies when that was all the original "publishers" had produced. He also received translations—horribly expensive, but paid for by the agency, out of their apparently limitless bank account—of at least the abstracts from those journals that happened to be in languages Ranjit had no hope of ever comprehending.

What was wrong was that he had nothing to *do*.

The first few days were busy enough, because Ranjit had to be walked through the places where red tape was generated so that they could generate Ranjit's own contribution to the supply—identity badge to prepare, documents to sign, all the unavoidable flotsam of any large enterprise in the twenty-first century. Then nothing.

By the end of the first month, Ranjit, who was never grumpy, was waking up grumpy almost every workday morning. There was a cure. A prescribed dose of Natasha, along with one of Myra, usually cleared the symptoms up before he finished breakfast, but then by the time he came home for dinner, he was morose again. Apologetic about it, of course: "I don't mean to take it out on Tashy and you, Myra, but I'm just wasting time here. No one will tell me what I'm supposed to be doing. When I find someone to ask, he just gets all mock-deferential and says, Well, that would be up to me, wouldn't it?" But then, by the time he had finished dinner, and given Tashy her bath or changed her diaper or just dandled her on his knee, who could stay morose? Not Ranjit, and he was then his usual cheery self until the next time he had to get up to go to his nonwork.

By the end of the second month the depression was deeper. It took longer to lift, because, as Ranjit told his wife—over and over!—"It's worse than ever! I cornered Bledsoe today—not easy to do, because he's hardly ever in his office—and asked him point-blank what kind of work I was supposed to be doing. He gave me a dirty look, and do you know what he said? He said, 'If you ever find out, please tell me.' It seems he had orders from high up to hire me, but nobody ever told him what my job was to be."

"They wanted you because you're famous and you add class to the operation," his wife informed him.

"Good guess. I sort of had the same idea myself, but it can't be right. That whole operation's so secret nobody knows who's working in the next office."

"So do you want to quit?" Myra asked.

"Huh. Well, I don't think so. Don't know if I can, really, because I'm not sure what all I signed, but anyway I promised Gamini."

"Then," she said, "let's just learn to love it. Why don't you solve that P equals NP problem you talk about? And anyway, tomorrow's Saturday, so why don't we take Tashy to the zoo?"

The zoo, of course, was a delight, although in the rest of the world things were going as badly as ever. Recent developments? Well, Argentina's vast herds of cattle were keeling over by the thousands with a new variety of the old disease called bluetongue. It had just been confirmed that the plague was a biowarfare strain. What wasn't clear was who had spread it. Maybe Venezuela or Colombia, some people around the agency thought, because Argentina had contributed heavily to the international force that was trying to keep the Venezuelan and the Colombian armies apart. (They weren't very successful at it, but the Venezuelans and the Colombians hated them for trying.) The rest of the world was as unquiet as ever. In Iraq nightly outbreaks of car-bombings and beheadings showed that the two kinds of Iraqi Muslims were again trying to ensure that there was only one true Islamic faith by exterminating each other. In Africa the number of officially recognized wars had grown to fourteen, not counting several dozen tribal skirmishes. In Asia the Adorable Leader's North Koreans were issuing communiqué after communiqué charging most of the world's other states with spreading lies about them.

But in Pasadena nobody was fighting anybody, and little Tashy Subramanian was delighting her parents. What other infant so precociously tried to turn herself over in her crib at such an early age? Or even more precociously, at that same early age, slept nearly halfway through the night, on many nights, sometimes? Natasha Subramanian was bound to be a person of high intelligence, Myra and Ranjit agreed, no matter that Jingting Jian, the baby doctor the office's advisory service had helped them find, swore that you could tell nothing about a child's intelligence until it was at least four or five months old.

Though weak in that area, Dr. Jian was a very comforting pediatrician to have, full of tips on the diagnosis of infant crying. Some crying meant you had to do something right away; some could be ignored until the baby had cried itself out. Dr. Jian even had recordings of many of the possible crying styles to help them figure which was which. In fact, the advisers had done nearly everything that had had to be done for Myra and Ranjit. They had located for them the pretty little apartment in a gated development—four rooms, washer-dryer installed, access to the community swimming pool, its own plant-bedecked balcony that looked down on the city of Los Angeles from above, and, maybe most important of all in these times, its twenty-four-hour guard service to check every last person going in or out. The advisers had done more than that, too, helping them choose the best dry cleaners, pizza deliverers, banks, and car rental services (until the time when they might choose to buy a couple of cars for themselves, which time had not yet arrived).

They had even provided Myra with the names of three separate maid services, but Myra chose to decline them all. "The apartment's not that big," she told Ranjit. "What kind of housework is there to do? Vacuuming, cooking, laundry, dishes—just for the two of us there's not that much work involved."

Ranjit strongly agreed. "I'm sure you can handle it," he said, which got him a slightly frosty look.

"I'm sure we can," she corrected him. "Let's see. I'd better be the cook, because I'm better at it than you are, so you can clean up afterward? That would be good. Laundry—you can operate a washer and dryer, can't you? They've got all the instructions written out in their manuals, anyway. Changing the baby, feeding the baby—when you're home we can take turns. When you're not, I can do it myself."

Item by item they ran through the list of domestic jobs, from replacing used lightbulbs and toilet paper rolls to paying the bills. It wasn't a problem. Neither one of them wanted the other stuck at some chore that would keep him or her away from the other for a minute longer than necessary, because neither wanted to be so deprived of the other's talk and company.

At this point the armada of One Point Fives was cruising at its maximum speed of .94c. By the time scale of most non-Earth beings, it would reach its destination in a mere blink of time. Of course, no human being knew this, so all nine billion went right on with their usual daily concerns.

Then one evening, as the Subramanians were finishing the dinner cleanup, the voice from their intercom spoke up. "Dr. Subramanian? This is Henry, down at the gate. There's a man here who'd like to see you. He says he doesn't want to give his name but you'll know him because he's Maggie's ex-boyfriend. All right to let him in?"

Ranjit jumped to his feet. "Gamini!" he shouted. "Sure, let the bastard come in, and ask him what he'd like to drink!"

But when the man arrived, he wasn't Gamini Bandara at all. He was a much older man, carrying a locked case that was chained to his right arm. When he opened it, he took out a chip and handed it to Ranjit. "Please play this," he said. "I'm not authorized to see it, so I'll have to wait outside, but Mrs. Subramanian is specifically permitted, and"—he offered them a polite smile—"I'm sure the baby won't tell any secrets."

When the courier was safely stowed in the hallway, Myra fed the chip into their player, and a grinning Gamini appeared on the screen. "Sorry to put you through all this cloak-and-dagger stuff, but we're walking a tightrope here. We're answering to five different national governments, plus the UN's own security staff, and—well, I'll tell you all about that another time. The thing is, that other job we've been talking about for you is all cleared now, if you want it. You will. You'd be crazy if you didn't. However, before I answer all those questions, there is one little thing— No, to tell the truth, there's one extremely big thing that has to happen first. I can't say what it is, but you'll know it when you see it on the news, and then you can say good-bye to Pasadena. So stay loose, Ranj. That's all those intelligence agencies will let me say now—except love to you all!"

The chip ended and the screen went blank.

Ten minutes later, when the courier had retrieved his chip and departed, Myra pulled down from the top of the cupboard the bottle of wine they saved for special occasions. She filled two glasses, cocked an ear to where Natasha was sleeping, and, when satisfied about that, said, "Do you know what's going on?"

Ranjit clinked her glass and took a sip from his own before he said, "No." He sat silently for a moment, and then grinned. "All the same, if I can't trust Gamini, who can I trust? So we'll just have to wait and see."

Myra nodded, finished her glass, got up to check on Natasha, and said, "At least it doesn't sound like the waiting will be much longer."

It wasn't. It was only three days before Ranjit—doing his best to find a few more really large prime numbers for the cryptographers to play with, because his conscience wouldn't let him do nothing at all—heard a huge commotion in the hallway and discovered that half the staff was trying to get into the lounge at the end of the corridor. Everybody was clustered before the news channels. What the channels were displaying was a procession of military vehicles, scores of them, pouring through a gap in an unfamiliar fence. "Korea," a man near the screen called to quiet the questions. "They're going into North Korea! Now shut up so we can hear what they're saying."

And North Korea was indeed where they were heading, and none of the Adorable Leader's huge army seemed interested in trying to stop them!

"But that's crazy!" the man next to Ranjit was saying. "Something must've happened!"

He hadn't been looking to Ranjit for an answer, but Ranjit gave him one anyway. "I'm sure something did happen," he told the man, grinning. "Something big."

25

SILENT THUNDER

It had a formal name in the records of the Pentagon, but to the people who invented it, the people who built it, and the people who sent it on its way, it was called Silent Thunder.

In the dark of midnight Silent Thunder took off from its birthplace, which was in the old Boeing field outside of Seattle, Washington, and cruised westward at a leisurely thousand kilometers an hour. The choice of darkness wasn't to keep it from being seen by some enemy. That would have been impossible. Every conceivable enemy, and everybody else as well, owned a sky full of observation satellites, and those were watching everybody's every move.

But it was still dark when, several hours later, Silent Thunder completed its great circle crossing of the Pacific Ocean and dropped—"like a rock," its pilot said later—almost to sea level. There it slid over the waters between the islands of Honshu and Hokkaido and entered the Sea of Japan.

It was then that the darkness became an advantage to the people who ran Silent Thunder. Darkness meant no nosy newscasters on one of the Japanese islands would get a good look at it, and therefore news of it would not be showing up at everybody's breakfast table. The radars belonging to Japan's tiny armed forces in Aomori and Hakodate did light up, of course. They didn't matter. Japan didn't have enough weaponry to do anything about something like Silent Thunder. Anyway, twelve hours earlier the Japanese generals had been notified, in strict secrecy, that America would be sending an experimental aircraft around there, and it would be courteous of them to look the other way.

Once well into the Sea of Japan, Silent Thunder climbed again, leveling off at twelve thousand meters. Of course, the western shores of the sea were Russian, and of course, the radars there were a lot more numerous and powerful than Japan's. They didn't matter, either. Russian top brass, too, knew that Silent Thunder was no threat—that is, to them.

When its pilot and navigator agreed they had reached their aiming point, Silent Thunder slowed to just enough velocity to keep it in the air and began to deploy its armaments. Those armaments—a modest-yield nuclear bomb and a hollow copper tube no wider than a man's body—would have baffled the weapons specialists of even a decade earlier, but they were all Silent Thunder needed to do its job.

Inside the weapon's guidance system, a map of the Adorable Leader's North Korea appeared, overlaid by the long, narrow oval that was the footprint of the weapon.

No human being in Silent Thunder looked at that map, because no human being was there. Its captain—all of its crew—was back in Washington state, observing the map on a TV screen. "It looks all right to me," the pilot, an American, said to the bombardier, who happened to be Russian. "Deploy the masks."

"Right," said the bombardier, fingers on his keypad. Black shapes formed around the edges of the oval, tracing the course of the Yalu River on its north and west, the Demarcation Line that was the border with South Korea, and then the Pacific coast to the south and east. Those shapes were nothing tangible, of course. Nothing made of matter could have survived what they needed to mask off, and devising the electronic fields that could do the masks' job had been one of the trickiest parts of building Silent Thunder. "All set," the bombardier reported to the pilot.

"Position still okay?" the pilot asked the Chinese navigator, and when the navigator reported that it was, the pilot crossed himself. (He thought of himself as a lapsed Catholic, but there were times when he didn't feel lapsed at all.) "Fire the weapon," he ordered the bombardier, and for the first time in the history of the world, a nation lost a war—totally, irrevocably lost it—without anyone getting hurt.

Actually, that wasn't quite true.

A few heart patients in the Adorable Leader's domain did die. They were the ones who were unlucky enough to be wearing pacemakers when the electromagnetic blast struck, carrying more energy than a stroke of lightning. (But about the only North Koreans with access to any technology that expensive—that *Western*—were high-ranking officials. They weren't missed.) Oh, and there were a handful of unfortunates flying in light planes who did not survive the consequent crashes. (As high-ranking as the others, and no more mourned.) In all, the latest regime change in North Korea came about with far fewer casualties than an average holiday weekend on the Western world's highways.

In a fraction of a second all the Adorable Leader's telephone systems were disabled. Most of his power lines were short-circuited. Every weapon his nation owned that was any more complex than a shotgun would fire no more—and the Adorable Leader's North Korean nation had owned a vast number of weapons of all kinds. Without telephones or radios no one knew what was happening any farther away than a shout could be heard. The nation was no longer a threat to anyone, because no real nation existed anymore on that plot of ground.

There was, it is true, one small actual battle in this nonwar.

That was because of one obdurate colonel stationed outside of Kaesong. He could not, of course, understand what had happened, but at least he recognized that his army was at risk. He did what many colonels would have done. He fell out his command, issued them whatever rifles and pistols would fire, and launched them on an attack across the line.

It didn't get very far.

It didn't even get them all the way through the dense minefields that bracketed the Demarcation Line. Half a dozen of his frontline soldiers fell when mines went off, a score more as the South Korean troops on the south side of the line saw them coming and opened fire . . . and then ceased fire again, when they saw that the North Koreans were still coming forward, but slowly and cautiously now, and with their hands above their heads.

By then, of course, the whole world was beginning to learn what was going on . . . and not just our own world, either.

The rest of the galaxy heard the electronic roar of that weapon only as it reached them by the sluggish crawl—a mere 300,000 kilometers (old-fashioned people, and Americans, still said 186,000 miles) per second—of the velocity of light.

The One Point Fives' armada, being fifteen light-years from Earth at the time of the blast, eventually crossed paths with the roar, which they detected had originated from those very beings they were on their way to annihilate.

No one on Earth knew that, of course.

Contrariwise, no one among the Machine-Stored, or any other part of the hegemony of the Grand Galactics, knew what had just occurred in North Korea, either. Therefore, when they heard that raucous electronic belch, they drew some reasonable, but wrong, conclusions.

It took years for that electromagnetic white noise to get to the home planets of any of the races subject to the Grand Galactics. Especially to that wrinkle in dark-matter flows that was home to the nearest cluster of the Grand Galactics themselves. And it had a bad effect. Potentially, indeed, it could have been a tragically, even terminally, bad one.

The difficulty was the nature of the weapon its owners called Silent Thunder.

Most human weapons were not a problem, since they depended either on chemical explosions or nuclear ones for their effect. Such puny events caused no fear in the nonbaryonic Grand Galactics. Silent Thunder, however, was a different kettle of particles. It could endanger parts of the Grand Galactics' own armorarium. Not, of course, the trivial early version that had just put the Adorable Leader out of business, but the more advanced specimens that these pesky humans were bound to come up with before long—if they were allowed to.

Of course, they weren't going to be allowed to. Their total annihilation was already on the schedule. When it had taken place, the problem would no longer exist.

Which meant, in the famous old words of William Schwenck Gilbert, as Ko-Ko explains his transgression to the Mikado, When an order is given, it's as good as done, so actually it is done.

Up until that point the question of the wiping-out of the human race had been, in some sense, not totally resolved. That is, the Grand Galactics themselves, having given the order, had continued checking up on the situation because of the remote possibility that circumstances would change and they might want to cancel the order.

They did that no more. They saw no reason to go on bothering their heads (that is, if they had had heads) with this particular question.

So they erased it from their consciousness (or consciousnesses) in favor of more urgent, and certainly more entertaining, matters. High on that list were, one, a white dwarf star just on the point of stealing enough matter from its red-giant partner to go Type Ia supernova, two, some communications from their opposite numbers in other galaxies that needed at least to be acknowledged, and three, the question of whether to split off another Bill-like fraction of themselves to pay closer attention to the small and fast-moving minor galaxy whose orbit would cause the galaxy to crash into their own at any moment now—well, within the next four or five million years at the latest.

Very low on their list was anything that might remind them of that nasty little planet that its occupants called Earth. Why should they care? All of this was not, after all, an unprecedented experience for the Grand Galactics. In the thousands of millions of years since they had become, willy-nilly, the overlords of that part of the universe, they had encountered some 254 similarly dangerous races, and terminated some 251 of them. (The other three, whose offenses were marginal, were given another chance.)

It was not likely that the humans of Earth would become a fourth.

26

ON THE THRESHOLD
OF PEACE

Back on Earth, there was confusion and worry. A mostly joyful confusion, to be sure, because hardly anybody in the world objected to the fact that the Adorable Leader—with his shyness and winsome apologetic public proclamations and, oh, yes, his million-man-strong army with all its rockets and nukes—was history. But questions were asked. By what right had America destroyed another country? And how the devil had they accomplished it?

No one answered. The American government merely said that the matter was under review and a statement would be issued, but didn't say when. Military scientists around the world wished they had the wreckage of Silent Thunder to study. They didn't, though. All that was left of Silent Thunder was a haze of white-hot liquid metal particles, rapidly cooling.

The news services were doing their best. Within an hour of when Silent Thunder had done its snuffing-out of the Adorable Leader's North Korea, news copters from South Korea and Japan were circling over the now electronically silent land.

There was nothing to hear, but much to see. Their cameras picked up the crowds milling around in the vast, and normally deserted, avenues of Pyongyang, or the smaller groups that stood helplessly beside their unworkable aircraft at now-useless air force bases, or the even tinier groups that, sometimes, could not control their rage and confusion and took it out by firing their impotent arms at the interlopers.

Some of those cameras picked up other things. A few detected other helicopters, for instance, also circling out of range of any persons with hand weapons.

These other aircraft came from the same cities as the news reporters. Their mission, however, was not to observe. It was to inform. Every one of them was equipped with powerful loudspeakers, and each loudspeaker was manned by a former North Korean refugee. Each of them circled over the towns and neighborhoods they had come from, and each speaker introduced himself by name as he repeated his (or her) four-part message:

"The reign of the so-called Adorable Leader is over. He will be tried for the crimes of betraying, mistreating, and starving a whole generation of our people.

"The North Korean army is now disbanded. It serves no useful purpose. No one is going to attack you. And all soldiers are now free to return to their homes and resume their peacetime occupations.

"Ample supplies of food and other necessities are on their way to you right now. Every one of you, from this day forward, is guaranteed, for life, a diet adequate for health and growth.

"Finally, you now will have the right to choose by secret ballot who will govern you."

And to that, many of the broadcasters added, often with tears running down their cheeks, "And I am coming *home!*"

27

PAX PER FIDEM

Gamini didn't keep his colleagues waiting for clarification. Not more than thirty-six hours, anyway, and for that particular length of time they—like the rest of the world—had plenty to keep them occupied. It wasn't work that obsessed them. It was the media, with their unending scenes of outside forces pouring in, unopposed and nearly unarmed, too, unless you counted their noisemakers and shock-givers, moving in on the previously impregnable fortress that had been the Adorable Leader's North Korea. Add to that the still more endless chatter of guess and supposition and bafflement that every commentator had to offer.

Then at last something appeared on the screen that at least promised to give some answers.

It was after dinner, and also after Myra had taken her turn at putting the baby to bed, that Ranjit again snapped on the TV. A moment later he gave a yelp of surprise that brought her back into the room. "Look," he said. "Maybe we're going to get some real information."

What the TV was displaying was an Asian-looking man who stood before a lectern. No one introduced him. He simply began to speak. "Hello," he said, voice educated and quite unflustered at being before the cameras. "My name is Aritsune Meyuda, and at one time I was Japan's ambassador to the United Nations. Now I am what I think you would call the personnel director for what we have been calling Pax per Fidem. That's short for Pax in Orbe Terrarum per Fidem, or World Peace Through Transparency. We are the ones who are responsible for the events on the Korean peninsula.

"Because that operation had to be conducted in secrecy, there has been much speculation about it, and about what has gone on there since. We can now supply some answers for you. To explain how those events came about, and what they mean, the person who made them all possible will speak."

Meyuda's face disappeared from the screen, replaced by the image of a tall, bronzed, and aged but strongly built figure, the sight of whom produced a gasp from Myra. "Oh my God," she said. "That's— That's—"

But before she got it out, Meyuda was already introducing him. "I give you," he said, "the secretary-general of the United Nations, Mr. Ro'onui Tearii."

Ro'onui Tearii troubled no more with prefacing remarks than had Meyuda. "Let me begin," he said, "by giving every one of you my assurance that nothing improper has occurred in Korea. This was not a war of conquest. It was a necessary police action, approved by a secret, but unanimous, vote of the United Nations Security Council.

"To explain how this came about I would like to clear up a matter that dates from a few years ago. Many of you will remember that at that time there was much discussion about the way in which the three most powerful nations in the world—that is, Russia, China, and the United States—were attempting to arrange a superpower conference, with the laudable stated aim of finding a solution to the many little wars that were breaking out all around the world. Many commentators thought that what then happened was ludicrous, even shameful, because of a story that was given out. The rumor was that their plan fell apart because the three nations could not agree on the city in which to hold the conference.

"In truth, however, I must now tell you that that whole episode was a deception. That was done at my request. It was needed to conceal the fact that the three presidents were actually conducting highly secret meetings on a subject of transcendental importance.

"Their subject was simply how—and when, and indeed whether—to employ a new nonlethal, but powerfully destructive, weapon, the one which we all now know by the name Silent Thunder.

"What caused them to take this exceptional action was that each of them had learned, through their quite effective intelligence services, that both of the other states had developed a Silent Thunder–like weapon and were rushing to make it operational. And all three of the presidents had advisers who were urging them to be the first to complete the development of the weapon, and then to use it to destroy the economies of their two adversaries and thus become the world's only superpower again.

"To their everlasting credit, they all rejected that plan. In their secret meetings they agreed to turn Silent Thunder over to the United Nations." He was somberly silent for a moment—a big and imposing man, said once to have been the strongest man on Maruputi, the tiny French Polynesian island where he had been born. Then he smiled. "And they did," he announced, "and so the world was spared a terrible conflict, with unguessable results."

By then Myra and Ranjit were giving each other startled looks almost as much as they were watching the screen. That was not the end of it. There was a great deal more, and, sleep deferred, indeed forgotten, they kept on listening. For nearly an hour, actually—for all the time Secretary-General Tearii was speaking, and then for the much longer time when all the world's political commentators went over every word of it in their own debates. And by the time Ranjit and Myra were preparing for bed, they were still trying to make sense of it.

"So what Tearii did," Ranjit called while brushing his teeth, "was to organize this Pax per Fidem thing, with its people from twenty different countries—"

"And all of them neutral ones," Myra pointed out from where she was fluffing up the pillows on their bed. "And not only that but they were all island nations that weren't big enough to be a threat to anybody else anyway."

Ranjit thoughtfully rinsed his mouth. "Actually," he said, drying his face, "when you look at the results, all of that doesn't sound all that bad, does it?"

"Not really," Myra conceded. "It's true that North Korea has always seemed to be a threat to world peace."

Ranjit stared at his reflection in the mirror. "Ah, well," he said at last. "If Gamini's coming, I wish he'd get here."

When Gamini did get there, he bore flowers for Myra, a giant Chinese rattle for the baby, a bottle of Korean whiskey for Ranjit, and a full load of apologies. "Sorry I took so long," he said, kissing Myra chastely on the cheek and sparing a hug for Ranjit. "I didn't mean to leave you hanging, but I was in Pyongyang with my father, just checking to see that it was all going all right, and then we had to make a quick trip to Washington. The president's mad at us."

Ranjit looked immediately concerned. "Mad how? Are you saying he didn't want you people to attack?"

"Oh, of course not. Nothing like that. The thing was that right along the border, at one stretch that was kind of kinky because of the terrain, there happened to be a couple of hectares of U.S. and South Korean defense matériel that got just as wiped out as the North's stuff." He shrugged.

"We couldn't help it, you know. Old Adorable had a lot of his meanest armaments right on his side of the line, and it's a pretty narrow line. We had to make sure we got it all. The president knows that, of course, but somebody made the mistake of guaranteeing him that nothing American would be touched. Meanwhile there's about fourteen billion dollars' worth of America's deadliest high-tech that doesn't work anymore. And, Ranj, are you ever going to open that bottle?"

Ranjit, who had been regarding his boyhood chum with unalloyed wonder, obeyed, while Myra collected glasses. As he poured, Ranjit said, "Does that mean trouble?"

"Oh, not enough to worry about. He'll get over it. And, listen, while he's what we're talking about, he gave me something to hand to you."

That something was an envelope embossed with the White House official seal. When they had all been served and Ranjit had taken his first sip—and made a face—he opened the letter. It said:

Dear Mr. Subramanian:

On behalf of the people of the United States I thank you for your service. I must now relieve you of your present post, however, and ask you to take on an even more important one, which, I am afraid, entails even more secrecy.

"He signed it with his own hand, too," Gamini said proudly. "Didn't use one of those machines. I saw him do it."

Ranjit set down the unfinished part of his drink, the part that was going to remain unfinished forever, and said, "Gamini, how much of this show are you personally running?"

Gamini laughed. "Me? Hardly any. I'm an errand boy for my father. He tells me what to do, and I do it. Like helping recruit the Nepalese."

"Which I've been wanting to ask you about," Myra said, tactfully sniffing the whiskey's bouquet without actually tasting any of it. "Why Nepalese?"

"Well, two reasons. First, their great-grandfathers used to serve in the British army—they were called the Gurkhas—and they were about the toughest and smartest soldiers they had. And, the most important part, just look at them. Nepalese don't look a bit like Americans, or Chinese, or Russians, so everybody in North Korea wasn't trained from birth to hate them." He sniffed his whiskey, sighed, and put it down. "They're like you and me, Ranj," he added. "One reason we can be so useful to Pax per Fidem. So what about it? Can I sign you up tonight?"

"Tell us more," Myra said quickly, before Ranjit had a chance to speak. "What would you want Ranjit to do?"

Gamini grinned. "Well, not what we were going to offer you way back when. What I was thinking of then was that you could help me be an assistant to my father, but you weren't famous then."

"But now?" Myra prompted.

"Actually, we'll have to work that out," Gamini confessed. "You'd go to work for the council and they would probably have some requests to make of you—speak for them at press conferences, sell the idea of Pax per Fidem to the world—"

Ranjit gave his friend a mock-frown that was not entirely imitation. "Wouldn't I have to know more about it to do that?"

Gamini sighed. "Good old Ranjit," he said. "I was hoping you'd see the light and sign up right away, but, yes, I suppose that, you being you, you certainly would need to know more. So I brought some reading for you."

He reached into his briefcase and pulled out an envelope of papers. "Let's call this your homework, Ranj. I guess the best thing would be for you to read it—both of you—and talk it over tonight, and then tomorrow I'll come by to take you to breakfast, and then I'll ask you the big question."

"And what question is that?" Ranjit asked.

"Why, whether you want to help us save the world. What did you think?"

Natasha got a little less playtime that night than she was used to. She gave her parents a few little wails to show that she had noticed the lack, but two minutes later she was asleep and Myra and Ranjit could go back to studying their homework.

There were two sets of papers. One seemed to be a sort of proposed constitution for (they supposed) the land that had formerly been the North Korea of one dictator or another. Both Ranjit and Myra read it attentively, of course, but most of it was procedural stuff—like the American constitution that both had read in school. Not entirely like the American, though. There were several paragraphs unlike anything in that document. One stated that the country would never go to war under any circumstances— that sounded more like the post–World War II Japanese constitution the Americans had written for them. Another wasn't in any constitution they had ever heard of before; it described some rather unusual methods of selecting their officeholders that involved heavy usage of computers. And a third pledged that every institution in the country—including not just their government legislatures at all levels, but educational, scientific, and even religious institutions—had to permit access of observers at all of their functions. ("I guess that's the 'transparency' Gamini was talking about," Ranjit observed.)

The other document was about more tangible things. It described how the secretary-general, with maximum secrecy, had set about creating his twenty-member independent council to run Pax per Fidem. It listed the members, ranging from the Bahamas, Brunei, and Cuba to Tonga and Vanuatu (with Sri Lanka tucked in just before). And it was a little more specific about the concept of transparency. In the interests of this "transparency" Pax per Fidem was charged to create an independent inspectorate for which the organization was pledged to offer that same transparency. "I guess that 'inspectorate' would be where you would go," Myra said as they turned the light out.

Ranjit yawned. "Maybe so, but I'm going to need a clearer picture of what I'd be supposed to do before I say I'll do it."

The next morning Gamini did his best to answer all their questions. "I talked to my father a little bit about how much freedom you'd have. It's a lot, Ranj. He's sure that you could go anywhere in Pax per Fidem and see anything we're doing, with the single exception of anything to do with Silent Thunder: You won't know how many of the weapons we have or what we'd like to do with them, because nobody below the council itself will. But anything else, sure. You can sit in on most council meetings, and if you've seen anything that you think is wrong, you can report it to them."

"And just suppose," Myra said, "that he did see something wrong and the council didn't do anything to fix it."

"Then he would be free to tell the world's press about it," Gamini said promptly. "That's what transparency is all about. So what do you say? Any other questions before you say if you'll join us?"

"A few," Ranjit said mildly. "This council. They meet, right? And what do they talk about when they do?"

"Well," Gamini said, "it's mostly planning for every contingency. You don't do a regime change without making sure the population has a viable society left after the change; we learned that from Germany after 1918 and Iraq after 2003. And it's not just making sure the population has its food, and as soon as possible its electrical power, and its working police force to prevent looting and so on; it's giving them a chance at forming their own government. And, of course, there's the future. There are plenty of brush-fire wars and threats of war going on, and the council keeps an eye on all of them."

"Wait a minute," Myra said. "Are you talking about doing that Silent Thunder thing in other parts of the world?"

Gamini gave her a fond smile. "Dear Myra," he said, "whatever made you think we were going to stop with North Korea?"

Then, taking notice of the expressions on their faces, he sounded hurt. "What's the matter? You aren't saying you don't trust us, are you?"

It was Myra who answered—or, more exactly, responded, because it certainly was not a specific answer to Gamini's specific question. "Gamini, did you ever happen to read the book *1984*? It was published in England around the middle of the last century, by a man named George Orwell."

Gamini looked offended. "Of course I read it. My father was a big Or-well fan. Are you trying to suggest we sound like Big Brother? Because, don't forget, the secretary-general had the unanimous approval of the Se-curity Council for everything we did!"

"That's not what I mean, dear Gamini. What I'm thinking about is the way Orwell had the world divided in his book. There were only three pow-ers, because they'd conquered everything else. Oceania, by which Orwell meant mostly America; Eurasia—that was Russia, then still the Soviet Union; and Eastasia. China."

Now Gamini was visibly annoyed. "Now, really, Myra! You don't think that the countries that created Pax per Fidem are going to try to divide the world among them, do you?"

And again Myra replied with a question of her own. "What any of them are planning I don't know, Gamini. I hope that's not it. But if they were, what could stop them?"

And when Gamini was gone—still a friend, a very dear friend, but now a friend they would not be seeing very often—Ranjit turned to his wife. "So," he said, "what do we do now? The president has fired me from the job here. I've turned down the job he—and Gamini—wanted me to take." He frowned at a thought. "His father wanted me to take it, too," he added. "I imagine he's not happy that I turned it down. I wonder if that offer of a job at the university is still open."

28

MAKING A LIFE

Well, the job was. Whatever faults Dr. Dhatusena Bandara might be charged with, vindictiveness was not among them. The university would be delighted to welcome Dr. (if only honorary) Ranjit Subramanian to the faculty as a full and tenured professor, with his employment (and thus his pay) to begin at once, actual work to start when the professor found it quite convenient. More than that, the university would be pleased to find a faculty position for Dr. (this time not honorary but fully earned) Myra de Soyza Subramanian as well. Of course, it went without saying, her title wouldn't be as elevated as her husband's, and neither would her pay scale. But still . . .

But still, they were going back to Sri Lanka!

If the president of the United States objected to Ranjit's walking out on the job offer, he didn't say anything about it. Neither did anyone else. Ranjit cleared out his few personal belongings at the office; true, there was a maintenance man, who happened also to be a security man, to help him pack everything up. True, he was required to turn in his passes and badges and IDs. But no one bothered them in their apartment, or at the air terminal, or on the planes they took. And Natasha rode in her cradle-seat between the two of them without a whimper.

Mevrouw Vorhulst, of course, was waiting for them at the Colombo airport, since it was obvious that the best thing was for them all to stay at her house again. "Just until we find an apartment," Myra said, while being hugged by her.

"As long as you like," said Mevrouw Vorhulst. "Joris wouldn't have it any other way."

There was a strange thing about those classrooms at the university, Ranjit found. When his principal dearest wish had been to get out of them, they had seemed oppressively small. Not now, not to a brand-new professor who had never faced a class before. Now the room was a vast jury box, packed with young men and women sitting in judgment on him. Their eyes were unerringly focused on his every move, their ears impatient for the great revelations Professor Subramanian would have for them of the innermost secrets of the world of mathematicians.

It wasn't just how to nurture this nest of hungry hatchlings that baffled Ranjit. It was what to nurture them with. When the university's search committee had welcomed him to the faculty, they had generously left the exact nature of his duties to his own good plan.

He didn't have one.

Ranjit was aware that he needed help. He even had a hope of finding it in the person of Dr. Davoodbhoy, the man who had behaved so exemplarily in the matter of the stolen math teacher's password.

He was not only still at the university. He had, in the natural attrition of deaths and retirements, already moved up a terrace or two along the slope of authority. All the same, when Ranjit applied to him for help, there wasn't much available. "Oh, Ranjit," he said. "May I still call you Ranjit? You know how it is. Our little university doesn't have many world-famous stars. The search committees want you here very much, but they don't have a clue about what to do with you. You do realize that you don't actually have to do much teaching? We don't have many faculty members who specialize in research instead, but that is a possibility."

"Huh," Ranjit said thoughtfully. He went on thinking for a moment, then said, "I suppose I might take a look at some of the famous old problems like Riemann, Goldbach, Collatz—"

"Certainly," Davoodbhoy said, "but don't give up on teaching until you try it. Why don't we set up a couple of quick seminars for practice? That sort of thing we can do on short notice." And then as Ranjit prepared to leave, turning that idea over in his mind, Davoodbhoy said, "Oh, and one more thing, Ranjit. You were right about Fermat and I was wrong. I haven't had to say that very often in my life. It leads me to want to trust your judgment."

It was pleasing for Ranjit to know that the provost trusted his judgment. Ranjit himself, however, was not quite as trusting. His first seminar was called Foundations of Number Theory. "I'll give them a sort of overview of the whole subject," he promised Davoodbhoy, who immediately started the wheels in motion. It would run for six weeks, four-hour classes, limited to juniors, seniors, and graduate students and a class size no larger than twenty-five.

The subject, of course, was one Ranjit had paid little attention to since he was fourteen and just beginning his fascination with Fermat's jotting. So he mined the university library for texts and taught out of them, trying to keep at least a dozen pages ahead of the dismayingly bright and worrisomely quick students who had signed up for the seminar.

Unfortunately, it didn't take them long to figure out what he was doing. That night he confessed to Myra, "I'm boring them. They can read from the book as well as I can."

"That," she said loyally, "is ridiculous." But then, as he repeated some of the quite respectful but unimpressed comments students had made, she thought more carefully. "I know," she said. "You need to make a little more personal contact with them. Do some of those binary arithmetic tricks for them, why don't you?"

Ranjit, having no better idea of his own, did. He did the Russian multiplication and the finger-counting and the one where he wrote down the heads-tails permutations of a row of coins of unknown length—he used actual coins, and let the students blindfold him while someone covered up a part of the row. Myra had been right. The students were amused. One or two of them begged for more, which sent Ranjit to the library's stacks, where he found an ancient copy of a Martin Gardner book on mathematical games and puzzles, and so he got through the six weeks of the seminar unscathed.

Or so he thought.

Then Dr. Davoodbhoy invited him to drop by for a chat. "I hope you won't mind, Ranjit," he said, pouring them each a stemmed glass of sherry, "but now and then, especially when we're trying something new, we ask the students themselves for comments. I've just been going over the comment sheets on your seminar."

"Huh," said Ranjit. "I hope they're all right."

The provost sighed. "Not entirely, I'm afraid," he said.

Indeed they were not entirely all right, Ranjit admitted that night at dinner. "Some of them said I was giving them nightclub magician tricks instead of math," he told his wife and Mevrouw. "And nearly all of them didn't like being taught right out of the book."

"But I thought they enjoyed the tricks," Mevrouw Vorhulst said, frowning.

"I suppose they did—in a way—but they said it wasn't what they had signed up for." He moodily peeled an orange. "I guess it wasn't, either. I just don't know what they want."

Myra patted his hand, accepting an orange wedge. "Well," she said, "that's why you did this seminar, isn't it? To see if this format would work? And apparently it didn't, so now you'll try something else." She wiped the orange juice from her lips, leaned forward, kissed the top of his head. "So let's give Tashy her bath, and then you and I can go for a swim in the pool to cheer ourselves up."

All of which they did. It did cheer them up, too. When you came right down to it, just about everything about living in the Vorhulst household was cheering. The staff was visibly proud of their distinguished guests and, of course, quite infatuated with Natasha as well. True, Myra was still spending an hour or two most days searching for a flat for the three of them to move into, but no such flat appeared. Some seemed promising at first encounter, but Mevrouw Vorhulst helpfully pointed out the hidden flaws: bad neighborhood, long commute to the university, rooms that were tiny or dark or both. Oh, there were a thousand flaws a flat might have that would make it wrong for the Subramanians, and Beatrix Vorhulst was assiduous at finding them. "Of course," Myra told her husband in one night's pillow talk, "she really just wants us to stay, you know. With Joris away I think she's lonely."

Ranjit drowsily said, "Huh." Then, yawning, "You know, there could be worse things than just staying here."

Which was inarguably true. Chez Vorhulst their every need was met without effort on their part, and the price was certainly right. Ranjit had pleaded to be allowed to reimburse the Vorhulst family for at least the out-of-pocket expenses involved in housing them. Mevrouw declined. Declined affectionately and fondly, but definitely declined. "Oh, well," Ranjit said to Myra as they lounged beside the pool that evening. "If it gives her pleasure to spoil us rotten, why should we deprive her?"

If Ranjit had a wish, it was that the outside world would be as pleasing. It wasn't. The example of Korea notwithstanding, the globe of Earth was still pockmarked with small wars and acts of violence. There had been a sort of hiccupy pause right after Silent Thunder, while combatants worldwide hesitated in case they were next. They weren't. Silent Thunder was not immediately repeated, and within a month the guns and the bombs outside North Korea were back to normal.

From time to time Ranjit wished that Gamini Bandara might drop by to give him the inside word on what was going on. He didn't. Probably too busy straightening things out in the former North Korea, Ranjit supposed. Indeed, a great deal was going on there. Power was flowing back into the country's struck transmission lines. Farms that had been abandoned because the men who would have worked them had been drafted into the army were being tilled once more. Even the actual manufacturing of consumer goods was beginning to happen. There were even puzzling reports of elections being planned. Curious ones, that neither the Subramanians nor anyone they spoke to could quite figure out. Computers seemed to be heavily involved, but in precisely what way no one could say.

Still, Myra and Ranjit admitted to each other, in their nightly wrapped-in-each-other's-arms dialogues, most events seemed to be going at least a little better, or at least a little less badly, than before Silent Thunder had deposed a regime. Most things, that is. Not necessarily including Ranjit's academic career.

The trouble with Ranjit's academic career was that he couldn't seem to get it started. After the dismal response to his first seminar, he was determined not to suffer a similar fate for his second attempt.

But what should it be? After much thought, he decided this one would be a recapitulation, step by step, of the long story of his involvement, and ultimate success, with Fermat's legacy. Dr. Davoodbhoy agreed to schedule it, remarking temperately that it was at least worth a try.

The students, however, didn't agree. Apparently, word had gotten around of his poor teaching skills, and although a few did sign up, a considerably larger number asked questions about it, temporized, and finally gave it a pass. Most seemed to think that Ranjit had already pretty well covered that ground, in speeches and interviews, anyway. The seminar was canceled.

Ranjit considered the research option. There were, to start, the famous seven unsolved problems proposed by the Clay Mathematics Institute at the dawn of the twenty-first century—not only interesting problems in themselves but, through the generosity of the institute, each one coming with a million-dollar reward for a solution.

So Ranjit accessed the list and thoughtfully pondered it. Some were pretty abstruse, even for him. Still, there was the Hodge conjecture and the Poincaré, the Riemann hypothesis—no, no, at least some of them had been solved and the prize collected. And, of course, the biggest of all: P = NP.

No matter how much Ranjit pondered over them, they remained remote. He could not work up the feeling that had gripped him the first time he'd seen what Fermat had scribbled in his margin. Myra offered one theory: "Maybe you just aren't fourteen anymore."

But that wasn't it. Fermat's proof had been an entirely different matter. It hadn't ever been presented to him as a problem that he should try to solve. One of the greatest minds in the history of mathematics had boasted that he had a proof for that final theorem. All Ranjit had to do was figure it out.

He tried to explain to Myra. "Did you ever hear of a man named George Dantzig? He was a graduate student at UC Berkeley in 1939. He came late to a class and saw two equations that the professor had written on the blackboard. Dantzig thought they were a homework assignment, so he copied them down and took them home and solved them.

"Only," he told her, "they weren't homework. The professor had put them up there as two problems in statistical mathematics that no one had been able to solve."

Myra pursed her lips. "So what you're saying," she said, "is if Dantzig had known that, he might not have been able to solve them. Is that right?"

Ranjit shrugged. "Maybe."

Myra availed herself of her husband's favorite reply to puzzling remarks. "Huh," she said.

Which made him grin. "Good," he said. "So now let's give Tashy a swimming lesson."

No one who knew little Natasha de Soyza Subramanian thought for one instant that she was not an exceptionally bright child. Toilet trained at under a year, first steps a month later, first clearly articulated word—it was "Myra"—less than a month after that. And all of those things Tashy had accomplished on her own.

It wasn't that her mother didn't have things she yearned to teach her daughter. She had many of them, but Myra was too intelligent to try to teach them all at once. So she limited parental lessons for her less-than-two-year-old to two subjects. One was singing, or at least vocalizing sounds that matched the ones Myra sang for her. The other was how to swim.

From the edge of the Vorhulst pool, his feet dangling in the water, Ranjit beamed at the two of them. He had learned not to rush to rescue his child whenever she slipped under the surface for a moment. "She'll always come up by herself," Myra promised, as indeed Natasha always did. "And anyway, I'm right here."

Later, when Tashy was dry and contentedly playing with her toes in her playpen beside the pool, while her mother frowned over the news reports on her portable screen, Ranjit peeked over Myra's shoulder. Of course the news was bad. When had it not been?

"It would be so nice," he said thoughtfully, "if something nice happened." And then something did.

Its name was Joris Vorhulst. When Ranjit walked in the door after another day of sitting in his little university office and trying to figure out how to earn his salary, he heard sounds of laughter. The ladylike elderly chuckle he quickly identified as Mevrouw Vorhulst, the less restrained giggles were his own dear wife, while the baritone and definitely male one was—

Ranjit very nearly ran the dozen meters to where they were gathered on the sunporch. "Joris!" he cried. "I mean, Dr. Vorhulst! I can't tell you how glad I am to see you!"

As soon as he said it, he realized how true it was. For days he had been wishing for someone like his old Astronomy 101 teacher—no, not someone like him! That specific person! That Joris Vorhulst who had made his astronomy course the only class in Ranjit's experience that he'd yearned to have taken sooner. And who—maybe—could help Ranjit solve his own teaching problems.

The first thing to be settled was that it wasn't to be "Dr. Vorhulst" anymore. "After all," he said, "it's one full professor talking to another now, even if I'm on extended leave to work on the Skyhook."

Which, of course, demanded that Vorhulst give everyone a report on just how the space ladder was getting along. Very well, he assured them. "We've already begun deploying the micron-size cable. Once we get a decent start on that, we'll start doubling up, and then things will really begin to move because we'll be able to start using the ladder itself to lift material to LEO instead of all those damn rockets. . . . Not," he added quickly, "that they're not doing a hell of a job. It moves fast because the big boys are all moving it. Russia, China, America—they've just about turned their whole space programs over to getting the ladder going. I've been checking all their launch sites for two months now." He held out his glass for a refill. "And they've already got started on the ground terminal down on the southeast coast. That's why I'm in Lanka today; I've got to go down there and prepare a report for the three presidents."

"I'd love to see that myself," Ranjit said wistfully.

"Sure you would. So would anybody from Astronomy 101, I hope, but don't go just yet. What's there now is a couple hundred pieces of earthmoving machinery, all going at once, and I think it's up to nearly three thousand construction workers getting in one another's way. Give it a few months and we'll go down for a visit together. Anyway, it's all top secret right now—I think the Americans are afraid the Bolivians or the Easter Islanders or somebody will steal their ideas and build a skyhook of their own. You would need really top security clearances to get in."

Ranjit was about to assure his old teacher that he had the best security clearances a human being could possess, when he stopped himself, wondering if they had all been revoked. And by then Vorhulst was saying, "And what about you, Ranjit? Outside of finding the Fermat proof and marrying the best-looking AI scientist in Sri Lanka, what've you been doing?"

It turned out that Joris Vorhulst had heard a great deal about the adventures of his former pupil and wanted to hear a lot more. That took them right up to dinner. Ranjit was hesitant about asking for help in front of the whole household, and anyway Aunt Beatrix had been watching news programs and had a lot of questions. "They're sending barges full of old tanks and self-propelled guns and things like that out into the China Sea and dumping them into the water," she informed the group. "To make false reefs where fish will breed, they say. And they showed clips of a kind of guillotine they have, like the ones from the French Revolution only they're five stories high, and they're using those to chop up their ICBMs. I imagine they drain the fuel and the warheads first."

"They strip them of recyclable metals first, too," Joris informed his mother. "I saw trainloads of the stuff going west through Siberia; the Russians called it part of Korea's reparations bill. And have you heard about the elections they've got scheduled?"

"Heard about them, certainly," Myra responded. "Understand them, not a chance."

Joris gave her a rueful grin. "Me, too. But in China I ran into a woman who'd been there, and she tried to explain it to me. The first thing is that the basic unit for voting isn't the town or precinct the voter lives in. It's an arbitrary group of ten thousand people, all over the country, who were born on the same day. And from those ten thousand there's a group of thirty-five, randomly computer-selected, who will run the group. Those thirty-five do meet; they spend one week a month in session somewhere in Korea, and they elect from their own membership a presider—sort of like a mayor—and a legislature to take care of things like issuing permits and planning construction projects. And they name judges and elect representatives to the national legislature and so on."

"Sounds complicated," his mother commented. "Also, that part about selecting them at random by computer? That was suggested thirty years or so ago by a science-fiction writer."

Joris nodded. "They have all the best ideas, don't they? Anyway, the system can't work until they get their communications back—at least another month or two, I think. Maybe by then we'll understand it."

After dinner the proud parents had to show Joris how well their infant could swim, and Mevrouw insisted that Joris go to bed when Tashy did. Since the last time he'd been in a bed, he had flown halfway around the world, and it was time he got some rest!

So there wasn't any chance to ask for Joris's help then, either. When both Natasha and his wife were sound asleep, Ranjit fretfully flipped on the news, sitting in their dressing room, volume too low to disturb the sleepers. The Security Council had issued a whole new bundle of stern warnings to countries that were engaging in, or seemed to be on the brink of, one of those brushfire wars; Silent Thunder was not mentioned but, Ranjit had no doubt, was present in the calculations of all the belligerents. It was possible, Ranjit told himself, that he had made a mistake in turning Gamini's offer down. Pax per Fidem had every appearance of being where the action was, while Colombo did not.

Irritated, he turned off the news. He thought he might as well get some sleep and perhaps get a word with Joris first thing in the morning, before Joris was off again on his way to the terminal's construction site.

But there was a faint sound of music coming from somewhere.

Ranjit pulled on a robe and investigated. There, on the balcony overlooking the gardens, Joris sat, sipping a tall drink and gazing at the moon while a radio softly played. When he saw Ranjit peering at him, he gave him a faintly embarrassed grin. "You caught me. I was just thinking where I'd like to land up there, oh, maybe five or six years from now, when the Skyhook's operational and I can get there. Mare Tranquillitatis, or Crisium, or maybe something on the far side, just to show off. Sit down, Ranjit. Would you care for a nightcap?"

Ranjit certainly would, and Joris had the fixings all ready for them. As he accepted the glass, Ranjit nodded toward the moon, nearly full, bright enough, almost, to read by. "Do you really think you'll be able to do that?" he asked.

"I don't think it; I guarantee it," Vorhulst promised. "Maybe it'll take a little longer for your average man in the street to buy a ticket. Not me. I'm an executive in the program, and rank has its privileges." He took note of a faintly quizzical expression on Ranjit's face. "What is it? You never expected me to take advantage of a position to get something I wanted? Well, for most things I wouldn't. But space travel is special. If the only way to get to the moon would be by robbing banks to finance the trip, I'd rob banks."

Ranjit shook his head. "I wish I liked my job as much as you like yours," he said, feeling a tiny stab of what he could recognize only as jealousy.

Dr. Vorhulst gave his former student a considering look. "Have a refill," he offered. And then, while he was mixing one, he said, "And while we're here, how would you like to tell me how you and the university are getting along?"

Ranjit would have, of course, liked nothing better. It didn't take long for him to unload his problems onto his former teacher, and not as long as that for Joris Vorhulst to get the picture. "So," he said thoughtfully, again replenishing their glasses, "let's get back to basics. You don't have any trouble filling a class, do you?"

Ranjit shook his head. "For the first seminar, they had a waiting list thirty or forty people long that couldn't get in."

"So then, why do people sign up for a class with you? It isn't because you're a great teacher—even if you were, they wouldn't have had any chance to find that out. It isn't because abstruse mathematics has suddenly got popular. No, Ranjit, the thing that pulls them in is you yourself, and how you plugged away at that problem for all those years. Why don't you teach them to do as you did?"

"Tried it," Ranjit said glumly. "They said they'd heard me lecture on that already. They wanted something new."

"All right," Joris said, "then why don't you show how someone else solved a problem like that, step by step. . . ."

Ranjit looked at him with dawning hope. "Huh," he said. "Yes, maybe. I know a lot about the way Sophie Germain tried to do Fermat herself—didn't succeed, of course, except partially."

"Fine," Joris said with satisfaction, but Ranjit was still thinking.

"Or, wait a minute," he was saying, suddenly excited, "do you know what I could do? I could take one of the grand old problems that nobody has solved—say, Euler's reworking of the Goldbach conjecture; you can explain that in words of one syllable that anybody can understand, though nobody's ever been able to produce a proof. What Goldbach proposed—"

Joris's hand was raised. "Please don't explain this Goldbach conjecture to me. But, yes, that sounds good. You could do it as a sort of class project. Everybody working on it together, the students and you as well. Who knows? Maybe you could even solve the thing!"

That produced an actual laugh from Ranjit. "That would be the day! But it doesn't matter; the students would at least get a feeling of what it takes to solve a big problem, and that ought to hold their interest." He nodded to himself, pleased. "I'll try it! But it's getting late and you have to get up in the morning, so thanks, but let's call it a night."

"We'd better do that before my mother catches me still up," Vorhulst agreed. "But there's something else I wanted to talk to you about, Ranjit."

Ranjit, on the point of getting up to leave, paused with his hands on the arms of his chair, ready to lift. "Oh?"

"I've been thinking about that committee you were invited to go to work for at old Peace Through Transparency. It occurs to me that maybe we need something like it for the ladder. Famous people keeping an eye on what we're doing and now and then telling the world about it. Famous people like you, Ranjit. Do you think you might consider—?"

Ranjit didn't let him finish. "Whatever you're asking," he said, "the answer is yes. After all, you've just saved my life!"

And "yes" it was . . . and years later Ranjit considered with wonder how that simple single word had changed his life.

Some light-years away the lives of the 140,000 One Point Fives in the Earth-depopulation fleet were also on the verge of a major change.

By the calculations of their Machine-Stored navigators the flotilla was within thirteen Earth years of their assault on the doomed human race. That was a meaningful point for the One Point Fives. It meant it was time for an important action to be taken.

So all over the fleet, in every corner of every ship, specially trained technical crews were checking every instrument or machine that was working, and turning most of them off. Basic drive, off; that meant the fleet was now simply drifting toward Earth—though already at such a great velocity that, under Einstein's laws, further acceleration was very difficult and very nearly pointless. Airborne waste filters: off. So beginning at once the exhalations of the One Point Fives themselves would begin to contaminate the air they breathed. Power pack chargers, off. Search beams, off. The instruments that monitored the running of all the machinery that couldn't be turned off even briefly—off.

Suddenly the armada of the One Point Fives was no longer a hard-driving fleet of warcraft aiming at a point of conflict; it had suddenly become a collection of derelicts, almost powerless and approaching the point where one ship might drift into another. The fleet could not maintain that condition for long.

The One Point Fives, however, didn't need it to be for long. As soon as the last crew reported that everything that could be shut down was shut down, the One Point Fives began slipping out of the last vestiges of their protective armor and life supports. Then began the wildest orgy of sexual activity any One Point Five could imagine.

For about an hour.

Then the pallid creatures that were the organic One Point Fives hurriedly clambered back into their armor. In each ship the technical crews hastily retraced their steps, turning back on everything they had turned off, and the orgy was over.

Why did the One Point Fives do that?

For a reason that most human beings would have understood very easily. One Point Fives, whether armored or stripped to their wasted little organic bodies, did not look in the least like any humans, but they had some traits in common. No One Point Five wanted to die without leaving a live descendant to take his place. In the struggle that lay ahead there was a definite and nonzero chance that some or all of them would die. So in that collective mating, many—with luck, maybe most—of the females would become pregnant. The fifteen Earth years before that final conflict was the minimum time it would take for them to deliver their wretched little newborns to the nursery machines, and then for the infants to grow and mature to the stage of puberty.

With that knowledge, their parents could afford to launch the attack.

Of course, no human being knew this, so all nine billion of them went right on with their usual daily tasks, none of them knowing that, from that day forward, their own newborns could only expect to experience the first inklings of sexual maturity before being wiped from the face of the earth.

29

BURGEONING HOPES

In the event, Ranjit did not begin his next seminar with Goldbach's conjecture. Myra had a different suggestion, and he had learned to listen to Myra.

The first day he faced the class, he spent most of the opening hour on housekeeping matters—answering questions on his testing and grading policies, announcing what days of class would be skipped for higher-echelon reasons, getting to begin to know some of the students. Then he asked, "How many of you know what a prime number is?"

Nearly every hand in the room went up. Half a dozen of the students didn't wait to be recognized but called out one version or another of the definition: a number that can be divided, without a remainder, only by one and itself.

It was a promising beginning. "Very good," Ranjit told them. "So two is a prime number and three is a prime number, but four can be divided not only by itself and by one but also by two. It is not, therefore, a prime number. Next question: How do you generate prime numbers?"

There was stirring in the classroom, but no hands immediately arose. Ranjit grinned at his students. "That's a hard question, isn't it? There are a bunch of shortcuts that people have suggested, many of them requiring large computers. But the one way that requires nothing but a brain, hand, and something to write with—but is guaranteed to generate every prime number there is up to any limit you care to set—is something called the sieve of Eratosthenes. Anybody can use the sieve. Anybody with a lot of time on his hands, that is."

He turned and began writing a line of numbers on the whiteboard, everything from one to twenty. As he was writing, he said, "There's a little mnemonic poem to help you remember it:

Strike the twos and strike the threes,
The sieve of Eratosthenes.

When the multiples sublime,
The numbers that are left are prime.

"That's the way it works," he went on. "Look at the list of numbers. Ignore the one; there's a sort of gentlemen's agreement among number theorists to pretend that the one doesn't belong there and shouldn't be called a prime, because just about every theorem about number theory goes all wonky if it includes the one. So the first number on the list is two. Now you go along the list and strike out every even number. That is, every number divisible by two, after the two itself—the four, six, eight, and so on." He did that. "So now the smallest number left, after the original two and the one that we're pretending never existed, is the three, so we strike out the nine and every later number left on the board that is divisible by three. So that leaves us with the two, the three, the five, the seven, and the eleven, and so on. And now you've generated a list of the first prime numbers.

"Now, we've only gone up to twenty because my hand gets tired when I write long lists, but the sieve works for any number of digits. If you were to write down the first ninety thousand numbers or so—I mean everything from one to around ninety thousand—your last surviving number would be the one-thousandth prime, and you would have written every prime before that as well.

"Now"—Ranjit glanced at the wall clock, as he had seen so many of his own teachers do—"because these are three-hour sessions, I'm declaring a ten-minute intermission now. Stretch your legs, use the facilities, chat with your neighbors—whatever you like, but please be back in your seats at half-past the hour, when we'll begin to take up the real business of the seminar."

He didn't wait to see them disperse but ducked quickly into the private door that led to faculty offices down the hall. He used his own facilities—pee whenever you get the chance, as, according to an urban legend, a queen of England had once counseled her subjects—and quickly called home. "How is it going?" Myra demanded.

"I don't know," he said honestly. "They've been quiet so far, but a fair number of them have put up their hands when I've asked questions." He considered for a moment. "I think you could say that I'm cautiously optimistic."

"Well," his wife said, "I'm not. Not cautious about it, I mean. I think you're going to knock them dead, and when you come home, we'll celebrate."

.   .   .

They were all in their seats when he returned to the podium, a minute before the big hand hit the six. A good sign, Ranjit thought hopefully, and plunged right in.

"How many prime numbers are there?" he asked, without preface.

This time the hands were slow in going up, but nearly all managed it. Ranjit pointed to a young girl in the first row. She stood and said, "I think there are an infinite number of prime numbers, sir." But when Ranjit asked why she thought that, she hung her head and sat down again without answering.

One of the other students, male and older than the rest, called out, "It's been proved!"

"Indeed it has," Ranjit agreed. "If you make a list of prime numbers, no matter how many are on the list or how big the biggest of them is, there will always be other primes that aren't on the list.

"Specifically, let's make believe that we're all pretty dumb about numbers and so we think that maybe the last term in that list, nineteen, is the biggest prime number that ever could be. So we make a list of all the primes smaller than nineteen—that is, two through seventeen above, and we multiply them all together. Two times three times five, et cetera. We can do this because, although we're pretty dumb, we have a really good calculator."

Ranjit allowed time for a few giggles to survive, then went on. "So we've done the multiplication and obtained a product. We then add one to it, leaving us with a number we will call N. Now, what do we know about N? We know that it might turn out to be a prime itself, because, by definition, if you divide by any of those numbers, you have one left over as a remainder. And if it happens to be a composite number, it can't have any factor that is on that list, for the same reason.

"So we've proved that no matter how many primes you put in a list, there are always primes larger still that aren't on the list, and thus the number of primes is infinite." He paused, looking the students over. "Any of you happen to know who gave us that proof?"

No hands were raised, but around the classroom names were called out: "Gauss?" "Euler?" "Lobachevsky?" And, from the back row, "Your old pal Fermat?"

Ranjit gave them a grin. "No, not Fermat, and not any of the others you mentioned. That proof goes way back. Almost as far as Eratosthenes, but not quite. The man's name was Euclid, and he did it somewhere around 300 B.C."

He held up an amiably cautionary hand. "Now let me show you something else. Look at the list of prime numbers. Notice how often there are two prime numbers that are consecutive odd ones. These are called prime pairs. Anyone care to guess how many prime pairs there are?"

There was a rustle of motion, but otherwise silence until some brave student called out, "An infinity?"

"Exactly," Ranjit said. "There is an infinite number of prime pairs . . . and for your homework assignment you can find a proof of that."

And so at dinner that night Ranjit was more spontaneously cheerful than Myra had seen him in some time. He informed the family, "They made jokes with me. It's going to work!"

"Of course it is," his wife said. "I had no doubt. Neither did Tashy."

And indeed little Natasha, now allowed to join the grown-ups at dinner, seemed to be listening attentively from her high chair when the butler came in. "Yes, Vijay?" Mevrouw said, looking up. "You look worried. Is there a difficulty below-stairs?"

He shook his head. "Not below-stairs, madam. There was something on the news that I thought you might want to know about, though. There's been another of those Silent Thunder attacks, in South America."

This time it wasn't a single nation that had been driven back to the pre-electronic age. This time there were two of them. Nowhere throughout the countries of Venezuela and Colombia did a telephone now ring, or a light go on when a switch was pressed, or a television display its picture.

So the rest of that meal was completed with little additional conversation about Ranjit's seminar, or even about the skillful way Natasha was manipulating her spoon. The room's own screens, never used during meals because Mevrouw thought that was barbarous, were full on now.

As with Korea, there were few scenes from inside either of the freshly subjugated countries, because the local facilities were all now blacked out. What was on the screens was a few sketchy displays of Pax per Fidem cargo planes—the kind with short takeoff and landing capabilities so they could dodge around the frozen aircraft on the runways—bringing in the same sort of troops and equipment that had poured over the border into North Korea. Mostly what was on the screens was talking heads—saying much the same things they had said about Korea—and a lot of stock footage to display the events that had brought on the current disaster.

The twenty-first century had not been good to either of the two countries. In Venezuela it was politics, in Colombia drugs; in both countries there had been violence and frequent governmental crises, capped by the decision of the former narcotics lords to take over some of their neighbor's now far more profitable oil business.

"Pax per Fidem took on North Korea first because it didn't have a real friend in the world," Ranjit told his wife. "This time they took on two countries at once because they had different friends—the U.S. has been propping Colombia up since the nineties, and Venezuela was close to both Russia and China."

"But there's a lot less killing going on now," Mevrouw said thoughtfully. "I can't feel unhappy about that."

Myra sighed. "But do you think we'll be better off when the whole world is run by Oceania, Eurasia, and Eastasia?" she asked.

30

BIG NEWS

When the seminar was over, no student had managed to produce a rigorous proof of the infinitude of twin primes, but then Ranjit hadn't expected one would. Neither had Dr. Davoodbhoy. At their postseminar conference, though, he was visibly happier than before. He flourished the student comment slips at Ranjit with a grin. "Listen to these. 'I had the feeling I wasn't just learning how to do mathematics; I was learning what doing mathematics was all about.' 'Good stuff. Dr. Subramanian doesn't treat us like children, more like we were new members of his research team.' 'Can I take his next seminar, too?' And what would you say to"—he glanced again at the slip—"this young lady, Ramya Salgado?"

Ranjit looked uncomfortable. "I know who she is; she was very active in the seminar. Maybe if we needed another warm body to fill the class out."

"Oh," said Dr. Davoodbhoy, "I don't think you need to worry about that. You do want to do another, don't you? Have you thought of a subject? Maybe something like the Riemann conjecture?"

"There are proofs of that," Ranjit reminded him.

"Some people don't think they're satisfactory. Anyway, there was a proof of Fermat, too—Wiles's—and that didn't keep you from finding a better one."

Ranjit considered, then shook his head. "I'm afraid Riemann is too complicated for anybody but a professional mathematician to care about. How are you going to get the average college student to care about what way the zeros in the Riemann zeta function are distributed? There are better ones around. Euler's reworking of the Goldbach conjecture, for instance. That's pure gold. 'All positive even integers greater than four can be expressed as the sum of two primes.' Six is three plus three, eight is five plus three, ten is five plus five—or seven plus three, if you like that better. Anybody can understand that! Only nobody has ever proved it—yet."

Davoodbhoy considered for one of the smaller fractions of a second, then nodded. "Go for it, Ranjit. I might even like to audit one of those sessions myself."

As the years flowed from that point in time onward, Ranjit began to realize that he truly loved teaching. Each semester brought a new flock of eager students, and of course he had his monthly reviews of the ladder to tend to, and Natasha was growing from a young, promising girl to a slightly older girl of significant promise. If anyone in the world shared Myra's concerns about the three Pax per Fidem sponsors' dividing the world among them, there was little sign of it. Silent Thunder was as gentle a conquistador in South America as it had been on the Korean peninsula. The casualty list was not much longer. The problems of feeding and caring for the suddenly technology-less populations were as quickly met. The outside world observed, and discussed, and seemed to think that Pax per Fidem had done a reasonably good thing.

Part of the reason why the affair had gone so well, Ranjit knew, was that the advance planning had been meticulous. Weeks before the attack the two surviving old American aircraft carriers had been loaded up with everything needed for the job, the goods supplied mostly by Russia and China. Fully prepared, they were deployed to the Gulf of Mexico—on "training missions," the routine Department of Defense announcement said—and in fact ready to start supplying emergency help almost before the echoes of Silent Thunder's nuclear blasts had died away. Even Myra had to admit that the effects had not been bad.

They were dawdling over a leisurely Sunday breakfast in the garden, just the three of them. Ranjit was checking some lecture possibilities on one screen, Myra idly following the news on another, while Natasha, who was nearing her twelfth birthday, practiced her backstroke in the pool. Then Myra looked up, sighing. "It looks like they're coming to an agreement," she told her husband. "Kenya and Egypt, and the other countries that depend on the Nile River water."

He gave her a comfortable smile. "I thought they would," he said. He had, in fact, all but guaranteed they would, at a time, no more than six months past, when the two principals had mobilized their not inconsiderable military might and sent the armies to glare at each other. But then the UN Security Council had favored them with one of its strongly worded warnings. "I guess they take the Security Council more seriously now, with Silent Thunder always looming," Myra ruminated.

Ranjit demonstrated what an intelligent husband he was by omitting any "I told you so." All he said was, "I'm glad they're working it out. Listen. What would you think if I said my next seminar would be on the Collatz conjecture?"

Myra looked puzzled. "I don't think I've ever heard of that one."

"Probably not," Ranjit agreed. "Most people haven't. Old Lothar Collatz never got the publicity he was entitled to. Here, I'll show you." He turned his screen so that they could both see it. "Take any number—something under three digits; it works with really big ones just as well, but it takes too long. Got the number?"

Myra essayed, "Well, how about, say, eight?"

"Good one. Now divide it by two, and keep on dividing by two until you can't get a whole-number answer anymore."

Obediently Myra said, "Eight, four, two, one. Is that what you mean?"

"That is exactly what I mean. Wait a minute while I put it on the screen. . . . All right. That is what we will call rule number one for Collatz: When it's an even number, divide it by two and keep on doing that until you don't have an even number anymore. Now take an odd number."

"Um . . . five?"

Ranjit sighed. "All right, we'll just do the easy ones. So now we apply rule number two. If the number is odd, you multiply it by three and add one."

"Fifteen . . . sixteen," Myra supplied.

"Good. Now you've got an even number again, so you go back to rule one. Let me put that on the screen."

As Ranjit quickly typed eight, four, two, one next to his other numbers, Myra raised her eyebrows. "Huh," she said. "They look the same."

Ranjit gave her a large smile. "That's the point. You take any number, even the largest number you can think of, and work on it with just those two rules. Divide by two if it's even, multiply by three and add one if it's odd, and you'll come down to one as a result every time. Even if the numbers you start with are pretty big—wait, I'll show you."

He typed some programming instructions onto the screen and gave it the number twenty-seven to start with. Alternating rules one and two as directed, the screen displayed "81 . . . 82 . . . 41 . . . 123 . . . 124 . . . 62 . . . 31 . . . 93 . . . 94 . . . 47 . . . 141 . . . 142 . . . 71 . . . 213 . . . 214 . . . 107 . . ." until Ranjit shut it off. "See how the number keeps bouncing up and down? It's sort of pretty to watch, and sometimes the numbers get really large—there were some people at Carnegie Mellon who got it up to numbers with more than fifty thousand digits—but in the long run it always collapses to one."

"Well," Myra said comfortably, "sure it does. Why wouldn't it?"

Ranjit gave her a hot look. "We mathematicians don't deal in the intuitively obvious. We want proof! And back in 1937 old Collatz made his conjecture, which is that that will happen to any number at all, all the way up to infinity. But it has never been proved."

Myra nodded absently. "Sounds like a good possibility." Then, shading her eyes as she looked toward the pool and raising her voice, she said, "Better take a break, Tashy! You don't want to get overtired."

Ranjit was quick to meet his daughter with a towel, but he was looking at his wife. Finally he said, "Myra? You sound a little bit distracted. Is anything wrong?"

She gave him a fond look, and then a real laugh. "Wrong? Not at all, Ranj. It's just that— Well, I haven't seen the doctor yet, but I'm pretty sure. I think I'm pregnant again."

31

SKYHOOK DAYS

For Myra de Soyza Subramanian, caring for her second infant was even more of a breeze than caring for her first. Her husband, for example, did not now come home depressed from a job he thought irrelevant; his students liked him, he liked his students, and Dr. Davoodbhoy was unfailingly pleased. The outside world was easier to take now, too. Oh, a few nations could not seem to break the habit of making threatening noises at their neighbors. Hardly anyone was actually getting killed, though.

And, over Beatrix Vorhulst's protest, they had finally moved into their own little house—"little" only by comparison with the Vorhulst mansion—just steps from one of the island's beautiful broad beaches, where the water was as warm and welcoming as ever. By the time they were settled in their new house, the world outside no longer seemed as threatening. Little Robert splashed in the shallowest part of the pool, while Natasha found deeper water to demonstrate her considerable (and, Ranjit maintained, clearly inherited) skill at swimming—or any other way—when she wasn't taking sailing lessons from a neighbor who owned a little Sunfish. What made being in their own home particularly pleasant was that Mevrouw Vorhulst had parted with her favorite cook and Natasha's favorite maid to save Myra the trouble of housework.

Another way in which Myra's second pregnancy was unlike the first went by the name of Natasha—well, more often it was Tashy. Tashy wasn't a problem. When she wasn't winning ribbons for swimming—only in children's events so far, but she was seen to watch adult races with narrowed eyes and obvious intentions—she was busy at being her mother's assistant, deputy, and sous-chef. Thus aided, Myra had a gratifying number of hours each day to spend catching up on what was going on in the field of artificial intelligence and autonomous prostheses.

That was quite a lot. By the time Myra had begun to evaluate each muscle twinge in the hope that it might be the beginnings of labor, she was pretty nearly up to speed again.

Of course, that wouldn't last. By the time the new baby was birthed, weaned, toilet trained, and off to school, Myra would have slipped behind her cohort again. That was inevitable.

Was Myra angry at this tyrannical law of childbearing? It was clearly unjust. It dictated that any woman who wanted a baby had to accept Mother Nature's inflexible decree that, for a period of time, the cognitive functions of her mind would have to take second place to mothering. It would have to be a fairly significant period, too. Ten years was the accepted minimum before a female AI nerd (or medical doctor or politician or, for that matter, pastry chef) could get back to her career.

Obviously that was unfair. But the world was chronically unfair in so many ways that Myra de Soyza Subramanian had no patience for wasting time in resentment. That was the unchangeable way the world was. What was the point in complaining? There would be a time when both her children were in college. Then she would be as free as any human could ever get, and then she would have twenty, thirty, maybe even fifty years of productive life in which to unravel the riddles of her chosen profession.

Deferred gratification was the name of that game. You didn't have to like its rules to play by them. And, one way or another, you might even win.

Both Myra and Ranjit considered themselves big winners when Robert Ganesh Subramanian was born. His parents thought they had hit the jackpot with two fine offspring. Robert was a vociferously healthy newborn who gained weight and strength as rapidly as Ranjit and Myra could have hoped for. He tried to turn himself over in his crib even earlier than Natasha had, and was toilet trained almost as early. All of their friends declared that he was the handsomest child they had ever seen, and they weren't really lying, either. Robert was the kind of infant for whose picture baby-food manufacturers would have paid handsomely to put on their labels.

Interestingly, if there was anyone who loved Baby Robert more than his parents did, that person was little Natasha, who wasn't all that little anymore and was already beginning to demonstrate a considerable aptitude for athletics, education, and getting her parents to do just about everything she might require of them.

Which, in this case, was to let her take care of Baby Robert.

Well, not quite all of his care. Not the part that involved situations that smelled really bad. But dressing Robert, pushing Robert around in his stroller, playing with Robert—Natasha demanded the privilege of taking care of those things, and after some early worried hesitation, Myra gave her daughter what she asked.

Actually, Natasha was good at the job. When Robert screamed or roared, it was Natasha who could usually fit words to his outcries. And when his mother took him away, Natasha had her own life to live, school or her daily swim sessions or just spending time with her friends . . . or most likely combining her interests, with her friends joining her at the pool, or Robert slumbering beside her as she studied English verbs or the history of India and its satellite nations.

All this, of course, was a good thing for Myra. With Natasha relieving her of so much of the work of raising Robert, Myra was not falling behind as rapidly as she might have feared in AI nerding. And what was good for Myra was certainly good for Ranjit, for whom his wife was as dear—and as unpredictably exciting—as she had been on the day they were wed.

All in all, things were going well for Ranjit Subramanian. One seminar per semester was all he needed to do, Dr. Davoodbhoy had decreed, but as long as he was going to do the one, they might as well make it a big one. So Ranjit's classroom had become the exact supersize theater in which he had thrilled to Joris Vorhulst's stories of the worlds of the solar system. Ranjit didn't have twenty students at a time anymore, either. Now he had a hundred. Which, Dr. Davoodbhoy assured him, entitled him to the luxury of a teaching assistant—that eager young woman, Ramya Salgado, now possessed of a master's degree of her own, who had so enriched his second seminar—and freedom to do his own "research" for the rest of each semester. Davoodbhoy intimated that that was so he could get a head start on whatever proof he was going to assign his next class.

Or, Ranjit realized, it was a good time to do some of that exploration of his native country that he had been intending to get around to ever since Myra had first chided him as overparochial.

That was a more attractive idea than it might have been some years earlier, for even tourist travel was looking more attractive in this post–Silent Thunder world. They could, for example, cruise the Nile River, as Myra had longed to do since she was ten; both Egypt and Kenya had furloughed large fractions of their militaries while the ecologists for all the countries involved worked out water-saving ways of containing their thirsts for Nile water. The Subramanians could have taken the children to London—or to Paris, or New York, or Rome—to get an idea of what a great city was like. They could have settled for Norwegian fjords or Swiss mountains or the jungles of Amazonia; they could indeed have gone almost anywhere, but what in fact happened was that, while they were still studying travel brochures, they got a text from Joris Vorhulst. It said:

> Mother tells me that you have some vacation time coming. I'll be down at the terminal for at least a week, starting the first of next month. Why don't you come see what we're doing these days?

"Actually," Myra said, "that would be fun." And Natasha said, "You bet!" And even Robert, hanging on to Natasha's chair and listening to every word, bellowed something that Natasha explained was a yes. And so the family of four prepared for its first long trip together.

It wasn't just Vorhulst's invitation that made Ranjit look forward to visiting the Skyhook terminal. There were actually two reasons, and the first was the advisory board that Vorhulst had talked him into joining a number of years ago. It had been as undemanding as Vorhulst had promised—no meetings to go to, not even any voting on any issues, because if there were any issues troublesome enough to require a decision, that decision was made for them by the real controllers of the enterprise, the governments of China, Russia, and the United States. Ranjit had, however, been the recipient of a monthly progress report. There too the heavy hand of the big three was felt, because most of each report's content was sternly secret, and even more of it was simply dismissed as what was cryptically called "development." He had only been to the site a handful of times, and those visits had been quite cursory. Whether he would learn more by being at the scene Ranjit could not say, but he was anxious to find out.

The other reason was a surprise to Ranjit himself. The Subramanians didn't have a car of their own—Ranjit and Myra biked to most places, sometimes with Natasha riding happily in front of them and Robert strapped into a child's seat behind his father, and when they needed more in the way of transport, there were always cabs. But the university had promised the loan of a car for the trip, and Ranjit picked it up from the grinning Dr. Davoodbhoy. "It's special for you," he said. "Pax per Fidem sent it. It's a new design from transparent Korea—with all those geniuses who used to build weapons now free for new civilian ideas, they've got a lot of stuff." And when he'd explained what the perky little four-seater could do, it sent Ranjit back to Myra grinning with pleasure.

"Get me a pitcher of water," he commanded as he pulled up at their house. Mystified, she obeyed. She was even more mystified when he cere-moniously opened the fuel tank and poured the water in, and when he then started the motor and listened pleasurably to its purr, she was totally baf-fled.

He gave her the explanation Davoodbhoy had given him. "Boron," he said. "It's called the Abu-Hamed drive, after I don't know who, maybe the person who invented it. You know the element boron is so hungry for oxy-gen that it'll pull it right out of compounds like water? And when you take the oxygen out of the water molecule, what do you have left?"

Myra frowned at him. "Hydrogen, but—"

Grinning, he touched a finger to her lips. "But boron's terribly expen-sive, and burning a carbon fuel's so much cheaper that nobody ever both-ered with it. But here it is! They've found out how to regenerate the boron so they can use it over and over. And so we're driving a car that not only is low-emission, it doesn't emit anything at all!"

"But—" Myra began again. This time he stopped his wife's lips with his own.

"Get Natasha and Robert, will you?" he coaxed. "And our baggage? And let's see how this hydrogen burner works."

Which turned out to be very well. They did have to stop twice to add water to the fuel tank, under the scandalized stares of the people running the filling stations they stopped at, but the little car performed as well as any fossil-fuel burner.

They were still ten kilometers from the terminal when Robert emitted one of his heart-stopping shrieks. Myra jammed on the brakes, but it wasn't a sudden danger. It was simply an exciting sight. What Robert was waving at (as he said "Spider!" and "Climb fast!" and "Many, many, many!") was the cable of the Skyhook itself, barely visible as something that glinted from the sun. But what it carried, once you knew what to look for, was visible enough. There were the cargo-carrying pods, one after an-other, marching up into the sky and disappearing into the first layer of clouds.

"Huh," Ranjit said. "Looks like they've really got it going, doesn't it?"

So they had.

The road to the terminal was paired up with a railroad track, and as they were approaching, a train—forty-two freight cars, Natasha counted excitedly—overtook them and disappeared into one of the terminal's giant sheds. There were guards at the car entrance, but they passed the Subramanian family with a friendly salute, and a wave in the direction of the VIP parking lot.

Where they were met by a handsome Asian woman who introduced herself as Joris Vorhulst's assistant. "Engineer Vorhulst was looking forward to seeing you very much," she informed them, "but he didn't expect you until tomorrow. He's on his way, though. Would you like something to eat?"

Ranjit opened his mouth to say what a good idea that was, but was overruled by his wife's faster response. "Not just yet. If we could just look around for a bit—"

They could. They were warned to stay out of the loading sheds and, of course, to beware of the trucks and tractors that were lugging around unidentifiable bits and pieces of no doubt excitingly interesting objects.

Ranjit contemplated all the activity with benign incomprehension. "I'd give a lot to know what some of these things are," he informed his family in general.

Young Natasha pursed her lips. "Well," she said, "that lumpy package there is the thruster for an ion rocket. I think the bale next to it is carbon nanotubes in sheet form—I'd say probably part of a solar sail—"

Ranjit gazed at his daughter, openmouthed. "What makes you so sure?" he demanded.

She grinned at him. "While you were talking to that lady, Robert and I poked around, and I read the bills of lading. I think they're building spaceships up there!"

"And," called a familiar voice from the unloading shed, "you're exactly right, Tashy! We've got a couple of them working already."

Joris Vorhulst wouldn't listen to any objections; he wanted food, decent Sri Lankan food, and if they didn't want to eat, they could just watch him doing so. Because, it turned out, he had been five weeks on the Skyhook himself, and was just now coming back from supervising the work of those very spacecraft whose existence Natasha had deduced.

"Skyhook is really beginning to pull its weight," he informed them happily. The two robot rocket ships that were already commissioned were working as scavengers, dedicated to combing LEO for abandoned spacecraft or even abandoned fuel tanks of ancient Russian and American ones. Once found, computer-controlled solar sails were mounted on them and they were programmed to sail themselves to Grand Central. There they were transformed. They were no longer dangerous free-flying spaceship killers. Now they were simply the raw materials for anything that needed to be built. "It's all very well to ship stuff up from the surface," Vorhulst declared, mouth full of what even Myra had to admit was a really good curry, "but why should we waste what's up there already?"

"And that's what you were doing up in LEO? Collecting scrap to build new things?"

Vorhulst looked embarrassed. "Actually," he said, "I was making sure the third ship was ready to go. That's the one that's headed for the moon. You know that the robot explorers have been busy there for a few years now? And they've found plenty of those lava tubes I used to talk about in my astronomy class?"

"Actually," Ranjit complained, "I didn't. The progress reports they sent the advisory council were pretty sketchy."

"Yes," Vorhulst conceded, "I know they were. We're hoping the big three will loosen up a little now, because those tubes are going to change everything. One of them is right under the Sinus Iridium—the 'Bay of Rainbows.' It's a beaut. It's eighteen hundred meters long, and ship three will be carrying the machinery to seal it up because Lunar Development has a plan for it. The big three want tourists, you see."

Myra looked skeptical. "Tourists? Last I heard there were about eleven people living in the lunar colony and it was costing a fortune just to keep them fed and supplied with air to breathe."

Vorhulst grinned. "In the old days, yes. That was when they had to be supported from Earth's surface, by rockets. But now we've got the Sky-hook! Oh, there'll be tourists, all right. And to give them a good reason to go there, the big three pulled a few strings, and now the Olympics association has made a deal."

Natasha, previously uncharacteristically silent, perked up. "What kind of a deal?"

"To hold the kind of events they can't do on Earth, Tashy. You see, lunar gravity's only 1.622 meters per second squared, so—"

Natasha held up her hands. "Please, Dr. Vorhulst!"

"Well, it's just about one sixth as much as Earth's at the surface. That means that the minute anybody does competitive sports on the moon, all the old records that involve running or jumping are just out the window. I'm not sure that even the Sinus Iridium tube is tall enough to let the high jumpers strut their stuff."

Ranjit was looking skeptical. "You think people are going to travel a couple of hundred thousand kilometers just to watch some athletes jump high?"

"I do," Vorhulst insisted. "So does Lunar Development. But that's not the star turn. What would you say to a contest that hasn't been possible on Earth? Like a race between humans in muscle-powered flight?"

If he expected Ranjit to answer, he was disappointed. There was a crash of dishes as Natasha jumped to her feet. "I would say I'm ready!" she cried. "I want to go! And, you'll see, I'll win!"

32

NATASHA'S GOLD

She did go there, too.

Not immediately, of course. A lot had to be done before that first-ever lunar Olympics could be held—a lot done to the moon to make it possible, for example, and a quite large lot that had to be done to the Skyhook to at least make it possible to carry passengers with a reasonable hope that they would get there alive. Now that the briefing texts had become more informative, Ranjit devoured them as soon as they arrived, all the space-cadet fever that Joris Vorhulst had awakened in him flashing back.

Fortunately for Ranjit's peace of mind the world seemed to have taken a turn for the better. The second dose of Silent Thunder had restrained some of the unruliest of the world's leaders. His seminars kept going well enough to keep Dr. Davoodbhoy pleased, and his little family continued to be an unfailing delight.

Especially Natasha. The prospect of college looming just a few years before her was no problem, but there was also the lunar Olympics Dr. Vorhulst had promised. Training for that was not easy. It made the athletes' training for every other Olympics look like ten minutes of morning jumping jacks to keep the love handles away.

Of course, Natasha was not the only one training for that unprecedented match. All over the world young athletes were wondering if they could get themselves fit enough for the flying events. Since the task of training would have to be accomplished within the tyranny of Earth's uncompromising 1-G gravity, a good deal of ingenuity was going to be required.

There were two lines of approach to the problem of muscle-powered flight. The "balloonatics" believed in employing gas bags of various shapes, so that the athlete was supported in flight, using all his muscle power to crank a propeller without the need of expending any effort simply to stay aloft. The sky-bikers, on the other hand, preferred to do everything by their muscles alone. For them sporting goods manufacturers had rapidly invented a whole array of propeller-driven devices. Thanks to carbon-60 nanotubes, the same molecules that made the Skyhook a working means of transportation instead of an idle dream, these devices were so light that even on Earth they could be lifted with one hand—on the moon, with a single finger!

What none of these ambitious athletes had was a true one-sixth gravity practice arena. They had to do the best they could, usually by using equipment counterweighted to give the equivalent of lunar gravity. All of which meant that it was not only ingenuity that was called for. Also required was quite a lot of money.

That would have exceeded the purchasing capacity of a college professor by a considerable margin, but for those purposes, Natasha's needs got considerable support from Sri Lankans in high places. Even those who had no particular interest in sporting events enjoyed calling attention to the fact that Sri Lanka had become the world's doorway to space. So the money was pledged, and a great lunar-gravity gym was built on the outskirts of Colombo. There Natasha practiced sky-biking to her heart's content.

The gym was only a ten-minute drive from their home, and so Natasha's family were often present as spectators. Sometimes more than spectators; Robert loved watching his big sister pump her way across the "sky" of the gym—loved even more when at last there was a little bit of open time on the machines. Then Robert, too, got his chance to fly.

Of course it was not only Natasha who was given the use of the low-grav gym. Hopeful candidates from all over the island begged for the chance to try their own skills on the machines, and more than thirty of them won the opportunity. But it was Natasha Subramanian who consistently outperformed every challenger.

And, on the day when the Sri Lankan team at last assembled at the Skyhook terminal to be elevated to their first experience of space, it was Natasha who carried the island's hope of victory.

When Myra got a look at the prices the tour companies were advertising for the lunar Olympics, she gasped. "Oh, Ranjit," she moaned, one hand pressed to her heart. "We can't let Tashy fly that race without us there, but how can we go?"

Ranjit, who had been expecting no less, was quick to reassure her. Families of contestants received a substantial discount. So did members of the advisory board, himself included, and when you put the two discounts together, the cost of the tickets was no more than outrageous.

Not impossible, though. Accordingly, Myra, Ranjit, and young Robert presented themselves at the terminal. Like everybody else in the world who owned a telescreen—which, to a close approximation, was pretty much everybody in the world—they had seen the rapturous news stories that had accompanied the Skyhook's evolution to passenger-carrying. They knew how the passenger capsules worked, and what it would feel like to be borne skyward at a steady rate of meters per second.

What they had not entirely appreciated, though, was quite how many seconds, even at that speed, it was going to take to get from Sri Lanka to the Sinus Iridium. This was not a weekend trip.

In the first half dozen days they had got only as far as the lower Van Allen belt, when the Subramanians—along with other families aboard, namely, the Kais, the Kosbas, and the unpronounceably named Norwegians—had to hustle into shelter against the murderous Van Allen radiation. The shelter consisted of the triple-walled sleep-and-sanitation chambers of the capsule. Those contained the toilets, the laughably named "baths," and twenty—count 'em, twenty—extraordinarily narrow bunks arrayed in ranks of five. When you had to head for the shelter, what you brought with you was the skimpy Skyhook special garments you were wearing (nearly weightless, to save on load, and as close to unsoilable as fabric technology could make them, since there was no hope of laundry), your medications, if any, and yourself. You could bring nothing else. Least of all, modesty.

Robert didn't care for the shelter. He cried. So did the Kai grandson. Ranjit didn't much care for it, either. When he was in the shelter, he yearned for the greater (though minimal) freedom of the unsheltered capsule, with its dark corners and its exercise elastics and its windows—long, narrow, and thick ones, but still rewardingly transparent. And, most of all, he yearned for their regular bunks that had their own lights and their own screens and almost as much space to turn around in as an average coffin. Enough, indeed, to allow for having company in them now and then, provided you were on extremely intimate terms with the company.

That first sentence to shelter was only for four days. Then they were in clear space again . . . for another nine days, until the warning squeals went off once more and it was time to seek shelter from the upper Van Allen.

Space travel had become possible for almost anyone. It certainly had not become easy, though. Or, come to that, particularly pleasant.

A funny thing happened as they came out of the upper Van Allen. Robert had made a dash for his favorite spot, the two-meter-long ribbon of thick plastic that was their main window to the universe outside. Myra was already climbing into the exercise straps and Ranjit was considering heading for his personal bunk and some untroubled sleep, when Robert came bouncing back to them, shrieking in excitement. Excited Robert was even harder to understand than the relaxed one. All either Myra or Ranjit could make out was the one word "fish." Robert could not, or would not, do much in the way of clarifying, and there was no Natasha on hand to translate. What there was was the three-year-old girl who had come with one of the other families in their capsule. She listened silently to their talk for a moment and then, still silent, took Robert away to learn how to do what Myra recognized as tai chi.

That was little Luo, daughter of the couple from Taipei, who were one fragment of their fellow passengers in the capsule. There were six of the Kais in all, including the elderly mothers of both Mr. and Mrs. Kai, who were in the hotel business. This had made them filthy rich, as they needed to be to afford being among the first of the actual tourists the Olympics people were counting on. So were the family from South Korea, so also the young couple from Kazakhstan. The Norwegians weren't, particularly, but they were the parents and siblings of one of their nation's broad jumpers and thus were entitled to the discounted fare.

What was wrong with the seventeen other human beings who shared their capsule was that not one of them spoke English, much less either Tamil or Sinhalese. The younger Mrs. Kai was fluent in French, so Myra had someone to talk to. The others talked to each other in Russian, Chinese, and what Ranjit thought was probably German, none of which were of much use to him.

Not at first, anyway. But what they had a lot of was time. Weeks to the midpoint, weeks more to the far end, where their capsule was whipped off on its lunar trajectory, and then a day or two more until their landing at Sinus Iridium.

It was during that last lap when the Subramanians were never more than a few steps from the news screens, because that was when the eliminations were taking place on the moon. The final race would be mano a mano, just one winged flyer against one balloonist. Seven wingers had made the trip to take part in the trials . . . and as the Subramanians were coming up on the end of their last flight, *luna* itself hanging gigantic out their windows, they heard their daughter announced as the winner of the trials.

By then all of the adults had become capable of speaking at least a few words each of all their home languages, and they used them to congratulate the Subramanians.

Natasha met her family at the elevator from the surface to Olympic Village, talkative, happy, and, Ranjit was a bit surprised to find, accompanied by a tall coffee-colored young man from Brazil. Both wore the minimal garments that everyone wore in an environment that never altered much from 23°C. "This is Ron," she told her parents. "That's short for Ronaldinho. He's hundred meter dash."

It wasn't until Ranjit made the experiment of trying to see his daughter through the eyes of Ronaldinho from Brazil that he really noticed how much a fifteen-year-old girl could resemble an attractive adult woman. To his surprise, Myra did not seem perturbed. She shook this Ronaldinho's hand with apparently genuine warmth, while young Robert took notice of the runner only to shove him out of the way as, roaring, he threw himself into the arms of his big sister.

After covering the top of Robert's head with kisses, Natasha said something in Ron's ear; he nodded, said to her parents, "It is a pleasing to meet you," and disappeared, loping in the slow-motion stretched-out walk that the lunar gravity encouraged.

"He's got to practice," Natasha said. "My own race is tomorrow, but his isn't till Wednesday. He'll get your bags and put them in your room, so we can get you something decent to eat." Holding Robert by the hand, she led the way. With Natasha's help the child quickly learned a decent approximation of Ron's gait. Ranjit was less fortunate. He found it was easier, if less graceful, to execute a slow-motion hop from point to point.

They didn't have far to go, and it was worth their while when they got there. The food was as unlike the extruded fodder of the Skyhook capsule as anyone could have hoped for: a salad; some kind of meat, perhaps ham, chopped and molded into croquettes; fresh fruit for dessert. "Most of it's shipped up from Earth," Natasha told them, "although the strawberries and most of the salad stuff are grown in another tube." It wasn't the food they wanted to hear about. It was what Natasha had been doing, and how she felt. What Natasha wanted was to hear all about their trip, listening with the somewhat amused patience of the veteran who had done all those things herself already. She paid attention when they told her about Robert's shrieking the word "fish," although when she queried Robert himself about it in their own personal dialect, he was more interested in his shortcake than giving her answers. "He just says he saw something out the window that looked like a fish. Funny. Some of the other people here said they saw something on the way up, too."

Myra yawned. "Probably frozen astronaut urine," she said drowsily. "Remember those stories about the Apollo crews seeing what they thought were space fireflies? Anyway, did you say we had a room? With a real bed?"

Natasha had said it, and they did have it—not just any bed, either, but a bed that was more than ninety centimeters across, which meant plenty of room for Myra and Ranjit to cuddle up. As soon as they saw it, they couldn't resist it. Just a nap, Ranjit told himself, one arm around his wife, who was asleep already. Then I'll get up and explore this fascinating place—oh, I mean after I take one of those real showers.

That was his definite intention. It wasn't his fault that when he woke it was with his wife gently shaking his shoulder and saying, "Ranj? Do you know you slept for fourteen hours? If you get up now, you'll have time for a decent breakfast and a look round the tube before we have to get to the race."

Some Olympic events have been witnessed by crowds in the hundreds of thousands. The in-person audience at these first lunar games, by comparison, was almost invisibly tiny. There were just enough people to fill the eighteen hundred lightweight seats that climbed the walls of the tube, and the Subramanians were lucky enough to have their seats less than a hundred meters from the finish line.

By the time they made their way to them along the footwalk, Ranjit was feeling about as good as he ever had in his life. A good long sleep, a quick shower in real, if reprocessed, water—only thirty seconds of the spray by its timer, but you could get really wet in thirty seconds—and a quick look around had marked the beginning of a good day. He was surprised to find that the living quarters weren't in the giant stadium tube itself but in a smaller one nearby, connected by a man-made tunnel.

But he was there! On the moon! With his dearly beloved wife and son, and on what might be his dearly beloved daughter's happiest day ever!

Although the man-made atmosphere in the tunnels was at only about half the pressure of sea-level Earth, it had been considerably oxygen-enriched. That was more important to the balloonatic who was Natasha's opponent, Piper Dugan, than to herself, although in the moon's one-sixth gravity he still needed a capacity of less than thirty cubic meters of hydrogen to lift him. He was, as it happened, Australian. As he entered, with three assistants on the ropes to make sure the machine didn't get away, his streamlined hydrogen cylinder floated overhead.

As Dugan entered, an invisible orchestra played what the program told Ranjit was Australia's national anthem, "Advance Australia Fair," and most of the audience on the far side of the tube went mad. "Uh-oh," Myra whispered into Ranjit's ear. "I don't think there are enough Sri Lankans here to equal that for Tashy."

There weren't, to be sure, but there was a big contingent from next-door India, and an even bigger one from people of any nationality who just happened to give their affection to a young girl from a tiny island. When Natasha came in to take her place, she had her own single assistant, this one carrying what looked like a bicycle without wheels but with flimsy, almost gossamer-like wings. There was music for her, too—if it was the Sri Lankan anthem, that was news to Ranjit, who hadn't known there was one—but it was almost drowned out by the yells of the spectators on her side of the tube. The yelling kept up while the handlers attached the racers to their machines—Piper Dugan suspended from his hydrogen tank, with his hands and feet free to pedal, Natasha seated at a forty-five-degree angle on the saddle of her sky-bike.

The music stopped. The yelling dwindled away. There was a moment of near silence . . . and then the sharp crack of the starter's pistol.

At first Dugan's blimp surged horizontally forward while Natasha's sky-bike dropped half a dozen meters before she could get it up to speed.

Then she began to overtake her competitor.

It was a neck-and-neck race almost to the end of the stadium, with both flyers being loudly cheered by everybody—and not just the handful of spectators in the tube but by the tens and hundreds of millions watching wherever in the solar system a human being possessed a screen.

Twenty meters from the finish line Natasha passed her opponent. When she crossed the line, it was no longer even close, and the howling, screaming, and shouting noises of the eighteen hundred spectators in the tube was quite the loudest sound the moon had heard in many a long year.

The trip back to Earth was quite as long and quite as restricted as the journey up, but at least they had Natasha with them this time—and Natasha had her rewards of victory.

Those were quite impressive, when you added them up. It seemed that her personal screen never darkened, with messages of congratulations from basically everyone she knew, as well as a very large number of people she didn't. The presidents of Russia, China, and the United States were among her well-wishers, not to mention the leaders of nearly every other country in the United Nations. And Dr. Dhatusena Bandara on behalf of Pax per Fidem, and just about every one of her old teachers and friends, and parents of friends. And the ones she really cared about, too, such as Beatrix Vorhulst and her whole domestic staff. And that is without mentioning the ones who wanted something from her—news programs seeking interviews, representatives of several dozen movements and charities begging for an endorsement. Not least, the International Olympic Committee itself was promising their new champion a place in the planned solar-sail spacecraft race, to be held as soon as enough viable solar-sail spaceships existed in LEO and could be spared from the urgent work of settling the solar system. "Now, that's because they're getting more pressure from the big three, I'll bet," Myra informed her family. "They want to get everything going at once for their own purposes."

Her husband patted her shoulder. "And what purposes are those?" he asked tolerantly. "According to you, they already own just about everything."

Myra wrinkled her nose at him. "You'll see," she said, though what it was he would see she did not say.

They were nearly to the upper Van Allen before the volume of calls dropped low enough for their traveling companions to catch up on some of their own neglected calls home. This time there were sixteen others sharing their capsule, two wealthy Bulgarian families, though what their wealth came from Ranjit had not been quite able to identify, and a handful of almost as wealthy Canadians. (In their case, the cash cow was petroleum from the Athabascan tar sands.) Ranjit felt an obligation to apologize to their fellow passengers for Natasha's hogging of the communications circuits. They were having none of that, though. "Bless her," said the oldest of the Canadian women. "Things like this don't come often in a young girl's life. Anyway, the news channels stayed open. Mostly that rash of new flying saucer stories, but did you hear about Egypt and Kenya?"

The Subramanians had not, and when they did, they were as delighted as any other. Kenya and Egypt had not only agreed on fairly sharing Nile water, but both countries, by a suddenly called plebiscite, had voted to join the transparency compact voluntarily.

"But that's very good!" Ranjit said.

However, just then the shrill radiation warnings sounded and it was time for them to get into the shelter once more.

Ranjit sighed and led the way, followed by Natasha in conversation with one of the Canadian girls, and his wife, with Robert by the hand.

It took several minutes for all twenty of them to check out their bunks, with the warning whistle sounding all the time. And while Myra was fluffing up their pitiful excuse for a pillow, she stopped, looked around, and then demanded, "Where's Robert?"

The answer came from one of the Canadians. "He was standing by the door a minute ago," she said.

She didn't have to say anything more. Ranjit was already out of that door himself, shouting Robert's name above the screeching warnings. It didn't take him long to find his son, interestedly gazing out of the window at the polychrome blur that was the Van Allen belt, and not even that long to drag him back inside the shelter, slamming the door behind them. "He's all right," he reassured his family—and the others, all worriedly gathered around the door together as well. "I asked him what the hell he thought he was doing, and he just said 'fish.' "

Among all the sounds of amused relief it was the Canadian grandmother who pursed her lips. "Was he saying he thought he saw a fish?" she asked. "Because it was on the news that other people have seen things from the Skyhook—metallic sorts of things, kind of pointy at both ends. I guess you could say that might look like a fish."

"The same things they've been claiming people saw all over," her son-in-law confirmed. "I thought it was all just another of those crazy things people get themselves into, but I don't know. I guess it's possible they could be real."

And at that same time those quite real Nine-Limbeds in their little canoe-shaped craft were having a great debate.

The decision to turn off the vision-deflecting shields so these Earth primitives could actually see them had seemed like a good idea at the time. Having done it, the Nine-Limbeds were all trying to talk at once over the tight-beam network that allowed them to communicate without being overheard by the humans on the ground. And there was only one subject for discussion: Had they done the right thing?

In order to try to answer that, the standing orders were refreshed and restored to visibility, and studied by all. The experts in communications between the Nine-Limbeds and the Grand Galactics meditated for prolonged periods before issuing an opinion. Since they had been trained from whelping to understand every nuance of every instruction ever handed down by the Grand Galactics, their opinions were listened to atten-tively, and their findings were nearly unanimous.

Expressed in the sort of terms a human lawyer might use, they were these: The Grand Galactics had flatly forbidden the Nine-Limbeds to enter into communication with the rogue race of humans. They had not, how-ever, ordered them to take any care to see that humans didn't suspect their presence.

Accordingly, the experts reasoned that the Grand Galactics could not in justice punish the Nine-Limbeds very severely for what they had done. And, the experts concurred, the record was clear that the Grand Galactics did have some concept of justice, or of something somewhat like it. So they might reprimand. They might even punish. But it was highly unlikely that they would respond by exterminating the entire Nine-Limbed race.

Other client races of the Grand Galactics wouldn't ever have taken that sort of chance in the first place. The One Point Fives wouldn't have. Nei-ther would the Machine-Stored. Not one of the Grand Galactics' subject races had that keen a sense of humor, nor had ever dared such a transgres-sion. Up until that point, that is.

33

PRIVATE PAIN IN A
REJOICING WORLD

The Nile waters might never threaten the world's peace again, because both Egypt and Kenya passed the Pax per Fidem vote with resounding margins. Even before Pax's peacekeepers were in place, teams of Kenyan hydrologists had begun setting up shop in the control buildings around the Aswân High Dam, and both countries had opened their (rather puny) missile sites to international control. Transparency of their heavy industry, such as it was, followed quickly.

They were not the last, either. The four countries in sub-Saharan Africa that had been contesting the waters of one medium-size lake saw what became of the one of their number that had sent a force to drive the other three away. When that one—properly warned, heedless of the warning—tasted Silent Thunder for itself, all three of the others joined the first in the contract.

And then there was a major breakthrough.

The Republic of Germany debated and argued and finally held a giant plebiscite of its own. Their terrible national memories of huge and violent lost battles trumped that sometimes troublesome German sense of destiny. They, too, signed up. They threw their borders open to the United Nations, disbanded the token armed forces they had retained, and signed on to Pax per Fidem's draft constitution for the world.

Those were times for rejoicing for the people of planet Earth.

There were only two things that dampened the joys of, say, the Subramanian family. The first was the one they shared with the whole human race, namely, those pesky little apparitions that kept showing themselves—in cities at night, in the air above seagoing vessels in broad daylight, even—perhaps like young Robert's "fish"—in space. Some people called them "bronzed bananas," some "flying midget submarines," some by names a lot less printable. What no one knew was exactly what they were. The devout UFO-ologists called them the final proof that flying saucers were real. The hardened skeptics suspected that one or more of Earth's sovereign states was developing a mystery weapon unlike anything that had gone before.

What everyone agreed on, however, was that none of these objects had done any human being any detectable harm. So comedians began joking about them, and human beings have never been able to be very afraid of things they laugh at.

But for the Subramanian family, at least, there was this one other thing.

Earlier than most, little Robert had begun walking on his own, but since they'd come back from the moon, his parents had noticed something odd. The whole family would be enjoying that happy playtime between baths and bed. Little Robert would let go of his mother's knee to wander over to where his big sister was coaxing him on. And then sometimes, without warning, Robert would drop in his tracks. Would fall like a sack of potatoes, and lie there, eyes closed, for just a moment. And then the eyes would open and he would scramble precariously to his feet and, grinning and murmuring to himself as always, head for where Natasha waited.

This was new . . . and frightening.

These little episodes didn't seem to bother Robert. He didn't even seem to notice that they happened. But then, another time, it would happen again. And again.

That was the place where there was a blemish on the otherwise nearly ideal happiness of Myra and Ranjit.

They weren't exactly worried, because Robert was so conspicuously healthy in every other respect. But they were concerned. They were feeling guilty, or at least Ranjit was, because he was the one who had let Robert escape the secure chamber when they were already entering the upper Van Allen. And who knew if there had been enough of the wrong kind of radiation to do the child harm?

Myra didn't believe that for one second, but she saw the worry in her husband's eyes. They decided to seek medical help.

So they got the best and most experienced there was, and a lot of it, too. Everywhere he and Myra took their son, Ranjit's fame was on their side. The member of the medical staff who came out to greet them was never some thirty-or-so-year-old, fresh out of medical school (and thus freshly exposed to the very latest in medical lore). It was some sixty-or-so-year-old, rich with the skills of an earlier generation and now at least a department head. All of them were honored to have the famous Dr. Ranjit

Subramanian come to their facility—hospital, clinic, laboratory, whatever—and all had the same dismal tidings to offer.

Robert was in almost every aspect a healthy child. Every aspect, that was, but one. Somewhere along the line something had gone wrong. "The brain is a very complex organ," they all said—or meant, although several of them found other ways to phrase the same bad news. There could have been an unsuspected allergy, a birth injury, an undetected infection. And then the next thing they all said was pretty much the same. There wasn't any medicine, or surgical procedure, or anything else that could make Robert "normal," because the one thing all their tests had agreed on was that the son of Ranjit Subramanian and Myra de Soyza had regressed. And now was developing intellectually somewhat more slowly than one would have expected.

By then the Subramanians had worked their way through a long list of specialists. It was one of those, a pediatric speech-language pathologist, who struck fear into the hearts of Robert's parents. "Robert has begun dropping consonants—' 'athroom' and ' 'inner,' for instance," she reported. "And have you noticed whether he talks the same way to you as to his play group?" Both his parents nodded. "By now most children modify their speech patterns according to whomever they're talking to. For one of you it might be 'give me that,' for another child 'gimme 'at.' And what about comprehensibility? I imagine you can understand what he's saying, but how about friends or relatives?"

"Not always," Ranjit admitted.

Myra corrected him. "Not usually," she said. "It upsets Robert sometimes, too. But isn't there any chance he'll outgrow it?"

"Oh, yes," the pathologist said decisively. "Albert Einstein didn't talk even that well as a child. But it's something we need to watch carefully."

But when Myra raised the question with the next doctor, he just said piously, "We can always hope, Dr. de Soyza."

And another said even more piously, "There are times when we just can't question God's will."

What no one said was, "Here are certain specific things you can do to help Robert improve."

If there were such things, the medical profession didn't seem to know what they were. And all this "progress" in understanding Robert's condition had been bought at the price of some dozens of unpleasant episodes. Like strapping Robert to a gurney while they x-rayed his head. Or shaving his hair so they could wrap his skull with sticky magnetic tape. Or pinning him to a wheeled stretcher that fed him centimeter by centimeter into an

MRI machine . . . all of which produced the effect that young Robert Subramanian, who had never been afraid of anything in his little life, began to cry as soon as anyone wearing white came anywhere near him.

There was one useful thing the medical profession had done, though. They had produced pharmaceuticals that controlled the falling down—they called it "petit mal," to distinguish it from the grand mal of epilepsy, which it was not. He didn't fall down anymore. But the doctors didn't have any pills to make Robert as smart as his quite ordinary playmates.

Then came the morning when there was a knock on the door. And when Ranjit, getting ready to bike to his office at the university, opened it, the man who was standing there was Gamini. "I would have called to see if I could come over, Ranj," he said, "but I was afraid you'd say no."

Ranjit's answer was to sweep him up in a thoroughgoing hug. "You are such a fool," he told his oldest and best friend. "I thought it was the other way around. I thought you were mad at us for turning your offer down so long ago."

Released, Gamini gave him a rueful grin. "Actually," he said, "I'm not so sure you were altogether wrong. Can I come in?"

Of course Gamini Bandara could come in, where he got hugs from Myra and little Robert as well. Robert got the most attention, because Gamini had never seen him before, but then Robert went off with the cook to play with his jigsaw puzzles, and the grown-ups settled down on the veranda. "I didn't see Tashy," Gamini remarked, accepting a cup of tea.

"She's out sailing," Ranjit informed him. "She does a lot of it—says it's practice for a big race she plans to be in. But what brings you to Lanka?"

Gamini pursed his lips. "You know Sri Lanka's got a presidential election coming up? My father's planning to resign from the Pax per Fidem board and come back to run. He's hoping that if he gets elected, he can bring Sri Lanka into the compact."

Ranjit looked genuinely pleased. "More power to him for that! He'd make a great president." He paused, and Myra said what Ranjit had been unwilling to.

"You look doubtful," she observed. "Is there a problem?"

"You bet there is," Gamini told her. "It's Cuba."

. . .

He didn't really need to say more, because naturally Myra and Ranjit had been following the events there. Cuba had been on the verge of a Pax per Fidem plebiscite of its own.

It had seemed pretty certain to pass, too. Cuba had been spared the usual third world horrors. Fidel Castro had caused much harm, but he had done a certain amount of good along the way—Cuba had an educated population; a copious supply of well-trained doctors, nurses, and other health professionals; an expert corps of pest-control people. And not a single Cuban dying of starvation in more than half a century.

But the other thing Castro had done was to inflame partisan passions. Some of the sons and grandsons—and daughters!—of the Cubans who had gone off to fight and die for the world revolution in a dozen different countries had not forgotten. Even a few of the ancient fighters themselves survived, though now at least in their eighties and more, but quite capable of pulling a trigger or setting the fuse on a bomb. How many of these were there? Not enough to put the verdict of the plebiscite in doubt, anyway. When the votes were counted, disarmament, peace, and a new constitution had achieved better than 80 percent of the ballots cast. But twelve of Pax per Fidem's workers had been shot at, nine of them had been hit—the old fighters for socialism knew how to handle a gun—and two of the wounded had died.

"Well," Ranjit said after a moment, "yes, tragic, but what does it have to do with Sri Lanka?"

"It has to do with America," Gamini said angrily. "And Russia and China, too, because they do nothing. But it's America who wants to send in about six companies of U.S. troops. Troops! With rapid-fire weapons and, I'm pretty sure, even tanks! When the whole point of Pax per Fidem is that we never use lethal force!"

Everyone was silent for a moment. Then, "I see," Myra said, and stopped there.

It was Ranjit who said: "Go ahead, Myra. You've got the right. Say 'I told you so.' "

34

PENTOMINOES AND CARS

Natasha Subramanian was practicing wind curls on the shallow seas near her parents' home when she saw the odd-looking yellow car. It was coming down one of the streets that led to the beach, hesitating at each intersection. When it turned off that one, the street it turned onto was the one that the Subramanian home was on. From her position standing on her windsurf board she couldn't see the house itself, but she could see the next street over clearly enough. The car didn't appear there. So it had to have stopped at one of the houses on their block, and Natasha couldn't help wondering if it had been theirs.

Since she was also aware that it was getting close to time for lunch, that made it a good time to come ashore. When she did, she saw that the yellow car was indeed parked in her driveway . . . but in the time it had taken her to get home, the car had suffered a peculiar change. Most of the front seat, including the space for the driver, was gone. Then, when she entered her kitchen, there was an old, old man in monks' robes sitting at their table, watching Robert solve one of his jigsaw puzzles. Next to him stood the missing fraction of the car, balanced on two rubber-tired wheels and emitting a gentle hum.

It had been years since Natasha had seen the old monk, but she knew him at once. "You're Surash, who used to change my father's diapers. I thought you were dying," she said.

Her mother gave her a sharp look, but Surash only smiled and patted her head. "I was indeed dying," he said. "I still am, and so are we all, but I'm not housebound anymore. Not since they gave me this." He dislodged Robert and pointed to the wheeled thing behind his chair. "I have promised to show your parents how it works. Come with us, Natasha."

When Surash made the transition from his chair at the table to the seat of his two-wheeled contraption, Natasha could see how frail and tottery he really was. But once in the seat he turned the vehicle's steering rod with a firm hand and wheeled it briskly through the door that her father had hurriedly opened for him.

When Surash backed his two-wheeler into the gap at the front of the waiting car, there were some quick sounds of turning gears. The main section of the car extruded strong grippers that locked the two-wheeled chair in place. A muted whistling sound came from the engine, and a cloud of pure white began to come out of the exhaust pipe at the rear. "Put your finger in it if you wish," Surash called. "All I burn in this thing, you see, is simple hydrogen."

"We know about hydrogen-fueled cars," Ranjit informed him.

The old monk nodded benignly. "But do you know about this?" he asked, and demonstrated how, once his two-wheeled personal chariot was attached, the whole thing became a road-drivable car that could take him in comfort wherever he might choose to go.

Then, Myra insisted, it was time for lunch. And friendly talk. A lot of it. Surash wanted to hear all about Ranjit's work at the university, and Natasha's hopes for using some of her sailing skills at the great solar-sail space race that was to take place in just over a year, and Robert's surprising skills at putting jigsaw puzzles together, and Myra's struggle to keep up with the rest of her cohort at her profession. And even more he wanted to tell them how things were at the great temple in Trincomalee and where he had been in his new car—all up and down the island, he boasted, in his effort to complete a long longed-for pilgrimage to Sri Lanka's most famous Hindu temples—and, most of all, how well the car had worked.

And where had this wonderful new machine come from? "Korea," Surash said promptly. "They've just begun marketing it, and one of our people was able to get this one for me. Oh," he said, almost jubilant, "isn't it fine that with so much less of our efforts going into wars and preparing for wars we're able to do so much more in other ways? Like that thing they call a nuclear quadrupole resonance detector that they use to find buried land mines, and then there's a thing like a little robot on caterpillar treads that comes along and clears the dirt off the mines and puts them away and no one gets hurt! They've cleaned up almost all the old battlefields near Trinco now. And they've got that gene-spliced hormone spray that's tuned to the DNA of the mosquitoes that carry the bending disease, and they've got little robot planes that go around and spray them dead. And much more. We owe a lot to that Silent Thunder!"

Ranjit nodded, looking at his wife. Who tossed her head and said, "I never said it was all bad, did I?"

. . .

When Surash was finally gone, his peculiarly complex car sputtering steam as it pulled away from the house, Ranjit came back inside. "He's a wonderful old man," Myra told him.

Ranjit agreed without hesitation. "Do you know where he's been in that contraption? He started at Naguleswaram, north of Jaffna. I don't know how many other temples he visited, but when he was at Munneswaram, he was just north of Colombo, and of course he could not visit the city and not stop to see us. Now he's heading south to Katirka-mam, although that temple's more likely to be used by Buddhists these days. And I think he's going to pay a visit to the Skyhook terminal, too." He hesitated, then added thoughtfully, "He's very interested in science, you know?"

Myra gave him a sharp look. "What is it, Ranjit?"

"Oh. . . ." He gave it a dismissive shrug that did not quite dismiss the subject. "Well, the first thing he said to me outside was he reminded me that I still owned my father's old house and it was just sitting there vacant."

"Well, but your work's here," Myra told him.

"Yes, I said that. Then he asked me if I was surprised that he talked about scientific things like his new car so fluently. And he said, 'But I learned from your father, Ranjit. One can believe in religion and still love science.' And then he looked really serious and said, 'So what about the opposite? Can one love science and still honor God? What of your children, Ranjit? What sort of religious education are you giving them?' And he didn't wait for an answer because he knew what the answer would be."

"Ah," Myra said, because she knew what the answer would have to be, too, and knew that hearing it would have hurt Surash. They had discussed the matter of religion long since, she and Ranjit, and they were of the same mind. If Ranjit quoted one obscure twentieth-century philosopher's "All religions were invented by the devil to hide God from mankind," she might retort with, "The greatest tragedy in mankind's entire history may be the hijacking of morality by the church. The church doesn't know what to do with morality. It thinks morality is defined by the will of a nonexistent person."

Still, Myra knew how fond her husband was of the old monk. Lacking any ideas that would satisfy them all, she changed the subject. "Did you see what Robert was doing for Surash when you were coming in?"

He blinked at her. "No—oh, wait a minute. He was doing one of his little jigsaws, wasn't he?"

"Not so little, Ranjit. That was a five-hundred-piecer he did in the kitchen. And there's something else he's been doing."

She stopped there, smiling. Ranjit took the bait. "Are you going to tell me what that is?" he demanded.

"I'd rather show you. Let's go up to his room." She wouldn't say anything more until they were there. Robert, sitting before his screen and its pictures of animals, looked up with a big smile on his face. "Robert, dear," his mother said, "why don't you show your dad your pentominoes?"

The news that his son was interested in pentominoes wasn't entirely a shock to Ranjit. He had been fascinated by them himself, at the age of five or six, and he was the one who had first tried to interest the boy in them. He had patiently explained the little tiles to Robert: "You know what a domino looks like, two squares stuck together. Well, if you stick three squares together, you call it a trimino, and it can take two shapes—one that looks like a capital *I*, the other a capital *L*. Do you see what I mean?"

Robert had peered gravely at his father's demonstration but wouldn't commit himself about understanding. Nevertheless Ranjit had plunged on. "If you go to four squares, together it's called a tetromino, and it can take four shapes—"

He drew swiftly:

```
X    X    X    XX
XX   X    X    XX
X    XX   X
          X
```

"Rotations and reflections don't count," he added, and then had to explain what rotations and reflections were. "None of the tetromino shapes is particularly exciting, but when you go to five squares stuck together, things start to happen!" Because, he said, there were twelve of the five-squared pentominoes. When you put them all together, you had a tiled surface of sixty squares.

Which immediately raised the question: Could you tile a surface of sixty squares—say, a five-by-twelve rectangle, or a long, skinny two-by-thirty rectangle—using all twelve pentominoes, so that the whole surface was covered and no squares were left over?

The answer—which had fascinated five-year-old Ranjit—was not only that you could but that you could do it in no less than 3,719 ways! The six-by-ten rectangles had 2,339 ways of tiling, the five-by-twelves had 1,010 ways, and so on.

How much of what he'd been saying had gotten past Robert's cheer-fully affectionate mask Ranjit could not have said. Then Robert had oblig-ingly switched the program on his learning computer. At once it had begun to roll off images of different pentomino tilings—all of the tilings for the five-by-twelves, then the six-by-tens, and so on to the very end.

Ranjit was now startled and delighted in almost equal amounts. The "handicapped" Robert had identified and displayed every last one of the pentomino tilings—a task that Ranjit himself had given up on all those years ago! "I—I—I think that's grand, Robert," he began, reaching out to his son for a hug.

And then he stopped, staring at the screen.

It had completed the display of pentomino patterns. What Ranjit ex-pected it to do then was to turn itself off. It didn't do that. It took the next step and went on to seek hexomino patterns.

Ranjit had never mentioned hexominoes to his son. It was too compli-cated a subject for Robert to have any hope of grasping it, Ranjit was sure. Why, there were thirty-five different hexominoes, and if you spread them all out, they covered a surface of two hundred ten units. And that was where young Ranjit had found them unwelcomely disappointing in those long-ago days of his childhood. Any rational person would think that a truly astronomical number of those two-hundred-ten-unit rectangles could be exactly covered by the thirty-five hexominoes. That person would be wrong. Not a single rectangle, whatever the ratio of its sides, could be tiled by the hexominoes in any pattern at all. Always, irreparably, there would be at least four empty spaces left over.

Obviously, that would have been too hard, and too frustrating, for the handicapped little Robert.

But evidently the real-world little Robert hadn't been deterred at all! His computer screen was rolling off hexomino pattern after hexomino pat-tern. Robert wasn't satisfied to just give up. He was going to check every one off for himself.

When Ranjit hugged his son, it was with almost bone-bending force; young Robert wriggled and grunted, though mostly with pleasure.

For years the people who were supposed to be helping Myra and Ran-jit with "the Robert problem" had offered the same, unsatisfying consola-tion: Don't think of him as disabled. Think of him as "differently abled."

But that had never made sense to Ranjit. Not until today, when he found something that his son not only could do, but could do better than almost anyone else Ranjit knew.

He found his cheeks damp—with tears of joy—as the family finally went downstairs to their postponed daily chores, and to the real world. And for the first time in his life, Ranjit Subramanian almost wished that there really had been a God—any kind of a God—that he could have believed in, so that there would have been someone he could thank.

It was at this point that "Bill," on his journey homeward, stopped for a brief period in the vicinity of that mildly troublesome planet whose inhabitants called it Earth. Though it was not a long stop, it was ample for him to be deluged with many billions of billions of bits of information concerning what the condemned inhabitants of Earth were currently doing and, more important by far, what egregious action the local representatives of the Grand Galactics, the Nine-Limbeds, had taken it upon themselves to commit.

One could not say that what the Nine-Limbeds had done was of a caliber to worry the Grand Galactics. The Grand Galactics had nothing to fear from a few billion ragtag mammalian humans, with their pitiful weaponry—the nuclear kind of weapons that exploded and knocked things around, or that other nuclear kind of weapon that generated electromagnetic pulses that interfered destructively with an opponent's own electromagnetic pulses. Such rudimentary matters were insignificant to the Grand Galactics. They would fear them about as much as some H-bomb-wielding human general might fear a gypsy woman's curse.

Nevertheless, in letting the humans know of their existence, the Nine-Limbeds had done something that, if not strictly prohibited for them, was not specifically allowed, either.

Actions would have to be taken. Decisions would have to be made.

For the first time ever Bill wondered whether he alone should make such decisions, or whether he needed to rejoin with the other Grand Galactics to meditate these decisions' implications.

35

THE USES OF
VACCINATION

Dr. Dhatusena Bandara did indeed resign from the Pax per Fidem board so he could run for the presidency of Sri Lanka. What left Ranjit open-mouthed was that the elder Bandara's replacement on the board was his son: Ranjit Subramanian's boyhood friend was now part of the team that wielded Silent Thunder.

So Ranjit went to bed filled with wonder, and when he woke up the next morning, there was something else to wonder at. The breakfast he could smell cooking was not the kind of breakfast Myra usually preferred. Even stranger, when he got out of the shower and had begun to dress, he heard the distant sound of his wife singing what appeared to be some hymn from her childhood memories of Sunday school. Mystified, he pulled on a shirt and hurried to the kitchen.

Myra was indeed singing cheerfully to herself. She stopped as Ranjit came into the room, pursed her lips for a good-morning kiss, and waved him to the breakfast table. "Start with the juice," she instructed. "I'll have your eggs in a minute."

Ranjit recognized what she was stirring up. "Scrambled eggs? And sausage, and those home-fried potatoes. What is it, Myra, are you home-sick for California?"

She gave him a fond smile. "No, but I know you like this kind of food now and then, and I wanted to celebrate. Ranj, I woke up with an idea! I know how to make Surash happy and keep our principles intact!"

Ranjit drained the juice glass and watched with pleasure as Myra heaped the solid parts of the menu onto his plate. "If you can do that," he declared, "I'm going to tell Gamini to put you on the Pax per Fidem board."

She gave him another smile, but all she said was, "Can you eat four sausages? Tashy wouldn't touch them. Said she'd get something at the university."

Ranjit returned the smile with a mock-scowl. "Myra! Stop this talk of sausages and tell me how we make Surash happy!"

"Well," she said, sitting down next to him and pouring herself a cup of tea, "today's the day I take Robert in for his booster shots, you know. And I had a dream about it. I dreamed Robert was home, playing with his computer things, only he was stuck all over with little rolled-up darts of paper, and when I pulled one out of his shoulder and looked at it, I saw that they were all Bible verses."

Ranjit's scowl deepened. "It would be perfectly normal to have a dream that expressed concern over our child's immunizations," he informed her.

"Oh, yes, my darling," she said affectionately, "but what was he being immunized against? We give the kids smallpox shots so they'll get immunized and won't be troubled with smallpox when they grow up. So if we inject them with Bible verses as children—I'm thinking of the kind of Sunday school I went to as a young girl—won't they be—"

"Immunized against grown-up religion!" Ranjit shouted. He stood up and wrapped his arms around her. "You're the best wife I ever had," he told her. "It's a great idea! Only—" He hesitated. "Do you think Natasha wants to take time from her busy schedule to go to Sunday school?"

"Yes," Myra admitted, "that's a problem. All we can do is try to persuade her."

But when Natasha came home from her stint at the university's solar-sail training center, she was radiant with joy. "It came!" she cried, waving a printout in the faces of her parents. "I'm confirmed for the race!"

Ranjit had never doubted that she would be, but he joined in the celebration, picking her up in a great bear hug . . . and then setting her down as soon as seemed proper, because his daughter was already three centimeters taller than he, with a body composed largely of muscle. Myra offered a congratulatory kiss, and then began studying the document that bore the official seal of the International Olympic Committee. "There are ten of you that are confirmed," she observed. "And who's this R. Olsos from Brazil? He's another solar-sail pilot. Sounds familiar."

Natasha produced what could only be called a giggle. "That's Ron," she told her mother. "Ronaldinho Olsos, the hundred-meter boy you met on the moon."

Myra gave her an inquisitorial look. "When did he stop being a runner and turn into a solar-sail pilot?"

"Oh," Natasha said idly, "it might be that I had something to do with it. He kept sounding jealous of what I was doing. We've sort of kept in touch ever since."

"I see," said Myra, who hadn't known anything of the kind. However, as Myra de Soyza had at one time been a teenage girl herself, and remembered quite well how little she had wanted her parents involved in her experimental dealings with boys, she didn't press the matter. She sent the maid out to the nearest decent bakery for a non-birthday but definitely celebratory cake for Natasha, which she herself decorated with an approximate sketch of the solar-sail ship Natasha would sail, and made a party out of that night's dinner.

The Subramanian family was used to parties. Out of considerable experience they had become very good at them, too, so by the time Natasha had blown out the candles on her cake and made her conventional wish (not to be told to anyone, especially her parents), they were all feeling warmly, affectionately jovial. That was when Robert threw his arms around his big sister and whispered in her ear.

Which made her look startled. She turned to her parents. "Is that true? You're going to make Robert go to church?"

"Not church," her father said. "It's a Sunday school. We've checked, and they have a class that would be good for him—learning the stories about Jesus and his Sermon on the Mount and all. And it would make Surash happy to know that my father's grandchildren aren't being kept entirely away from religion—"

Natasha shook her head crossly. "I don't mind being kept entirely away from religion. And Robert says you want me to go, too! Honestly, don't you think I have enough to do already? School, solar-sail practice—"

"It's only one evening a week," her mother informed her. "We aren't talking about Sunday school for you. You'd go to the church's teenager group. They do talk about the Bible now and then, yes, but most of their time is spent on projects to make the world a better place."

"Which, for now," her father added, "is mostly working for Bandara Senior's campaign for the presidency. I assume you might like to help with that."

That was unquestioned for Natasha, or any of the rest of her family, either. It was the elder Bandara who had persuaded the university to set up the solar-sail simulation laboratory that gave Natasha her best hope of doing well in the race to come. The solar-sail lab was orders of magnitude less expensive than the lunar-gravity chamber she had had to practice in for the moon race; it was little more than a chamber in which all six of the walls were screens. But the computer programs to run it were complex—and expensive. It was a major outlay for the university, and would have been totally impossible for the Subramanian family alone.

"And," her mother said, passing Natasha her personal screen, "I have a picture of the group when they had a beach party a few weeks ago. They look like kids you might want to be friendly with."

"Huh," Natasha said, studying the score or so of young people displayed on the screen.

She didn't comment on the fact that at least four of the boys in the picture were notably good-looking. Neither did her mother, although she was pretty sure that this unexpectedly reappearing Ron from Brazil wasn't nearly as handsome.

"Of course," Myra said, "it's completely up to you. If you really feel you'd rather not—"

"Oh," Natasha said, "I suppose I could try it out once or twice. As you say, it'd make Surash happy."

When Bill returned to unite himself once more with his cluster of Grand Galactics, he wasn't prepared for the joyous rush of feeling that came with the experience. All the time he had been detached for the running of his various errands, he had been something that was not a part of his previous life experience. He had been alone. And then, once again joined to his fellows, he wasn't alone anymore, and he was jubilant.

It was almost difficult for him to leave the cluster again.

There wasn't any choice, of course. The cluster had shared his concerns, and his need to be fair. Perhaps these wretched little humans no longer posed a threat to the galaxy's peace. If so, perhaps it was unfair to wipe them out.

The Grand Galactics were always stern and sometimes ruthless. But they did not deliberately choose to be unfair.

So Bill took the jumps that returned him to the neighborhood of the little yellow sun that their planet revolved around, and sent two messages.

The first was to the One Point Five armada, now only a small fraction of a light-year from the planet it had been instructed to depopulate. "Cancel instructions for depopulation," that message began. "Stop. Decelerate totally. Use emergency measures if necessary."

And the second message was to the armada, but also to the Nine-Limbeds themselves. It merely ordered that no further evidence of their presence should be given to the Earth humans—

Which made a small problem for the Machine-Stored operators of the armada's 154 ships.

They understood their orders, but those were much easier given than obeyed. In spacecraft you couldn't just slam on the brakes. There weren't any brakes. It was one thing to amp up the deceleration firing, which they did at once. That was terribly wasteful of electrical energy and working fluid, of course, but that didn't matter. Those commodities, like everything else in the observable universe, did after all belong to the Grand Galactics. If they chose to waste them, that was no one's business but their own.

No, it was the second part of their instruction that troubled the One Point Fives. They were commanded to avoid being observed by the subject species.

But never mind that the Nine-Limbeds had already blown their cover. When the One Point Fives were pouring gigajoules of energy into their exhausts, making a blazing beacon of ionized gases from 154 mammoth torches all firing at once, how could they remain unseen?

36

PREPARING FOR
THE RACE

Some people might have expected that the bon voyage party for the solar-sail contestants would have been held in some giant auditorium in a city like New York, or Beijing, or Moscow. It wasn't. True, the cameras were there, and everything that happened within their sight went out to the whole world's screens. But the place where the cameras were was only the terminal's little auditorium, and—counting everybody, the seven racers themselves, their handlers, their immediate families, and a very few VIP guests—there weren't more than two hundred people in the room.

Myra had her suspicions about why. No doubt no two of the big three were willing to let the other one have the event. She said nothing, however. Then she caught a glimpse of her daughter, standing serious and tall with the other six contestants as a judge gave them a last-minute review of the rules of the race. "Doesn't she look good?" she whispered to her husband, knowing the answer.

She got it. Ranjit had no more doubt than she that Natasha wasn't only the smartest and best of the solar-sail pilots, but that she looked astonishingly, even a little worrisomely, mature for her sixteen years. He focused on the most worrisome part of the scene. "There's that Brazilian, Olsos, standing right next to her," he pointed out to his wife.

She squeezed his hand. "Ron's all right," she told him, with the wisdom that came with once having been a sixteen-year-old girl herself. And then, "Oh, hello, Joris."

Vorhulst got a hug from her, and the two men shook hands. "They're going to start in a minute," Vorhulst told them. "I just wanted to say hello—and to tell you that we've got a little pool going among the Skyhook engineers. My money's on Natasha."

Myra said, "Is that what you engineers were getting excited about a little while ago?"

Vorhulst blinked at her. "Oh, that. No. It was an all-points message from the Sky Events center in Massachusetts. There's been a hell of a bright supernova just observed in Centaurus, but it's got some funny features." He grinned. "Almost makes me wish I'd stayed with astronomy." And then, as the chairman of the event mounted the podium and all the members of the audience began the move toward their chairs, he said, "See you later!"

There was only one speaker at the ceremony, and that was the newly elected president of the Republic of Sri Lanka, Dhatusena Bandara. He looked presidential, all right, with a strong old face and the slim figure of a man who had never let himself go soft. But what he said was informal, almost jocular. "There were several nations," he told the select few who were his audience, "who wanted this event to be held in some great city, but you are here. That isn't because my country is more deserving than any other. It's simply because, through the good fortune of geography, Sri Lanka is the site for the Skyhook. Without the Skyhook this race could never be. It is the Skyhook that you seven wonderful young men and women will board to take you to low earth orbit. It was the Skyhook that carried each one of your spacecraft up to that point, piece by piece, and now those pieces are nearly completely assembled into the craft that you will fly in this greatest of all races. May God bless you all, and see you safely home when the race is over."

And that was the end of it, except for the good-bye hugs and kisses before the pilots and their handlers moved toward the Skyhook loading platform. Ranjit observed, not with displeasure, that this Ronaldinho Olsos from Brazil was boarding the first capsule, while Natasha was among those going in the third.

When they had kissed Natasha good-bye for the fourth or fifth time, and had at last successfully untangled Robert from her arms, the remainder of the Subramanian family, like everyone else, began to head for the buses.

There, squarely in their way, was Joris Vorhulst, standing by himself and talking agitatedly into his pocket screen. "So, Joris," Myra said as they came up to him, "what are you worrying about now? Did they find another supernova?"

Her tone was jocular. Vorhulst's expression was not. He folded his screen shut and shook his head. "Not exactly. What they saw may not be a supernova at all, now that the space telescopes are lining up to get a good look at it. And it's a lot closer than any supernova should be. It may even be right in the Oort cloud."

Myra stopped, her hand to her breast. "It isn't going to bother the racers—?"

Vorhulst shook his head. "Oh, there's no danger of that. No. The solar sailers will be in low earth orbit. This thing, whatever it is, is a long, long way from there. But I wish I knew what it was."

Up where the solar sailers were nearly completely assembled, their riggers were not alone.

No one saw the tiny spacecraft of the Nine-Limbeds, because they had restored their photon-shifters long since. But their Nine-Limbed crews were nearly as puzzled as Joris Vorhulst, though about an entirely different matter. These seven nearly completed sail ships—what were they for? They bore no sign of any kind of weaponry. That relieved the Nine-Limbeds of one sort of worry, but another kind remained. None among the Nine-Limbeds had any idea of what these spacecraft were up to. And that was not a fact that the Nine-Limbeds wanted to report to their Grand Galactic masters.

37

THE RACE

Her ship's name was *Diana,* chosen by Natasha Subramanian herself. It had never flown. Now it was ready. It lay moored to its mother ship with its enormous disk of sail straining at the rigging, already filled with the great, silent wind that blew between the worlds. The race was ready to begin.

"T minus two minutes," said her cabin radio. "Cross-check to confirm readiness."

One by one the other skippers answered. Natasha recognized every voice—some tense, some almost inhumanly calm—for they were the voices of her friends and rivals. In all of the places where humanity dwelt there were scarcely a score of men and women who owned the skills needed to sail a sun yacht. Every one of them was here, at the starting line like Natasha or aboard the escort vessels, orbiting thirty-six thousand kilometers above Earth's equator.

"Number One, *Gossamer.* Ready to go!"

"Number Two, *Woomera,* all okay."

"Number Three, *Sunbeam.* Okay!"

"Number Four, *Santa Maria,* all systems go." Natasha smiled. That one was Ron Olsos, of course, whom she liked, though perhaps not as much as he seemed to like her. The Brazilian's reply had been an ancient echo from the early days of astronautics, typical of Ron's tendency toward the theatrical.

"Number Five, *Lebedev.* We're ready." That was the Russian, Efremy.

"Number Six, *Arachne.* Also okay." Hsi Liang, the young woman from some village north of Chengdu, in the shadow of the Himalayas. And then, at the end of the line, it was Natasha's turn to say the words that would be heard around the world and in every human outpost:

"Number Seven, *Diana.* Ready to win!"

And let old Ronaldinho take that, she thought as she turned to make one last check of the tensions in her rigging.

To Natasha, floating weightless in her tiny cabin, *Diana*'s sail seemed to fill the sky. Well it might. Out there, ready to take her free of Earth's gravitational bonds, were more than five million square meters of sail, webbed to her command capsule by almost a hundred kilometers of bucky-cord rigging. Those square kilometers of aluminized plastic sail, though only a few millionths of a centimeter thick, would exert enough force—she hoped!—to put her first across the lunar-orbit finish line.

The wall speaker again: "T minus ten seconds. All recording instruments on!"

Eyes still fixed on the vast billow of sail, Natasha touched the switch that turned on all *Diana*'s cameras and instrument recorders. It was the sail that held her imagination. Something that was at once so huge and so frail was difficult for the mind to grasp. Harder still was to believe that this mirrored wisp could tow her ever faster through space by nothing more than the power of the sunlight it would trap.

". . . five, four, three, two, one. Detach!"

Seven diamond-edged computer-controlled knife blades sliced through seven thin tethers at once. Then the yachts were free. Until this moment yachts and servicing vessels had circled the Earth as a single unit, firmly held together. Now the yachts would begin to disperse like dandelion seeds drifting before a breeze.

And the one that first drifted past the orbit of the moon would be the winner.

Aboard *Diana* nothing among the senses of Natasha's body registered a change. She had not expected anything would; the only thing that showed that any thrust at all was being exerted was the dial on her instrument board, now registering an acceleration that was almost one one-thousandth of one Earth gravity.

That was, of course, almost ludicrously tiny. Yet it was more than any manned solar-sail vessel had ever managed before, just as *Diana*'s designers and builders had promised it would be. Such accelerations had never been achieved in any but toy-size rigs, but there it was now. At this rate—she calculated quickly, smiled as the result appeared on her board—she would need only two circuits of Earth to build up enough velocity to leave low earth orbit and head for the moon. And then the full force of the sun's radiation would be behind her.

The full force of the sun's radiation . . .

Natasha's smile persisted as she thought of all the attempts she had made to explain solar sailing to audiences of potential backers and the merely curious on Earth. "Hold your hand to the sun, palm up," she would tell them. "What do you feel?" And then, when there was no answer beyond, perhaps, "a little heat," she would spring the rationale for solar sailing on them. "But there is something else. There's pressure. Not much of it, no. In fact so little that you can't possibly feel it, far less than a milligram's thrust on your palms. But see what that tiny pressure can do!"

And then she would pull out a few square meters of sail material and toss it toward her audience. The silvery film would coil and twist like smoke, and then drift toward the ceiling on the rising plume of warm air the human bodies made. And Natasha would continue:

"You can see how light the sail is. The whole square kilometer my yacht will deploy weighs less than a ton. That's all we need. It's enough to collect two kilograms of radiation pressure, so the sail will start to move . . . and the rigging will pull my *Diana* right along with it. Of course, the acceleration will be tiny—less than a thousandth of a G—but let's see what that pitiful little thrust can do.

"In the first second, *Diana* will move about half a centimeter. Not even that much, really, because the rigging will stretch enough so that that first move can't even be measured."

She would turn toward the screen on the wall of the room, snapping her fingers to set it alight. It would display the vast, if almost impalpable, semi-cylindrical span of the sail, then zoom down to the passenger capsule—not much bigger than a motel shower stall—that would be Natasha's home for the weeks in transit.

She would then go on. "After a minute, though, the motion is quite detectable. By then we've covered twenty meters, and our velocity has become nearly one kilometer per hour . . . with only a few hundred thousand more kilometers to go to reach the orbit of the moon."

Then there would often be a faint titter from the audience. Natasha would smile back good-naturedly until it had died away, before going on. "That's not bad, you know. After the first hour we'll be sixty kilometers from our starting point, and by then we'll be moving at a hundred kilometers an hour. And please remember where we are! All of this will be taking place in space, where there is no friction. Once you start something to move, it will move forever, with nothing slowing it down but the gravity of distant objects. You'll be surprised when I tell you what kind of velocity our thousandth-of-a-G sailboat will be giving us by the end of its first day's run. Almost three thousand kilometers an hour, all from the thrust of a sunlight pressure that you can't even feel!"

Well, she'd convinced them. In the end the whole world had been convinced, or at least the people in high places, the decision makers, had been. Foundations, individuals, the treasuries of three great nations (and smaller amounts from dozens of smaller treasuries) had come together to meet the staggering bills for this event. It was paying off, though. The free-flying race in that old lunar lava tube had successfully sparked a trickle of actual lunar tourism. Now this new event already owned the biggest audience in history. And the big boys were already commissioning their prospector vessels, many of them solar-sail-driven themselves, to begin to investigate the raw material wealth of the solar system.

And here was young Natasha de Soyza Subramanian, right in the middle of it all!

Diana had made a good start. Now Natasha had time to take a look at the opposition. For starters she shrugged out of most of her clothing, since there was no one else around to see. Then, moving very cautiously—there were shock absorbers between her control capsule and the delicate rigging of the sail, but Natasha was determined to take no risks at all—she stationed herself at the periscope.

There the other spacecraft were, looking like strange silvery flowers planted in the dark fields of space. There was South America's *Santa Maria,* Ron Olsos at the helm, only eighty kilometers away. *Santa Maria* bore a close resemblance to a boy's kite, though a kite that measured more than a kilometer on a side. Beyond *Santa Maria* was the Russian Cosmodyne Corporation's *Lebedev,* looking like a Maltese cross; the theory, Natasha knew, was that the sails that formed its four fat arms could be used for steering purposes. In contrast, the Australian *Woomera* was a simple old-fashioned round parachute, though one that was five kilometers in circumference. General Spacecraft's *Arachne,* as its name suggested, looked like a spider's web—and had been built on the same principles, by robot shuttles spiraling out from a central point. Eurospace's *Gossamer* was an identical design, though slightly smaller. And the People's Republic of China's *Sunbeam* was a flat ring, with a kilometer-wide hole in the center, spinning slowly so that it was stiffened by centrifugal force. That was an old idea, Natasha knew, but no one had ever made it work well. She was fairly sure the Asian vessel would have trouble when *Sunbeam* started to turn.

That, of course, would not be for another six hours, after all seven of the solar yachts had moved through the first quarter of their twenty-four-hour geosynchronous orbit. Here, at the beginning of the race, they were all headed directly away from the sun—running, as it were, before the solar wind. Each of them had to make the most of that first lap, before the laws of orbital motion swung them around Earth. When that point was reached, they would suddenly be heading directly back toward the sun. That was when expert pilotage would really count.

Not now, though. Now Natasha had no navigational worries. With the periscope she made a careful examination of her sail, checking each attachment point for the rigging. The shroud lines, narrow bands of unsilvered plastic film, would have been quite invisible had they not been coated with fluorescent dye. Now, in Natasha's periscope, they were taut lines of colored light, dwindling away for hundreds of meters toward the gigantic span of the sail. Each line had its own little electric windlass, not much bigger than the reel on a fly fisherman's rod. The windlasses, computer-controlled, were constantly turning, playing lines in or out as the autopilot kept the sail trimmed to the correct angle to the sun.

To Natasha, the play of sunlight on her great mirrored sail was beautiful to watch. The sail undulated in stately oscillations, sending multiple images of the sun marching across it until they faded at the edges. Those oscillations, of course, were not a problem. Such leisurely vibrations were inevitable in so vast and flimsy a structure, and usually quite harmless. Nevertheless, Natasha watched them carefully, alert for signs that they might ultimately build up to the catastrophic waves that were known as "wriggles." Those could tear a sail to pieces, but her computer reassured her that the present pattern posed no danger.

When she was satisfied that everything was shipshape—and not before!—she allowed herself to access her personal screen. Since everything passed through the command craft before it got to her, and they were careful to pass on only messages from an approved list, she was spared the endless flood of good luck wishes and begging pleas for some favor or other. There was one message from her family, one from Gamini, and one from Joris Vorhulst. No more. She was glad to get them. None required any answer.

Natasha thought for a moment of going to sleep. Of course, the race had just started, but sleeping was something she needed to ration adequately to herself. All the other yachts had two-person crews. They could take turns asleep, but Natasha Subramanian had no one to relieve her.

That had been her own decision, of course—remembering that other solitary sailer, Joshua Slocum, who long ago had single-handedly taken his tiny sailboat, *Spray,* around the world. If Slocum could do it, she maintained, she could. There was a good reason to try it, too. The performance of a sun yacht depended inversely on the mass it had to move. A second person, with all her supplies, would have meant adding another three hundred kilos, and that could easily have been the difference between winning and losing.

So Natasha snapped the elastic bands of the cabin seat around her waist and legs. She hesitated for a moment. It might be interesting, she thought, to look in on some of the news broadcasts, particularly to see if any astronomer had yet made any sense of that peculiar not-a-supernova that had blossomed astonishingly bright in the southern sky and then simply disappeared. . . .

Discipline won out over curiosity. She placed the electrodes of the sleep-inducer onto her forehead, set the time for three hours, and relaxed. Very gently, the hypnotic pulses throbbed in the frontal lobes of her brain. Colored spirals of light expanded beneath her closed eyelids, widening outward to infinity.

Then nothing.

What dragged Natasha back from her dreamless sleep was the brazen clamor of the alarm. Instantly she was awake, her eyes scanning the instrument board. Only two hours had passed . . . but above the accelerometer a red light was flashing.

Thrust was failing. The *Diana* was losing power.

Training brought discipline. Discipline prevented panic. Nevertheless, Natasha's heart was in her mouth as she cast off her restraining straps to act. Her first thought was that something had happened to the sail. Perhaps the anti-spin devices had failed and the rigging was twisting itself up. But as she checked the meters that read out the tensions of the shroud lines, what they told her was strange. On one side of the sail the meters were reading normally. On the other the value was dropping slowly before her eyes.

Then understanding came. Natasha grabbed the periscope for a wide-angle scan of the edges of the sail. Yes! There was the trouble . . . and it could have come from only one cause.

The huge sharp-edged shadow that had begun to slide across the gleaming silver of *Diana*'s sail told the story. Darkness was spreading over one edge of Natasha's ship as though a cloud had passed between her and the sun, cutting off light, putting a stop to the tiny pressure that drove the craft.

There were no such clouds in space.

Natasha grinned as she swung the periscope sunward. Optical filters clicked automatically into position to save her from instant blindness, and what she saw was precisely what she had expected to see. It looked as though a giant boy's kite were sliding across the face of the sun.

Natasha recognized the shape at once. Thirty kilometers astern, South America's *Santa Maria* was trying to produce an artificial eclipse for Natasha.

"Ha, Senhor Ronaldinho Olsos," Natasha whispered, "that's the oldest trick in the book!"

So it was, and a perfectly legal one, too. Back in the days of ocean racing, skippers had done their best to rob opponents of their wind.

But only the incompetents were caught that way, and incompetent, Natasha de Soyza Subramanian was not. Her tiny computer—the size of a matchbook but the equivalent of a thousand human number-crunching experts—considered the problem for a brief fraction of a moment and quickly spat out course corrections.

Two could play at that game. Grinning, Natasha reached out to disable the autopilot and make the adjustments to the trim in her rigging. . . .

That didn't happen.

The tiny windlasses stayed frozen. Suddenly they were receiving no orders at all, either from the autopilot computer or from the human being that should have been controlling everything.

Solar yacht *Diana* was no longer under way. The vast sail began to tip. . . .

And then to bend. . . .

And then the ripples in the fabric began to grow into great, irregular billows. And the flimsy material that was the sail reached, and passed, its maximum tolerated stress.

The commodore saw at once that *Diana* was in trouble. Indeed, the whole fleet did, and radio discipline evaporated in a flash. Ron Olsos was the first to demand a chemical-powered tender to take him off his own ship so that he could help search for Natasha Subramanian in the collapsing ruin that had been the space yacht *Diana*. He wasn't the last. Within another hour the race had dissolved into more than a score of vessels of all kinds milling about the crumpled mass that had once been beautiful *Diana,* doing their best to avoid colliding with one another. The spacecraft that possessed the capability of man-in-space technology suited up as many of their crews as they could and searched.

38

THE HUNT FOR
NATASHA SUBRAMANIAN

three fourths of the Subramanian family that remained on Earth
ved to do was carry on with as normal a life as was possible, with
quarter of the family gallivanting through cislunar space in a con-
of plastic and buckyball carbon. Accordingly, once they had sent
their final good luck message, Ranjit had got on his bike to head
ffice. Myra had seen the possibility of a whole hour, maybe two,
try to catch up on what her increasing backlog of journals had to
t some of the hotter subjects in the area of AI and prostheses. Such
a few personal hours were not frequent. They came when young
was asleep, or when he was at his special school, or when he was,
dutifully following the housemaid around, helping her—or, more
ly, "helping" her—with her early-morning tasks of making beds
ing rooms.

with a cooling cup of tea on the table before her—and, of course,
news programs playing on her room screen in case, however im-
y, something unexpected occurred in Natasha's race—Myra was
make sense of some of her journals when she heard the sound of
s heartbroken sobbing.

looked up and saw the maid carrying him into the room. "I don't
hat happened, missus," the maid said, sounding struck. "We were
g out the wastebaskets when Robert suddenly sat down and began
Robert never cries, missus!"

ich Myra, of course, knew as well as she did. But there it was. So
d what untold billions of other mothers have done, all the way from
ralopithecines. She took her son in her arms and rocked him sooth-
murmuring into his ear. It didn't stop the crying, no, but the tears
ed down to sobs. Myra was asking herself whether this unusual and
g—but certainly not life-threatening—development warranted
her husband at his office, when there was a stifled shriek from the
Myra looked up.

They searched every fold of the immense crumpled sail—visually when they had to, and with infrared viewers when those were present. These viewers would instantly pick up the tiny signal of a warm human body anywhere in the destroyed sail.

They searched all the space around destroyed *Diana,* on the chance that somehow Natasha had been flung free through some unknown accident. . . .

Above all, they searched *Diana*'s tiny cabin.

That didn't take long. With only herself aboard there was no need for privacy; *Diana*'s capsule amounted to only a few cubic meters of space, and no possible place to hide.

But she wasn't there. As far as the searchers could tell, Natasha Subramanian wasn't anywhere at all.

38

THE HUNT FOR
NATASHA SUBRAMANIAN

What the three fourths of the Subramanian family that remained on Earth had resolved to do was carry on with as normal a life as was possible, with the other quarter of the family gallivanting through cislunar space in a contraption of plastic and buckyball carbon. Accordingly, once they had sent Natasha their final good luck message, Ranjit had got on his bike to head for his office. Myra had seen the possibility of a whole hour, maybe two, for her to try to catch up on what her increasing backlog of journals had to say about some of the hotter subjects in the area of AI and prostheses. Such gifts of a few personal hours were not frequent. They came when young Robert was asleep, or when he was at his special school, or when he was, as now, dutifully following the housemaid around, helping her—or, more accurately, "helping" her—with her early-morning tasks of making beds and tidying rooms.

So, with a cooling cup of tea on the table before her—and, of course, with the news programs playing on her room screen in case, however improbably, something unexpected occurred in Natasha's race—Myra was trying to make sense of some of her journals when she heard the sound of her son's heartbroken sobbing.

She looked up and saw the maid carrying him into the room. "I don't know what happened, missus," the maid said, sounding struck. "We were emptying out the wastebaskets when Robert suddenly sat down and began to cry. Robert never cries, missus!"

Which Myra, of course, knew as well as she did. But there it was. So Myra did what untold billions of other mothers have done, all the way from the australopithecines. She took her son in her arms and rocked him soothingly, murmuring into his ear. It didn't stop the crying, no, but the tears simmered down to sobs. Myra was asking herself whether this unusual and troubling—but certainly not life-threatening—development warranted calling her husband at his office, when there was a stifled shriek from the maid. Myra looked up.

There on the screen was the image of her daughter's solar yacht. Apart from the fact that one edge was, ever so slightly, tipped up, it looked exactly as it had an hour earlier. But now there was a red banner underneath the image that said "Accident in lunar race?" And when the audio volume was turned up, there was no question mark in the agitated remarks of the newscaster. Something bad had happened to *Diana*. Worst of all, *Diana*'s pilot—which was to say, Myra's beloved daughter—was not answering distress calls from the commodore, and it seemed that whatever had gone wrong with the solar yacht had somehow abducted its pilot.

Myra Subramanian's terrible worry was perhaps the most personal distress anyone in the world can feel, but she was not alone. The more the tender vessels dug into the puzzle of what had happened to *Diana,* the more hopelessly unanswerable the puzzle seemed.

Emergency workers from the commodore's yacht had long since suited up and reached *Diana*'s command capsule. They managed to gain entrance, searched it, found no trace of its pilot. But that was not the worst. More detailed examination showed that the register on the capsule's one air lock showed unequivocally that it had not been opened since Natasha herself had entered, to begin the race. So Natasha was not only missing; she had never even left her command capsule.

All of which, of course, was quite impossible. And also unarguably true.

Also of course, the commodore and his staff had several dozen other problems to try to solve, all at once. There were the six other solar yachts, no longer in an orderly line, now in some danger of colliding with one another as their pilots were distracted by what had happened to the seventh of their group. The order went out to each of them to furl their sails and await pickup. That would leave the craft as six little bullets of matter that would have to be followed and somehow steered into parking orbits that would not threaten other space traffic . . . but not right away. Those problems could be dealt with in an orderly fashion, when time permitted.

There was nothing orderly, however, in what had become of Natasha Subramanian. Her disappearance, in the circumstances in which it had occurred, was simply impossible. And all of that was very bad for everyone concerned, and then it got worse.

For the next thirty-six hours the whole remaining Subramanian family was gathered in their kitchen, maid and cook as well. When Robert woke up from his nap, the crying spell was over, though he didn't seem able to tell his parents what it had been about—until they asked him if it had something to do with his sister and he replied, " 'Atasha 'appy asleep."

When dinner arrived, he ate with a good appetite, although no one else did. They didn't sleep much, either, drowsing in their chairs or stretching out for half an hour or so on the couch under the kitchen's windows. But none of the adults dared walk away from the news screens for more than a couple of minutes, lest some explanation of what had happened might suddenly be announced.

None was.

Oh, there was news, all right. One worrying bulletin came from the searchers in low earth orbit to say that now they were being escorted by several dozen of those little copper-colored flying things that had given the world its first solid indication that flying saucers, or something like flying saucers, were real. Why were they there? What did they want? Speculation was intense, but no explanation emerged, and so the world's attention turned to other matters. Attention turned to that spot in the Oort where astronomers had seen something that looked a little like, but wasn't, a supernova. Now the longer photographic exposures, with more powerful clusters of telescopes hooked together, showed that there was indeed some low-level radiation going on that positively had not been there in earlier studies of the same area. Attention turned to the tugs that were gradually herding all seven of the racing yachts into safe orbits—the six that were unharmed as well as the ball of crumpled fabric that had been Natasha's *Diana*. Attention turned to all the world's capitals and major cities, not one of which lacked a collection of "experts" capable of endlessly discussing what was going on—without ever increasing anyone's understanding of it.

And then the phone started ringing. It got no better the next day, nor the day after that.

The last thing Myra Subramanian wanted to do was let her one remaining child out of her sight, but when she and Ranjit talked it over, they agreed that it would be even worse to upset Robert any more than he had been upset already. That next day was a Sunday. On Sundays, Robert went to Sunday school. This Sunday was no different—though Myra sat in an empty room nearby during the whole time that Robert, like the other handicapped children in the church's special group, listened politely as the woman who was the assistant pastor read them Bible stories and they colored the line drawings of what the little girl next to Robert called "Jesus

Christ on a crisscross." And on Monday there was the workshop that one of their advisers had thought Robert would enjoy. There, Robert Subramanian—the boy who had discovered hexominoes for himself!—patiently and apparently pleasurably learned how to fill a decorative pencil box with one of each color of crayon, for sale in the workshop's little gift store.

At least Robert's crying was over. The worry, the puzzlement, the terrible pain of loss, however—they weren't over for either Myra or Ranjit. The calls never stopped coming in, either, from everyone they knew, and from an unbelievable number of people they didn't know at all. Some were actual pests. Ronaldinho Olsos, for instance, begging their forgiveness in case they felt he was in any way responsible; T. Orion Bledsoe, from Pasadena, to offer cursory sympathy but mostly to ask if Ranjit had any idea, any idea at all that for any reason he hadn't already communicated to the authorities, of what might have happened to his daughter.

Then there were the reporters.

Ranjit had believed that the absolute maximum invasion of his privacy had taken place after *Nature* had published his proof of Fermat's Last Theorem. He was wrong about that. What happened now was much worse. Although President-Elect Bandara had arranged for police to guard the approaches to the Subramanian home, they were effective only there and nowhere else. Once Ranjit got onto his bike to leave, he was fair game. So he didn't go into his university any more often than was unavoidable. After dinner he left Myra studying her journal reports and Robert stacking marbles on the floor beside her and retreated to the master bedroom to plan his next seminar.

That was when it happened.

Myra looked up from her screen, frowning. She had heard something—a distant electronic squeal, perhaps—and at the same moment had seen a flash of golden light coming under the door.

The next thing she heard was her husband's voice, his tone a mixture of joy and terror. "My God!" he cried. "Tashy, is that really you?"

After that there was nothing that could have kept Myra de Soyza Subramanian out of that room. When she flung the door open, she saw her husband staring at someone standing by the window. It was a young woman. What she wore was the bare minimum that any girl might wear who knew perfectly well that no outside party was going to see her.

It was a costume Myra had often enough seen her daughter wear around the house. She echoed her husband's cry—"Tashy!"—and did what any mother might have done in these preposterous circumstances, threw herself at the girl, trying to wrap her arms around her.

That, it turned out, was impossible.

A meter from the figure of the girl something slowed Myra down, a dozen centimeters later it stopped her cold. It wasn't anything like a wall. It wasn't anything tangible at all. Perhaps one could say that it was something like a warm and irresistible breeze.

Whatever it was, Myra was stopped cold, right there, at arm's length from any part of this figure that wore the face of the child she had borne, and raised, and loved.

And who now did not even look at her. Its eyes were fixed on Ranjit. When it spoke, it said, "It is not of interest to discuss who I am, Dr. Subramanian. What is important is that I must ask you many questions, all of which you must answer."

And then, without waiting for a response from Ranjit, without any explanations or even simple courtesy, the questioning began.

"Many" questions?

Yes, that was definitely the right word. They went on forever—for, by actual clock time, nearly four hours—and they covered, well, everything. "Why are many of your tribes destroying their weapons?" "Has your species ever lived at peace?" "What is the meaning of 'proof' as applied to your earlier researches on the Fermat theorem?" And even stranger ones: "Why do your males and females often copulate even when the female cannot conceive?" And "Have you not calculated an optimal population for your planet?" And "Why do your actual numbers so greatly exceed it?" And, "There are areas of many square kilometers on your planet that have very small human populations. Why have you not resettled some of your people there from crowded urban areas?"

Through it all, Myra stood there, frozen. She could see everything. She couldn't move. She saw, and yearned to help, her husband's struggles to deal with the interrogation in spite of his own helpless bafflement.

And such questions! "Sometimes," she—or it—was asking, in that uninflected voice that might have come from a reanimated corpse, "the word you use for an assemblage of humans is 'country' and sometimes 'nation.' Are the two concepts differentiated by, perhaps, size?"

The figure's putative father shook his head. "Not at all. There are some countries with as few as some hundreds of thousands of inhabitants and some—China, for instance—with nearly two billion. But they're both sovereign states—nations, that is," he corrected himself.

The figure was silent for a moment. Then, "How was the decision made to annihilate the electronic capabilities of the nations, countries, or sovereign states of North Korea, Colombia, Venezuela, and others?"

Ranjit sighed. "By the council of Pax per Fidem, I suppose. You'd probably have to ask one of them for a more reliable answer—Gamini Bandara, say, or his father." When the figure was silent again, he added nervously, "Of course, I can speculate. Would you like me to do that?"

The eyes that were not Natasha's eyes regarded him for a long moment. Then the figure said, "No." There was an ear-piercing electronic squeal, and a quick stir in the air, and the figure was gone.

Myra could move again, and did. She ran to her husband's side and threw her arms around him. They sat silent, hugging each other, until a banging at the front door startled everyone. When the maid answered it, at least a dozen police came racing in, looking for something to arrest. The captain, out of breath, panted, "Sorry. The duty constable saw what was happening through a window and alerted us, but when we got here, we just couldn't get close to the house. Couldn't even touch the wall— Excuse me." He lifted his own screen to his ear, while Myra was assuring the police, diligently searching every part of the house, that none of them had been harmed.

Then the police captain replaced his pocket screen on his belt. "Dr. Subramanian? Did you mention Gamini Bandara, the president-elect's son, in your conversation with that—" He stopped, searching for the right noun to complete the sentence and not finding it. "With that," he finished.

Ranjit nodded. "Yes, I think I did."

"I thought so," the cop said heavily. "Now he's getting the same kind of questioning you were, from the same person."

All of that news went out to every human being who owned or had access to a screen. It did not give much understanding to anyone, though. Not to what was left of the Subramanian family, nor to the rest of the human race. Not even to the horde of One Point Fives who hung trapped in their troop transports, drifting through the Oort cloud.

Those beings had concerns much more immediate than those of the human race. To the One Point Fives it was all very well to be ordered to postpone their annihilation of the human race, but the orders the Grand Galactics had handed down did not seem to take full cognizance of what obeying those orders entailed.

It was a question of numbers. Some 140,000 One Point Fives had originally boarded the transports. That number had not changed for more than a dozen years. But then, unwilling to die without descendants to carry on their genetic line, the One Point Fives had given themselves the luxury of that brief and violent flurry of sexuality.

The results of that orgy had already been born. Indeed, they now were nearly fully adult. . . .

But the armada had not been equipped to keep so large a number alive for a prolonged period.

The mechanical replenishers that had been built to supply air, water, and food for 140,000 One Point Fives had been forced to cope with nearly twice that number. Now they were beginning to crumble under that stress. Soon there would be shortages. Soon after that, deaths.

And what were the Grand Galactics going to do about that?

39

THE INTERROGATIONS

There wasn't much sleep that night for the Subramanian family—for anybody, really, whatever their time zone, because most of the world sat enthralled before their screens regardless of the hour. What they saw at first was Gamini Bandara, wearing only a huge bath towel, sitting on the edge of a tub and being questioned by that same close copy of Natasha Subramanian who had interrogated her father. There was no immediate explanation of how this event came to be.

The subject matter of these particular questions had mostly to do with the founding of Pax per Fidem, the development of the Silent Thunder weapon, and the command structure of the groups that planned and executed its missions. Gamini answered every question as best he could. For the technical details of Silent Thunder he shook his head and named one of the team of engineers who had built it. For the inside story of who said what to whom to get the project started, he referred the questioning to the UN secretary-general. When the questioning turned to the human race's eternal propensity for fighting wars with neighboring bodies, Gamini apologized. That went back as far as human history did, he said, but he had failed the one ancient history course he had ever taken. The professor who taught it, however, was still at the London School of Economics.

So she was, though at the moment on sabbatical in the tiny country of Belize. The inquisitor tracked her down at a local collection of ruins called Altun Ha. There, in broad and sweaty daylight, with a hundred anthropologists, tourists, guides, and (finally) Belizean police watching and hearing every word that was spoken but unable to approach the participants, the pseudo-Natasha demanded and got a summary of the military history of the human race. The professor gave her everything she wanted. She started with the first nations on record—Sumerians, Akkadians, Old Babylonians, and Hittites—in those earliest years before what was called "civilization" exploded out of the Fertile Crescent that lay between the Rivers Tigris and Euphrates to conquer Egypt, China, Europe, and ultimately the whole world. Wherever human beings went, whatever their neighbors, however rich their lives, yes, they still fought their regular ration of bloody and murderous wars.

Taken all in all the simulacrum of Natasha Subramanian interviewed nearly twenty people. Whatever she asked, they answered—not necessarily on first being asked. The slowest to answer her was a nuclear bomb designer from Amarillo, Texas, who flatly refused to give any details about the design of the nuclear weapon in Silent Thunder. Wouldn't answer even when he was denied food, water, or the use of a bathroom . . . until he finally admitted that if the president of the United States gave him permission to talk, he would obey. The interview with the president that followed took less than twenty minutes before the president, grasping the situation and its likely impact on his own life and comfort, said, "Oh, hell, tell her whatever she wants."

The simulacrum's nonstop interrogations altogether took some fifty-one hours. Then she simply disappeared. And when Ranjit and Myra compared tapes of the last questioning and the first, they were astonished to see that her curls were still in place. There was no fatigue in her face or in the sound of her voice. Her sketchy garments weren't stained with the inevitable drop of food (what food? she hadn't been seen to eat any) or involuntary brushing against a powdery wall. "She just isn't real," Ranjit marveled.

His wife said, "No, she isn't. But where is the real one?"

Because Myra and Ranjit were, after all, merely human, they needed rest. They weren't getting it. So Myra left strict orders with the servants that they were not to be disturbed before ten A.M. unless the end of the world was at hand.

Then, when Myra opened one eye to see the cook's worried face bent over hers and discovered it was only a little past seven, she gave her unmoving husband a quick elbow to the ribs. That was just in case the world really was ending, since she didn't want him to miss that.

And really, who was to say it was not? The news the cook had for them was that the "supernova" in the Oort had come to life again, though at only a tiny fraction of the energy displayed before. As more and more of Earth's biggest light buckets swung themselves to get a better look, it turned out that there wasn't a single source for this new radiation, either. There were more than a hundred and fifty sources, and (so the news reader said, sounding both worried and very confused) Doppler analysis showed one more fact about them. They were all moving. And they were moving in the general direction of the inner solar system, indeed in the direction of Earth itself.

Ranjit's response was typically Ranjit. He stared into space for a long moment. Then he said, "Huh," and rolled over, presumably to go back to sleep.

Myra thought of trying to do the same, but a brief trial established that that was impossible. Laboriously she went through her morning rituals and wound up in the kitchen to accept a cup of tea, but not a conversation, with the cook. To avoid that she took her tea out on the patio to think.

Thinking was something that Dr. Myra de Soyza Subramanian did quite well. This morning, though, it wasn't going properly. Perhaps that was because the cook had left the news on in the kitchen, and even from outside Myra could hear the muffled voices—saying nothing that was of interest, really, because the news services didn't know anything of interest that they hadn't said in their first announcement. Perhaps it was because what she really wanted to think about was the puzzle of the inexplicable appearance of what looked so much like her daughter but wasn't. Perhaps it was just the warmth of the morning sun, taken together with her near exhaustion.

Myra fell asleep.

How long she slept, lying on their all-weather recliner in the bright sun, she could not say. When something woke her, she noticed at once that the sun was markedly higher in the sky, and the cook and the maid were making a ridiculous amount of noise in the kitchen.

Then she heard the faint voice from the news screen that they were making the noise about. It was a broadcast, by chance caught by one of the monitors in low earth orbit, and it came from that orbiting collection of space yachts that once had been the contestants in the first-ever solar-sail race. And the voice was one both Myra and Ranjit knew well.

"Help," the familiar voice said. "I need someone to get me out of this capsule before the emergency air runs out." The voice finished with another bit of information quite unnecessary for either Myra or Ranjit: "This is Natasha de Soyza Subramanian, formerly the skipper of the solar yacht *Diana,* and I have no idea what I'm doing here."

40

THE PORTRAIT GALLERY

Twenty-four hours earlier Myra Subramanian would have taken an oath that there was only one thing that she desired in the world, and that was to learn that, against all the odds, her daughter was alive and well. That was then. Now she had that word. She even had the word of the emergency crews who had instantly responded to Natasha's SOS. They radioed to the waiting world that the missing young woman was not only alive and as far as they could determine quite well, but she was now even safe, because they had her in their rockets, already heading for the LEO juncture point of the Skyhook.

That wasn't enough for Myra. What she wanted now was for her daughter to be in her arms. Not thousands of kilometers away, and with no chance of physically getting there for all the weeks it would take Skyhook to get her home.

But then, that evening, Myra was studying the news screens in the hopes of finding one item that wasn't either frightening or incomprehensible, when her scream brought Ranjit running. "Look!" she cried, waving at the image on the screen. That nearly got a yell out of Ranjit, too, because what she was looking at was their daughter, Natasha—and not, she was sure, that unreal copy of her Natasha that had spent fifty-odd hours questioning all those members of the human race.

What she was saying Ranjit didn't know and didn't at that moment care about. He headed for his study, Myra by his side, leaving the image on the news screen behind. He didn't waste time trying to get a regular phone call through to the Skyhook car that contained his real returning daughter, either. Rank had its privileges. He called on the executive channels that were open to him as a member of the Skyhook board, and it was less than a minute before he had his own actual daughter looking out at him from her tiny bunk in the car's radiation-shielded capsule. It took longer than that for the actual Natasha to reassure her mother that this Natasha—hair mussed, bra stained, nothing like the immaculacy of the narrator-Natasha—was really the specific Natasha that Myra had wanted.

She was also, she finally succeeded in persuading her parents, alive and unharmed, though totally unable to say how she had come to wind up in the capsule that she had definitely not been in when it was searched.

That was all good, but not quite good enough to satisfy Myra. Having frighteningly, and seemingly irrevocably, lost her daughter once, she was not prepared to give up the present contact. Might indeed not have done so for hours, except that it was actually Natasha who ended their talk. She looked up from the camera first in irritation, then in startlement, and finally in something that was almost fear. "Oh my God," she cried. "Is that the copy of me they were talking about? On the news channels—go see for yourself!"

They did, and then they dialed back to the beginnings of the thing's message. It started with a blaze of light. Then the Natasha figure began to speak without introduction. "Hello, members of the Earth human race," it said. "We have three matters to communicate to you, and they are as follows.

"One, the member of the Grand Galactics formerly nearby has left this astronomical neighborhood, we suppose to rejoin its fellows. It is not known when it will return or what it will then do.

"Two, our principal decision makers have concluded that you will find it easier to converse with us if you know what we look like. Accordingly, we will display images of about fifty-five of the races most active on behalf of the Grand Galactics, beginning with ourselves, who are known as the Nine-Limbeds.

"Three, and final, the One Point Fives cannot return to their home at present because of inadequate supplies. The Machine-Stored prefer not to leave without them. Both species will therefore come to your planet. Those three species just mentioned include all of the species charged with dealing with the problems arising from your kind. Do not be alarmed, though. The Grand Galactics have rescinded their orders to sterilize your planet. In any case, when the One Point Fives arrive, they will be occupying areas that your people do not use. That ends this communication."

It did. Myra and Ranjit looked at each other in bafflement. "What areas are they going to occupy, do you think?" Myra asked.

Ranjit didn't try to answer her, because he had a more urgent question of his own. "What do you suppose they meant about sterilizing our planet?" he asked.

The creatures who called themselves the Nine-Limbeds not only showed all the beings they had promised—over and over, on all the world's screens—they gave a running commentary. "We are called Nine-Limbeds," the voice said, "because, as you see, we have nine limbs. There are four on each side used mainly for transportation. The one at the rear is used for everything else."

And on each screen was a picture of the creature the voice was describing. "It looks like a beetle!" the cook exclaimed. Indeed it did, provided a beetle might wear girdles of bright metallic fabric between each of its four pairs of limbs. As the voice promised, there was another limb at the end of its body, a thing like an elephant's trunk, Myra thought, but skinnier and long enough to reach to the front end, where there seemed to be a mouth and eyes.

And if the Nine-Limbeds looked bizarre—well, face it, they really were quite bizarre enough for any normal purpose—the next contestants down the runway were markedly weirder still. The second species displayed most suggested something like a skinned baby rabbit, though one of an unhealthy pale lavender color instead of the more familiar pink. (The accompanying commentary referred to them as the One Point Fives, though it was some time before any human being knew why.) The third was the nearest to human-looking (though not very) of mankind's newly discovered galaxy mates. Some of the species displayed later in the broadcast enjoyed up to a dozen limbs or perhaps even more tentacles (it was sometimes hard to be sure). This third species, though, oddly termed the Machine-Stored, had only the familiar two arms, two legs, and single head. There was no way of judging scale. It could have been marmoset-tiny or circus-freak huge, but it was certainly not the kind of thing one would like to meet on a dark night. It was hideous. In fact the kindest adjective any of the world's news commentators used to describe it was "diabolical."

Then the displays got weirder still. The creatures that followed were of every imaginable color, and often of many colors clashing against one another in eye-aching camouflage-like patterns. They had scales or sparse and wispy feathers; they were of every imaginable architecture; and those were only the carbon-based forms. The ones that looked, more than anything else, like stubby alligators in old-fashioned divers' suits were not that comprehensible, until it was revealed that they came from a world with an atmosphere as brutal as an earthly sea bottom, and the working fluid of their biologies was supercritical carbon dioxide.

Actually, the display that Myra couldn't help calling "the freak show" didn't stop with displaying all fifty-five of the galaxy's most advanced races. It was a continuous performance. Once every one of the species had had its moment of fame on Earth's screens, the procession started over, again with the Nine-Limbeds. The difference was that this time there was a context. The aliens were displayed along with their banana-shaped spacecraft and other parts of their world, and there was a different running commentary.

It was all interesting, of course. By the third time around, the Subramanians had learned that, measured against the approximate size of one of their spacecraft, the average Nine-Limbed couldn't be much more than eighteen or twenty centimeters long. And, according to the commentary with the second showing of the Machine-Stored, that name described precisely what they were. They were machine-stored. The biological bodies shown were a historical fact, but now every member of that race survived only in electronic storage. So Myra informed Ranjit as he returned from carrying the sleeping Robert off to bed.

"Huh," he said, returning to his favorite armchair. "That's convenient. I guess then you can live pretty much forever, wouldn't you say?"

"Probably so," she agreed. "I'm going to make myself a cup of tea. Want some?"

He did. When she came back with the two cups, the screen was displaying one of the Nine-Limbeds removing the fabric from between two of another's hip joints and then rubbing the exposed flesh with his own ninth limb. "Hey," Myra said, setting a cup before her husband. "What's he doing, giving the other one a bath?"

"Maybe changing his oil," Ranjit said. "Who knows? Listen, all this is recorded, so why don't we turn it off for now and we can come back to it when we want to?"

"Good idea," Myra said, reaching out and doing it for him. "I wanted to ask you something anyway. What is it that we haven't seen in this parade?"

Ranjit nodded. "I know. The ones they were talking about. The ones they call the Grand Galactics."

"They're the ones, and they sound important. And yet they're not showing them to us."

41

HOME AGAIN

By the time Natasha, the real Natasha, was back in her own bed at the Colombo house, one would have expected that the running commentary delivered to the world by the not-Natasha would be long over. Well, it was . . . sort of. That is, all sixty-two hours of it had been repeated three times and then stopped, but for reasons of their own the Nine-Limbeds gave encore performances every few days.

The human race did not consider this a blessing. The Nine-Limbeds' voice-over was not delivered in English only. It was repeated in just about every language and dialect used by any group of people large enough to command some broadcast time somewhere. That was a large number, large enough to tie up much of the world's satellite links to the detriment of human affairs.

The other effect this had was to give young Natasha plenty of time to study her simulated self as it appeared on the screen—skimpy halter top and errant curl over her left ear and all. It never changed. It wasn't a spectacle Natasha enjoyed watching, either. "Gives me the cold shivers," she admitted to her parents. "There I am, saying things I know I never said, and it's me!"

"But it isn't, hon," her mother said reasonably. "They just somehow copied you, I guess so that they could have someone to speak for them who didn't look like a nightmare."

"But where was I while they were doing that? I don't remember a thing! I saw Ron Olsos trying to steal my solar wind, and then all of a sudden I was— Well, I don't know where. Sort of nowhere at all. Only warm and comfortable—possibly the way I was when I was still inside you, Mother."

Myra shook her head in puzzlement. "Robert told us you were happy."

"I guess I was. And then the next thing I knew I was sitting at the controls, yelling for help, with *Diana* all collapsed around me."

Myra patted her arm. "And you got help, love, because here you are.

And speaking of the Olsos boy, there are four more texts that came in from him while you were sleeping. All saying how sorry he was and asking if he can see you to apologize."

That made Natasha grin at last. "Sure he can," she said. "Just not right away. And right now, is there any breakfast?"

For most of the human race those senseless repetitions of the alien roll call were a terrible waste of time and communications facilities. Not for all, though. The tiny church of satanists had seen the pre-storage images of the Machine-Stored and immediately decided that the spiky-furred humanoid was indeed the image of the devil—just as a few million other viewers had at once decided—but, they argued, that wasn't a bad thing. His Satanic Majesty was to be worshipped, not loathed. Scripture proved it, if read with proper understanding, for Lucifer had been driven from heaven because of character assassination by rival angels. "He isn't our enemy," said one of their bishops rhapsodically. "He is our king!"

What the church's scrawny handful of members, mostly in the American Southwest, chose to believe would not have greatly concerned most of the human race—except for two factors. First, there was that worrisome remark about "sterilizing" Earth. That implied that those alien horrors did have the capacity to wipe humanity out if they chose, and that was not a thing easy to forget. And, second, the satanists weren't just a handful of nutcases anymore. Even a nutcase knew what the sound of opportunity knocking at the door was like. They grasped their chance. Every satanist who had any status in the organization higher than pew-polisher went immediately on every talk program that would have them. Their hope was that the world was full of other nutcases like themselves who just had never been recruited to Satan worship because they had not yet been convinced there actually was a Satan. The satanists hoped these nutcases would be swung into line by the sight of the demonic Machine-Stored.

They were right. By the third showing of the horrid creatures called Machine-Stored, nearly a hundred thousand instant converts were begging for Satan's sacraments. By the time of the first rerun, the congregation of the church of satanists was already in the high millions, and two competing—that is to say, heretical—satanist churches were already battling them for membership. Other cults and pseudo-religions prospered as well, but none prospered nearly as much as the satanists.

They were all, of course, crazy. "Or the next thing to it," Ranjit told Gamini Bandara when he called. "Why are you worrying about it?"

"Because even a crazy person can pull a trigger, Ranj. Isn't it true that Natasha has had death threats?"

Ranjit thought that over for a moment before he answered. His daughter had been very emphatic about not telling anyone about that, but still—"Well, yes," he admitted. "Stupid stuff. She doesn't take them seriously."

"Well, I do," Gamini informed him, "and so does my father. He's ordering twenty-four-hour guards around your house and to go with any of you who goes out."

Ranjit was shaking his head. "I don't think that's necessary—" he began.

"Doesn't matter what you think," Gamini said cheerfully. "Dad's the president now, so he's the one who gives the orders. Anyway, if it wasn't the Feds, it'd be somebody else. Your pal Joris Vorhulst is getting threats, too. He's already got a bunch of armed guards around the Skyhook base. Now he's talking about putting Skyhook security forces around everybody connected with the project. You included."

Ranjit opened his mouth to protest—not as much because he couldn't stand the idea of being guarded twenty-four hours a day as because he anticipated his daughter's reaction—but Gamini didn't give him the chance. "So you see, Ranj," he said reasonably, "it's going to happen. There's no sense in fighting it. And, you know, it just might save all your lives."

Ranjit sighed. "How long?" he asked.

"Well, until those One Point Fives get here, at least," Gamini said thoughtfully. "After that, who knows?"

And that was a really good question, Ranjit admitted to himself. Leaving only that quite different question of how he was going to tell Myra and Natasha about the plan.

The chance came almost at once. Once off the phone with Gamini, he went looking for his family and found them on the back porch with binoculars in the dark, studying the constellation that held much of the Oort cloud. Passing the glasses to Natasha, Myra said to her husband, "They're getting close. Tashy? Give your father a look." And she did. Ranjit had no difficulty in finding the bright splash of light that—so said the experts—was the exhaust of the deceleration rockets of the approaching One Point Five armada. It wasn't the first time he had seen it. Even before the announcement that these One Point Fives were coming to stay, Earth's giant telescopes had been providing much brighter and more detailed images for the world's news screens.

But they were getting closer.

Ranjit lowered the glasses and cleared his throat. "That was Gamini on the phone," he said, and relayed what had been said. But if he had expected his daughter to object to grown-up interference with her life, he had been mistaken. She listened patiently, but all she said was, "These guards are to protect us against the nut satanists, right? But who"—she waved at the gentle starry patterns overhead—"is going to protect us from them?"

That was the question the whole world was asking—asking itself and even trying to ask of the invaders, as half of the world's most important people began talking into microphones that beamed their question in the direction of the approaching armada. There were many questions, covering their plans, their intentions, their reasons for coming to Earth in the first place—many, many questions, in many languages, from many people great and small.

They received no answers at all.

This wasn't easy for the human race to handle. All over planet Earth—and in the lava tubes of the moon, and in orbit, and wherever else human beings had established a foothold—people were showing the strain of what was coming. Even the Subramanian family was not immune. Myra was biting her nails again, as she hadn't done since her early teens. Ranjit was spending hours on the phone to almost every important person he knew (and that was a lot of important people), on the chance that any of them might have some wisdom to share that hadn't occurred to himself. (They didn't.) Meanwhile, Natasha was obsessively trying to teach young Robert how to read Portuguese. And then one morning, while they were all at breakfast, there was a sudden eruption of raised voices from outside. When Ranjit opened the door to look, what he saw was four of their uniformed guards with their guns drawn and pointed at half a dozen strangers. Well, not all strangers. Most of them were young, scowling, their hands in the air, but in their center was someone whom, though somewhat older than the last time he'd seen him, Ranjit recognized at once. "Colonel Bledsoe," he said. "What are you doing here?"

The situation took a little negotiating. The way it worked out, Lt. Col. Bledsoe (retired) was allowed to come into the house, although only with the captain of the guard standing by with his gun in his hand. Bledsoe's escort remained outside, sitting on the ground with their hands on their heads, with the rest of the Sri Lankan detail making sure they stayed that way.

One might have supposed that Bledsoe would feel he was at some sort of a disadvantage. He didn't. "Thanks for letting me come in and talk to you," he said. "I didn't want to have to turn my boys loose on your guards."

Ranjit wasn't sure whether he should be amused or angry but decided not to try to figure that out. He went right to the point. "Talk about what?" he asked.

Bledsoe nodded. "Right, let's not waste time. I'm here representing the president of the United States, and he has determined that the human race can't afford to let these alien assassins land on Earth."

It was Ranjit's intention to ask how the president of the United States proposed to prevent it, but his wife got in first. "What makes your president think he can speak for the whole human race? Don't—for instance—Russia and China have something to say about it?"

To Ranjit's surprise, Bledsoe seemed to expect the question. "You're living in the past, Mrs. Subramanian. You act like there still was a big three. There isn't. Russia and China are nothing but paper tigers anymore! They don't need to be considered."

He went on to explain, his tone scornful, that they were both preoccupied with internal problems they tried to keep secret. "The People's Republic of China," he lectured, "has just about lost control of Jilin province to the Falun Gong movement, and they can't afford that. Oh, sure, you never heard of Jilin province, did you? But it's where the Chinese government gets a lot of its grain, not to mention a lot of its automobiles and railway cars. You heard me. Agriculture *and* manufacturing! And Falun Gong's spreading across the border to Inner Mongolia."

He shook his head in a manner that might have been sympathetic, if the little grin at the corners of his mouth hadn't been so obviously gloating. "And what about the Russians?" he asked. "They're even worse off. Chechnya is a running sore. There are Muslims there, and every Islamic jihadist anywhere in the world who still wants to kill heretics is going to flock to Chechnya to pick up a gun—and there goes some of Russia's most important oil pipelines. And if Chechnya finally does get loose, there are a bunch of other provinces that would like nothing better than to go the same way."

Myra commented, "You look happy about it."

Bledsoe pursed his lips. "Happy? No. What do I care what kind of trouble the Chinks and the Russkis have? But it sure simplifies things when action has to be taken and the president doesn't have to worry about getting them on board. And that's where you and your family come in, Subramanian. The president has a plan. And you're all part of it."

The mood Ranjit and his family had toward their uninvited guest had never been warmer than tepid. Now it congealed to brittle antarctic ice.

"What do you want?" Ranjit asked, in a tone that suggested that whatever it was, there was small chance he would get it.

"It's simple," Bledsoe said. "I want your daughter, Natasha, to go on a broadcast to say that while she was their prisoner, they let her know that 'sterilizing' the Earth meant killing every human being so their aliens can take possession of it."

Natasha spoke up at once. "That never happened, Mr. Bledsoe. I don't remember anything at all of being a captive."

Her father raised one hand. "He knows it's a lie, hon," he told her. "All right, Bledsoe. Why do you want to whip up the hatred for these creatures?"

"Because sooner or later we're going to have to wipe them out. What else? Oh, we'll let them land, all right. But then you go on the air, Subramanian, to say your daughter has confided things in you that you think the world needs to know, and then Natasha comes on and tells her story."

He was looking actually pleased about the prospect, Ranjit thought. "And then what?" he demanded.

Bledsoe shrugged. "We wipe 'em out," he said. "Hit them first with a Silent Thunder so they can't do anything about it. Then we turn the entire American air force on them with every bomb and rocket they can carry, and all the ICBMs, too. Nuclear and all. I guarantee there won't be anything bigger than the tip of your little finger left when we're through."

Myra snorted, but it was Ranjit who spoke. "Bledsoe," he said, "you're crazy. Do you think these people don't have their own weapons? All you're going to do is get a few thousand air crew killed—and make the aliens mad."

"Wrong twice," Bledsoe said scornfully. "Every one of those American planes is fly-by-wire, with all the crews safely on the ground. And it doesn't matter if those things get mad. We've got a saying in the States, Subramanian. 'Live free or die.' Or don't you believe in that?"

Myra opened her mouth to answer for all of them, but Ranjit forestalled her. "What I don't believe in," he said, "is telling lies that are going to get people killed, even if they aren't human people. We aren't going to do what you want, Bledsoe. What I think we ought to do is get on the screens, all right, but what we ought to do is tell the world what you proposed."

Bledsoe gave him a poisonous look. "You think that would make any difference? Hell, Subramanian, do you know what 'deniable' means? I'm deniable. If this gets out, the president just shakes his head and says, 'Poor old Colonel Bledsoe. He was doing what he thought was right, but completely on his own initiative. I never authorized any such plan.' And maybe some reporters pester me for a while, but I just don't talk to them and pretty soon it all blows over. As leader of the predominant force on this planet, it's the president's duty to defend the weaker states, and he has determined that to attack is the best course to follow. I serve at the pleasure of the president. What do you say to that?"

Ranjit stood up. "I want to live free, all right, but that isn't on offer here, is it? If the choice is between living in a world where people like you are in charge and one run by scaly green monsters from space, why, I just might pick the monsters. And now get out of my house!"

42

A GREAT DEPRESSION

When at last the One Point Five fleet came down to the surface of Earth, they were accompanied by an enormous fireworks show. That pyrotechnical display did not come about for the same reasons a returning human fleet of spacecraft might produce such a display, though. All those old human-built Mercury capsules and Soyuzes and space shuttles struck Earth's air in an eye-straining blaze of fire when they came home, and the reason was simple. They had no choice about it. They had to slow down for reentry, and nothing but friction with the atmosphere could brake their descent enough to allow safe landing on the ground.

The spacecraft of the One Point Fives, on the other hand, had no need for air friction. Their descent was slowed by a completely different mechanism. They simply fired their ionic rockets in a forward direction, at full power, to serve as brakes. It was a gentler way to land, and one that offered more accurate control on a landing site.

It also required immensely more energy, but conserving energy was not a priority for the One Point Fives.

A problem for human observers was figuring out just where the armada had chosen to set down. An early guess was somewhere in the Libyan desert, perhaps on the beaches along the Mediterranean. That was quickly revised to somewhere a bit farther east and north, perhaps somewhere in the otherwise empty northwestern desert provinces of Egypt.

It didn't take the news channels' experts long to come up with the name "Qattara Depression."

Then it took Myra and Ranjit less time than that to get their search engines going. "This Qattara thing is the world's fifth deepest depression," Myra called, reading from her screen. "It goes down as low as 133 meters below sea level."

"And it's only fifty-six kilometers from the sea," Ranjit added, eyes on his own screen. "And—wait a minute!—in some ways it's the world's biggest depression of the Earth's surface there is on land, with more than forty thousand square kilometers that are below sea level." And it was un-inhabited, they both learned at once, except for wandering bedouin tribes and their flocks, and of no apparent value to anyone—at least not to any human. The only thing about it that seemed ever to have mattered to human beings was that at least for a few weeks it had been really important in one of those twentieth-century wars, the one between the Germans and the English. Then the impassable Qattara Depression had trapped the Germans where the English could inflict heavy losses on them in what was called the Battle of El Alamein.

At that point Myra and Ranjit gave up the search as unproductive. "I don't think that's why these aliens picked it," Ranjit said at last. "Because it's easy to defend against an army, I mean."

"But what, then?" Myra asked.

For that Ranjit frowned but did not answer. They spent the next quarter of an hour inventing increasingly unlikely motives, until the news screen broke in. What the reporter had to tell them was that the first official bluster had just come in from Cairo. Its tone was belligerent.

Well, that's not quite giving the true picture. The broadcast came from Cairo, all right, but it wasn't delivered by an Egyptian. The speaker was the American ambassador. The Egyptian government, he informed the world, had asked him to give the official reply for them. That area called Munkhafad al-Qattar-ah, he said, was an integral part of the sovereign state of the Arab Republic of Egypt. The intruders had no right to be there. They were commanded to leave Egyptian territory at once or face the consequences.

It was obvious that secret meetings had been going on, and the ambassador's next words left no doubt of what they had been about. "The Arab Republic of Egypt," he proclaimed, "is one of America's oldest and closest allies. Trespassers will have to face Egypt's military might as well as that of the United States."

"Oh my God," Ranjit murmured. "I smell T. Orion Bledsoe again."

"And heaven help us now," said the irreligious Myra to her even less religious husband.

It might have eased the situation if the alien beings landing on Earth had taken time to announce what their long-range plans actually were. No explanation was offered. Perhaps the aliens couldn't handle more than one thing at a time—or thought that these primitive Earth humans couldn't—because what they did do, incessantly, was keep their promise to show humanity, all over again, every last one of the galaxy's assorted races of beings.

This had been quite interesting at one time. That time, however, was past. About the only viewers who stayed tuned in were producers of low-budget horror films, eagerly seeking ideas to pass on to their makeup departments, plus what remained of the world's dwindling corps of taxonomists, each of whom had been intoxicated by a sudden breathtaking vision of becoming the Carolus Linnaeus (subclass Alien Biota) of the twenty-first century.

Of course, none of that was a problem for the human race. There was a problem, though, and it came in two parts.

First was the inordinate demand being made on the world's communications bandwidths. The mere broadcast of the catalog of galactic sentients itself made no real dent in these. What made a difference was the aliens' courteous habit of broadcasting everything they had to say in a large fraction of the world's 6,900-odd languages.

But even that discommoded only the handful of people whose favorite game show was squeezed off the air. Far more serious was the interference with communications, particularly the behind-the-scenes negotiations among many of the world's military forces.

A quick call to Gamini Bandara confirmed what Ranjit was already sure of. No, it hadn't been a voluntary decision of the Egyptian government that had produced the saber-rattling remarks of the American ambassador. The old Egyptian friend of Dhatusena Bandara, now Egyptian ambassador to Sri Lanka, Hameed Al-Zasr, had explained it all by phone to Gamini's father. "He managed to get a personal call through to Dad. It was American pressure and they couldn't fight it. There was some American cloak-and-dagger guy, Dad said—"

"Of course there was. Your old pal Colonel Bledsoe, I bet."

Gamini sounded startled when he said, "You're probably right. Anyway, Al-Zasr says Egypt wasn't forgetting its Pax per Fidem obligations, but it's still in the middle of implementing them. The changeover isn't complete, and Egypt's too poor to antagonize the U.S. Billions of dollars in American aid are involved."

"Hell," said Ranjit. And when he reported the conversation to Myra, she said much the same.

"We should have guessed," she said. "Let's hope it doesn't get any worse."

43

LANDED IMMIGRANTS

In the Subramanian family it might have been young Robert who was the least affected by the scary developments in the world they lived in. He cried a bit more these days, true. It didn't seem to be the state of the outside world that was saddening him, though. Rather, it was the obvious distress of his parents. Robert's way of dealing with the problem was to be especially good—patting them, cuddling with them, even eating all his vegetables without argument and going to bed without protest when told it was time. And trying to cheer them up by repeating words and phrases from his Sunday school. " 'Olden 'Ule," he would say reassuringly, and, " 'Oo unto others."

Of course, hearing Robert's recollections of Sunday school lessons about the Golden Rule didn't really make things better for Ranjit and Myra. They were not displeased when he began to take an interest in things that were showing on the world's news screens—when he could find a channel that was not overrun with the quaint denizens of the galaxy.

What was showing there was what these One Point Five invaders were doing in the Qattara Depression. Every human spy satellite not hijacked by reruns of the galactic bestiary was brought to bear on that almost forgotten part of the world.

As soon as the One Point Five armada had landed, it became clear why they had used rockets to decelerate instead of simple air friction. Air friction would have shredded their spacecraft. They weren't streamlined. They weren't even simple tube shapes, like the pygmy vessels of the Nine-Limbeds. The One Point Fives' ships looked more like Christmas trees than any aerodynamic design, with cubes and balls and polygons hanging off the main bodies at all sorts of angles.

That explained their willingness to expend fuel on a slow-down. A shuttle-type reentry would have turned them into the brightest shooting star display ever, quickly followed by glowing fields of debris covering thousands of hectares.

Once they were landed in orderly ranks, the One Point Fives showed what all those grotesque add-ons were for. Some of them were tentacle-like in appearance; these detached themselves, waved indecisively for a moment, and then squirmed away to explore their new surroundings. Others linked together and headed for the brackish waters of the oasis, to do what, Ranjit could not guess. "That's not potable water," he said. "I hope they're aware of that."

Myra studied his face. "You know," she said meditatively, "you're looking a lot more cheerful since Joris called to say the dynamiters gave up. Now you're worried about what these One Point Five creatures have to drink."

Since what his wife said was true, Ranjit made no attempt to argue. "It's like Robert keeps telling us," he said. "We should 'oo unto others as we would have others 'oo unto us. I personally would not like any others to be shooting me."

Myra grinned and then was caught by what was now going on on the screen. Some of the alien bits and pieces of machinery had detached themselves from their spacecraft, had crawled to a dune, and had begun chewing at it. "They're digging a tunnel," Myra marveled. "What do you think, maybe a kind of bomb shelter in case anyone attacks them?"

Ranjit didn't answer that. The idea that the aliens might be expecting armed attack was all too plausible, but he didn't want to say as much. . . .

And didn't need to, because all the news screens that still belonged to the human race at once went dark. They were quickly replaced by a flustered newscaster, hurriedly informing the audience that the president of the United States had requested immediate air time to make an announcement of "world importance." "Those were the president's words," the newscaster on the Subramanian screen nervously informed her audience. "We know nothing beyond that here, except that this is almost unprecedented in— What?"

She was asking the question of someone invisible, but the answer was obvious. All she had time to say was, "Ladies and gentlemen, the president of the—"

And then the screen went briefly to black. When it lighted up again, it was showing a group of important-looking (but also worried-looking) men and women clustered around a table that bore a forest of microphones. Ranjit looked with some puzzlement at the scene; it was not the usual Rose Garden setting, or the Oval Office, or any of the other backgrounds the president usually preferred. There was, it was true, the giant American flag behind the standing group, as the president almost always required. But what Ranjit could see of the chamber they were in was unfamiliar to him—windowless, harshly lit with floodlights, with a corporal's guard of armed United States Marines standing at attention, their fingers on the triggers of their weapons.

"Oh my God," Myra whispered. "They're in their nuke shelter."

But Ranjit hardly heard her. He had made a discovery of his own. "Look who's standing between the president and the Egyptian ambassador. Isn't that Orion Bledsoe?"

It was. They had no time to discuss his presence, though, because the president had begun to speak. "My friends," he said, "it is with a heavy heart that I come before you to say that the invasion—yes, invasion; I can find no other word to describe what has happened—of our planet by these beings from space has passed the point at which it can be tolerated. The government of the Arab Republic of Egypt has explicitly demanded that those who have committed this act of aggression stop their preparations for war at once and begin to withdraw from Egyptian territory. The aggressors not only have failed to comply with this demand, which is according to international law, they haven't even had the courtesy to acknowledge receiving it.

"Accordingly the government of our ally, the Arab Republic of Egypt, is preparing an armored column to cross the desert and drive the invaders off their soil. Furthermore, the president of the Arab Republic of Egypt has called upon the United States to comply with existing treaties by aiding in the military effort to drive them out.

"You will understand that I have no option but to comply with this demand. Accordingly, I have ordered the sixth, twelfth, fourteenth, and eighteenth air forces to destroy the alien encampment." He permitted himself a slight smile. "Under most circumstances that would be a highly classified decision, but I feel that showing the actual forces that have been brought to bear on the aggressors will help convince these alien invaders that they must immediately cease their provocative activities and declare their intention to depart Egyptian territory."

The president turned to look at his own screen, just in time for the scene on the screens in the rest of the world to show the reality of what the president had promised. From all directions warplanes, arranged in precise flights and *V*s, were heading in toward a single target, the Qattara Depression. Ranjit recognized some of them—supersonic flying wings; immense old B-52s, originally deployed in the Vietnam War and still going strong;

the tiny, fast stealth fighter-bombers—Ranjit counted at least a dozen different types of aircraft, all heading to the same point on the map—

And then, suddenly and without warning, they weren't.

To Ranjit it looked like nothing as much as one of those radio dog fences, where the animal gets a shock from buried wiring any time he tries to pass a certain point in his run. The planes did the same thing. As they reached a certain point along the perimeter of a circle drawn with the Qattara Depression as its center, the orderly patterns of *V*s faltered, ceased to be coherent, one by one lost power. Nothing exploded. There were no flames, and no sign of enemy action. All that happened was that the mighty air fleet no longer displayed the torches of flame that were their jet exhausts. Those had winked out.

Lacking thrust, the planes did their best to glide to the ground, but their best was very poor. Within a matter of minutes the screens were displaying five or six hundred funeral pyres, each marking the point at which a member of the mighty striking force had hit the ground, the fuel that remained in its tanks immediately exploding.

And within the perimeter of the invaders' camp, the various bits of busy machinery, paying no attention at all, kept right on with their arcane tasks.

For the One Point Fives themselves the Qattara Depression was pure heaven.

They particularly loved the brackish water of the oasis. It was purer than any water they had seen for generations on their own planet. Oh, sure, there were a few chemicals that had to be filtered out. But there were hardly any radioactive contaminants, and no positron emitters at all!

And the air! You could very nearly breathe it without a filter! True, it was on the warmish side—around 45°C, or perhaps 110°F, in the several confusing ways the human population had of measuring temperatures—but once they had finished digging their tunnel from the depression to the sea, there would be plenty of cooling Mediterranean waters to make the climate livable.

They were, in fact, about as happy as an enslaved race of largely prosthetic beings can be, except for one annoying thing.

As usual it was the Nine-Limbeds who were making trouble. The Nine-Limbeds had agreed to the destruction of the attacking aircraft because no actual local sentients' lives were endangered, all of the war planes being of course remotely controlled. But, infuriatingly, the attack had destroyed some human life anyway.

A party of oil prospectors had had the bad luck to be setting up their seismometers just where one of the American bombers crashed. True, only eleven human beings had been killed, less than 0.0000001 percent of the human race. By any rational count that was hardly enough to worry about.

But the Nine-Limbeds kept caterwauling about it. Human ideas of justice and reparations were not the same as their own, as they knew from eavesdropping on every major human activity and a good many minor ones. Finally the council of the One Point Fives gave in. "What can we do to heal the situation?" they asked. "That is, other than leaving this extraordinarily inviting place to go back to our own planet, which we are not going to do."

"Reparations," said the experts of the Nine-Limbeds at once. "You must pay them. Through our eavesdropping program we have ascertained that nearly anything that goes wrong in the affairs of these human beings can be repaired by paying reparations, in the form of money. Would you be willing to do that?"

It didn't take the One Point Fives long to answer that question. "Of course we will," their leaders said at once. "What is 'money'?"

44

INTERNATIONAL DISAGREEMENTS

A day later and quite a distance from Qattara, the Subramanian family was finishing breakfast. Natasha and Robert were already in their swimsuits, just waiting out the statutory, and mother-enforced, period of thirty minutes of delay after a meal before they could head for the beach. Ranjit, a cooling cup of tea in his hand, was frowning at the screen. What it showed was the bustling One Point Five colony as seen from one of the few still-human-controlled satellites, and Ranjit had been frowning at it for some time.

When Myra thought about it at all, she did wonder what her husband found so absorbing on the screen, though her mind was mostly on the morning's assortment of incoming texts. She held one up for a better look and called to Ranjit. "Harvard wants to know if you're interested in doing their commencement address again. Oh, and here's one from Joris. He says they keep getting threatening messages, but if there actually are any satanists planning to really attack Skyhook, they're not within twenty kilometers of the base. And— Wait! What's that?"

What stopped Myra right there was a startled "Huh!" from her husband, and when she looked up, she saw why. The aerial view was gone, the satellite had been preempted again by the aliens for their own purposes, and a familiar figure was taking shape on the screen. Behind Myra her daughter snapped, "Oh, hell! It's me again!"

It was. Or at least it was that indestructible not-Natasha, little curl hanging over her left ear, that had been displayed so frequently since the world had begun to fall apart. Myra sighed. "I do wish you'd had a little more clothes on," she offered, and was spared her daughter's withering reply as the figure began to speak.

"I am bringing you a message from the persons identified as the One Point Fives, currently located in what is called the Qattara Depression on the planet you call Earth. The message is as follows:

" 'We are deeply regretting loss of human life in defense against attack. We will pay reparations up to one thousand metric tons of ninety-nine and five nines pure metallic gold, but require ninety days for processing metal from seawater. Please inform that offer is accepted.' This ends their message."

The figure disappeared, the shiny structures of the colony popped up, and Ranjit turned around to gaze at his wife and children. He said incredulously, "I guess they've really made a sort of stock copy of Tashy they can use to make their announcements."

Myra was diffidently smiling. "I don't know, but did you hear what they said? It almost sounds good. If they're willing to try to make up for what happened, there's some hope."

Ranjit nodded thoughtfully. "You know," he said in wonder, "it's been so long since there was any good news that I don't know how to celebrate it. A drink all around?"

"It's too early," Natasha said at once. "Anyway, Robert doesn't drink and neither do I, much. You people do what you want. He and I are going to the beach."

"And I think I'll call the office. I wonder what Davoodbhoy thinks about it," Ranjit said, kissing his wife's hand.

"Go, then, all of you," Myra said. She sat silently thoughtful for a moment. Then she sighed, poured herself some fresh tea, and allowed herself to relapse into what was beginning to look like a once-again normal world.

Thoughts of destruction and disaster had not entirely vanished from her mind. They were bearable now, though, no more distracting than the occasional twinge in a molar that reminds you to make an appointment with the dentist—oh, not for next month, necessarily, but maybe the month after. So Myra went back to the morning's texts. There was one from her niece Ada Labrooy to say hopefully that this "machine-stored" state the alien creatures talked about sounded a lot like something resembling the artificial intelligence she herself had been working on for what seemed like her whole life, and did Natasha have any possible way, any way at all, of asking them for details? A dozen texts from other people, all sharing the delusion that the real Natasha might somehow be able to get a message to the aliens. And, worryingly, a text from the Trincomalee temple, reporting that the old monk, Surash, had come through his most recent surgery well enough but that the long-range outlook was doubtful at best.

Lips pursed in concern, Myra reread the saddening words. Surash himself had called to tell them that he would have to have another procedure, but he had made it sound like the approximate equivalent of a tonsillectomy. This text sounded a good deal more serious. She sighed and turned to the next one—

And scowled. This one was addressed to Ranjit personally. It came from Orion Bledsoe, and what it said was, "This is to remind you of the obligations under the Uniform Military Service Act of 2014 of the American citizen Natasha de Soyza Subramanian. She may report to any U.S. army installation for the purpose of evaluation. This must be done within the next eight days or penalties will be incurred."

It was too late to catch Natasha to tell her about this new proposal for her life's career. Ranjit, however, was within shouting range, and when Myra had got him off the phone and handed him the message, he said, "Huh!" And then, to clarify his meaning, "Hell!"

So now the Subramanian family had a new and totally unexpected set of worries. It had never occurred to either Ranjit or Myra that the geographic fact of their daughter's birth on American soil had ever given America any right to commandeer her services. There was one clear step to be taken, and they took it.

When Ranjit urgently sought help from Gamini Bandara, his old friend put him on hold for a moment, and then, with apologies, for a much longer period.

When he came back, though, he sounded less worried. "Ranjit?" he said. "You're still there. Good. Well, I've spoken to my father and he's already on the phone with his legal people. He wants you to come down here." He paused for a moment, and when he went on, he sounded almost embarrassed. "The problem is that slimeball Bledsoe. We need to talk about him, Ranj. Dad'll send a plane for you. Bring Myra. And Natasha. And, oh, hell, Robert, for that matter. We'll be waiting."

The plane that arrived for them that evening wasn't anywhere nearly as big as the one that had rescued Ranjit from rendition. It had only one stewardess, and she was nowhere near as pretty as the others, but it did have something unexpected, though. It had an old friend, standing in the doorway to welcome them. Myra looked at him twice, and then broke into a smile. "Dr. De Saram, what a nice surprise!"

Nigel De Saram, the man who had once been Ranjit's lawyer, now President Bandara's secretary of state, submitted to a hug, and then waved everyone to the seats that surrounded a long table. "We'll talk on the way," he said, strapping himself in. While the plane was racing down the takeoff strip, he read the text Myra had brought for him, and by the time they were approaching cruising altitude, he was ready. He turned to Natasha. "I believe what must be done is clear; I accessed all the U.S. law and court decisions that bear on this matter while I was on the way down. The first thing for you to do is renounce American citizenship; the papers should be drawn up by my office by the time we arrive. It would be better if you'd done it years ago, of course," he added. "My fault for not making sure you did."

"Then that's all we have to do to settle this?" Ranjit asked incredulously. If the mightiest power on Earth was trying to put his daughter into its uniform, he was not prepared to take chances.

The old lawyer looked shocked. "Of course not! It just means the whole matter gets fought out in the American courts. But that will take years, and—I don't know if you've been paying attention—there's a presidential election coming up in America. It looks like the present administration isn't likely to win. I'm hoping the next one won't have quite the same policies. Meanwhile, you should stay out of America, please."

Natasha threw her arms around him. "Thank you," she breathed.

Her father, sounding embarrassed, echoed the thanks and added, "I guess we didn't need to drag you down here."

"Ah," the lawyer said, "that's another question, isn't it? President Bandara wants to talk to you about the American ex-marine named Orion Bledsoe."

That was when Myra came in. "He's the one who cooked up the idea of drafting Tashy."

The lawyer shook his head. "It's unclear whether it was his idea or if it came from higher up. What I do know is that he's the one who is now in Brussels to talk to people at the World Bank."

Myra looked more worried. "What about?" she asked.

"He's giving them their orders from the Americans," the lawyer said grimly. "They're preparing a statement to release tomorrow morning and it's going to say that such an influx of gold can't be permitted because it would unbalance the world's financial structure."

Ranjit frowned, pursing his lips. "It might at that," he conceded. "That would amount to an overnight injection of—what? Trillions of dollars of new capital. There would be serious repercussions. Not to mention what it would do to the price of gold on the world markets." Then he shrugged. "I don't envy you, sir. I don't see how to deal with that kind of problem."

But the lawyer was shaking his head. "I think the president would not agree. At least he hopes that you can help—all of you. He'll be joining you shortly, and he wants to hear all about this Bledsoe person. Then he wants to try to work out some solutions."

The president of Sri Lanka was not the only world leader to convene a sort of brain trust. All over the planet some of the world's smartest and best-informed people were wrestling with the same questions. Pax per Fidem had convened gatherings of their own, and their headquarters was working what satellites it could command to collect these best and brightest voices. . . .

And, who knows, they might have succeeded, if the Americans had not had one more monkey wrench to throw into the works. It was an announcement, presented as routine by the administration's usual spokesperson, but not routine at all in its effect on the situation:

"The president would like it understood," the spokesperson said, smiling into the camera the girl-next-door smile that had served her through a hundred unpalatable announcements, "that America, too, has a valid claim for reparations due to the unnecessarily severe damage inflicted on its peacekeeping aircraft."

45

SEARCHING FOR
A SOLUTION

When Nigel De Saram escorted the Subramanian family into the presidential offices, what struck Ranjit first was how much Dhatusena Bandara had aged. That wasn't entirely unexpected. The president had to be pushing ninety. But now he seemed a good deal more fragile than the last time Ranjit had been in a room with him, at his inaugural. Though, when he welcomed them, his voice was clear and strong. He kissed both Myra and Natasha and gave an impressively youthful handshake to both Ranjit and Robert—a performance followed by his son, with the difference that Gamini gave both of the male Subramanians hugs instead of handshakes. "Thanks for coming," Gamini said. "We've got tea coming for the grownups"—he winked at Natasha, who returned an appreciative smile for her promotion—"and fruit juice for Robert. And if Robert gets tired of hearing us talk, there's a game machine by the window."

"That will be fine," Myra told him. "He likes to play 3-D chess against the machine."

"Good, then. Did Nigel straighten out your problems with the draft?"

"I think so. Hope so, anyway," Ranjit said.

"Then let's get down to business. Old Orion Bledsoe is giving us a lot of trouble. Let's start, please, with hearing what he's doing with you."

Nigel De Saram answered that one, quickly and concisely. Gamini bobbed his head and addressed the Subramanians. "Did you happen to notice where his message came from?"

Myra shook her head. Ranjit frowned. "Actually, I did notice something. It wasn't from Washington. Wasn't from his California office, either. I think it might've been someplace in Europe."

Gamini glanced at his father, who nodded soberly. "It was Brussels," the president said. "Because of American pressure, the World Bank has ordered the Egyptians to refuse the gold offer, and it was Colonel Bledsoe who applied the pressure."

Gamini Bandara spoke up. "That whole thing is my fault," he said.

"Bledsoe looked like the man I could use to get you the clearance you needed to join us at Pax per Fidem. That whole clearance thing was the American government's doing, of course: They didn't want anybody involved with Silent Thunder who didn't have maximum security clearance, and Bledsoe looked like somebody who could get it for you." He shook his head gloomily. "Bad decision. I should've gone a different way. He's been trouble ever since."

His father said, "There's no point talking about blame. The thing is, what can be done? Egypt really needs money."

Myra was frowning. "Why do they have to listen to the World Bank? Why not just accept the space people's offer?"

"Ah, my dear Myra," the president said ruefully, "if only they could. The bank would have to retaliate—canceling funds it has the power to cancel, withholding grants it can withhold, and just slowing down everything else." He shook his head. "Sadly, the Americans are not wrong about the effects of such an infusion of new capital; it would cause terrible problems in the international markets. It would bankrupt us here."

He looked down. Seated cross-legged on the floor next to him, Natasha Subramanian was giving signs of distress. "Did you want to say something, my dear?" he asked.

"Well, yes," she confessed. "I mean, why is Egypt poor? I thought the high dam at Aswân made them rich."

The president smiled, sadly. "A good many people thought that. Aswân can produce a great deal of electric power, but it can't do two things at once. When it's maxing the power production, it is cutting power from agriculture, and they need food even more." He shook his head. "The money could do wonders for Egypt. Build hundreds of new power plants, for instance."

"Why can't they do that anyway?" Natasha asked.

The president gave her a tolerant look. "They'd love to," he said. "They can't. They don't have the money. They haven't had it for a long time. So the only way they've been able to build new plants is what they call the BOOT scheme—build, own, operate, transfer. Private industry pays for building the plants, and it owns them, collecting all the profits, for a period of years before transferring them to the state. But by then they're pretty elderly plants and maybe not quite as safe as they should be." He shook his head again. "All this," he added, "is what my old friend Hameed told me in confidence. It would be unpleasant for him if the Americans found out he told me about it."

Natasha sighed. "So, what can we do, then?"

She got an answer from an unexpected source. Robert looked up from his work screen. " 'Olden 'Ule," he said reprovingly.

Nigel De Saram gave him an affectionate look. "You could be right about that, Robert," he said.

Gamini Bandara frowned. "What's he right about?"

"Why, the Golden Rule. You know, 'Do unto others as you would have them do unto you.' That's the simplest description of a benevolent world I know, and if everybody did it—us, the Americans, the space aliens, everyone—I'm sure a good many problems would simply vanish."

Gamini looked doubtfully at his father's old friend. "No disrespect, sir, but do you really think these One Point Fives are going to be moved by an ancient saying from some primitive people's supersti—some people's religion, I mean?"

"Oh, but I do," the lawyer said firmly. "That Golden Rule is not just a religious notion. Others have said the same thing in other words, without invoking supernatural authority. There was Immanuel Kant, the pure reason man, for example. What he said was—" De Saram closed his eyes for a moment, then repeated the well-learned sentences: " 'Act only according to that maxim whereby you can at the same time will that it should become a universal law.' Isn't that Robert's Golden Rule, exactly? What Kant called it was his 'categorical imperative.' By that he meant that it was what every human being—and, I guess, every space alien, too, if Kant had ever let himself imagine such things—should establish as his basic rule of behavior, with no exceptions." He tousled Robert's hair affectionately. "Now, Robert," he said, "all you have to do is get your father to prove that particular theorem and the world will become a better place." He glanced across the room to where Ranjit had placed himself before the screen that displayed the One Point Fives' multitudinous activities. "Care to try it, Ranjit?" he called.

When Ranjit looked up at last, the expression on his face was seraphic, but he wasn't looking at Nigel De Saram. "Gamini," he said, "do you remember when, years and years ago, you and I were discussing something from a lecture I'd wandered into? About an idea the Israelis had—they called it a hydro-solar project—for generating power at the Dead Sea?"

Gamini took no more than half a second to search his ancient memories. "No," he said. "What are you talking about?"

"I finally figured out why the One Point Fives might be digging that tunnel!" Ranjit said triumphantly. "Perhaps they're building a power plant! All right, the Americans won't let the aliens give the Egyptians all that money, but the Americans can't object to the aliens' sharing some of the electrical power the Egyptians really need!"

46

DEAL-MAKING

Since important decisions were to be made, some eighteen or twenty of the visitors from space were crowded together—Nine-Limbeds and One Point Fives alike, even including a couple of the Machine-Stored who were the armada's pilots. The place they were in had once been the equivalent of an admiral's bridge for the One Point Fives' invading armada. Now it was the approximate equivalent of a Kremlin or an Oval Office. The crowding was distasteful to the One Point Fives, since most of them were wearing only the minimal protective garb and thus were more exposed than ever before to the sounds, sights, and smells of all these others.

Of all the One Point Fives, the one least happy with all those unwanted sensory inputs was the one charged with keeping them out of trouble. Her official title was "Identifier of Undesirable Outcomes," but she was usually called just "Worrier." Actually, what Worrier disliked most of all was being compelled to sit through a lecture on antique human technology as delivered by the chief arbitrator of the Nine-Limbeds. When you came right down to it, Worrier didn't really care for Nine-Limbeds in any relationship, especially one that might involve touching their nasty little ninth limbs. But sometimes she had no choice.

The bit of human gadget-building they were now being taught was quite important to the humans. Actually, it was not uningenious, Worrier admitted to herself. Water would come from the sea, drop to the floor of Qattara, and there turn turbines to generate electricity. "And this electricity," Worrier said to the speaker for the Nine-Limbeds, "is what these creatures want?"

The Nine-Limbed said, "It is what you promised them. I have a copy of the agreement if you wish to see it."

The creature was actually holding out a data rod in its manipulating limb. Worrier shuddered and moved a bit away. Since she did not want these negotiations to fail, she offered a more constructive comment: "When you first proposed this," she said, "I thought you were considering teaching them the harvesting of vacuum energy as we do it. I am glad we aren't doing that. When the Grand Galactics come back, it might anger them."

The Nine-Limbed did not respond. Worrier pressed. "And this matter of what they call the categorical imperative?"

The Nine-Limbed covered a yawn. "It is how these creatures wish to run their planet. They want us to do the same. And actually"—it leveled its ninth limb at one of the Machine-Stored pilots, who was following the conversation with his own Nine-Limbed translator—"some technology transfer has already begun."

Worrier, who knew that quite well, sighed. "And when the Grand Galactics come back, what will we tell them?"

The Nine-Limbed gave her an impatient hiss. "They will return one second from now, perhaps, or in ten thousand years. Time is not the same for them. You know the Grand Galactics."

Worrier gazed at the Nine-Limbed in silence for a moment. Then, shivering inside her light armor, she said, "Actually, we don't know them at all. However, having no better alternative, we accept the proposal. And, if we are lucky, by the time the Grand Galactics come back, we may all be dead."

Before Worrier would come back into the command center, she insisted that it be flushed with ionized gases. Even so she paused in the doorway to sniff before entering.

This caused the other occupants to do the One Point Five equivalent of exchanging amused smiles. The one called Manager, however, was the only one who spoke up. "They are gone, Worrier," he called to her. "Even their smells are gone. There is no longer anything to be afraid of."

Worrier gave him a reproving look as she took her seat. But he was, after all, not only her superior in the One Point Five hierarchy but, when possible, her mate. "You know I am not afraid of the Nine-Limbeds," she informed him and, even more, the others in the room. "Would you like me to tell you why I dislike them?"

Manager said meekly, "Please do, Worrier."

"It is not because of their offensive odor," she said, "and not because their ninth limb, which is their organ for manipulating things, is also their sexual organ. These things are unpleasant. Sometimes they even use that limb to touch me, which is offensive. But they cannot help their biology, can they?"

"No, Worrier, they cannot," Manager confirmed, and there were shrill hisses of agreement from the others in the room.

"What they can help, however, is the way in which we can teach and mentor the aborigines of this planet as they grow to be as civilized as we are. We can no longer accept that all our dealings with them must be through the Nine-Limbeds, since only they can speak their languages."

The hisses abruptly dried up. Even Manager was silent for a moment before venturing, "Our superiors do not want us to be able to talk to other races directly. That is why only the Nine-Limbeds have been authorized language skills."

Worrier was steadfast. "But our superiors are not here now. We have only one proper course for the future. We must begin at once to learn human languages. . . . Or would you prefer that when these human beings grow up they take after the Nine-Limbeds instead of us?"

47

PARTING

When Ranjit and Myra went back to see Surash, it was quite a bit after their previous meeting—two surgeries later, by the way the old monk had come to count time. By then their world—the world of everyone alive on Earth—was new twice over, and still changing.

"It's not just the technology, either," Ranjit told his wife. "It's, well, friendlier than that. All the Egyptians hoped for was a share of the Qattara power. The One Point Fives didn't have to give them all of it."

Myra didn't immediately respond, so Ranjit gave her a quick look. She was gazing out at the waters of the Bay of Bengal, with what might have been a slight smile on her face. When she felt her husband's eye on her, the smile broadened. "Huh," she said.

Ranjit, laughing, turned his attention back to the road. "My darling," he said, "you are full of surprises. Have you run out of things to be suspicious of?"

Myra considered. "Probably not. Right now I can't think of any big ones, though."

"Not even the Americans?"

She pursed her lips. "Now that that horrid Bledsoe man is a fugitive from justice, no. I think the president isn't going to make any more waves for a while. Bledsoe is what deniability was invented for."

Ranjit listened quietly, but what he was thinking was not really about what she was saying. More than anything else he was thinking about Myra herself, and in particular what incredibly good fortune he had to have her. He almost didn't hear the next thing she said to him. "What?"

"I said, do you think he can get reelected?"

Before he answered, Ranjit made the turn onto the uphill road where Surash waited. "No. But I don't think it matters. He's played the hard-as-nails role about as long as he can. Now he's going to want to show himself caring."

Myra didn't respond to that until Ranjit had parked the car. Then she put an affectionate hand on his arm. "Ranj, do you know what? I'm feeling really relaxed."

The old monk's days of freedom were over. He lay on a narrow cot, his left arm immobilized so that a forest of tubing could stream unimpeded, from a wildflower bed of multicolored bags of medications at the head of the bed to the veins in his wrist. "Hello, my dears," he said as they came in, his voice fuzzed and metallic because of the throat mike taped to his larynx. "I am grateful that you came. I have a decision to make, Ranjit, and I don't know what to do. If your father were still alive, I could ask him, but he is gone and I turn to you. Shall I let them store me in a machine?"

Myra caught her breath. "Ada has been here," she said.

The old monk couldn't nod his head, but he managed a movement of the chin. "Indeed she has," he agreed. "I invited Dr. Labrooy. There is nothing more that medicine can do for me except let the machines continue to breathe for me and continue me in this great pain. In the news it said that Ada Labrooy had another possibility. She says she can do as these people from space have taught her. I can leave my body but live on as a computer program. I wouldn't hurt anymore." He was silent for a moment before he found the strength to go on. "However," he said, "there would be costs. The way to salvation through doing good works in karma yoga would no longer be possible for me, I think, but jnana yoga and bhakti yoga—the way of knowledge and the way of devotion—are still there. But do you know what that sounds like to me?"

Ranjit shook his head.

"Nirvana," said the old monk. "My soul would be released from the cycle of eternities."

Ranjit cleared his throat. "But that is what everyone seeks, my father used to say. Don't you want it?"

"With all my heart, yes! But what if this is a deception? I can't trick Brahman!"

He lay back in the bed, the ancient eyes fixed on Ranjit and Myra imploringly.

Ranjit frowned. It was Myra, however, who spoke. She laid one hand on his shrunken wrist and said, "Dear Surash, we know you would never do anything for a base motive. You must simply do what you think is right. It will be."

And that was the end of their talk.

When they were outside again, Ranjit took a deep breath. "I didn't know Ada was ready to try recording a human being."

"Neither did I," Myra said. "Last time we spoke, she told me they were getting ready to record a white rat."

Ranjit winced. "And if Surash is wrong, that's what he'll be reborn as."

"Well," Myra said practically, "if he is going to be reborn at all—which is his belief, not mine—I am sure it would not be as a bad thing."

She was silent for a moment, then smiled. "Let's see how they're coming with our house."

The house that had been Ranjit's father's had now begun to show the effects of Myra's reshaping—one big bedroom for Ranjit and Myra to share where there had been two smaller ones, three baths (and a half bath on the ground floor for visitors as well) where there had been only one. None of it, however, was finished, and sidestepping all the piles of tiling and plumbing and general refurbishing was thirsty work. And Myra said, "What would you think about a quick swim?"

It was a great idea, and Ranjit admitted as much at once. Within twenty minutes they were in their suits and on their bikes on the way to the raft anchored nearest to Swami Rock.

Since the waters nearby quickly fell off to a depth of a hundred meters and more, they took along their diving gear. That included the latest carbon-fiber tanks, capable of holding air at a pressure of a thousand atmospheres. They had no particular plans for going that deep, but there was always the brutal history of the area to view underwater. It was here that—nearly four centuries back, when Trinco was dominated by the Portuguese invaders—their sea captain had destroyed the original temple in a fit of religious fury. (The fact that some of her own ancestors had been among the vandals didn't diminish Myra's interest at all.) The seabed around the rock was still littered with recognizable carved columns.

Once underwater, Ranjit and Myra paused to inspect an elaborate doorway. Ranjit was giving his wife a mock-reproachful shake of the head as he traced a crack that defaced the lotus carvings, when the light above them suddenly dimmed.

Looking up through the brilliantly clear water, Ranjit saw an enormous shape passing just above them.

"It's a whale shark!" he shouted through his aquaphone, so loudly that his voice was distorted into something resembling the old monk's as reshaped by his throat mike. "Let's go and make friends with it!"

Myra grinned and nodded. It was not the first time she and Ranjit had encountered these huge and entirely harmless plankton eaters in the waters around Trincomalee. As much as ten meters long, they were capital ships attended by a retinue of remoras, some attached to them by their suction pads, others swimming hopefully near the enormous mouths in the expectation of table scraps to feast on.

Ranjit started to inflate his buoyancy compensator, rising slowly up the shot line. He expected that Myra would follow at the same pace and was startled when he heard her voice, tightly controlled but clearly under a strain. "Something's wrong with my inflator," she gasped. "Be with you in a moment." Then there was a violent hiss of air as her flotation bag suddenly filled. Ranjit was thrust aside as she was dragged violently upward.

It was in moments such as that when even the most experienced divers could panic. Myra made the fatal mistake of trying to hold her breath.

When Ranjit caught up with her on the raft, it was already too late. Blood was trickling from her mouth and he was not sure if he had caught her last whispered words.

He replayed them in his mind until he was standing on the pontoon of the air-medic helicopter that had arrived just in time to confirm what he already knew.

What she had said was, "See you in the next world." He bent to kiss her chilled forehead.

Then to the helicopter pilot he said, "Let me use your phone. I need to talk to Dr. Ada Labrooy right away."

48

THE SOUL IN THE MACHINE

If there was any patient for whom Dr. Ada Labrooy would pull out all the stops, it was certainly her beloved aunt Myra. It wasn't entirely up to her, however. The alien machines that could do the job were fortunately nearby, getting ready to transform old Surash into the abstract of himself that would live on in the machines. But the parts had not yet been assembled together. Some were stacked in the hall outside Surash's hospital room, some were on pallets in the yard, a couple were still on the trucks that had brought them from the Skyhook. It would take time to put them all together.

Time in which the remorseless agents of decay would be doing their best to make Myra's body unusable.

They had to buy time. There was only one way to do it. When Ranjit bullied his way into the chamber where what was left of his wife was being worked on, he at last understood why they had tried so hard to keep him out. Myra wasn't in a hospital bed. She was submerged in a tank of water with half-melted ice cubes floating on its surface. Rubber cuffs at her neck and groin gave work space to the preservation techs, each perfusing Myra's body with some chill liquid while Myra's actual scarlet blood ran into a—toilet? But yes, that was where it was going!

From behind him a voice said, "Ranjit."

He turned, his expression still horrified. The tone of Dr. Ada Labrooy's voice had been kind, but the look on her face was stern. "You shouldn't be here. None of this is pretty." She glanced at a dial and added, "I think we're in time, but you should get out of here and let us work."

He didn't argue. He had seen all he could stand to see. Over a long and happy marriage he had seen his wife's naked body many times, pink-tinged and healthy, but now it was a bluish-violetish shade that he could not bear to look at.

The waiting time was forever, or seemed like it, but at last it came to an end. Ranjit was sitting in an anteroom, staring into space, when Dr.

Labrooy came in, looking flushed and even happy. "It's going well, Ranjit," she said, taking a seat beside him. "We were able to establish all the interfaces. Now we're just waiting while the data transfer is going on."

Ranjit translated that for himself. "That means Myra's being stored in the machine? Shouldn't someone be there while that's happening?"

"Someone is, Ranjit." She lifted her arm to display a wrist screen. "I'm monitoring the flow. You know we're lucky that the Grand Galactics have a habit of storing a few samples of every race they exterminate, so the Machine-Stored were already tooling up for the job before they got here."

Ranjit scowled at a word. "What do you mean, 'storing'? Are you talking about something like, I don't know, some kind of coffin or urn or something?"

Ada scowled back. "Haven't you been keeping up with the news, Ranjit? It's nothing like that. It's like the Machine-Stored themselves. They're what you might call stage two machines. Stage one is just making exact copies of people and tucking them away for samples. Stage two is giving them life within the machine—no, wait," she said as there was a tiny bell-like sound. Her eyes were on the news screen as she lifted her arm and spoke into the contraption on her wrist. A moment later the screen went black. When it lighted up again, Ranjit's heart stopped, for what it was displaying was his wife as he had seen her last, wearing her swimsuit as before but now lying motionless on a surgical cot. . . .

No, not motionless. Her eyes opened. Her expression was puzzled but interested as she lifted her hand and rotated it to study the fingers.

"You're seeing her in her simulation," Ada informed him proudly. "Later on she'll learn how to simulate any surround she likes, and how to interact with others in the simulation." Then she whispered again into the thing on her wrist. The screen went black once more. "We aren't being fair to her, though. Let's let her have her privacy while she gets used to what's happened to her. You and I can get a cup of tea, and I'll try to answer all your questions, assuming you have some."

Oh, Ranjit had questions, all right. The tea in his cup, undrunk, grew cold while he tried to make sense of what had happened. At last there was another tiny bell and Ada smiled. "I think you can talk to her now," she said, and nodded toward the screen, which abruptly displayed Myra again. "Hello, Aunt Myra," Ada said to the screen. "Has the briefing program told you all you need to know?"

"Almost." Myra touched her hair, untended since she'd come out of the water that had killed her. "I need to know how to fix myself up a little, but I didn't want to wait any longer. Hello, Ranjit. Thanks for saving my—well, my meta-life, I guess, or whatever you can call it."

"You are very welcome," was all Ranjit could find to say. And then, as Ada got up to let the two of them talk in private, he said to Ada, "Wait a minute. You don't have to be dead to be stored like this, do you? I mean, if I wanted to, you could put me right in the scene with her? And then it would be just as though we were flesh-and-blood people together?"

Ada looked alarmed. "Well, yes," she said. She would have gone on, but Myra, speaking from the screen, was ahead of her.

"Dear Ranjit," she said, "forget it. Much as I'd like to have you here with me, you mustn't. It wouldn't be fair to Tashy, or to Robert, or— Hell, let's face it. It wouldn't be fair to the world."

Ranjit stared at the screen. "Huh," he said. And then, after a moment's pondering, "But I miss you already," he complained.

"Of course. And I miss you. It's not as though we could never see each other, though. The briefing program says we can talk like this as often as we like."

"Huh," Ranjit said again. "But we can't touch, and I may live for years."

"Many years, I hope, my darling. But it will give us something to look forward to."

∞

THE FIRST POSTAMBLE

The Long, Long Life of Ranjit Subramanian

That is the end of our story of Ranjit Subramanian.

This is not to say that he didn't live—or "live"—for quite a long time after that. He did, first in his "normal" life and then in machine storage. What's more, he had many fascinating and colorful occurrences in that postmortem "life" as a collection of electronic patterns. Most of these, however, we will not set down here. It isn't that they aren't of interest, for they are. It's just that there were so many of them. There are other things for us to do that are more significant than recounting everything that happened to what incorporeal fragment of the original organic Ranjit Subramanian was stored and continued to live during the next large number of years.

There was, however, this one thing.

It happened much later in his machine-stored life, at a time when Ranjit had already done most of the touristy things he had always wanted to do. (That is, explored nearly all of the surface of Mars, as well as its even more interesting network of subsurface caverns, plus most other planets and major satellites of the solar system and a number of the larger objects in the Oort cloud.) At that particular time Myra had gone off on a trip to the core because she had always wanted to see a black hole close up. For the few thousand years she would be gone, Ranjit himself was occupying a virtual spun-glass mountainside while relaxing. (The way he was relaxing was by considering the theorem P = NP. This had kept him entertained for a fair number of decades already, with no end in sight.) Ranjit had created that virtual mountain within his surround in order to be alone, and it was a surprise to him to observe someone trudging up its slope in his direction.

The intruder was not only a stranger but a very odd-looking one. His eyes were tiny, his facial bone structure deeply carved, and he was a good three meters tall. When he reached the outcropping where Ranjit waited, he threw himself onto a deck chair (which had not existed before the stranger's arrival), drew a couple of exaggeratedly deep breaths, and said,

"Let me see. 'That was quite a climb, wasn't it?' Was that the right thing for me to say?"

Ranjit had been bothered by too many strangers over the last few millennia to have much courtesy left over. He didn't answer that. He simply asked, "Who are you and what do you want?"

The stranger looked both surprised and pleased. "I see," he said. "You go directly to the point. Very well. Then I suppose I must say, 'My name is—' "

He didn't actually say a name, though. He simply emitted a blast of inarticulate sound, followed by, "but you may simply call me 'Student,' as I am here to study your thought processes and mannerisms."

Ranjit considered throwing this interloper out of his carefully constructed private surround, but there was something amusing about him. "Oh," he said, "all right, study away. Why do you want to do that?"

The stranger puffed out his cheeks. "How do I explain this? It is a sort of commemoration of the return of the Grand Galactics—"

"Wait," Ranjit said. "The Grand Galactics did finally come back?"

"Of course they did, after—let me see, in your counting—some thirteen thousand years. Not very long in terms of Grand Galactic time, but enough for some major changes for human beings like me. Oh, like you, too, of course," he added graciously. "Therefore we have begun a re-creation of those events, and as you were a minor figure in some of them, I have been chosen to re-create you."

"You mean you're making a kind of movie about it and you're going to play me?"

"Oh, certainly not a 'movie.' But, yes, I am to 'play' you."

"Huh," Ranjit said. "I haven't been paying a lot of attention to events lately. I didn't know the Grand Galactics had come back, even."

The stranger looked surprised. "But of course they did. They had told the Nine-Limbeds and the One Point Fives that they would be gone for only a short time. So they were. Of course, although thirteen thousand years was only a short time by their standards, it wasn't by ours. The Grand Galactics were, it seems, quite surprised to find that we had developed so fast. They had had no experience of a sentient species' being allowed to evolve at its own pace, having methodically prevented any such evolution with every other species they'd discovered. But I don't think they minded being relieved of their burden." He moved his lips experimentally for a moment, and then said, "Would you say 'huh' one more time for me, please?"

"Huh," Ranjit said, not only to grant the request but because he could think of no other response to what he had just heard. "What do you mean? Relieved of what burden?"

"Oh, running things," the stranger said, studying the look on Ranjit's face and trying to reproduce it on his own. "Not that they didn't do a good job, mostly. But it was wrong to prevent the development of so many interesting species. And although the technical stuff was generally all right, you have to admit that what they did with the cosmological constant was simply embarrassing."

Ranjit sat up straight. "Well," he said, "if the Grand Galactics aren't running things anymore, shouldn't somebody else be taking over for them?"

"Of course," the stranger said impatiently. "I thought you knew. Someone is. It's us."

∞

THE SECOND POSTAMBLE

Acknowledgments, and Other Acknowledgments

As one of us has noted elsewhere, there is a definition of a gentleman that describes him as "one who is never rude by accident." In the same way, we feel a proper science-fiction writer should never misstate a canonical scientific truth by accident.

The significant words here, however, are "by accident," because there are times in the writing of a science-fiction story when the author is forced to take a scientific liberty because otherwise his, or her, story won't work. (For example, we all know that traveling faster than light is pretty much out of the question. However, if we don't let our characters do it anyway, there are whole classes of interesting stories that we can never write.)

So when such liberties are taken, we think it only fair that the writers admit to them. In the present work there are three such cases:

1. There is in this early twenty-first-century time no such spacecraft as the high-speed one Joris Vorhulst describes as visiting the Oort cloud. We wish there were, but there isn't.

2. There is no five-page proof of Fermat's Last Theorem such as the one Ranjit Subramanian is described as having produced, and one of us thinks it is possible there never can be because the question may be formally undecidable.

3. Sri Lanka could never really be the ground terminal for a Skyhook because it isn't really on the equator. In a previous work one of us dealt with that problem by moving Sri Lanka farther south. Rather than repeat that, however, in the present case we have chosen a somewhat different solution. The equator, after all, is nothing but an imaginary line. So we have simply chosen to imagine it a few hundred kilometers farther north.

Finally we would like to acknowledge certain kindnesses, such as the elucidation provided by Dr. Wilkinson of the Drexel Math Forum of what

Andrew Wiles really accomplished with his one-hundred-fifty-page proof, and such as the assistance beyond the call of duty provided by our friend Robert Silverberg and, through him, the principal orator of Oxford University in the UK.

∞

THE THIRD POSTAMBLE

Fermat's Last Theorem

We felt it would be useful to give more details of what Fermat's Last Theorem was all about, but we could not find an earlier place for this discussion that did not wound, almost fatally, the story's narrative pace. So here
it is at the end . . . and, if you are part of that large fraction of humanity
who doesn't know it all already, we do think you will find that it was worth
waiting for.

The story of the most famous problem in mathematics began with a casual
jotting by a seventeenth-century French attorney from Toulouse. The attorney's name was Pierre de Fermat. Lawyering did not take up all of Fermat's
time, and so he dabbled in mathematics as an amateur—or, to give him his
due, actually as a person with a solid claim to being called one of the greatest mathematicians of all time.

The name of that famous problem is Fermat's Last Theorem.

One of that theorem's greatest appeals is that it is not at all hard to understand. In fact, for most people coming to it for the first time, it is hard
to believe that proving something so elementary that it can be demonstrated by counting on one's fingers had defied all the world's mathematicians for more than three centuries. In fact the problem's origins go back a
lot further than that, because it was Pythagoras himself, around five hundred B.C., who defined it in the words of the only mathematical theorem
that has ever become a cliché:

"The square of the hypotenuse of a right triangle equals the sum of the
squares of the opposite sides."

For those of us who got as far as high school freshman math, we can
visualize a right triangle and thus write the Pythagorean theorem as $a^2 + b^2
= c^2$.

Other mathematicians began investigating matters related to Pythagoras's statement about as soon as Pythagoras stated it (that is what mathe-

maticians do). One discovery was that there were many right triangles with whole-number sides that fit the equation. Such a triangle with sides of five units and twelve units, for instance, will have a hypotenuse measuring thirteen units . . . and, of course, 5^2 plus 12^2 does in fact equal 13^2. Some people looked at other possibilities. Was there, for example, any whole-number triangle with a similar relation to the cubes of the arms? That is, could a^3 plus b^3 ever equal c^3? And what about fourth-power numbers, or indeed numbers with an exponent of any number other than two?

In the days before mechanical calculators, let alone electronic ones, people spent lifetimes squandering acres of paper with the calculations necessary to try to find the answers to such questions. So they did on this problem. No one found any answers. The amusing little equation worked for squares but not for any other exponent.

Then everyone stopped looking, because Fermat had stopped them with a single scrawled line. That charming little equation that worked for squares would never work for any other exponent, he said. Positively.

Now, most mathematicians would have published that statement in some mathematical journal. Fermat, however, was in some ways a rather odd duck, and that wasn't his style. What he did was make a little note in the white space of a page of his copy of the ancient Greek mathematics book called *Arithmetica*. The note said:

"I have discovered a truly marvelous proof of this proposition which this margin is too narrow to contain."

What made this offhand jotting important was that it contained the magic word "proof."

A proof is powerful medicine for mathematicians. The requirement of a proof—that is, of a logical demonstration that a given statement must always and necessarily be true—is what distinguishes mathematicians from most "hard" scientists. Physicists, for instance, have it pretty easy. If a physicist splatters a bunch of high-velocity protons onto an aluminum target ten or a hundred times and always gets the same mix of other particles flying out, he is allowed to assume that some other physicist doing the same experiment somewhere else will always get the same selection of particles.

The mathematician is allowed no such ease. His theorems aren't statistical. They must be definitive. No mathematician is allowed to say that any mathematical statement is "true" until he has, with impeccable and unarguable logic, constructed a proof that shows that this must always be the case—perhaps by showing that if it were not, it would lead to an obvious and absurd contradiction.

So then the real search began. Now what the mathematicians were looking for was the proof that Fermat had claimed to possess. Many of the greatest mathematicians—Euler, Goldbach, Dirichlet, Sophie Germain—did their best to find that elusive proof. So did lesser names by the hundreds. From time to time some weary one of their number would leap to his feet with a cry of joy and a claim to have found the solution. Such alleged "proofs" turned up in the hundreds; there were a thousand of them in one four-year stretch of the early twentieth century alone.

But they were all quickly slain by other mathematicians who found the writers had made fundamental mistakes in fact or in logic. It began to seem to the mathematical world that great Fermat had stumbled and that no proof of his scribble would ever be found.

In that conclusion, however, they were not entirely right.

A true and final proof of Fermat's theorem came at last at almost the end of the twentieth century. It happened in the years 1993 to 1995, when a British mathematician named Andrew Wiles, working at Princeton University in the United States, published a final, complete, error-free, and definitive proof of Fermat's 350-odd-year-old conjecture. The problem had been solved.

Hardly anyone, however, was satisfied.

In the first place, Wiles's proof was ridiculously long—one hundred fifty densely written pages. Worse still, there were parts of it that no human being could read—and thereby confirm that they were error-free. Only a computer program could check them. Worst of all, Wiles's proof could not have been the one that Fermat claimed, because it relied on proofs and procedures that had not been known to Fermat or anyone else anywhere near that time. So, many great mathematicians refused to accept it. . . .

Including, as we have just seen, one truly superb, if fictitious, one. We are speaking of one whose home was far from Fermat's in both time and space, namely the one named Ranjit Subramanian, whom this book has been about.

∞

THE FOURTH POSTAMBLE

The Authors

Both SIR ARTHUR C. CLARKE and FREDERIK POHL have won large numbers of awards for their work. Both have been declared "Grand Masters of Science Fiction" by SFWA, the formal organization of science-fiction writers, and both have collaborated with a number of other writers over the years. They have, however, never before collaborated on a novel together.

ABOUT THE TYPE

This book was set in Times New Roman, designed by Stanley Morison specifically for *The Times* of London. The typeface was introduced in the newspaper in 1932. Times New Roman has had its greatest success in the United States as a book and commercial typeface rather than one used in newspapers.